The O. Henry Prize Stories 2015

WITHDRAWN

The O. Henry Prize Stories 2015

Chosen and with an Introduction by
Laura Furman

With Essays by Jurors
Tessa Hadley
Kristen Iskandrian
Michael Parker
on the Stories They Admire Most

Anchor Books
A Division of Penguin Random House LLC
New York

AN ANCHOR BOOKS ORIGINAL, SEPTEMBER 2015

*Copyright © 2015 by Vintage Anchor Publishing, a division of
Penguin Random House LLC
Introduction copyright © 2015 by Laura Furman*

**Anchor Books Trade Paperback ISBN: 978-1-101-87231-4
eBook ISBN: 978-1-101-87232-1**

www.anchorbooks.com

Printed in the United States of America
10 9 8 7 6 5 4 3 2 1

To Ellen and Karl Sklar with sisterly love

The staff of Anchor Books is devoted to publishing excellent books. Their collective intelligence, dedication, and professional skill make it a pleasure to work with them. Jennifer Marshall's unflagging enthusiasm and experience reveal *The O. Henry Prize Stories* to the world each year anew. Diana Secker Tesdell shows the series editor each year how it should be done.

Taylor Flory Ogletree and Marissa Colon-Margolies were the editorial assistants for *The O. Henry Prize Stories 2015*. The series editor is grateful to them for their sharpness and honesty, and for the fun of being with them.

The graduate school and Department of English of the University of Texas at Austin support *The O. Henry Prize Stories* in many ways. The series editor thanks the university and especially Elizabeth Cullingford and Oscar Cásares.

—LF

Publisher's Note

A BRIEF HISTORY OF
THE O. HENRY PRIZE STORIES

Many readers have come to love the short story through the simple characters, easy narrative voice and humor, and compelling plotting in the work of William Sydney Porter (1862–1910), best known as O. Henry. His surprise endings entertain readers, including those back for a second, third, or fourth look. Even now one can say "Gift of the Magi" in a conversation about a love affair or marriage, and almost any literate person will know what is meant. It's hard to think of many other American writers whose work has been so incorporated into our national shorthand.

O. Henry was a newspaperman, skilled at hiding from his editors at deadline. A prolific writer, he wrote to make a living and to make sense of his life. He spent his childhood in Greensboro, North Carolina, his adolescence and young manhood in Texas, and his mature years in New York City. In between Texas and New York, he served out a prison sentence for bank fraud in Columbus, Ohio. Accounts of the origin of his pen name vary:

One story dates from his days in Austin, where he was said to call the wandering family cat "Oh! Henry!"; another states that the name was inspired by the captain of the guard at the Ohio State Penitentiary, Orrin Henry.

Porter had devoted friends, and it's not hard to see why. He was charming and had an attractively gallant attitude. He drank too much and neglected his health, which caused his friends concern. He was often short of money; in a letter to a friend asking for a loan of $15 (his banker was out of town, he wrote), Porter added a postscript: "If it isn't convenient, I'll love you just the same." His banker was unavailable most of Porter's life. His sense of humor was always with him.

Reportedly, Porter's last words were from a popular song: "Turn up the light, for I don't want to go home in the dark."

Eight years after O. Henry's death, in April 1918, the Twilight Club (founded in 1883 and later known as the Society of Arts and Letters) held a dinner in his honor at the Hotel McAlpin in New York City. His friends remembered him so enthusiastically that a group of them met at the Biltmore Hotel in December of that year to establish some kind of memorial to him. They decided to award annual prizes in his name for short-story writers, and formed a committee of award to read the short stories published in a year and to pick the winners. In the words of Blanche Colton Williams (1879–1944), the first of the nine series editors, the memorial was intended to "strengthen the art of the short story and to stimulate younger authors."

Doubleday, Page & Company was chosen to publish the first volume, *O. Henry Memorial Award Prize Stories 1919*. In 1927, the society sold all rights to the annual collection to Doubleday, Doran & Company. Doubleday published *The O. Henry Prize Stories*, as it came to be known, in hardcover, and from 1984 to 1996 its subsidiary, Anchor Books, published it simultaneously in paperback. Since 1997 *The O. Henry Prize Stories* has been published as an original Anchor Books paperback.

HOW THE STORIES ARE CHOSEN

All stories originally written in the English language and published in an American or Canadian periodical are eligible for consideration. Individual stories may not be nominated; magazines must submit the year's issues in their entirety by July 1. Editors are invited to submit online fiction for consideration. Such submissions must be sent to the series editor in hard copy. (Please see pp. 379–80 for details.)

As of 2003, the series editor chooses the twenty O. Henry Prize Stories, and each year three writers distinguished for their fiction are asked to evaluate the entire collection and to write an appreciation of the story they most admire. These three writers receive the twenty prize stories in manuscript form with no identification of author or publication. They make their choices independent of one another and the series editor.

The goal of *The O. Henry Prize Stories* remains to strengthen the art of the short story.

To V. S. Pritchett (1900–1997)

The shelf within arm's reach of my desk holds several books by V. S. Pritchett, though not all by any means; his life's work includes many volumes of story collections, essays, criticism, and biographies. My acquaintance with Pritchett's writing began when I was too young to know anything but that he was the real thing. Nowadays, what once seemed a harsh view of mankind strikes me as calm and clear-sighted.

Late in life Pritchett wrote a biography of Anton Chekhov, a writer to whom he is often compared. The impetus for the book might have come from fellow feeling. Both Chekhov and Pritchett are praised for their compassion, which means to this reader that neither ever loses interest or sums up a character in a dismissive way. Both are scrupulous in their portrayals of minor characters, the lower class of the fictional world. Both are unsentimental and see their characters whole.

Pritchett's characters are often motivated by desire, especially sexual desire, and he is alert to signals and cross-signals, frustration and cunning. The latter plays a special role in the celebrated story "On the Edge of the Cliff." Harry is in his seventies and his beautiful lover, Rowena, in her twenties. He's a widower and has always had young lovers: "When young girls turned into women, they lost his interest; he had always lived for reverie." At the story's beginning, Rowena and Harry are preparing to leave his house, first to go to a fair for Rowena's enjoyment, and then to walk on a cliff above a cove where Harry went when he was younger and his wife alive. Rowena loves the tales he tells her about his past, which she glamorizes for her own reasons.

Harry is on guard and takes care to keep Rowena from seeing him as a decrepit old man, and he's right to be careful. En route to the carnival he entertains her with historical facts and fancies about "carnival, Celtic gods and devils. He was old Father Time, she said now, and he humored her with a small laugh. It was part of the game. He was not Father Time, for in one's seventies one is a miser of time, putting it by, hiding the minutes, while she spent it fast, not knowing she was living in time at all."

At the fair they encounter Doris, a former fling and now a widow, and her handsome young companion, Steven, who they take to be her son. Harry is thrown off his stride by the chance meeting and snubs Doris. Later, he descends the hillside to the cove, strips off his clothes, and triumphantly swims in the cold sea, breaking a rule of his old man's game by letting Rowena see him naked. They return home, and for the first time she comes into Harry's bed. He guesses that she's jealous of Doris and of his past. Harry's game is almost despicable, almost touching, manipulative, and a little desperate; he knows that this girl might be his last.

The story shifts when Doris comes to visit while Rowena is away. In another writer's hand, the middle of the story might center on Rowena and Harry. Is she restless or disenchanted after his stumbles in the old man's game? Looking down into the cove reminds Rowena of looking into the empty hole of his mouth when he wasn't wearing his dentures. Or does Rowena, as Harry imagines, love him? If so, what does Harry make of that and might he be able to tolerate her aging into a woman?

By mirroring Harry and Rowena with Doris and Steven, Pritchett takes another path. He complicates the story with Doris, who reveals that at the fair she wasn't with her son but her much younger lover; she insists that she and Harry keep their lovers apart because they are beautiful and young, and attraction would be inevitable. Hers is an old woman's game, one more realistic than Harry's. Doris isn't dreaming and she isn't playing. If her young lover leaves her, she'll throw herself off that cliff. She would choose death rather than try to fool time.

Doris leaves, Rowena returns, and Harry makes another mistake. He tells Rowena that the young man they saw wasn't Doris's son but her lover, and Rowena protests: "She's old enough—" She stops herself from finishing the sentence, but it's the beginning of the end for her and Harry: "Instead of giving him one of her light hugs, she rumpled his hair."

That small detail indicates greater changes to come, and disaster for the old man. Harry is vain, manipulative, and human, for who wants to grow old and who wants to die?

Like him or not, we can't stop watching.

Contents

Introduction

What is great prose to one person is wallpaper to another. As readers, we are all subjective and that is one of the pleasures of being a reader.

This particular reader likes writing best when it is free of the looming presence of the writer, who, reasonably and humanly, wants the work to be liked, appreciated, praised, and rewarded. Sometimes that understandable desire casts a shadow. The best short stories don't necessarily have the cleverest plots or the most ingenious twists, but they do have the best prose and a full creation of a fictional world.

The reader of the short story often feels two things simultaneously, as with Russell Banks's "A Permanent Member of the Family." Just as you're starting to understand how the characters are put together, you recognize the ways in which they're unraveling. Banks's narrator is driven by his desire to keep everything the same at the moment when everything is changing. He acknowledges that his actions are disrupting family life, but he and his soon-to-be ex-wife are working out their arrangements and disarrangements smoothly. A bit of self-congratulation seems only right. The bump comes when the family dog, Sarge, makes it known that she isn't about to change her ways. The family is her pack, the narrator is the leader of the pack, and so Sarge goes where the narrator does, all human agreements aside. Sarge's doggy devotion to family life as it used to be is the rift in the lute of the enlightened divorce.

The pleasures of "A Permanent Member of the Family" are many. The narrator wants to "set the record straight, get the story told truthfully once and for all, even if it does in a vague way reflect badly on" him. He is thoughtful, judicious, and still, thirty-five years after the events of the story, hoping for a pass. He's kidding himself about a number of things. If his version of the truth were the only one, that would be one thing; Banks's skill and intelligence make it clear that his is only one version among several, and not the most important at that.

The narrator of Emily Ruskovich's "Owl" is devoted to his wife, Jane. At first we see her as a victim; a neighbor boy shot her, mistaking her for an owl. For much of the story the narrator seems to be his wife's nurse and keeper, and while Jane appreciates his care, at the same time she keeps secrets and holds herself apart emotionally. Her actions and feelings are as opaque to the reader as they are to the narrator, though she grows less mysterious when we learn the harsh story of how they came to marry twelve years earlier and farm in Bonner's Ferry, Idaho.

Several boys from neighboring farms are also devoted to Jane, and the reader senses something dangerous about the boys and about Jane, though it isn't clear at first if the danger originates with Jane herself, the boys, or the hapless narrator. "Owl" is a triumphant, heartbreaking visit to isolated rural life at the turn of the twentieth century. Occasionally the narrator harks back to worse times, to the one-room, dirt-floored house he grew up in, where dust destroyed his mother's lungs. The difficulties of frontier life turned him into a workhorse, a man without vision or hope. When he marries fifteen-year-old Jane, who is pregnant by another man, she brings beauty to his narrow life. He tells us: "She was polite to me, my Jane." The reader intuits that she's been waiting all twelve years to make her escape, even if her adoring husband doesn't.

Lynn Freed's chilling "The Way Things Are Going" is set in contemporary South Africa and California. The story is about transitions, all of them difficult: A fierce mother ages from a resourceful pirate to a fragile and delusional old woman; a country develops from unjust tyranny to lawlessness; love devolves into a memory.

The narrator tries to make sense of her own story, in which she is both victim and perpetrator, an appendage of her failing mother and manipulative sister. She knows that her passivity and her allegiance to an idea of manners make her a witness to her own life, but she will not help herself. The disaster that's befallen the narrator isn't the violent incident that sets chaos in motion. It's the title of the story that defines her. Freed has a gift for exposing the roots of her characters' individual disaster, roots so deep that each one is inevitable. We might not like where the narrator of "The Way Things Are Going" ends up any more than she does but we can see no way out for her.

Lionel Shriver starts her story "Kilifi Creek" in a more idyllic African setting. Liana, a tourist, is young and pretty enough to wheedle her way around East Africa in the care of distant acquaintances older and richer than herself. "Mature adulthood—and the experience of being imposed upon herself—might have encouraged her to consider what showing up as an uninvited, impecunious houseguest would require of her hosts." Shriver narrates with an Olympian knowledge of her character's fate and way of being; Liana in all her obliviousness is fun to watch as she risks her life and then forgets whatever lesson might have been gained from the experience. The combination of entertainment and lesson-drawing makes "Kilifi Creek" intriguing and, because of its ending, satisfying and shocking. What is the use of lessons in manners when life is so fragile and so temporary, and youth so much fun?

In Dina Nayeri's "A Ride Out of Phrao" the main character, Shirin Khalilipour-Anderson, might have learned some lessons along the way but everything in her resists conventional wisdom. Shirin carries her chaos wherever she goes. An exile from Iran after the fall of the shah, she goes to America and lives for fifteen years in Cedar Rapids. After she's fired from her job, and lies shamelessly about why she's unemployed, she joins the Peace Corps and is sent to a village in northern Thailand.

The story revolves around a visit to the Thai village by Shirin's estranged daughter, a young woman so exhausted by her mother's lies that she believes almost nothing her mother says. Their relationship—tenuous and tentative, loving and hostile—is the heart of the story, for Shirin wishes above all else that her daughter would believe her, though Shirin lies the way other people breathe. As she sees it, her lies are for the convenience or pleasure of others. "A Ride Out of Phrao" is juror Tessa Hadley's favorite story in this year's collection, and she explains why in eloquent terms (pp. 351–53).

Brenda Peynado's "The History of Happiness" is about another traveler, who started her journey with her boyfriend. "We were both computer science majors and once we got a job we would spend the rest of our lives in a five-by-five box controlling machines and we wanted to see the real, human world." Along the way, when it's time to move on, the boyfriend decides to remain in India with Hindu monks. The narrator tells us, "I was angry at myself and doing things like couch surfing with strangers, stealing wallets, and lifting bank account passwords from Internet café computers, and I dared some terrible consequence to happen." She's absorbed by her dilemma of having no money, and by her loneliness and anger, interested in her boyfriend's spiritual crisis only to make fun of it. She is tilting toward becoming a criminal perhaps destined for a confinement far worse than the five-by-five box of a computer programmer, or for worse punishment. The story takes place in Singapore, where, as one character says, "no one would be foolish enough to steal anything."

At the end of "The History of Happiness" Peynado creates an explosion and a revelation: The narrator's anger breaks open, and she understands that she, like the boyfriend who stayed with the monks, must struggle with questions too large to answer or ignore. The peacefulness of the conclusion is both welcome and unexpected, and explains the word *happiness* in the title.

Manuel Muñoz's "The Happiest Girl in the Whole USA" is the story of two women who meet by chance as they travel on the same mission: to find their husbands, who've just crossed the US-Mexico border illegally. The narrator, Griselda, knows her way around from long experience. She knows where to go, what shoes to wear, which motel to stay in for the night when her man doesn't show up, and she knows too that happiness is temporary. The younger woman, Natalia, is naive, wears high heels she can hardly walk in, and has nowhere to spend the night; in short, she needs looking after, and Griselda reluctantly shares what she has. She stops short of advising the other woman to forget her man, and keeps to herself the many difficulties of "the whole drama of deportation and return" and the sacrifices she's made. *"Do something with your life, Griselda,"* an observant teacher once told her, but she couldn't follow that urgent advice, and she was too shy to ask how in the world she could. Once she fell in love with Timoteo, her options were even more constricted.

In part, the story is about the many difficulties and limits of the particular life the characters—women, Mexican-American, poor—are leading, and that is enough, given the beauty of the writing, to make a fine story. But the story is an even greater gift to the reader for, with grace, generosity, and wisdom, Manuel Muñoz is telling us about the cost of love.

"I, Buffalo" by Vauhini Vara begins on a bus in San Francisco. The narrator is horribly, blindingly, painfully hungover, and she engages in a conversation with a mother and her little boy that ends with the boy lobbing an imaginary hand grenade her way. There are faint echoes of Flannery O'Connor's "Everything That Rises Must Converge" in its dark humor and edginess.

The narrator, however impaired, is eager to share her story. She's unlucky in love, she tells us, and now that she's alone there is "a great and holy emptiness. It resembled the alarming emptiness that cathedrals and mosques hold for those of us who believe in nothing beyond what is proven to exist." The narrator's exuberance and delightful language seduce the reader, even as she details her drinking, which is the kind that ends up in blackouts. Slapstick ensues as the narrator tries to hide her condition from her visiting family. Little by little, the reader understands how dangerous the narrator is to herself and others, and the comedy thins and disappears. The mellifluous narrator reaches a stopping point where nothing will do but the silence of truth: "Enough with all these words. Enough with the endless questions and endless answers."

Thomas Pierce's "Ba Baboon" has a similarly ingenious combination of tragedy and comedy, beginning as it does with a brother and sister—Brooks and Mary—trapped in the pantry of a house they've more or less broken into. The house belongs to a former lover of Mary's and she is there to collect an embarrassing video. Brooks is there because he's in her care. He's recovering from a head injury; someone hit him with a brick. "'A random act of violence,' his mother called it. 'A totally senseless thing.' Unnecessary qualifiers, he sometimes wants to tell her, as the universe is inherently a random and senseless place."

Mary's lover is away with his family, but he's left behind a vicious pair of guard dogs who have trapped Mary and Brooks in the pantry. There are some code words that will make the dogs retreat but Mary and Brooks don't know them. In a random and senseless universe, the existence of the powerful words makes complete sense, as does Mary and Brooks's ignorance of them. They won't be trapped in this situation forever, but the effects of Brooks's brain injury are probably permanent. He might enjoy a "fuller" recovery, or he might not. His doctor assures him that whatever happens, Brooks will still be Brooks, in some form. If he can accept that, he might be happy. Or happier.

"Ba Baboon" is filled with hopelessness and loss, and also with humor and affection. Maybe there are some magic words that will heal the damaged brain and the old Brooks will return. In a random and senseless universe, can there be limits to what might happen?

Christopher Merkner's "Cabins" is about men and divorce, written in numbered chapters and set in hookah bars, basketball courts, a men's penitentiary, a house decorated with the heads of dead animals, and an imaginary cabin where the narrator is alone. (Juror Michael Parker chose "Cabins" as his favorite story and discusses it on pp. 356–58.) The cabin of solitary existence isn't, of course, an exclusively masculine province. It is imagined in opposition to the elusive intimacy and inexorable commitment of marriage. The narrator is surrounded, he believes, by men who are divorcing, friends he thought he knew and doesn't. There are other threats to the narrator's peace: He had a heart attack a year before and his wife is about to give birth to their first child. The story is a disquisition on fear and various ways of trying to talk your way out of being afraid, and it ends with tenderness and loneliness in equal measure.

In Becky Hagenston's "The Upside-Down World," Jim has flown to Nice to rescue his sister, Gertrude. The middle-aged pair is not especially close, and the story's jaunty title is at odds with the emotions at play between brother and sister—crippling anxiety, frustration, fretfulness, and bewilderment. Jim last saw Gertrude three years before but she's called him in the middle of the night to ask his opinion: "'I just took a seven-hundred-euro taxi ride to Monte Carlo in my nightgown. Do you think I'm losing it again?'" Jim's wife, Jeannie, is offended by his willingness to rescue Gertrude. Jeannie can always predict precisely how things will go wrong, and as the story moves along, her self-assurance works nicely against Jim's hesitations. He's come on a rescue mission but his sister is an octopus of evasion. Time and again, Jim tries to understand how she must feel, as though his understanding will bring him closer to getting her back to a psychiatric hospital in America.

The second thread of the story concerns Elodie, a French run-away, and her companion Ted, who spot Jim and Gertrude as easy marks. They have their own form of disorder, not in mental confusion but in lethal mutual misunderstanding. Elodie is running from her mother's death; she witnesses a terrible accident and perceives nothing but the advantage it might give her. In the end, Elodie is the character most at risk of being turned upside down permanently.

In Lydia Davis's "The Seals" the narrator mourns her older sister, once beloved and now dead, as are their parents. The narrator questions why she loved her sister so much and wonders what they shared—a love of animals, perhaps, for she remembers "animal-themed presents" and wonders about them. There was a "mobile made of china penguins—why? Another time, a seagull of balsa wood that hung on strings . . . Another time, a dish towel with badgers on it." She seems to be describing someone she knew only in the distant past but as the story goes on we learn that though she saw her sister infrequently, they always kept in touch.

Part of the beauty of "The Seals" is the slow meditative consideration of the sister, of her death, her life, her gifts, her witholdings, and then of what it feels like to miss her. "There was also some confusion in my mind, in the months afterward. It was not that I thought she was still alive. But at the same time I couldn't believe that she was actually gone. Suddenly the choice wasn't so simple: either alive or not alive. It was as though not being alive did not have to mean she was dead, as though there were some third possibility."

Molly Antopol's "My Grandmother Tells Me This Story" is also a meditation on the past punctuated by brief returns to the present, during which the grandmother-narrator questions why the granddaughter wants to know about the part she and her husband played as teenagers in the Jewish resistance to the Nazis in Belarus, and how she met her husband, and how they came to America. Her granddaughter's curiosity is as incomprehensible to her as it is that she hasn't made an adult life for herself and clings to family history as if there's an answer in it for her own young troubles.

Though the grandmother has a war story of courage and daring, of risking death and surviving when so many died, she doesn't have a love story to tell. Whether or not she even likes her husband, the courageous resistance fighter and immigrant failure, is in question. The raw passion we feel in the story is for her lost youth and opportunities, for a world gone by, and for her choice-lessness in the world she's in now. The story ends with a final harangue at her granddaughter's failures to make friends, find a husband, make her way, be happy, her insistence on "scratching at ugly things that have nothing to do with" her. The granddaughter is silent, yet we argue on her behalf that these things have everything to do with who she is. All these "horrible things that happened before [she was] born" speak to trust and love, and to the damage that was done and preserved like a sacred relic.

In Percival Everett's "Finding Billy White Feather," set in Wyoming, Oliver Campbell finds a note on his door, left maybe by a ghost; Oliver's dog doesn't alert him to a visitor. The note is from Billy White Feather, which sounds like an Indian name, though Oliver finds out soon enough from people in town that Billy White Feather (not his real name) is "a tall, skinny white boy with blue eyes and a blond ponytail and he come up here a couple of years ago and started hanging around acting like he was a full blood or something." Or he's "a big guy with red hair and a big mustache." Or else he's "an Indian. Got a jet-black braid down to his narrow ass."

Still, Billy's note told the truth about twin Appaloosa foals born on the reservation. The story rolls on, taking Oliver to the unusual twins and their mother, and to more stories about Billy White Feather's shortcomings. Little by little, in the vastness of the western landscape, Oliver comes to see the elusive Billy as a threat. He tells his wife, "He came to our home, Lauren. Stood on our porch." The story pulls you right into the life of the characters and to the odd pursuit of a phantom by the solid citizen

Oliver Campbell. The shift in the story's tone from beginning to end is a demonstration both of Percival Everett's mastery and of the difference between the pull of curiosity and the power of the shape-shifting unknown.

Emma Törzs's "Word of Mouth" is another Western, this one set in Montana. The narrator, Jenny, tells us: "I'd been raised in the city . . . and I still couldn't believe I was allowed to live here among healthy streams and molting birches and the constant upsurge of rocky earth. The land made me feel blindly cared for." Recently, Jenny was the caretaker of her grandmother, a woman who didn't take anything easily. When her grandmother dies, Jenny is free, though for what she isn't sure. She finds a job as a waitress at the Whole Hog, an unsuccessful restaurant whose owner abhors advertising and waits for word of mouth to kick in, showing a faith in things invisible. There's a woman missing from the area, possibly murdered, and her husband, possibly her murderer, comes to the Whole Hog.

Törzs's story deals with various forms of power: one lover over another, men over women, a terrible disease over a body, Jenny's grandmother over her. The writing is clear and down-to-earth, and "Word of Mouth" ends with a great tenderness that encloses the story, the characters, and even Montana.

In Elizabeth Strout's "Snow Blind," the Appleby family is a study in secret-keeping. The youngest child, Annie, is an imaginative chatterbox:

> *"Our teacher says if you look at the fields right after it snows and the sun is shining hard you can get blind." Annie craned her neck to see out the window.*
> *"Then don't look," her grandmother said.*

What should the Appleby children look at? What should they avoid seeing? There's a mystery in their family life that's like the rumble of far-off thunder. At first, "Snow Blind" seems to be about the whole family and their rural world. In a swerve in narrative direction, the story concentrates on Annie, the only one of the Appleby children to notice that an unnamed shame holds the family together. Annie leaves home and establishes a celebrated life far away, returning to face the revelations of her family's secrets. By the end, she knows what it costs to dare to look at the light.

Naira Kuzmich's "The Kingsley Drive Chorus" is told in first-person plural, appropriate because the community's eyes, hearts, and voices are one—all are the immigrant mothers of daring young men. In Greek tragedy, the chorus sees all, knows past and present, and is helpless to change anything. "We had done what we could, all the things we told ourselves we could have done. We resigned ourselves to our windows. We wiped down the glass. We waved."

The tragic hero enacts and embodies the community's dangers and suffers for everybody. In the Armenian community Kuzmich has created, the enormous sacrifice of one mother resonates through all of them and makes them question if indeed they really did all they could or if they lacked the courage of their love.

Another community comes under scrutiny in "The Golden Rule," by Lynne Sharon Schwartz, a previous O. Henry winner. Every aspect of the dictum "Do unto others as you would have them do unto you" is examined through the story of Amanda, a sensible, chic widow who seems to be doing unto herself very well. She has her own business, a successful boutique, a boyfriend whose company and lovemaking she enjoys, and a good relationship with her only child, a daughter who lives abroad. Amanda "felt herself in a permanent battle with time and nature, and though in the end she would lose, as everyone does, she resolved to fight valiantly to the death."

Amanda is good to the "frail old neighbor" who lives on the same floor in their apartment house, and does Maria the kind of small favors that can make another's life easier and cost one little to perform. Maria is a complainer, ten years older than Amanda, and a little bit paranoid; such qualities don't seem at first to matter. "How could she refuse?" As Maria's health deteriorates and her demands grow, Amanda begins to compare herself to Maria, and, it seems, her own troubles also increase. She misses her daughter but refuses to ask for more contact. She might be faced soon with closing her business. The boyfriend is fine but at heart Amanda is haunted by the illness and death of her beloved husband; worst of all, she misses him. As Schwartz moves the story along irresistibly, the reader begins to see Amanda's own demise coming, if not actually caused by her querulous neighbor. The ending of "The Golden Rule" is a convincing cry of courage against inevitable defeat.

Joan Silber has been an O. Henry winner before, and her work is widely praised for its honesty, ingenuity, and beauty. The reader is immediately involved in the questions Reyna, the narrator of "About My Aunt," asks about life in general and in particular. There's a lot to say about Reyna's aunt Kiki—the eight years she lived in rural Turkey, her ability to recover and even triumph in tight spot after tight spot, including Hurricane Sandy. Reyna, who has a young son, Oliver, is less adept at landing on her feet. In talking about a new tattoo, she says, "Some people design their body art so it all fits together, but I did mine piecemeal, like my life, and it looked fine." Reyna's boyfriend, Boyd, is in jail on Rikers Island, and the complications of visiting him bring Reyna and Kiki together in a new intimacy. Eventually, Kiki tries to get Reyna to leave New York and Boyd. As the conflict plays out, the reader contemplates the differences between the women. Both are worth caring about, and each has wishes for the other one's life, wishes that, the reader knows, will never come true.

"Birdsong from the Radio" by Elizabeth McCracken, according to juror Kristen Iskandrian, who chose it as her favorite (pp. 354–56), "has the aura of a fairy tale." Fairy tales fascinate, enchant, and frighten us. Leonora is a loving mother who wants to eat her children. "Children long to be eaten," the authorial voice tells us. "Everyone knows that." But Leonora terrorizes her children, Dolly, Marco, and Rosa, and then she becomes another kind of monster altogether, a monster of grief. McCracken merges the impossible with the all-too-real in her story of a woman bolstering herself against the worst of all possible losses.

"Details," V. S. Pritchett tells us, "make stories human, and the more human a story can be, the better."

As you read *The O. Henry Prize Stories 2015*, look for the details that fill all the stories with human beings.

—*Laura Furman*
Austin, Texas

The O. Henry Prize Stories 2015

Percival Everett
Finding Billy White Feather

OLIVER CAMPBELL HAD NEVER met Billy White Feather. He had never heard the name. But the note tacked to his back door had him out on the reservation at nine on a raw Sunday morning. *Twin Appaloosa foals at Arapaho Ranch*, the note said. *To purchase, find Billy White Feather.* The note was signed, *Billy White Feather.* He'd stepped out to find the note and no sign of anyone. He looked at his dog on the seat next to him. The twelve-year-old Lab's big head hung over the edge of the seat.

"You're not much of a watchdog, Tuck," Oliver said. "You're supposed to let me know when somebody's in the yard."

The dog said nothing.

Oliver didn't want to make the drive all the way up to the reservation ranch just to find no one there, so he stopped at the flashing yellow traffic signal in Ethete. Ethete was a gas station/store and a flashing yellow light. He got out of his pickup and walked through the fresh snow and into the store. He stomped his feet on the mud-caked rubber mat. The young clerk didn't look up. Oliver moved through one of the narrow aisles to the back and poured himself a large cup of coffee. He picked up a packaged blueberry muffin on his way back and set it on the counter.

"Three dollars," the young woman yawned.

"Three dollars?" Oliver said in mock surprise.

"Okay, two-fifty," the woman said, without a pause or interest.

He gave her three dollars. "I'm looking for Billy White Feather."

"Why?"

"He left me a note about a horse."

"No, I mean why are you looking here?"

"I think he lives here. On the reservation, I mean."

"Indians live on the reservation."

Oliver tore open his muffin and pinched off a bite, looked outside at the snow that was falling again. "Do you know Billy White Feather?"

"I do."

"But he's not an Indian?"

She nodded.

"His name is White Feather?"

"That's something you're going to have to talk to him about. He ain't no Arapaho and he ain't no Shoshone and he ain't no Crow and he ain't no Cheyenne. That's what I know."

"So, he might be Sioux."

"Ain't no Sioux or Blackfoot or Gros Ventre or Paiute neither."

"Okay."

"He's a tall, skinny white boy with blue eyes and a blond ponytail and he come up here a couple of years ago and started hanging around acting like he was a full-blood or something."

Oliver sipped his coffee.

"He liked on Indian girls and dated a bunch of them. Bought them all doughnuts 'til they got fat and then ran out on them. Now he's in town liking on Mexican girls. That's what I hear."

"His note said there are some twin foals up at the ranch," Oliver said. "Heard anything about that?"

"I heard. It's big news. Twins. That means good luck."

"So, what's White Feather have to do with the horses?"

"I ain't got no idea. I don't care. Long he don't come in here I got no problem with Billy whatever-his-name-is."

Oliver looked at her.

"Because it sure ain't no White Feather."

Oliver nodded. "Well, thanks for talking to me."

"Good luck."

The door opened and in with a shock of frigid air came Hiram Shakespeare. He was a big man with a soft voice that didn't quite fit him.

"Hiram," Oliver said.

"Hiya," Hiram said. "What are you doing up this way, brown man?"

"I came to see the twins."

"Word travels fast. Twins. Something, that. How'd you find out?"

"I got a note from somebody named Billy White Feather."

"You know him?"

"Never met him."

"Stay away from him, though. He's bad medicine."

"I'm gathering that." Oliver looked at his cup. "I'll buy you a cup of coffee if you take me up to see the foals."

"You drive."

"You bet," Oliver said.

"I hate driving in snow," Hiram said. "Can't see shit in the snow. Course I can't see shit in the bright sunshine."

Hiram grabbed his extra-large tub of coffee, and Oliver paid for it. They walked out into the wet falling snow and climbed into Oliver's truck. Tuck moved to the middle and sat, his head level with the humans.

Hiram rubbed the dog's head. "He's looking good."

"For an old guy," Oliver said.

"I wish somebody would say that about me."

"I'm saying."

Hiram looked through the back window into the bed of the truck. Oliver had thrown a bunch of cinder blocks into the bed over the rear wheels to keep the truck from fishtailing on the ice. Hiram nodded. "That's good, them blocks." He then started to fiddle with the radio. He settled on a country station.

"You like that crap?" Oliver asked.

"It's country music," Hiram said. "Indians are country people." He sang along with the song. "So, how do you know Billy White Feather?"

"I don't know him. Never heard of him until today when I got the note saying to contact him about buying the foals. When were they born?"

"Last night. It's George Big Elk's mare."

"So, they don't belong to Billy White Feather."

Hiram laughed loudly. "Billy White Feather?"

"His note said that if I was interested in buying the foals, I should contact Billy White Feather."

"More like Billy White Man. He doesn't own the shirt he's wearing. If he's wearing a shirt."

"George's, eh. Did George know she was having twins?"

Hiram shook his head. "The mare looked plenty big, but not crazy big, you know? Nobody up here was going to pay for a scan. Nobody does that. You know how much them scans cost?"

Oliver nodded. He turned his defroster on high and used his glove to wipe the windshield. "You must breathe a lot or something."

"Indians breathe a third more than white people. A quarter more than black people."

"Why is that?"

"This is FBI air."

"FBI?"

Hiram laughed. "Full-Blooded Indian."

"I wonder why that guy put that note on my door."

"Bad medicine. I wonder how he knew about the foals. I heard tell that Danny Moss and Wilson O'Neil run him off the reservation a few weeks ago. Beat him up pretty good."

"I wonder if I've seen the guy without knowing who he was," Oliver said.

"You'd remember him, all right. He's a big guy with red hair and a big mustache."

Oliver took the turn onto a dirt road that had not been plowed. "Think we'll be okay on this road?" he asked.

Hiram shrugged. "Long as the tribe hasn't plowed it yet. Those guys come by and make everything impassable."

"County does the same thing. They can take a messy run and turn it into impassable in a few hours."

"Two gallons of shit in a one-gallon bucket. Probably go to the same classes."

"Have you seen the foals yet?"

Hiram shook his head. "I hear tell they're damn near the same size and pretty strong."

"That's unusual."

"I heard that. I haven't seen them. They say the mare's good, too. Vet came up and couldn't believe it."

"Who's the vet?"

"Sam Innis."

Oliver nodded.

The snow let up a bit.

Hiram was looking out the window at the Owl Creek Hills. "My father wouldn't set foot in these mountains," he said. "Scared him. Said there were witches out here." Then he laughed.

"What's funny?" Oliver asked.

"That priest over at Saint whatever-it's-called asked me the other day if I believed in God. I looked him in the eye and said, 'Why the hell not.' Then I told him the question is, does He believe in me. He didn't like that. I don't think he liked me saying *hell* in church."

"What were you doing in the church?"

"I go in there for that communion wine. It's the only booze I get. My wife won't let me have beer or nothing."

"Mine, either."

"You're married? Who would marry you?"

"She's crazy," Oliver said.

Oliver pulled the truck into the yard of the ranch. There were several people standing outside the barn corral. The snow had stopped falling, and the sun was even breaking through in the west. They got out and walked over to the huddle of men standing near the gate. Tuck stayed close to Oliver.

The foals were standing, spindly-legged clichés next to their mother, a fat-rumped, well-blanketed Appaloosa. The two colts were identical, buckskin in color, with matching blazes. Like the sire, Oliver was told. Who could tell yet whether they would thrive, but they were standing.

"What was the birth like?" Oliver asked.

A fat man named Oscar threw his cigarette butt into the snow. "I knew it was happening at about nine last night. I called Innis and he drove up, got here about ten. Then it went real fast. Vet pulled the first one out, but it wasn't easy. The head and hoof were showing. He said a bunch of stuff, talking to himself. You know how he is. He reached his hands in there to untwist her leg and I heard him say, 'What the fuck.' I never heard Innis swear before. He said he couldn't believe it, but he felt another head. I couldn't believe it, either."

A couple of the men whistled even though they'd heard the story.

"Vet said there was another one and there he stands. He gave them some shots and left a couple of hours ago."

Oscar looked at Oliver. "What are you doing here?"

"I got a note about these guys."

"Sam Innis was here all night," Oscar said.

"The note was from Billy White Feather."

The men grew quiet.

"How do you know him?" one of the men asked.

"Never met him," Oliver said.

"Why is he leaving you notes?"

"I don't know."

"He's an asshole," Oscar said. "He owes Mary Willow two hundred dollars."

"For what?" Hiram asked.

"Something about a horse trailer. She paid him to rewire it, but I guess he skipped with the money. Asshole."

"So, nobody suspected twins," Oliver said.

"Naw," Oscar said.

George Big Elk, a Northern Cheyenne man, came out of the house and moved to the rail. He greeted Oliver. "News travels fast," he said.

"Around here," Oliver said.

"Looks like they're okay."

"They're beautiful. Has she thrown before?"

"Twice. Lost the first one. Almost lost her, too. It was a mess. I thought she was all torn up inside, but then she had a foal the next year."

Oliver looked at the mare. She was tall for an App, with great conformation. "The sire as pretty as she is?"

"You bet," George said. "Handsome. He's handsome."

"Billy White Feather offered to sell them to ol' Ollie," Hiram said.

"I wish that wasichu would come around here," George said.

The men laughed.

"Well, I can now say I've seen the twins," Oliver said. "I will see you men later. Hiram, do you need a ride back down to Ethete?"

"I'm all right. But if you want to come back later, I'll have some buffalo triplets to sell to you."

"Come on, Tuck."

It was snowing again when Oliver arrived home to find Lauren rearranging the furniture in the living room. The rug was rolled up and shoved to one side. She had put towels under the feet of the sofa so that she could slide it across the floor.

"You're going to hurt yourself," he said.

"I won't complain if you help me."

"Do you know what you're doing?"

"No."

"Well, okay then." He helped her move the sofa across the room and turn it. He stood away with her and looked at it. "What do you think?" he asked.

"Nope. Back where it was."

They pushed it back.

"So, where'd you run off to this morning?"

"Went to see twin foals up on the rez."

"That's cool."

"It was pretty cool. Big App mare, identical babies, mother and children doing well. A real beautiful scene."

"Somebody's going to die," she said.

"You got that right."

"Why are you such a pessimist?" she asked.

"Hey, I didn't say it, you did."

"I only said it because I knew you were thinking it."

"Seriously though, I hope those babies make it. They looked strong."

"So, who called you?" She followed him into the kitchen.

Oliver grabbed a couple of mugs and poured coffee from the pot that was sitting out. "Got a note. Tacked to the back door when I came in from feeding. It was from Billy White Feather."

"Who the hell is Billy White Feather?"

"Some white boy with an Indian fetish from what I gather. I'd never heard of him."

"So, why'd he leave you a note?"

"Beats me. It's pretty weird."

"While you're in town I want you to pick up a package waiting at the post office." Lauren sipped her coffee.

"Who said I'm going into town? I just got back. I've got work to do around here."

"Please? It's snowing. I hate driving in the snow."

"Everybody hates driving in the snow," he said.

"Pretty please?"

"I love it when you beg. I'm leaving Tuck here." He looked at the dog. "Be a watchdog. Watch."

"Hey, he's old."

"He's still employed." He gave the dog's head a rub.

The new post office was right beside the old post office. Oliver wondered if a post office needed an address. The only part of the old one used was its parking lot. It wasn't that the new lot was ever crowded, but the lines of the spaces had been so closely painted that no one could fit a truck into one. Oliver walked inside and handed the slip to Pam, the clerk, a large woman with large hair.

"You don't look like a Lauren," Pam said, looking at the paper.

"Haircut."

He watched as she waded through the piles of boxes in the back. He looked at the bulletin board beside him and wondered when they quit putting wanted posters on the wall. Someone was missing a tabby cat. There were some free shepherd-mix puppies to a good home. And there was a sheet with tear-off numbers offering guitar lessons from one Billy White Feather. Oliver tore off one of the tabs.

Pam came back with the box. "Here it is, Lauren."

"Thank you, ma'am."

"Just sign right here."

"Pam, have you come across a Billy White Feather?"

"Jerk."

"You've met him?"

"No. He came in here and caused a ruckus a while back while I was out to lunch. Drunk."

"You know his address?"

"Yeah, Ethete."

"Ethete? But he's a white guy."

"You get kicked by a horse? His name is White Feather."

"Folks up at Ethete say he's a white guy."

"Well, maybe he ain't Arapaho, but he's an Indian. Got a jet-black braid down to his narrow ass."

"Then, you've seen him."

"I wish I would see him. After what he said to that Dwight girl."

"Duncan Dwight's daughter?"

"Yeah."

"What did he say?" Oliver asked.

"I can't repeat it. But Duncan Dwight will shoot him if he sees him. And I wouldn't blame him."

Oliver picked up the package. "Thanks, Pam."

"You have a nice day now. Barn journey, as the French say."

Behind the wheel of his truck, Oliver called the guitar-lesson number on his mobile phone. A recording informed him that the line was not in service. Of course, he thought. He put the phone away and stared ahead through his windshield at the old post office. He was near laughing at himself, taken, as he was, by what seemed to be a mystery. The irony was double-sided, as he on one hand really had no interest in Billy White Feather, whether Indian or white, and on the other he recognized that pursuing an answer here was the same as falling for whatever con game this Billy White Feather was running around playing. But why had this guy left him a note? Why had he been at his place?

Oliver felt uneasy and so he called Lauren.

"You get my package?"

"Yep." He didn't want to alarm her, but he had to ask. "Has anybody come by today?"

"No. Why?"

"Just asking. Keep an eye out."

"Ollie?"

"I'll be home directly."

Even though he was anxious about getting home, his next stop was Duncan Dwight's office. He was an attorney and a cattle detective. He'd done Oliver's will and living trust. He was a short man who was comfortable with his size. He never rode a horse, but he was a real cowboy.

Duncan was chatting with his receptionist when Oliver walked in. "Howdo, Oliver. What brings you around?"

"Just came from the reservation. An App just dropped twins."

"Really?" He led the way into his office. "Come on in."

"All healthy so far," Oliver reported.

"Pretty cool."

"They're gorgeous. Born last night. And somebody tacked a note to my door telling me about it."

Oliver watched Duncan respond to his tone. "Okay, a note," Duncan said. "Why are you saying it like that?"

"A note from Billy White Feather."

Duncan pulled a cigar from the box on his desk, snipped off the end, and put it in his mouth. "Billy White Feather."

"You know him?" Oliver asked.

"Never met him."

Oliver walked over and looked at a wall of photos. Duncan posed with various people, maybe famous. There were a couple of pictures of Duncan standing with prized beef. "Do you know anything about him?"

"Heard some people talking about him. Nobody seems to like the guy very much, if at all."

"I heard he said something to your daughter."

"I heard that too, but she says she never saw him." Duncan lit his cigar. "What are you after, Oliver?"

"You know the folks up on the rez say Billy White Feather is a white guy?"

Duncan blew out a cloud of smoke. "White Feather sounds awfully Indian to me. What's eating at you?"

"This guy left me a note about buying horses that weren't his to sell. Left the note tacked to my door." He sighed, thought about Lauren at home, and said, "I'd better get home."

"Maybe Billy White Feather isn't Shoshone or Arapaho, but everybody described him as an Indian guy to me," Duncan said.

"What else did they say about him?"

"Great big guy."

"Fat?"

"I heard big. Could be he's fat."

"Woman up at Ethete described him as a skinny blond man to me."

Oliver and Duncan stared out the same window.

"Well, I gotta go," Oliver said.

"I'll ask around some," Duncan said.

Oliver nodded and left.

Oliver arrived home to find Lauren dragging a bag of fertilizer across the yard. He got out of the truck and picked it up for her. "You're going to hurt yourself," he said. "This shit is heavy."

"You can carry my shit any day, cowboy," she said.

"Where do you want it?"

"By the hydrangeas."

"And which ones might those be?"

Lauren pointed.

Oliver put down the bag.

"What was that phone call all about?" she asked. "You got me all nervous and scared."

"Sorry about that. It's just that I found out about the twins up on the reservation from a note left on our door. And I started worrying because someone had been on the place."

"Well, you got yourself another note." Lauren pulled a paper from her sweater pocket, handed it to him. "It's from Billy White Feather."

"He was here?"

"No, some woman brought it by."

"Indian woman?"

"White. Never saw her before, but she was wearing one of those pale blue uniforms from that fast-food place near the grocery store. What's it called?" She searched. "Tastee Freez."

"What did she look like?"

"Twenty-five, maybe a little older. Thick body, but not fat. Blond hair. Bad makeup."

"Did she say her name?"

"No, but her name tag said *Billie* with an *i-e*."

"Very funny."

"I kid you not."

Oliver looked at the note. *Sorry about this morning. Beautiful twins, but not mine. Call me if you need a ranch hand.*

"You sure you don't know this guy?"

"Now I'm not so sure. Maybe from a while ago. Maybe he used a different name. I'm trying to remember if I know any tall, short, skinny, fat, white Indians with black blond hair."

That night Oliver couldn't sleep. He pulled on some jeans and a sweatshirt and walked downstairs. Tuck raised his head from his bed when Oliver sat in the mudroom to put on his boots. He told the dog to stay and Tuck put his head back down. The snow had stopped and the clouds had blown clear, allowing the temperature to take a serious drop. He folded his arms over his chest and walked out into the pasture with his donkeys. They stirred at the bottom of the hill and plodded their way up, investigating, hoping for treats.

Oliver thought about the twin foals and hoped they would be all right. He then considered Billy White Feather, or rather he tried to consider him, tried to imagine him. He wouldn't have cared at all, except that the note had been left on the door of his home. It irked him even now that a stranger had stood on his porch without his knowledge. He worried for Lauren. Then the fragility of it all, everything, became so apparent. Strangers always had access to one's home. He could not be there all the time. He decided to find a companion for Tuck.

The donkeys came and stood around him, became still and peaceful. One of them lay down. Perhaps they were asleep. Who could tell? Perhaps he was still asleep and only dreaming that he was standing out in a pasture. The cold air bit at him some more and he decided, dream or not, he'd go back inside.

The next morning, after feeding the horses, after fixing a near-downed section of fence, and after a light breakfast of yogurt and toast, Oliver drove into town to the Tastee Freez. He arrived at a little after eight to discover they opened at eight thirty. He sat in his truck with his dog and listened to the news and weather on the radio. It seemed winter was coming early and hard.

An old-model blue Buick 225 rolled in and parked in a spot on the far side of the lot beside the Dumpsters. A man got out and walked toward the restaurant. Oliver got out and waved to him.

"We'll be open in about twenty minutes," the man said.

"Does Billie work here?" Oliver asked.

"Who wants to know?" The man was rightly suspicious.

"My name is Oliver Campbell. Billie brought a note by my place yesterday, and I just want to ask her about it."

The man looked Oliver up and down. "What kind of note?"

"It was a note about some horses. She delivered it to my place for Billy White Feather."

"Fuck Billy White Feather. If you're a friend of his, then you ain't no friend of mine." The man started to move away.

"I've never even seen Billy White Feather. I just want to know why I'm getting these notes."

"Yeah, well, that guy's got problems."

"You know him then," Oliver said.

"He came around here about three months ago messing with every waitress he could talk to."

"White guy?"

"Hispanic, I think. Anyway, that's what the girls told me."

"You never saw him?"

"I wish I had."

Oliver nodded. "Does Billie work today?"

"She should be here soon."

"Mind if I wait?"

"Suit yourself."

Oliver returned to his truck.

Another man arrived by bicycle. A tall, skinny, older woman parked her late-sixties Cadillac Coupe de Ville beside the Buick.

A stout young woman with blond hair was dropped off by a man in a white dually pickup.

Oliver got out of his truck and called to her. "Excuse me, ma'am. Are you Billie?"

The woman looked at Oliver and then at the door of the Tastee Freez as if she was considering running. When he was closer he could see that her name tag did indeed read BILLIE.

"It's okay," Oliver said. "I just want to ask you a couple of questions. You left a note with my wife yesterday. The note from Billy White Feather."

The woman's face showed some kind of relief, but she was still uncomfortable. "And?" she said.

"I just wanted to ask you about Billy White Feather."

"I delivered that note for my idiot roommate. I don't even know Billy White Feather."

"Your roommate."

"Yes, my roommate."

"And where might I find your roommate?" Oliver asked. He felt suddenly exhausted and perhaps overwhelmed. He certainly had no idea what he was doing in the parking lot of the Tastee Freez.

"Not here," she said.

"You think I can drop by and see her?"

"Not here meaning not in town. She's gone. She's on her way to Denver to meet up with that guy."

"Billy White Feather."

"Yeah."

"Listen, I'd really like to track down this guy. Did she give you a forwarding address or anything?"

"I can't tell you that. I don't know you."

"I understand." He looked at the sky. "But you've seen my place, my wife. You know I'm not some crazy killer."

"I don't know that."

"I'll give you ten dollars for the address."

"Listen, I'm late for work."

"Twenty dollars."

"You're not a crazy?"

"No, ma'am."

She gave Oliver the address and walked on into the restaurant.

Oliver returned home to do his chores. It was time for his horses to have their shots and so he waited for Sam Innis, the vet. Innis always delivered the vaccine and left it to Oliver to administer the shots. He drove in while Oliver was combing out his mare's tail.

"I've got the drugs," Innis said, conspiratorially, stepping out of his rig.

"Thanks."

"First one's free." Innis looked around, then at the sky. "Any animals need looking at?"

"Everybody is standing. Got time for coffee?"

"A quick cup sounds good." The vet followed Oliver across the yard and into the house.

Innis sat at the table in the kitchen. Oliver pulled some mugs from the cupboard and reached for the pot.

"Where's Lauren?"

"Food shopping."

"Shoot. The only reason I come all the way out here is to see her. You can tell her I said that."

"I will."

Oliver poured the coffee.

Innis yawned. "Sorry. Late night."

"Out partying?"

"I wish. Some foals died up on the reservation."

"The twins?"

"Yup."

"Damn. What happened?"

"Beats me. Failure to thrive. They looked good, real good. I can't believe both failed. Twins are difficult." Innis sipped his coffee. He handled the information like someone used to death.

Oliver was shaken by what he'd just heard. "I can't believe it," he said. He sat at the table, too. "They looked good."

"I'm going to do autopsies on them, but nothing is going to turn up. It just happens."

Oliver looked out the window at Tuck sniffing at the vet's tires. "George must be pretty disappointed."

"I think he is, but who can tell with him."

They drank for a couple minutes without talking.

"It's a tough thing, all right," Innis said. "Twins are a complicated business. Complicated."

"Yeah, I guess so."

"Well, gotta run."

"Thanks for bringing the meds over," Oliver said.

Oliver checked the tractor and the plow blade. He would apparently be needing them soon. The sky had become fat and gray. Like a city pigeon. That was how his father had described a snow sky. He'd told Lauren the news about the foals and her eyes had welled up, but she didn't cry. She'd seemed more worried about him. Then he'd started talking about Billy White Feather again. She hadn't laughed at him, but she did stare at him with concern. She'd watched him unfold and fold the piece of paper with the Denver address.

Now he walked into the house to find on the kitchen table a paper sack and a tall thermos bottle standing next to it. Lauren was sitting, drinking tea.

"What's this?" he asked.

"Some sandwiches, some cookies, some coffee." She looked him in the eye and offered a weak smile. "How long have we been married? That was a rhetorical question."

"I thought so."

"I know you, Oliver Campbell. Go to Denver. Figure this out. Otherwise you're going to drive me crazy."

"I thought I did that anyway."

"It's a long drive, so stop for the night in Laramie."

"You've got this all figured out."

"Pretty much."

"Well, bolt the doors. I'll put the twelve-gauge by the bed."

"You're scaring me again. I won't need it."

"Humor me."

Lauren nodded.

"Want to ride with me?" he asked.

"And who's going to take care of this place?"

"Just what am I looking for?"

"Billy White Feather."

"And why?"

"Beats me."

Oliver started toward the stairs, stopped. "He came to our home, Lauren. Stood on our porch."

"I know."

The drive to Denver, though long, was a familiar one. He knew when he promised Lauren that he would stop for the night that he would not. It was only two in the afternoon when he reached Laramie and with only three more hours of driving it made little sense to lay up for the better part of a day. He grabbed a hot dog at Dick's Dogs, a place that he could never visit if he were with Lauren, then continued on. He reached Denver just about in the middle of rush hour.

Sitting in the traffic turned out to be better for his thinking than the driving. He looked at the faces of the other drivers. Any one of them could have been Billy White Feather. He had decided that Billy White Feather was actually a middle-aged, wheelchair-bound Filipina. Or a tall black man with a disfiguring scar down the center of his face.

If he found the man, what was he going to say? "Hey, why are you leaving me notes?" Or maybe, "Stay out of my yard." Being there felt suddenly stupid. He had half a mind to turn around and head back to Laramie for the night. But it was only half a mind, after all. The rest of his mind wanted to see what a Billy

White Feather looked like. Was he a native guy or was he white? Oliver knew he wouldn't be able to tell by looking. Maybe everybody had him wrong. Maybe he was an Indian, but he sure wasn't Arapaho or Shoshone. Maybe he was a white guy with dark skin and a ponytail going around telling all the wasichus that he was an Indian. None of this thinking answered the question of what he was going to say if he found the man.

He got off the freeway and made his way through town. He found the street and the address. It was a dingy neighborhood, made dingier by the fact that it was dusk now. Oliver parked in front of the small white house. A couple of teenagers eyed him as they walked by. He decided that sitting in his truck like that might get him into trouble, so he got out and walked to the door.

No one answered his knock. He walked around back, feeling uncomfortable as his head passed windows. He expected a pit bull to come running at him at any moment. In the back was a poorly maintained rectangle of grass, one of those circular clothes-drying racks, and a partially disassembled motorcycle under a cheap aluminum cover. He tripped a motion-activated yard light over the paint-peeled screen door. His hands were shaking, but once he realized it, they stopped. He knocked on the back door and still there was no response. He sat on the concrete steps and looked at the battered Honda bike. It was fast becoming dark now. He looked again at the door.

Oliver got up and went back to his truck. He found some paper, the back of something on the floor, and wrote a note. He walked around to the back of the house again. As he attempted to wedge his note between the screen door and the jamb, the back door opened. A woman in a dingy yellow terry-cloth robe stood rubbing her eyes.

"Who the fuck are you?" she asked. She was tall and extremely skinny. Oliver thought she looked like a user of some kind of drug, but decided he didn't know enough to tell. She had small features set on a narrow face with a sharp nose that was pointed at Oliver.

"Is this where Billy White Feather lives?"

"It's where he's supposed to live soon," she said.

"I was leaving him a note. Are you his girlfriend?"

"I'm her roommate." She sniffed like she had a cold. "What do you want with Billy?"

"Billy left me a note at my place up in Wyoming," Oliver said.

"Yeah?"

"I don't know this Billy and I want to know why he left me a note."

"You drove all the way from Wyoming for that?"

When she said it, it did sound sort of crazy.

"I'm calling the cops if you don't leave," she said.

"Do you know Billy?"

"Suppose I do?"

"Is Billy White Feather white or Indian?"

"What kind of question is that? You'd better get away from here."

"He put a note on my door and I don't know him. I just want to know what he looks like. Tall? Short? What?"

"Fuck you," she said, and slammed the door.

Oliver left the note wedged inside the screen. He walked back to his truck and fell in behind the wheel. The teenagers were walking back in his direction. He heard a siren in the distance. He cranked his engine and drove away.

Lydia Davis

The Seals

I KNOW WE'RE SUPPOSED TO be happy on this day. How odd that is. When you're very young, you're usually happy, at least you're ready to be. You get older and see things more clearly and there's less to be happy about. Also, you start losing people— your family. Ours weren't necessarily easy, but they were ours, the hand we were dealt. There were five of us, actually, like a poker hand—I never thought of that before.

We're beyond the river and into New Jersey now, we'll be in Philadelphia in about an hour, we pulled out of the station on time.

I'm thinking especially about her—older than me and older than our brother, and so often responsible for us, always the most responsible, at least till we were all grown up. By the time I was grown up, she already had her first child. Actually, by the time I was twenty-one, she had both of them.

Most of the time I don't think about her, because I don't like to feel sad. Her broad cheeks, soft skin, lovely features, large eyes, her light complexion, blonde hair, colored but natural, with a little gray in it. She always looked a little tired, a little sad, when she paused in a conversation, when she rested for a moment, and especially in a photograph. I've searched and searched for a photo in which she doesn't look tired or sad, but I can find only one.

They said she looked young, and peaceful, in her coma, day after day. It went on and on—no one knew exactly when it would end. My brother told me she had a glow over her face, a damp sheen—she was sweating lightly. The plan was to let her breathe on her own, with a little oxygen, until she stopped breathing. I never saw her in the coma, I never saw her at the end. I'm sorry about that now. I thought I should stay with our mother and wait it out here, holding her hand, till the phone call came. At least that's what I told myself. The phone call came in the middle of the night. My mother and I both got out of bed, and then stood there together in the dark living room, the only light coming from outside, from the street lamps.

I miss her so much. Maybe you miss someone even more when you can't figure out what your relationship was. Or when it seemed unfinished. When I was little, I thought I loved her more than our mother. Then she left home.

I think she left right after she was done with college. She moved away to the city. I would have been about seven. I have some memories of her in that house, before she moved away. I remember her playing music in the living room, I remember her standing by the piano, bent a little forward, her lips pursed around the mouthpiece of her clarinet, her eyes on the sheet music. She played very well then. There were always little family dramas about the reeds she needed for the mouthpiece of her clarinet. Years later, miles away from there, when I was visiting her, she would bring out the clarinet again, not having played it in a long time, and we would try to play something together, we would work our way, hit or miss, through something. You could sometimes hear the full, round tones that she had learned how to make, and her perfect sense of the shape of a line of music, but the muscles of her lips had weakened and sometimes she lost control. The instrument would squeak or remain silent. Playing, she would force the air into the mouthpiece, pressing hard, and then, when there was a rest, she would lower the instrument for a moment, expel the air in a rush, and then take a quick breath before starting to play again.

I remember where the piano was in our house, just inside the archway into that long, low-ceilinged room shadowed by pine trees outside the front windows, with sun coming in the side windows, on the open side, from the sunny yard, where the rose-bushes grew against the house and the beds of iris lay out in the middle of the lawn, but I don't remember her there on this holiday. Maybe she didn't come home for that. She was too far away to come back very often. We didn't have a lot of money, so there probably wasn't much for train fares. And maybe she didn't want to come back very often. I wouldn't have understood that then. I told our mother I would give up all the few dollars I had saved if it would bring her home again for a visit. I was very serious about this, I thought it would help, but our mother just smiled.

I missed her so much. When she still lived at home she often looked after us, my brother and me. On the day I was born, on that hot summer afternoon, she was the one who stayed with my brother. They were dropped off at the county fair. She led him around the rides and booths for hours and hours, both of them hot and thirsty and tired, in that flat basin of fairground, where years later we watched the fireworks. My father and mother were miles away, across town, at the hospital on top of the hill.

When I was ten, the rest of us moved, too, to the same city, so for a few years we all lived close by. She would come over to our apartment and stay for a while, but I don't think she came very often, and I don't really understand why not. I don't remember family meals together with her, I don't remember excursions in the city together. When she was at the apartment, she would listen carefully when I practiced the piano. She would tell me when I played a wrong note, but sometimes she was wrong about that. She taught me my first word in French: She made me say it over and over till I had the pronunciation right. Our mother is gone now, too, so I can't ask her why we didn't see her more often.

There won't be any more animal-themed presents from her. There won't be any more presents from her at all.

Why those animal-themed presents? Why did she want to remind me of animals? She once gave me a mobile made of china penguins—why? Another time, a seagull of balsa wood that hung on strings and bobbed its wings up and down in the breeze. Another time, a dish towel with badgers on it. I still have that. Why badgers?

TRENTON MAKES, THE WORLD TAKES—out the window. How many advertising slogans will I stare at out the window today? Now there are poles falling over into the water with all their wires still strung on them—what happened to them, and why were they left there?

It's always the ones without families who get asked to work on this day. I could have claimed that I was spending it with my brother, but he's in Mexico. Four hours, a little more. I'll be there around dinnertime. I'll eat in the hotel restaurant, if there is one. That's always the easiest. The food is never really very good, but the people are friendly. They have to be, it's part of their job. Friendly sometimes meaning they'll turn the music down for me. Or they'll say they can't, but smile.

Was a love of animals something we shared? She must have liked them or she wouldn't have sent me those presents. I can't remember how she was with animals. I try to remember her different moods: so often worried, sometimes more relaxed and smiling (at the table, after a drink of wine), sometimes laughing at a joke, sometimes playful (years ago, with her children), at those times filled with sudden physical energy, lunging at someone across the lawn, under the bay tree, in the walled garden that her husband cared for so patiently.

She worried about so many things. She would imagine a bad outcome and she would elaborate on it until it grew into a story and moved far away from where it started. It could start with a prediction of rain. To one of her grown daughters she might say something like, It's going to rain. Don't forget your raincoat. If you get wet you might catch cold, and then you might miss the performance tomorrow. That would be too bad. Bill would be so disappointed. He's looking forward to hearing what you think of the play. You and he have talked about it so much . . .

I think about that a lot—how tense she was. It's something that must have started very early, she had such a complicated childhood. Three fathers by the time she was six years old—or two, I suppose, if you don't count her actual father. He knew her only when she was a baby. Our mother kept leaving her with other people—a nanny, a cousin. For a morning or a day, usually, but once, at least, for weeks and weeks. Our mother had to work—it was always for a good reason.

I didn't see her often, a long time would go by, because she lived so far away. When we saw each other again, she would put her arms around me and give me a strong hug, pressing me against her soft chest, my cheek against her shoulder. She was half a head taller, and she was broader. I was not only younger, but smaller. She had been there as long as I could remember. I always felt she would protect me or look out for me, even when I was grown up. I still sometimes think, with a pang of longing, before I realize what I'm thinking, that some older woman I see somewhere, about fourteen years older, will take care of me. When she drew back from hugging me, she would be looking off to the side or over my head. She seemed to be thinking of something else. Then, when her eyes rested on me, I wasn't sure she saw me. I didn't know what her feelings for me really were.

What was my place in her life? I sometimes thought that to her daughters, and even to her, I didn't matter. The sensation would come over me suddenly, an emptiness, as if I didn't even exist. There were just the three of them, her two girls and her, after their father died, after her second husband left. I was peripheral, our brother was, too, though he and I had been such a large part of her life early on.

I was never sure how she felt about anyone except her daughters. I could tell how much she missed them, when they were away, because she would suddenly become so quiet. Or when they were about to go away—from the rented house at the beach, saying good-bye on the front doorstep, the shiny dune grass growing in the sand beyond the cars, the gray shingle of the roof in the sun, the smell of fish and creosote, the sun reflecting off the cars, then the slam of one car door, the slam of the other car door, and her silence as she watched. It was when she was quiet that I felt I had more access to the truth of her feelings, a way to see into them, and those times were mostly in relation to her daughters.

But I think her feelings about our mother were a heavy burden in her life, at least when they were together. When our mother was far away, maybe she could forget her. Our mother was always stepping on her to get up higher, always needing to be right, always needing to be better than her, and than all of us, most of the time. The terrible innocence of our mother, too, as she did that. She had no idea, most of the time.

Our last conversation—it was on the phone, long-distance. She said she was having trouble seeing things on the right side of her field of vision. On a form she was filling out, she saw the word *date* and wrote in the day's date, not seeing that there were more words to the right of it, and that she was supposed to fill in *date of birth*. We talked for a while, and toward the end of the conversation I must have said something about talking again in a few days, or staying in touch about her condition, because then, in answer to that, she said she didn't want to talk again, because she wanted to save all her strength for talking to her daughters. As she said it, her voice sounded to me distant, or exhausted, she did not soften what she was saying, or apologize. We never talked again after that. I felt pushed away, pushed out of her life. But her coolness was the sound of her own fear, her preoccupation with what was happening to her, not anything against me.

After she died, I kept going over and over it, trying to see what she felt about me, trying to measure it, find the affection or the love, measure that, make sure of it. She must have had mixed feelings about me, her much younger sister—my life at home was easier than hers had ever been. She probably felt some jealousy that went on and on, year after year, and yet she did want to be with me, she came to where I lived, she visited me, she slept in my living room, it was two nights, at least. She came more than once. Was it on one of those visits that I heard her little radio going half the night, close beside her next to the bed, muttering and singing, or was it in one of the rented beach places during the summer vacation, sand on the floor, someone else's furniture, someone else's art on the walls? She had trouble sleeping, she kept the radio on and read a detective novel late into the night.

And she did have me come and stay with her, and once I lived with her for a while, when I had to get away from my parents. Sometimes I thought she took me in from a sense of duty to me, her younger sister, since I was always having my own problems.

She always sent a package well ahead of time. Inside, each present was wrapped in soft tissue paper, or stiffer wrapping paper. All these presents—she picked them out, bought them, wrapped them in cheerful paper, labeled them in her large script with black or colored marker directly on the gift wrap, and sent them a couple of weeks in advance.

I know I always cared too much about my presents. This holiday was the high point of the year for me when I was a child, and that has never changed. The year culminates in this holiday and the turning of the old year to the new year, and then the circle of the year begins again, always leading up to this holiday.

The seagull ended up in a closet, the strings tangled. From time to time, I would try to untangle it, and at last I succeeded. Then I hung it from a rafter in the barn with a piece of duct tape. After a while, in the heat of the summer, the tape loosened and it fell down.

Then there was that little green stuffed elephant with sequins, from India, quite pretty. With two little cords on it, to hang it up somewhere. I hung it in a window and the green material on one side of it faded after a while in the sunlight. And a thing made of felt, with pockets, to hang on the back of a door and put things in—I'm not sure what. It had elephants on it, too, embroidered on the felt.

Now I remember—she would get these things at special handicraft fairs to benefit some organization of indigenous people. That was part of her kindness, and her conscientiousness, and part of the reason the things were a little odd and sometimes a strange match for us.

So there was always the excitement of her package arriving in the mail. The coarse brown paper a little battered from the trip overseas. The brown paper was even more exciting than the wrappings inside, because it was so drab, yet you knew that inside there would be that explosion of little packages, each wrapped in colored paper, each paper different.

She chose my presents with me in mind, I think, but twisting the facts a little, in an optimistic sort of way, thinking I would find this thing useful or decorative. I think a lot of people, when they pick out a gift, twist the facts optimistically. But I'm not saying I'm against people trying out a different kind of gift on someone, and I'm certainly not against those handicraft fairs. Now that a few years have gone by, and I've changed, too, I would buy my gifts at a handicraft fair. I would do it at least in her memory.

She wouldn't spend a lot of money on a gift. That was her conscience. She wouldn't spend a lot on herself, either. I also believe that, deep down, she probably didn't think she deserved any better.

But she spent a lot on us at other times. Her gifts then would come out of the blue. Once, she wrote to me and asked if I wanted to go on a skiing trip in the mountains with her and the children. It was early spring and the snow was melting in muddy patches on the slopes. We skied on what snow there was. I sometimes went off on long walks. She thought I shouldn't go by myself—if something happened to me, I would be alone and without help. But she could not forbid me to go, so I went. On the paths I took, in fact, there were many people hiking up and down, passing each other with a friendly greeting.

Years later, when I was long past the age when I should have needed any help from her, she bought me my first computer. I could have refused, but I still did not have much money. And there was something exciting about her sudden offer one afternoon, over the phone. It was late in the evening where she was. Her offer was an enveloping burst of generosity, I wanted to sink into it and stay inside it. Yes, she said, yes, she insisted, she would send me the money. The next day she called again, a little calmer—she wanted to help, she would send me some money, but not the whole amount, which was a lot in those days. I know how it must have been—late in the evening, she was thinking of me, and missing me, and the feeling grew in her and turned into a desire to do something for me, even something dramatic.

Starting at about that time, she would rent a house for us each summer, or at least pay for most of it, a house at the beach, for a week or two, a different one each year, and we would all go there and be there together. The last time we did this was the last year of my father's life, though he didn't come to the beach house—we left him behind in the nursing home. The next summer, he was gone, and she was gone, too.

Nearly to Philadelphia—rounding the bend, by the river, there are the boathouses on the other side, that big museum on the cliff across the water, like a building from ancient Greece. I won't see the station this time—its high ceiling and long wooden benches and archways and preserved old signs. I could just stand there looking at it for a while, the deep space of it—I do, now and then, if I have time. Our own Penn Station was even grander. It's gone now—that always hurts, to think about. And then when you're walking around there in that underground concourse, killing time before your train, you keep passing the photos they put up on the columns, of the old Penn Station, the long shafts of sunlight falling through the tall windows down the flights of marble stairs. As if they want to remind us of what we're missing—strange.

Then we'll be passing through Amish country. I never remember to watch for it, it always takes me by surprise. In the spring, the teams of mules and horses plowing the sloping fields up to the horizon—none of that today. The wash on the lines—maybe. It's cloudy, but dry and windy. What was that I read about salting your wash in winter? Anyway, it's not freezing today. A warm winter.

Again and again, she tried to pay our brother's way over, to go visit her. He never went. He never said why. He finally went when she was dying, when she didn't know it, it was too late for her to have that satisfaction—that at last he had agreed to come. He stayed there until the end. When he was not with her, he walked around the city. He took care of some of the practical things that had to be done. Then he stayed on for the funeral. I did not go over for the funeral. I had good reasons, to me they seemed good, anyway, having to do with our old mother, and the shock of it, and how far away it was, across the ocean. Really, it had more to do with the strangers who would be at the funeral, and the tenderness of my own feelings, which I did not want to share with strangers.

I could share her when she was alive. When she was alive, her presence was endless, time with her was endless, time was endless. Our mother was very old already, and when we children stopped to think about how long we might live, we thought we would live to be just as old. Then, suddenly, there was that strange problem with her vision, which turned out to be a problem not with her vision but in her brain, and then, without warning, the bleeding and the coma, and the doctors announcing that she did not have long to live.

Once she was gone, every memory was suddenly precious, even

the bad ones, even the times I was irritated with her, or she was irritated with me. Then it seemed a luxury to be irritated.

I did not want to share her, I did not want to hear a stranger say something about her, a minister in front of the congregation, or a friend of hers who would see her in a different way. To stay with her, in my mind, to remain with her, was not easy, since it was all in my mind, since she wasn't really there, and for that, it had to be just the two of us, no one else. There would have been strangers at the funeral, people she knew but I didn't know, or people I knew but didn't like, people who had cared about her or had not cared about her but thought they should attend the funeral. But now I'm sorry, or rather, I'm sorry I couldn't have done both—gone to the funeral and also stayed home to be with our mother and nurse my own grief and my own memories.

Suddenly, after she was gone, things of hers became more valuable to me than they had been before—her letters, of course, though there weren't many of them, but also things she had left behind in my house after her last visit, like her jacket, a dark blue windbreaker with some logo on it. And a detective novel I tried to read and couldn't. A tub of frozen clams in the freezer, and a jar of tartar sauce, marked down, in the door of the fridge.

We're moving pretty fast now. When you slide by it all so quickly, you think you won't ever have to get bogged down in it again— the traffic, the neighborhoods, the stores, waiting in lines. We're really speeding. The ride is smooth. Just a little squeaking from some metal part in the car that's jiggling. We're all jiggling a little.

There aren't many people in the car, and they're pretty quiet today. I don't mind telling someone if he talks too long on his cell phone. I did that once. I gave this man ten minutes, maybe even more, maybe twenty, and then I went and stood there next to him in the aisle. He was hunched over with his finger pressed against his free ear. He didn't get angry. He looked up at me, smiled, waved his hand in the air, and ended the call before I was back in my seat. I don't do business on my cell phone on the train. They should know better.

There were also gifts of a different kind that she gave—the effort she went to for other people, the work she put into preparing meals for friends. The wanderers she took into her house, to live for weeks or months—kids passing through, but also, one year, that thin old Indian who spent every day arranging her books in the bookcases, and who ate so little and meditated so long. And later her old father, her actual father, the one she first met when she was already grown up, not my father, not the father who raised her. She had had a dream about him, that he was very ill. She had set out to find him, she had found him, and it turned out that he was very ill.

She was so tired by the end of the day that whenever I was there visiting, when we all sat watching some program or movie on television in the evening, she would fall asleep. First she was awake for a while, curious about the actors—Who is that, didn't we see him in . . . ?—and then she would grow quiet, she was quiet for so long that you would look over and see that her head was leaning to the side, the lamplight shining on her light hair, or her head was bowed over her chest, and she would sleep until we all stood up to go to bed.

What was the last present she gave me? Seven years ago. If I had known it was the last, I would have given it such careful attention.

If it wasn't animal themed or made by some indigenous person, then it was probably some kind of a bag, not an expensive bag, but one that had a special feature, a trick to it, like it folded into itself when it was empty, and then zipped up and had a little clip on it so you could clip it onto another bag. I have a few of those stored away.

She carried them herself, and other kinds of bags, always open and full of things—an extra sweater, another bag, a couple of books, a box of crackers, a bottle of something to drink. There was a generosity in how much she packed and carried with her.

One time when she came to visit—I'm thinking of her bags leaning in a group against a chair of mine. I was nearly paralyzed, not knowing what to do. I don't know why. I didn't want to leave her alone, that wouldn't have been right, but I also wasn't used to having company. After a while, the panicky feeling passed, maybe just because time passed, but there was a moment when I thought I was going to collapse.

Now I can look at that same bed where she slept and wish she would come back at least for a little while. We wouldn't have to talk, we wouldn't even have to look at each other, but I just want to see her arms, her broad shoulders, her hair.

I want to say to her, Yes, there were problems, our relationship was difficult to understand, and complicated, but still, I would like just to have you sitting there on the daybed where you did sleep for a few nights once, it's your part of the living room now, I'd like to just look at your cheeks, your shoulders, your arms, your wrist with the gold watchband on it, a little tight, pressing into the flesh, your strong hands, the gold wedding ring, your short fingernails, I don't have to look you in the eyes or have any sort of communion, complete or incomplete, but to have you there in person, in the flesh, for a while, pressing down the mattress, making folds in the cover, the sun coming in behind you, would be very nice. Maybe you would stretch out on the daybed and read for a while in the afternoon, maybe fall asleep. I would be in the next room, nearby.

Sometimes, after dinner, if she was very relaxed and I was sitting next to her, she would put her hand on my shoulder and let it rest there for a while, so that I felt it warmer and warmer through the cotton of my shirt.

I sensed then that she did love me in a way that wouldn't change, whatever her mood might be.

That fall, after the summer when they both died, she and my father, there was a point when I wanted to say to them, All right, you have died, I know that, and you've been dead for a while, we have all absorbed this and we've explored the feelings we had at first, in reaction to it, surprising feelings, some of them, and the feelings we're having now that a few months have gone by—but now it's time for you to come back. You have been away long enough.

Because after the dramas of the deaths themselves, those complicated dramas that went on for days, for both of them, there was the quieter and simpler fact of missing them. He would not be there to come out of his room at home with a picture or a letter to show us, he would not be there to tell us the same stories over again, about when he was a young boy—pronouncing the names that meant so much to him and so little to us: Clinton Street where he was born, Winter Island where they went in the summers when he was little, him watching the back of the horse that trotted ahead of them pulling their carriage, his pneumonia when he was a child, weakened and lying in bed reading, day after day, in that cousin's house in Salem, going to the Y on Saturdays to swim with the other boys, where it was the usual thing for all the boys to swim naked, and how that bothered him, the Perkins family next door. He would not be there having his first cup of coffee in the morning at eleven o'clock, or reading by the light from the window in an armchair. She would not be making pancakes for us in the mornings at the rented beach house, wide fat blueberry pancakes a little underdone in the middle, standing over the pan, quiet and concentrating, or talking as she worked, in her flowered blouse and straight pants, her comfortable flats or her moccasins, the familiar shape of her toes in them stretching the fabric or the leather. She would not go out swimming in the rough waves of the harbor, even in stormy weather, her eyes a lighter blue than the water. She would not stand with our mother waist-deep in the water near the shore talking with a little frown on her face either from the sunlight or from concentrating on what they were talking about. She would never again make oyster stew the way she did one Christmas Eve, on that visit to our mother and father's house after her husband died, the crunch of sand in our mouths in the milky broth, sand in the bottoms of our spoons. She would not take a child on her lap, her own child, as on that same visit, when they were all so sad and confused, or someone else's child, and rock that child quietly back and forth, her broad strong arms around the child's chest, resting her cheek against the child's hair, her face sad and thoughtful, her eyes distant. She would not be there on the sofa in the evenings, exclaiming in surprise when she saw an actor she knew in a movie or a show, she would not fall asleep there, suddenly quiet, later in the evening.

The first New Year after they died felt like another betrayal—we were leaving behind the last year in which they had lived, a year they had known, and starting on a year which they would never experience.

There was also some confusion in my mind, in the months afterward. It was not that I thought she was still alive. But at the same time I couldn't believe that she was actually gone. Suddenly the choice wasn't so simple: either alive or not alive. It was as though not being alive did not have to mean she was dead, as though there were some third possibility.

Her visit, that time—now I don't know why it seemed so complicated. You just go out and do something together, or sit and talk if you stay inside. Talking would have been easy enough, since she liked to talk. Of course it's too simple to say that she liked to talk. There was something frantic about the way she talked. As though she were afraid of something, underneath, fending something off. After she died, that was one thing we all said—we used to wish she would stop talking for a while, or talk a little less, but now we would have given anything to hear her voice.

I wanted to talk, too, I had things to say in answer to her, but it wasn't possible, or it was difficult. She wouldn't let me, or I would have to force my way into the conversation.

I wish I could try again—I wish she would come and visit again. I think I would be calmer. I'd be so glad to see her. But it doesn't work that way. If she came back, she'd be back for more than just a little while, and maybe I wouldn't know what to do, after all, any better than the last time I saw her. Still, I'd like to try. But it's too late.

Another present was a board game involving endangered species. A board game—there was that optimism again. Or she was doing what our mother used to do—giving me something that required another person, so that I would have to bring another person into my life. I actually meet plenty of people. I even meet them traveling. Most people are basically pretty friendly. It's true that I still live alone, I'm just more comfortable that way, I like having everything the way I want it. But having a board game wasn't going to encourage me to bring someone home to play it with me.

There aren't that many of us in the car, though more than I would have expected on this particular day. Of course I think they're all on their way to some place that's welcoming and friendly, where people are waiting for them with things to eat and drink, like little sausages and eggnog. But that may not be true. And they may be thinking the same thing about me—if they are thinking anything about me.

And some of them who may not be going anywhere special may be glad, though that's a little hard to believe, because you're made to feel, by all the hype, by all the advertising, really, but also by the things your friends say, that you should be somewhere special, with your family, or with your friends. If you're not, you get that old feeling of being left out, another feeling you learned when you were a child, in school probably, at the same time that you learned to get excited seeing all those wrapped presents, no matter what you eventually found in them, besides what you wanted.

I'm not as cheerful as I used to be, I know. A friend of mine said something about it, after I lost both of them, three weeks apart, that summer: He said, Your grief spreads into all sorts of different areas of your life. Your grief turns into depression. And after a while you just don't want to do anything. You just can't be bothered.

Another friend—when I told him, he said, "I didn't know you had a sister." So strange. By the time he found out I had a sister, I no longer had a sister.

Now it's beginning to rain, it's raining after all—little drops driven sideways across the windowpane. Streaks and dots across the glass. The sky outside is darker and the lights in the car, the ceiling light and the little reading lights over the seats, seem brighter. The farms are passing now. There's no wash hanging out, but I can see the clotheslines stretched between the back porches and the barns. The farms are on both sides of the tracks, there are wide-open spaces between them, the silos far apart over the landscape, with the farm buildings clustered around them, like churches in their little villages in the distance.

Sometimes the grief was nearby, waiting, just barely held back, and I could ignore it for a while. But at other times it was like a cup that was always full and kept spilling over.

For a while, it was hard for me to think or speak about one of them separate from the other. For a while, though not any-more, they were always linked together in my mind because they died so close to each other in time. It was hard not to imagine her waiting for him somewhere, and him coming. We were even comforted by it—we imagined that she would take care of him, wherever they were. She was younger and more alert than he was. She was taller and stronger. But would he be pleased, or would he be annoyed? Would he want to be by himself?

I didn't even know if he wanted me to stay there next to the bed while he was dying. I had taken the bus to the city where he and my mother lived, to be with him. There would be no chance of recovery, for him, or going back from where he was, because they had stopped feeding him. He wasn't speaking or hearing, or even seeing anymore, so there was no way to know what he wanted. He didn't look like himself. His eyes were half open, but they didn't see anything. His mouth was half open. He didn't have his teeth in. Once, I put a little wet sponge to his lower lip, because of the dryness, and his mouth clamped shut on it suddenly.

You think you should sit with someone who is dying, you think it must be a comfort to him, or to her. But when he was alive, when we were lingering at the dinner table, or in the living room talking and laughing, after a while our father always got up and left us and went into his own room. Later, when he was doing the dishes, he would say no, he didn't want any help. Even when we were visiting him in the nursing home, after an hour or two he would ask us to leave.

Our mother consulted a psychic, later, after they were gone, to see if she could get in touch with them. She didn't really believe in that sort of thing, but some friend of hers had recommended this psychic, and she thought it might be interesting and couldn't hurt to try, so she met with the woman and told her things about them, and let her try to communicate with them.

The woman said she reached both of them. Our father was agreeable and cooperative, though he didn't say much, something noncommittal, that he was "all right." My mother thought that after the trouble they had gone to, trying to reach him, he might have said more. But our sister turned away and was cross, and didn't want to have anything to do with it. We were very interested in this, even though we had trouble believing it. We felt that at least the psychic believed it and thought she had had that experience.

The two kinds of grief were different. One kind, for him, was for an end that came at the right time, that was in the natural order of things. The other kind of grief, for her, was for an end that came unexpectedly and much too soon. She and I were just beginning a good correspondence—now it will never continue. She was just beginning a project of her own that meant a lot to her. She had just rented a house near us where we would be able to see her much more often. A different phase of her life was just beginning.

Strange, the way things look when you're watching them out a train window. I don't get tired of that. Just now I saw an island in the river, a small one with a grove of trees on it, and I was going to look more carefully at it, because I like islands, but then I looked away for a moment and when I looked back it was gone. Now we're passing some woods again. Now the woods are gone and I can see the river again and the hills in the distance. The things close to the tracks flash by so fast, and the things in the middle distance flow past more quietly and steadily, and the things in the far distance stay still, or sometimes they seem to be moving forward, just because the things in the middle distance are moving backward.

Actually, even though things in the far distance seem to be staying still, or even moving forward a little, they are moving back very slowly. Those treetops on a hill in the far distance were even with us for a while, but when I looked again, they were behind us, though not far behind.

I kept noticing things in the days after she died and then after he died: A white bird flying up seemed to mean something, or a white bird landing nearby. Three crows on the branch of a tree meant something. Three days after he died, I woke up from a dream about Elysian fields, as though he had now gone into them, as though he had hovered near us for a while, for three days, even floating over our mother's living room, and had then gone on, into the Elysian fields, maybe before going farther, to whatever place he was going to go and stay.

I wanted to believe all this, I tried hard to believe it. After all, we don't know what happens. It's such a strange thing—that once you are dead, you do know the answer, if you know anything at all. But whatever the answer is, you can't communicate it to the ones who are still alive. And before you die, you can't know, whether we live on in some form, after we die, or just come to an end.

It's like what that woman in the store said to me the other day. We were talking about the little expressions our mothers liked to use over and over again—"To each his own," or "They meant well." She said her mother was Christian, and devout, and that she believed in an afterlife of the soul. But this woman herself did not believe, and would gently make fun of her mother. And whenever that happened, her mother would say to her, with a good-humored smile, When we die, one of us is going to be very surprised!

Our father himself believed that it was all in the body, and specifically in the brain, that it was all physical—the mind, the soul, our feelings. He had once seen a man's brains spread over the asphalt of a driveway after an accident. He had stopped his car on the street and got out to look. My sister was a little girl then. He told her to wait for him in the car. When the body was finished, he said, it was all over. But I wasn't so sure.

There was the terror I felt one night as I was going to sleep— the sudden question that woke me up. Where was she going now? I sensed very strongly that she was going somewhere or had gone somewhere, not that she had simply stopped existing. That she, like him, had stayed nearby for a while, and then she was going— down, maybe, but also out somewhere, as though out to sea.

First, while she was still alive, but dying, I kept wondering what was happening to her. I did not hear much about it. One thing they said was that when her reflexes were worse, according to the doctors, she would move toward the pinch or the prick instead of away from it. I thought that meant that her body wanted the pain, that she wanted to feel something. I thought it meant she wanted to stay alive.

There was also that slow, dark dream I had about five days after her death. I may have had the dream just as her funeral was taking place, or just after. In the dream, I was making my way down from one level to the next in a kind of arena, the levels were wider and deeper than steps, down into a large, deep, high-ceilinged, ornately furnished and decorated room, or hall—I had an impression of dark furniture, sumptuous ornamentation, it was a hall intended for ceremony, not for any daily use. I was holding a small lantern that fit tightly over my thumb and extended outward, with a tiny flame burning in it. This was the only illumination in the vast place, a flame that wavered and flickered and had already gone out or nearly gone out once or twice. I was afraid that as I went down, as I climbed down with such difficulty, over levels that were too wide and deep to be easily straddled, the light would go out and I would be left in that deep well of darkness, that dark hall. The door I had come in by was far above me, and if I called out, no one would hear me. Without a light, I would not be able to climb back up those difficult levels.

I later realized that, given the day and the hour when I woke up from the dream, it was quite possible that I dreamt it just at the time she was being cremated. The cremation was to begin right after the funeral, my brother told me, and he told me when the funeral had ended. I thought the flickering light was her life, as she held on to it those last few days. The difficult levels descending into the hall must have been the stages of her decline, day by day. The vast and ornate hall might have been death itself, in all its ceremony, as it lay ahead, or below.

The odd problem we had afterward was whether or not to tell our father. Our father was vague in his mind, by then, and puzzled by many things. We would wheel him up and down the hallway of his nursing home. He liked to greet the other residents with a smile and a nod. We would stop in front of the door to his room. In June, the last year he was alive, he looked at the HAPPY BIRTHDAY sign on the door and waved at it with his long, pale, freckled hand and asked me a question about it. He couldn't articulate his words very well anymore. Unless you had heard him

all your life, you wouldn't know what he was saying. He was mar-
veling over the sign, and smiling. He was probably wondering
how they knew when his birthday was.

He still recognized us, but there was a lot he didn't understand. He was not going to live much longer, though we didn't
know then how little time was left. It seemed to us important
for him to know that she had died—his daughter, though she
was really his stepdaughter. And yet, would he understand, if we
told him? And wouldn't it only distress him terribly, if he did
understand? Or maybe he would have both reactions at once—he
might understand some part of what we were saying, and then
feel terrible distress at both what we had told him and his inability to understand it completely. Should his last days be filled with
this distress and grief?

But the alternative seemed wrong, too—that he should end
his life not knowing this important thing, that his daughter had
died. Wrong that he, who had once been the head of our small
family, the one who, with our mother, made the most important
family decisions, the one who drove the car when we went out on
a little excursion, who helped our sister with her homework when
she was a teenager, who walked her to school every morning when
she was in her first year of school, while our mother rested or
worked, who refused or gave permission, who played jokes at the
dinner table that made her and her little friends laugh, who was
busy out in the backyard for a few weeks building a playhouse—
that he should not be shown the respect of being told that such an
important thing had happened in his own family.

He had so little time left, and we were the ones deciding something about the end of his life—that he would die knowing or
not knowing. And now I'm not sure what we did, it was so many
years ago. Which probably means that nothing very dramatic
happened. Maybe we did tell him, out of a sense of duty, but hast-
ily, and nervously, not wanting him to understand, and maybe
there was a look of incomprehension on his face, because some-

thing was going by too quickly. But I don't know if I'm remembering that or making it up.

On one of her visits to me, she gave me a red sweater, a red skirt, and a round clay tile for baking bread. She took a picture of me wearing the red sweater and the skirt. I think the last thing she gave me was those little white seals with perforated backs. They're filled with charcoal, which is supposed to absorb odors. You put them in your refrigerator. I guess she thought that because I live alone, my refrigerator would be neglected and smell bad, or maybe she just thought that anyone might need this.

When did she leave the tartar sauce? You wouldn't think a person could become attached to something like a jar of tartar sauce. But I guess you can—I didn't want to throw it out, because she had left it. Throwing it out would mean that the days had passed, time had moved on and left her behind. Just as it was hard for me to see the new month begin, the month of July, because she would never experience that new month. Then the month of August came, and he was gone by then, too.

Well, the little seals are useful to me, at least they were seven years ago. I did put them in my refrigerator, though at the back of a shelf, where I wouldn't have to look at their cheerful little faces and black eyes every time I opened the door. I even took them with me when I moved.

I doubt if they absorb anything anymore, after all this time. But they don't take up much room, and there isn't much in there anyway. I like having them, because they remind me of her. If I bend down and move things around, I can see them lying back there under the light that shines through some dried spilled things on the shelf above. There are two of them. They have black smiles painted on their faces. Or at least a line painted on their faces that looks like a smile.

Really, the only present I ever wanted, after I grew up, was something for work, like a reference book. Or something old.

Now there's a lot of noise coming from the café car—people

laughing. They sell alcohol there. I've never bought a drink on a train—I like to drink, but not here. Our brother used to have a drink on the train sometimes, on his way home from seeing our mother. He told me that once. This year he's in Acapulco—he likes Mexico.

We have a couple of hours to go, still. It's dark out. I'm glad it was light when we passed the farms. Maybe there's a big family in the café car, or a group traveling to a conference. I see that all the time. Or to a sporting event. Well, that doesn't actually make much sense, not today. Now someone's coming this way, staring at me. She's smiling a little—but she looks embarrassed. Now what? She's lurching. Oh, a party. It's a party—in the café car, she tells me. Everyone's invited.

Lionel Shriver

Kilifi Creek

It was a brand of imposition of which young people like Liana thought nothing: showing up on an older couple's doorstep, the home of friends of friends of friends, playing on a tentative enough connection that she'd have had difficulty constructing the sequence of referrals. If there was anything to that six-degrees-of-separation folderol, she must have been equally related to the entire population of the continent.

Typically, she'd given short notice, first announcing her intention to visit in a voice mail only a few days before bumming a ride with another party she hardly knew. (Well, the group had spent a long, hard-drinking night in Nairobi at a sprawling house with mangy dead animals on the walls that the guy with the ponytail was caretaking. In this footloose crowd of journalists and foreign-aid workers between famines, trust-fund layabouts, and tourists who didn't think of themselves as tourists, if only because they never did anything, the evening qualified them all as fast friends.) Ponytail Guy was driving to Malindi, on the Kenyan coast, for an expat bash that sounded a little druggy for Liana's Midwestern tastes. But the last available seat in his Land Rover would take her a stone's throw from this purportedly more-the-merrier couple and their gorgeously situated crash pad. It was nice of the guy to divert to Kilifi to drop her off, but then Liana was attractive, and knew it.

Mature adulthood—and the experience of being imposed upon herself—might have encouraged her to consider what showing up as an uninvited, impecunious houseguest would require of her hosts. Though Liana imagined herself undemanding, even the easy to please required fresh sheets, which would have to be laundered after her departure, then dried and folded. She would require a towel for swimming, a second for her shower. She would expect dinner, replete with discreet refreshments of her wineglass, strong filtered coffee every morning, and—what cost older people more than a sponger in her early twenties realized—steady conversational energy channeled in her direction for the duration of her stay.

For her part, Liana always repaid such hospitality with brightness and enthusiasm. On arrival at the Henleys' airy, weathered wooden house nestled in the coastal woods, she made a point of admiring soapstone knickknacks, cooing over framed black-and-whites of Masai initiation ceremonies, and telling comical tales about the European riffraff she'd met in Nairobi. Her effervescence came naturally. She would never have characterized it as an effort, until—and unless—she grew older herself.

While she'd have been reluctant to form the vain conceit outright, it was perhaps tempting to regard the sheer insertion of her physical presence as a gift, one akin to showing up at the door with roses. Supposedly a world-famous photographer, Regent Henley carried herself as if she used to be a looker, but she'd let her long dry hair go gray. Her crusty husband, Beano (the handle may have worked when he was a boy, but now that he was over sixty it sounded absurd), could probably use a little eye candy twitching onto their screened-in porch for sundowners: some narrow hips wrapped tightly in a fresh kikoi, long wet hair slicked back from a tanned, exertion-flushed face after a shower. Had Liana needed further rationalization of her amiable freeloading, she might also have reasoned that in Kenya every white household was overrun with underemployed servants. Not Regent and Beano but their African help would knot the mosquito netting over the guest bed. So Liana's impromptu visit would provide the domestics with something to do, helping to justify the fact that bwana paid their children's school fees.

But Liana thought none of these things. She thought only that this was another opportunity for adventure on the cheap, and at that time economy trumped all other considerations. Not because she was rude, or prone to take advantage by nature. She was merely young. A perfectly pleasant girl on her first big excursion abroad, she would doubtless grow into a better-socialized woman who would make exorbitant hotel reservations rather than dream of dumping herself on total strangers.

Yet midway through this casual mooching off the teeny-tiny-bit-pretentious photographer and her retired safari-guide husband (who likewise seemed rather self-impressed, considering that Liana had already run into a dozen masters of the savanna just like him), Liana entered one eerily elongated window during which her eventual capacity to make sterner judgments of her youthful impositions from the perspective of a more worldly adulthood became imperiled. A window after which there might be no woman. There might only, ever, have been a girl—remembered, guiltily, uneasily, resentfully, by her aging, unwilling hosts more often than they would have preferred.

Day Four. She was staying only six nights—an eyeblink for a twenty-three-year-old, a "bloody long time" for the Brit who had groused to his wife under-breath about putting up "another dewy-eyed Yank who confuses a flight to Africa with a trip to the zoo." Innocent of Beano's less-than-charmed characterizations, Liana had already established a routine. Mornings were consumed with texting friends back in Milwaukee about her exotic situation, with regular refills of passion-fruit juice. After lunch, she'd pile into the jeep with Regent to head to town for supplies, after tolerating the photographer's ritual admonishment that Kilifi was heavily Muslim and it would be prudent to "cover up." (Afternoons were hot. Even her muscle T clung uncomfortably, and Liana considered it a concession not to strip down to her running bra. She wasn't about to drag on long pants to pander to a bunch of uptight foreigners she'd never see again; career expats like Regent were forever showing off how they're hip to local customs and you're not.) She never proffered a few hundred shillings to contribute to the grocery bill, not because she was cheap—though she was; at her age, that went without saying—but because the gesture never occurred to her. Back "home," she would mobilize for a long, vigorous swim in Kilifi Creek, where she would work up an appetite for dinner.

As she sidled around the house in her bikini—gulping more passion-fruit juice at the counter, grabbing a fresh towel—her exhibitionism was unconscious; call it instinctive, suggesting an inborn feel for barter. She lingered with Beano, inquiring about the biggest animal he'd ever shot, then commiserating about ivory poaching (always a crowd-pleaser) as she bound back her long blond hair, now bleached almost white. Raised arms made her stomach look flatter. Turning with a "cheerio!" that she'd picked up in Nairobi, Liana sashayed out the back porch and down the splintered wooden steps before cursing herself, because she should have worn flip-flops. Returning for shoes would ruin her exit, so she picked her way carefully down the overgrown dirt track to the beach in bare feet.

In Wisconsin, a "creek" was a shallow, burbling dribble with tadpoles that purled over rocks. Where Liana was from, you wouldn't go for a serious swim in a "creek." You'd splash up to your ankles while cupping your arches over mossy stones, arms extended for balance, though you almost always fell in. But everything in Africa was bigger. Emptying into the Indian Ocean, Kilifi Creek was a river—an impressively wide river at that—which opened into a giant lake sort of thing when she swam to the left and under the bridge. This time, in the interest of variety, she would strike out to the right.

The water was cold. Yipping at every advance, Liana struggled out to the depth of her upper thighs, gingerly avoiding sharp rocks. Regent and Beano may have referred to the shoreline as a "beach," but there wasn't a grain of sand in sight, and with all the green gunk along the bank the obstacles were hard to spot. Chiding herself not to be a wimp, she plunged forward. This was a familiar ritual of her childhood trips to Lake Winnebago: the shriek of inhalation, the hyperventilation, the panicked splashing to get the blood running, the soft surprise of how quickly the water feels warm.

Liana considered herself a strong swimmer, of a kind. That is, she'd never been comfortable with the gasping and thrashing of the crawl, which felt frenetic. But she was a virtuoso of the sidestroke, with a powerful scissor kick whose thrust carried her faster than many swimmers with inefficient crawls (much to their annoyance, as she'd verified in her college pool). The sidestroke was contemplative. Its rhythm was ideally calibrated for a breath on every other kick, and resting only one cheek in the water allowed her to look around. It was less rigorous than the butterfly but not as geriatric as the breaststroke, and after long enough you still got tired—marvelously so.

Pulling out far enough from the riverbank so that she shouldn't have to worry about hitting rocks with that scissor kick, Liana rounded to the right and rapidly hit her stride. The late-afternoon light had just begun to mellow. The shores were forested, with richly shaded inlets and copses. She didn't know the names of the trees, but now that she was alone, with no one trying to make her feel ignorant about a continent of which white people tended to be curiously possessive, she didn't care if those were acacias or junipers. They were green: good enough. Though Kilifi was renowned as a resort area for high-end tourists, and secreted any number of capacious houses like her hosts', the canopy hid them well. It looked like wilderness: good enough. Gloriously, Liana didn't have to watch out for the powerboats and Jet Skis that terrorized Lake Winnebago, and she was the only swimmer in sight. Africans, she'd been told (lord, how much she'd been told; every backpacker three days out of Jomo Kenyatta Airport was an expert), didn't swim. Not only was the affluent safari set too lazy to get in the water; by this late in the afternoon they were already drunk.

This was the best part of the day. No more enthusiastic chatter about Regent's latest work. For heaven's sake, you'd think she might have finally discovered color photography at this late date. Blazing with yellow flora, red earth, and, at least outside Nairobi, unsullied azure sky, Africa was wasted on the woman. All she photographed was dust and poor people. It was a relief, too, not to have to seem fascinated as Beano lamented the unsustainable growth of the human population and the demise of Kenyan game, all the while having to pretend that she hadn't heard variations on this same dirge dozens of times in a mere three weeks. Though she did hope that, before she hopped a ride back to Nairobi with Ponytail Guy, the couple would opt for a repeat of that antelope steak from the first night. The meat had been lean; rare in both senses of the word, it gave good text the next morning. There wasn't much point in going all the way to Africa and then sitting around eating another hamburger.

Liana paused her reverie to check her position, and sure enough she'd drifted farther from the shore than was probably wise. She knew from the lake swims of childhood vacations that distance over water was hard to judge. If anything, the shore was farther away than it looked. So she pulled heavily to the right, and was struck by how long it took to make the trees appear appreciably larger. Just when she'd determined that land was within safe reach, she gave one more stiff kick, and her right foot struck rock.

The pain was sharp. Liana hated interrupting a swim, and she didn't have much time before the equatorial sun set, as if someone had flicked a light switch. Nevertheless, she dropped her feet and discovered that this section of the creek was barely a foot and a half deep. No wonder she'd hit a rock. Sloshing to a sun-warmed outcrop, she examined the top of her foot, which began to gush blood as soon as she lifted it out of the water. There was a flap. Something of a mess.

Even if she headed straight back to the Henleys', all she could see was thicket—no path, much less a road. The only way to return and put some kind of dressing on this stupid thing was to swim. As she stumbled through the shallows, her foot smarted. Yet, bathed in the cool water, it quickly grew numb. Once she had slogged in deep enough to resume her sidestroke, Liana reasoned, *Big deal, I cut my foot.* The water would keep the laceration clean; the chill would stanch the bleeding. It didn't really hurt much now, and the only decision was whether to cut the swim short. The silence pierced by tropical birdcalls was a relief, and Liana didn't feel like showing up back at the house with too much time to kill with enraptured blah-blah before dinner. She'd promised herself that she'd swim at least a mile, and she couldn't have done more than a quarter.

So Liana continued to the right, making damned sure to swim out far enough so that she was in no danger of hitting another rock. Still, the cut had left her rattled. Her idyll had been violated. No longer gentle and welcoming, the shoreline shadows undulated with a hint of menace. The creek had bitten her. Having grown fitful, the sidestroke had transformed from luxury to chore. Possibly she'd tightened up from a queer encroaching fearfulness, or perhaps she was suffering from a trace of shock—unless, that is, the water had genuinely got colder. Once in a while she felt a flitter against her foot, like a fish, but it wasn't a fish. It was the flap. Kind of creepy.

Liana resigned herself: This expedition was no longer fun. The light had taken a turn from golden to vermillion—a modulation she'd have found transfixing if only she were on dry land—and she still had to swim all the way back. Churning a short length farther to satisfy pride, she turned around.

And got nowhere. Stroking at full power, Liana could swear she was going backward. As long as she'd been swimming roughly in the same direction, the current hadn't been noticeable. This was a creek, right? But an African creek. As for her having failed to detect the violent surge running at a forty-five-degree angle to the shoreline, an aphorism must have applied—something about never being aware of forces that are on your side until you defy them.

Liana made another assessment of her position. Her best guess was that the shore had drifted farther away again. Very much farther. The current had been pulling her out while she'd been dithering about the fish-flutter flap of her foot. Which was now the least of her problems. Because the shore was not only distant. It stopped.

Beyond the end of the land was nothing but water. Indian Ocean water. If she did not get out of the grip of the current, it would sweep her past that last little nub of the continent and out to sea. Suddenly the dearth of boats, Jet Skis, fellow swimmers, and visible residents or tourists, drunken or not, seemed far less glorious.

The sensation that descended was calm, determined, and quiet, though it was underwritten by a suppressed hysteria that it was not in her interest to indulge. Had she concentration to spare, she might have worked out that this whole emotional package was one of her first true tastes of adulthood: what happens when you realize that a great deal, or even everything, is at stake and that no one is going to help you. It was a feeling that some children probably did experience but shouldn't. At least solitude discouraged theatrics. She had no audience to panic for. No one to exclaim to, no one to whom she might bemoan her quandary. It was all do, no say.

Swimming directly against the current had proved fruitless. Instead, Liana angled sharply toward the shore, so that she was cutting across the current. Though she was still pointed backward, in the direction of Regent and Beano's place, this riptide would keep dragging her body to the left. Had she known her exact speed, and the exact rate at which the current was carrying her in the direction of the Indian Ocean, she would have been able to answer the question of whether she was about to die by solving a simple geometry problem: A point travels at a set speed at a set angle toward a plane of a set width while moving at a set speed to the left. Either it will intersect the plane or it will miss the plane and keep traveling into wide-open space. Liquid space, in this case.

Of course, she wasn't in possession of these variables. So she swam as hard and as steadily as she knew how. There was little likelihood that suddenly adopting the crawl, at which she'd never been any good, would improve her chances, so the sidestroke it would remain. She trained her eyes on a distinctive rock formation as a navigational guide. Thinking about her foot wouldn't help, so she did not. Thinking about how exhausted she was wouldn't help, so she did not. Thinking about never having been all that proficient at geometry was hardly an assist, either, so she proceeded in a state of dumb animal optimism.

The last of the sun glinted through the trees and winked out. Technically, the residual threads of pink and gray in the early-evening sky were very pretty.

"Where is that blooming girl?" Beano said, and threw one of the leopard-print cushions onto the sofa. "She should have been back two hours ago. It's dark. It's Africa, she's a baby, she knows absolutely nothing, and it's dark."

"Maybe she met someone, went for a drink," Regent said.

"Our fetching little interloper's *meeting someone* is exactly what I'm afraid of. And how's she to go to town with some local rapist in only a bikini?"

"You would remember the bikini," Regent said, dryly.

"Damned if I understand why all these people rock up and suddenly they're our problem."

"I don't like it any more than you do, but if she floats off into the night air never to be seen again she is our problem. Maybe someone picked her up in a boat. Carried her round the southern bend to one of the resorts."

"She'll not have her phone on a swim, so she's no means of giving us a shout if she's in trouble. She'll not have her wallet, either—if she even has one. Never so much as volunteers a bottle of wine, while hoovering up my best Cabernet like there's no tomorrow."

"If anything has happened, you'll regret having said that sort of thing."

"Might as well gripe while I still can, then. You know, I don't even know the girl's surname? Much less who to ring if she's vanished. I can see it: having to comb through her kit, search out her passport. Bringing in the sodding police, who'll expect chai just for answering the phone. No good ever comes from involving those thieving idiots in your life, and then there'll be a manhunt. Thrashing the bush, prodding the shallows. And you know how the locals thrive on a mystery, especially when it involves a young lady—"

"They're bored. We're all bored. Which is why you're letting your imagination run away with you. It's not that late yet. I'm sure there's a simple explanation."

"I'm not bored, I'm hungry. Aziza probably started dinner at four—since she *is* bored—and you can bet it's muck by now."

Regent fetched a bowl of fried-chickpea snacks, but despite Beano's claims of an appetite he left them untouched. "Christ, I can see the whole thing," he said, pacing. "It'll turn into one of those cases. With the parents flying out and grilling all the servants and having meetings with the police. Expecting to stay here, of course, tearing hair and getting emotional while we urge them to please do eat some lunch. Going on tirades about how the local law enforcement is ineffectual and corrupt, and bringing in the FBI. Telling childhood anecdotes about their darling and expecting us to get tearful with them over the disappearance of some, I concede, quite agreeable twentysomething, but still a girl we'd barely met."

"You like her," Regent said. "You're just ranting because you're anxious."

"She has a certain intrepid quality, which may be deadly, but which until it's frightened out of her I rather admire," he begrudged, then resumed the rant. "Oh, and there'll be media. CNN and that. You know the Americans—they love innocent-abroad stories. But you'd think they'd learn their lesson. It beats me why their families keep letting kids holiday in Africa as if the whole world is a happy-clappy theme park. With all those car-jackings on the coast road—"

"Ordinarily I'd agree with you, but there's nothing especially *African* about going for a swim in a creek. She's done it every other afternoon, so I've assumed she's a passable swimmer. Do you think—would it help if we got a torch and went down to the dock? We could flash it about, shout her name out. She might just be lost."

"My throat hurts just thinking about it." Still, Beano was heading to the entryway for his jacket when the back-porch screen door creaked.

"Hi," Liana said, shyly. With luck, streaks of mud and a strong tan disguised what her weak, light-headed sensation suggested was a shocking pallor. She steadied herself by holding on to the sofa and got mud on the upholstery. "Sorry, I—swam a little farther than I'd planned. I hope you didn't worry."

"We *did* worry," Regent said sternly. Her face flickered between anger and relief, an expression that reminded Liana of her mother. "It's after dark."

"I guess with the stars, the moon . . . ," Liana covered. "It was so . . . peaceful."

The moon, in fact, had been obscured by cloud for the bulk of her wet grope back. Most of which had been conducted on her hands and knees in shallow water along the shore—land she was not about to let out of her clutches for one minute. The muck had been treacherous with more biting rocks. For long periods, the vista had been so inky that she'd found the Henleys' rickety rowboat dock only because she had bumped into it.

"What happened to your *foot*?" Regent cried.

"Oh, that. Oh, nuts. I'm getting blood on your floor."

"Looks like a proper war wound, that," Beano said boisterously.

"We're going to get that cleaned right up." Examining the wound, Regent exclaimed, "My dear girl, you're shaking!"

"Yes, I may have gotten—a little chill." Perhaps it was never too late to master the famously British knack for understatement.

"Let's get you into a nice hot shower first, and then we'll bandage your foot. That cut looks deep, Liana. You really shouldn't be so casual about it."

Liana weaved to the other side of the house, leaving red footprints down the hall. In previous showers here, she'd had trouble with scalding, but this time she couldn't get the water hot enough. She huddled under the dribble until finally the water grew tepid, and then, with a shudder, wrapped herself in one of their big white bath sheets, trying to keep from getting blood on the towel.

Emerging in jeans and an unseasonably warm sweater she'd found in the guest room's dresser, Liana was grateful for the cut on her foot, which gave Regent something to fuss over and distracted her hostess from the fact that she was still trembling. Regent trickled the oozing inch-long gash with antiseptic and bound it with gauze and adhesive tape, whose excessive swaddling didn't make up for its being several years old; the tape was discolored, and barely stuck. Meanwhile, Liana threw the couple a bone: She told them how she had injured her foot, embellishing just enough to make it a serviceable story.

The foot story was a decoy. It obviated telling the other one. At twenty-three, Liana hadn't accumulated many stories; until now, she had hungered for more. Vastly superior to carvings of hippos, stories were the souvenirs that this bold stint in Africa had been designed to provide. Whenever she'd scored a proper experience in the past, like the time she'd dated a man who confided that he'd always felt like a woman, or even when she'd had her e-mail hacked, she'd traded on the tale at every opportunity.

Perhaps if she'd returned to her parents after this latest ordeal, she'd have burst into tears and delivered the blow-by-blow. But she was abruptly aware that these people were virtual strangers. She'd only make them even more nervous about whether she was irresponsible or lead them to believe that she was an attention-seeker with a tendency to exaggerate. It was funny how when some little nothing went down you played it for all it was worth, but when a truly momentous occurrence shifted the tectonic plates in your mind you kept your mouth shut. Because instinct dictated that this one was private. Now she knew: There was such a thing as private.

Having aged far more than a few hours this evening, Liana was disheartened to discover that maturity could involve getting smaller. She had been reduced. She was a weaker, more fragile girl than the one who'd piled into Regent's jeep that afternoon, and in some manner that she couldn't put her finger on she also felt less real—less here—since in a highly plausible alternative reality she was not here.

The couple made a to-do over the importance of getting hot food inside her, but before the dinner had warmed Liana curled around the leopard-print pillow on the sofa and dropped into a comatose slumber. Intuiting something—Beano himself had survived any number of close calls, the worst of which he had kept from Regent, lest she lay down the law that he had to stop hunting in Botswana even sooner than she did—he discouraged his wife from rousing the girl even to go to bed, draping her gently in a mohair blanket and carefully tucking the fringe around her pretty wet head.

Predictably, Liana grew into a civilized woman with a regard for the impositions of laundry. She pursued a practical career in marketing in New York, and, after three years, ended an impetuous marriage to an Afghan. Meantime, starting with Kilifi Creek, she assembled an offbeat collection. It was a class of moments that most adults stockpile: the times they almost died. Rarely was there a good reason, or any warning. No majestic life lessons presented themselves in compensation for having been given a fright. Most of these incidents were in no way heroic, like the rescue of a child from a fire. They were more a matter of stepping distractedly off a curb, only to feel the draft of the M4 bus flattening your hair.

Not living close to a public pool, Liana took up running in her late twenties. One evening, along her usual route, a minivan shot out of a parking garage without checking for pedestrians and missed her by a whisker. Had she not stopped to double-knot her left running shoe before leaving her apartment, she would be dead. Later: She was taking a scuba-diving course on Cape Cod when a surge about a hundred feet deep dislodged her mask and knocked her regulator from her mouth. The Atlantic was unnervingly murky, and her panic was absolute. Sure, they taught you to make regular decompression stops, and to exhale evenly as you ascended, but it was early in her training. If her instructor hadn't managed to grab her before she bolted for the surface while holding her breath, her lungs would have exploded and she would be dead. Still later: Had she not unaccountably thought better of shooting forward on her Citi Bike on Seventh Avenue when the light turned green, the garbage truck would still have taken a sharp left onto Sixteenth Street without signaling, and she would be dead. There was nothing else to learn, though that was something to learn, something inchoate and large.

The scar on her right foot, wormy and white (the flap should have been stitched), became a totem of this not-really-a-lesson. Oh, she'd considered the episode, and felt free to conclude that she had overestimated her swimming ability, or underestimated the insidious, bigger-than-you powers of water. She could also sensibly have decided that swimming alone anywhere was tempting fate. She might have concocted a loftier version, wherein she had been rescued by an almighty presence who had grand plans for her—grander than marketing. But that wasn't it. Any of those interpretations would have been plastered on top, like the poorly adhering bandage on that gash. The message was bigger and dumber and blunter than that, and she was a bright woman, with no desire to disguise it.

After Liana was promoted to director of marketing at Brace-Yourself—a rapidly expanding firm that made the neoprene joint supports popular with aging boomers still pounding the pavement—she moved from Brooklyn to Manhattan, where she could now afford a stylish one-bedroom on the twenty-sixth floor, facing Broadway. The awful Afghan behind her, she'd started dating again. The age of thirty-seven marked a good time in her life: She was well paid and roundly liked in the office; she relished New York; though she'd regained an interest in men, she didn't feel desperate. Many a summer evening without plans she would pour a glass of wine, take the elevator to the top floor, and slip up a last flight of stairs; roof access was one of the reasons she'd chosen the apartment. Lounging against the railing sipping Chenin Blanc, Liana would bask in the lights and echoing taxi horns of the city, sometimes sneaking a cigarette. This time of year, the regal overlook made her feel rich beyond measure. The air was fat and soft in her hair—which was shorter now, with a becoming cut. So when she finally met a man whom she actually liked, she invited him to her building's traditional Fourth of July potluck picnic on the roof to show it off.

"Are you sure you're safe, sitting there?" David said, solicitously. They had sifted away from the tables of wheat-berry salad and smoked-tofu patties to talk.

His concern was touching; perhaps he liked her, too. But she was perfectly stable—lodged against the perpendicular railing on a northern corner, feet braced on a bolted-down bench, weight firmly forward—and her consort had nothing to fear. Liana may have grown warier of water, but heights had never induced the vertigo from which others suffered. Besides, David was awfully tall, and the small boost in altitude was equalizing.

"You're just worried that I'll have a better view of the fireworks. Refill?" She leaned down for the Merlot on the bench for a generous pour into their plastic glasses. A standard fallback for a first date, they had been exchanging travel stories, and impetuously—there was something about this guy that she trusted—she told him about Kilifi Creek. Having never shared the tale, she was startled by how little time it took to tell. But that was the nature of these stories: They were about what could have happened, or should have happened, but didn't. They were very nearly not stories at all.

"That must have been pretty scary," he said dutifully. He sounded let down, as if she'd told a joke without a punch line.

"I wasn't scared," she reflected. "I couldn't afford to be. Only later, and then there was no longer anything to be afraid of. That's part of what was interesting: having been cheated of feeling afraid. Usually, when you have a near-miss, it's an instant. A little flash, like, *Wow. That was weird.* This one went on forever, or seemed to. I was going to die, floating off on the Indian Ocean until I lost consciousness, or I wasn't. It was a long time to be in this . . . in-between state." She laughed. "I don't know, don't make me embarrassed. I've no idea what I'm trying to say."

Attempting to seem captivated by the waning sunset, Liana no more than shifted her hips, by way of expressing her discomfort that her story had landed flat. Nothing foolhardy. For the oddest moment, she thought that David had pushed her, and was therefore not a nice man at all but a lunatic. Because what happened next was both enormously subtle and plain enormous—the way the difference between knocking over a glass and not knocking over a glass could be a matter of upsetting its angle by a single greater or lesser degree. Greater, this time. Throw any body of mass that one extra increment off its axis, and rather than barely brush against it you might as well have hurled it at a wall.

With the same quiet clarity with which she had registered, in Kilifi, *I am being swept out to sea*, she grasped simply, *Oh. I lost my balance.* For she was now executing the perfect backflip that she'd never been able to pull off on a high dive. The air rushed in her ears like water. This time the feeling was different—that is, the starkness was there, the calmness was there also, but these clean, serene sensations were spiked with a sharp surprise, which quickly morphed to perplexity, and then to sorrow. She fit in a wisp of disappointment before the fall was through. Her eyes tearing, the lights of high-rises blurred. Above, the evening sky rippled into the infinite ocean that had waited to greet her for fourteen years: largely good years, really—gravy, a long and lucky reprieve. Then, of course, what had mattered was her body striking the plane, and now what mattered was not striking it—and what were the chances of that? By the time she reached the sidewalk, Liana had taken back her surprise. At some point there was no *almost*. That had always been the message. There were bystanders, and they would get the message, too.

Manuel Muñoz

The Happiest Girl in the Whole USA

TIMOTEO REALLY IS NOTHING special, shorter than me and rounder, and hardly even a smile to break the dark moon of his face. I say no one special because it is still, after all these years, just me and him. No one special because I'm no different from any of the women who line up at the town bank, ready to exchange my saved collection of coins for a wad of sweaty bills. It takes money to get a man back from the border, more money than anyone might think.

Some of us have rings on our fingers and some of us don't, but we all know what it means to watch the calendar turn to the last of the month. We know what some of the farmers do on final Fridays, and we know what to do on Saturday mornings. The farmers put their dusty hands on a phone receiver and very calmly place a call to the migra. Then the men in the green uniforms arrive at the rows of whatever crops are in season—grapes or peaches or plums—and round up the men into vans. No one ends up paid for the week's labor, and everyone gets a standard booking in either Visalia or Fresno before being hustled back onto the vehicles. By nighttime, the vans reach Bakersfield and start the slow ascent into the mountains. They will head through

Los Angeles—where all our men know it's easy to get lost, but expensive to live—then on to San Diego, where it's just expensive to live. Finally, they'll reach the border itself, and Tijuana, where the van doors open to let all of the men out so they can start over again.

The bank teller counts out the bills as quickly as she can. She is a very pretty white girl who always wears skirts, her hair pulled up with simple barrettes. She knows the bus from Fresno stops once a week in our town now, Saturday midafternoon in front of the barbershop, as if the whole drama of deportation and return were a big plan between the migra and the charter companies. She hurries, and though she never says much of a pleasant word to any of us, I think it is because she doesn't want us to miss the only bus going out of town, the only way to get our men back. I often wonder about the history of her good luck. I don't always know what to think of the fact that she doesn't have a ring on her finger, if it is a good or a bad thing.

It's always the same when I board the bus—it's already half full, mostly women from Fresno and the little towns just south of it, like Fowler and Selma. I get a seat alone and the bus moves on to Goshen, then Tulare and Delano, each woman who boards more weary than the last. They're all like me. Or at least, they look like me. I don't know their histories. I don't know if they came from South Texas like I did, were taken from school in the third grade to work in the fields like me. I was resentful of my parents for giving me the life of a dumb mule, and I left them almost to the minute of my eighteenth birthday, with only a scrap of paper with their address and phone number that I never ended up using. I walk around with a lot of pride because I did that, because I proved that I could support myself in a hard world. I did all right for myself for a while. Then I fell in love.

When we get to Bakersfield, the bus is packed, and a young woman boards with a big sigh and looks at the seat beside me.

"Con permiso," she says, before she moves to sit down.

I know just from looking at her that this is her first trip. She carries a cheap white purse in one hand and a bulky shopping bag in the other. She reminds me of all the women in town who everybody knows have just recently arrived from Mexico, because they go to the grocery store in high heels and tight dresses, doing their best to be like the American women they see on television.

She's wearing a purple dress and white high heels, and just by that I know she spends too much time watching the afternoon soap operas, not understanding that the women on those shows only scheme because they have no jobs to go to. It will take a while for her to someday let the TV station rest on the evening news with Jessica Savitch—the kind of person I wish I were smart enough to sound like—when the need to listen to English for practice turns into a wish to look like an intelligent and confident woman.

She sits down quickly as the bus begins to pull out of the station, and when she adjusts the shopping bag under her legs, I look at her hands, but there isn't a ring to be found.

The bus is back on the road and, soon enough, I can feel the rise into the mountains, the climb into Los Angeles. My stomach flutters like the times when Timoteo and I boarded the cheap traveling carnival rides that sometimes set up in the town park, and I place my hand on my ribs, remembering.

"Are you hungry?" the young girl says to me in Spanish.

I didn't know she had been looking at me, and before I can answer, she reaches into the shopping bag and brings out something wrapped in foil. When I don't take it immediately, she begins to unwrap it—a taco of corn tortilla and something orange—and tears off a piece for herself.

"Take it," she says, handing me the part still in the foil. It's cold, but delicious: chorizo and potato. I nod my thanks. "Where are you headed?" she asks.

"Los Angeles." I think to ask where she might be headed but I already know.

She says nothing for a moment, and just when I feel bad that I haven't asked her a question, she finishes her food and carefully pulls a tissue from her bra to wipe her fingers. "Do you know Los Angeles very well?" she asks.

"What do you mean?"

"Do you know the city? Do you know your way around?"

"I know some places. Around the bus station, I mean."

She dabs at her lips with the tissue before balling it into her fist. "Would you help me when we get there?"

"Help you how?"

She reaches for her cheap white purse and pulls out a folded piece of paper.

The bus has darkened with the coming of sundown and the road's curve into the high walls of the mountains. She shows me the paper—a map—in the bare light.

"He told me to look for the park," she says.

I know the park and I know the agreed routine: Pershing Square, where I know to wait overnight to see if Timoteo might show up from Tijuana, spending a night at a motel near Seventh Street where the door opens out to the city's loud darkness. If Timoteo doesn't show, then I know to board the bus to San Diego, this time to the bus station almost within sight of the border, as if both countries wanted to make everything easier on everyone. Nearby is a park just like the one in Los Angeles, where everyone waits and waits and waits.

If I don't show up there, Timoteo always tells me, then you know it's over.

"I know that park," I say to her. "It's very close by."

"Would you mind showing me?"

"Of course," I say, but maybe I don't say it with much conviction.

"No, really," she says. "I don't know where I'm going. I've never had to stop in Los Angeles, and it's a scary city."

"It's big, but not scary when you get used to it."

"You've been there a lot? When did you cross over?"

"I was born here," I tell her in English. Then I say it again to her in Spanish, then I let her stay silent for a moment so she can know who she's talking to. To me, she's a young girl without a name. She's someone who might not have anything in her purse except the folded-up map, who might not know how much money to take on a trip like this.

I take the map from her hand. "Who are you going to see?" I tilt the paper toward the fading light of the bus window and follow the map with my clean finger. She doesn't answer.

"You don't have to be married to be in love," I tell her. "I understand."

She leans her head toward me, as if to study the map together. But there's nothing to study. The street is a straight shot from the bus station to the park, and I trace it on the map with my finger. "When we get off at the station, a lot of people will head here, along this street, over to the park. It's a long walk in the dark, but if you stay close to the group you can feel safe. You can take a taxi if you want to, but I think it's a waste of money. And sometimes the drivers circle around just to cheat you, so be careful."

"Thank you—" she says to me, and I can tell by how she says it that she wants to insist, one more time, that I show her. But I meant to say we and a lot of people and stay close to let her know that she should just follow everyone, all of us on the same trip, the same type of man at the other end. She's too young to understand though.

"My name is Natalia," she says.

"Good to meet you," I tell Natalia. The bus has gone dark and I can feel some of the gradual descent toward Los Angeles, so I lean my head against the window. I close my eyes as if to nap, but I don't offer my name.

She's quiet while I pretend to nap and with my eyes closed, I think back to a Natalia I knew in South Texas, one of two other girls in my third-grade class. They were good friends to me, both of them, Natalia and the other one, and we sat in the last row of the classroom while the rowdy boys tried to impress the teacher. I remember third grade because it was the last year I ever had in school. I was a smart girl. I was smarter than the boys, and I was filled with a need to prove I was better than them. One day, our teacher asked the class a simple question. Which weighed more, a pound of feathers or a pound of gold? The boys went out of their way to explain why one would be heavier than the other, until I finally raised my hand. When the teacher called on me, I said, without hesitation, "A pound is a pound, no matter what."

On the bus, I open my eyes again to the silence I remember from the classroom. In the dark, all the women are sleeping, this new Natalia next to me, not the same girl, but the same thinking: Latch on to someone who can move around in the world, someone who can help you. I can't imagine whatever happened to those girlhood friends, if they ever got out of South Texas, but I remember they were sweet to me after the teacher opened the top drawer of her desk, then came down the aisle with a white ribbon in her hand. The room went silent, almost dark, from everyone's watching, and the teacher placed the ribbon in front of me. *Do something with your life, Griselda.*

When we arrive at the station, I have to goad Natalia ahead so we can get off the bus. She stands so bewildered with her two bags at the rush of the station that it's all I can do to not take her hand in mine. "Come," I tell her, as a group of our fellow passengers makes its way to the exit, and she follows me through the grimy bustle of the station, the sleepy eyes, the baby strollers, the impatience. The better part of me says I should turn around to make sure she is close behind, that she hasn't been swallowed up by what is, for her, the surprise of so many people at nine in the evening. I don't ask if she's hungry or if she'd like a drink or if she needs the restroom—there is never time for anything on a trip like this—and she follows me past the coffee-dispensing machines, the bank of pay phones, the ticket counters with their long lines of arguments. We follow the other passengers who had been on the bus, all of us a flock of birds swerving onto the street.

Natalia is having trouble keeping up. She's figured out that her white shoes are not made for walking, but I tell her nothing about the stupidity of wearing a dress. She should be smart enough for this world on her own, I think to myself, for the day that demands she do this trip alone with no one to help her. I can hear the click-click of her heels along the sidewalk, so I know she's behind me. The sweat on my brow appears quickly; sometimes, the Los Angeles nights are balmy and bearable, but tonight it feels as if we brought the Valley heat with us. I can hear her breathing heavily behind me, but I don't turn around. We hardly need the other passengers as our guides anymore. We're walking quickly enough to show we are determined, not lost or tired, and our pace blends us into the life on the sidewalk: the late-shift week-end workers waiting at the city bus benches; the exhaust of the taxicabs idling at the corners; boys on bikes who are too young to be out so late; the hot fluorescence of a bodega, its vegetables wilting in the heat.

"How much more?" Natalia finally says, and when I turn around, I can see the sweat stains in dark circles under her arms, how hard she tries to not show a slight limp in her right foot, a blister no doubt.

"Two more blocks," I tell her. The other passengers—we were never really a group at all—have long reached the park, fanned out to look for their men. We've almost reached it, and not once along the way were we spoken to or looked at, the street always humming with traffic, inviting what I know is a false sense of safety. "Will you remember the way back to the station?"

"Yes," she says, looking around, and she says it so confidently that I have to believe her, even though I wonder about the man who she is coming to meet, if he would lead her by the hand back to the station. She says it so confidently that I know immediately that it has never occurred to her that her man might not have made it to the park to begin with.

That's when I know she is truly lost.

"Come," I tell her again, when we reach the edge of the park, and here, I know, is where her eyes will be opened, where she'll learn to never again wear a purple dress on such a trip. "Stay with me," I tell her as we approach the benches filled with men in T-shirts so white they glow in the dark, all of them waiting. I don't call out Timoteo's name—I learned a long time ago never to do that—and Natalia's fear gets the better of her. She stays silent as we near the benches, close enough to the small groups to make out faces, sometimes a cigarette lighter briefly illuminating a circle of tired, anxious men. "Mamasita," I can hear someone mutter, and the single word is followed by the ugly laughter of too many men to count. "¿Dónde me llevas?" says another one, and Natalia takes my hand out of sheer fright, her grip tighter than mine. If she wore a ring, it would have dug into me.

We circle the park twice, then cut across it once, but Timoteo is not in any of the usual spots. I stand looking back at the darkness, thinking about whether I should go back in, or to give it another hour. But I know Timoteo has not made it to Los Angeles tonight, and that I need to board the bus in the morning and head to San Diego.

"What do we do now?" Natalia asks. "He said he would be here."

"It's hard," I tell her. "You remember." I have done this so many times that Timoteo's failure to show up at the park only means I have to spend more money to get him back home. But for Natalia, I know, it means her hand-drawn map is useless, as if she were standing not at a park entrance, but at the edge of the world.

"What do we do now?" she asks again. She looks at the dark park and, in the dim streetlight, I think I can see tears forming in her eyes. "He said he would be here."

"Things happen," I tell her. "Did you bring any money?" I ask her, keeping my voice low. "For a motel?"

"He said he would be here . . . ," she says, trailing off.

Despite everything, I am a smart person in the world. I could have been even smarter and better if life had turned out a certain way. If I could have stayed in school, there may have been more than just white ribbons. I think of the young Natalia from my girl days and I take this one's hands, and then the name of the other girl comes to me—Carla!—as if her spirit knew that someone had been thinking of her. Such sweet girls, wherever they wound up.

"Come with me," I tell her, and we turn and walk back in the direction of the station. Natalia follows me without a word, and I eventually take a left toward the motel I always stay at when I need to. But first, I direct Natalia into the corner bodega just out of eyeshot of the motel office. "Go in there and pretend to look at the vegetables," I tell her, and her eyes widen, her hands stiff around my wrist when she realizes I am about to leave her. "No," I tell her. "The motel charges per person."

"Please don't leave me," she says.

"I promise," I tell her, and I know I don't say it with much kindness in my voice. But I don't rush away and I don't turn back to look at her. If she chooses to follow me to the motel instead of waiting, I won't pay the extra lodging fee. If Natalia chooses to leave the safety of the bodega, then she's on her own.

With the key gripped in my hand, I walk back to the bodega and find her cradling a box of saltines and two tins of Vienna sausages. I know the packaged sandwiches—salty ham and American cheese—are half off at night, so I get one and a tall bottle of soda. When I place them on the counter, I tell the clerk, "Just these," to see if Natalia can fish any money out of her purse.

"I'll wait for you outside," I tell her, as she counts out change to the clerk and waits for him to bag her items. When she click-clicks her way back out to the sidewalk, everything is set, and I know she'll be with me for the rest of the night and a good part of the morning.

"Now listen," I tell her. "Just stay a little ways behind me on the other side of the street, and don't cross until you pass the main office window. If the owner thinks we're together, it's going to cost me." I give her the room number and point to where we're headed, her heels so faint in the night I think for a moment that I've already lost her. I could've done the right thing and taken one of her bags, but then she'd never learn how to travel with hardly anything.

I go into the motel room and set my dinner on the table with the television, leaving the door slightly ajar and the light off. Her heels gradually click-click from across the street and into the parking lot, a greater racket than I thought, and I wave at her to rush quickly to the door. She slips in and when I close the door behind her, I do so as quietly as I can, hesitating to turn on the light. When I finally let out a sigh of relief and slip the lock on, she hears my frustration.

"I'm sorry," she says.

I turn on the light. "Keep your voice down," I say, and open my paper bag from the bodega. "Let's eat."

She kicks off her white high heels and rubs her feet while I eat my sandwich. I can see the red patches where blisters will appear in the morning. "Eat," I tell her. "We need to be up early."

I'm surprised when she doesn't open the Vienna sausage tins or the saltines, but takes out her last two cold tacos, as if standing in the glare of the bodega taught her that the only food she should ever bring along is the kind that can keep.

"I don't have any money—" Natalia starts.

"I had to spend it on a room anyway," I tell her. "But tomorrow, you're on your own." The moment I say it, the words sound cruel, but there is no way to explain to her what self-reliance means without bringing up the past. She doesn't need to know my past. She doesn't even know my name.

"You're lucky," I tell her. "Sometimes people are not kind. Especially other women who are by themselves."

"I hope my luck doesn't run out tomorrow."

"He'll show up," I say, but he may not, and the better part of me is already thinking ahead, to the kind of person I am if Timoteo shows up in the morning and I go back to my life by forgetting about her.

"So why aren't you married?" I ask her. I'm looking at her hands again, her fingers, and thinking about the man she's come to get.

"I want to get married," Natalia answers. "But I have to wait for him to ask."

"Do you have children?"

"No," she says. "Not yet."

"You better marry him," I say, hearing the longing in her voice, knowing how much harder it will be if he saddles her with his children before disappearing.

"But you're not married."

So she noticed my bare hands, too.

"He's too afraid to marry me."

"Men are always afraid."

"No," I say. "He's not afraid of marriage. I'm a citizen. I've been telling him for years that marriage would solve a lot of our problems. When he asks me what we have to do, I tell him we have to go to city hall and get a license, and that's when he gets afraid. Like a lot of people, he's scared of the government."

"Everyone should be afraid of the government."

"Maybe in Mexico," I tell her. "But I was born here and I don't let anybody push me around."

Natalia looks at me as if this revelation is beyond belief. She puts down the last bite of her taco and smooths the empty shopping bag flat against the little table. I can see from her face that a wave of relief has crossed it, that my determination comes from a place she can name, maybe even get to.

"I was born in Texas," I tell her. "I went to school for a little bit. That's how I know English." For once, this means something, and all the despair I've ever had about being no better off than where I came from dims in the light of Natalia's silence, the futility of her white shoes and her purple dress, with no one in this new world to show her how to survive.

"Eat," I tell her, motioning to the last bite. My sandwich is almost gone, the soda flat and warm, and as soon as I take the last mouthful, I know I'm going to rise and prepare for bed. I look down at Natalia's reddened feet. "We have the same shoe size, I bet."

"You think so?"

I lean down and hand her my sneaker. "Try it on." When it fits her like a glove, I get up from the chair and go to the bathroom, taking off my socks. I turn on the water and plug the sink. "Why don't you wear the sneakers tomorrow?" I tell her, dipping the socks in the water and unwrapping the motel soap to wash them for her. She's silent in the next room, maybe with the sneaker still on her single foot, maybe with the taco unfinished on the table, but she can hear my determination in the splashing of the water and the soap. Natalia must be no more than nineteen or twenty years old. Even if her man shows up, I know he won't be much to worry over. It's not my place to correct her mistake in placing so much trust in one man, but at least I can see that she knows how to spot the resilience in another woman and learn from it, like my two schoolyard friends, the little Natalia, the little Carla, wherever my poor girls ended up.

I close the bathroom door to wash up and prepare for bed, hang the socks to dry. On any other night, I could take off my bra and panties to wash in the sink and dry overnight, sleep in some comfort, but I would be a fool to trust Natalia completely. Now I'll have to hide the money in one of the bra cups safe next to me once I drift off, dead tired. My panties are tattered—I don't have to impress Timoteo anymore—but I hate that I'll have to wear them two days in a row without washing.

"We need to sleep soon," I say, when I walk back out, and Natalia complies. She tidies the table and washes up in the bathroom, but when she emerges, she still has her purple dress on. She crosses the room to turn out the light before she undresses, and the darkness amplifies the street noise of late-night Los Angeles, the far-off sirens, men's voices faint on the street, always sinister no matter what they might be talking about. Natalia takes her side of the bed and doesn't move for the longest time, but I can tell by her breathing that she can't sleep, that she's afraid of tomorrow.

I can't sleep either, not sure of what to do in the morning. I don't toss around, though. I stay rigid in bed, thinking of my old stern teacher from South Texas, the way she walked down the row of desks with her back straight. She walked with determination. She walked as if everything in her life had gone as planned. Her face comes to me, clearer and clearer, the white ribbon in her hand, and when my eyes finally close, her name comes to me—Mrs. Rolnik—and almost as suddenly, I can see the faint gray light of the morning through the ugly mustard-colored drapes.

Timoteo will be there this morning. I know it in my bones. I rouse Natalia and tell her to shower, and while she's in the bathroom, I take out the motel's pen and paper from the nightstand and write my own name and phone number and address. I do it because Timoteo will come back—he always does—and I do it because everyone needs someone in this world. I take just enough bills to cover either a bus ticket back home or another night in the motel and I pray to the god I don't believe in that she'll make the right decision.

Natalia emerges from the bathroom in a lime-green dress, the same style as the purple one, which tells me she knows a good bargain. Later, she'll understand that it means little to suffer the indignity of wearing the same clothes two or three days in a row. When we're ready, I send her across the street ahead of me while I go to turn in the key. She walks briskly now that she's wearing the sneakers, but the socks weren't dry yet. I'll have to remind her to take them off for a moment when we sit at the park, let them air out in the sunlight. I have to cuff my jeans so the hems won't stick on the heels of her white shoes and when I click-click along to the motel office, key in hand, the sound betrays her ridiculous wish to be the white women on the soap operas, at the county offices, at the J. C. Penney's.

Los Angeles is different in the daytime, but it is Sunday morning just like everywhere else, quiet, just a few cars on the street, older ladies walking to church. The Mexican bakery a block from the park is busy, people coming out with white bags, and I remember the days when Timoteo has shown up early enough to get some sweet bread and coffee, already waiting for me.

But it's too early and we make only one round at the park before my feet start to hurt. There are men around, but not very many yet. I motion her to an empty bench.

"You should put your purse in the shopping bag if it fits," I tell her.

"It might," she says, about to try, but I put my hand on her arm.

"Put this in your purse," I say, reaching into my bra and pulling out the little wad of bills and the piece of paper tucked between them. "Quickly. And don't lose it."

"You don't have to—"

"Quickly," I say again, and she opens her purse and I drop the money inside, a deep pocket of nothing, just as I had suspected: No wallet, which means no identification. No address book either, no gum, no mints, no tissues, no rolls of coins for the coffee machine, for the tampon dispenser, no nothing.

"I left home when I was eighteen," I tell her. "And somehow I made it here—" I sigh just from how good it feels to tell someone who I am, how good it feels to admit to myself that I want her to know someone like me can help. But I know enough to let it rest, to not say the rest of the story. It's too long anyway, and we don't have all day.

All around us, the park starts to bustle with people. I know that most of us are waiting, but not everyone. Some are citizens, some are not. Some are out walking to their Sunday jobs, lucky to have something to do. Some are out walking just to relieve themselves of the boredom of being stuck at home, unemployed. To walk in the park, to sit in it as we are doing—it doesn't feel like a luxury, like I imagine it does to all those women on the television. They lounge on a beach and wish time would never end. Here, it ends the minute my man shows up.

And here he comes. I can spot Timoteo's small round shape

even if his T-shirt is just as white and plain as everyone else's, and I raise my hand to capture his attention. But I don't wave it. I leave it straight up in the air like a flag.

Timoteo doesn't hug me or kiss me, but he grabs my hand and squeezes it briefly in greeting. He looks at Natalia for a moment, trying to decide if we're friendly or simply sharing space, and then I introduce her.

"Natalia," I tell him. "Mi amiga."

Timoteo nods at her and takes my hand again, impatient to get going. He asks her no questions, ready to move on with our lives. The day is early and I could invite Natalia to come with us to the Mexican bakery or to one of the food carts a few blocks away, where Timoteo likes to get a grilled corncob sprinkled with chile and lime. But she has her life to live, and I have mine.

"Bueno," I tell her. "Suerte," and I say it with enough certainty and finality for her to know that she need do nothing—not return the shoes, not thank me for the money—except make the right choice when her man fails to show up in the park. I turn quickly before I have to see her eyes water from the fear of being all alone, and I clutch Timoteo's elbow when he turns around to look at her, a flash of what might be alarm on his face. "Come," I tell him.

We walk back to the bus station and it's only when Timoteo sees that I'm having trouble walking that he spots the high heels. "There's too many men in that park for you to be wearing shoes like that."

His comment is neither stern nor kind: He knows my temperament well enough not to raise his voice to me. Even so, he's quiet for the few hours we wait in the bus station for our afternoon departure. He sits hunched over, elbows on his knees, as if he's contemplating Natalia more than me. He lets me have my silence. What we must look like to people, I wonder, neither one of us with a ring on our fingers.

Once we're on the bus, he takes the window seat, and it's only then that I see how exhausted he is. Nothing new is ever in his stories of how he got back—the coming back is always stressful, always tense—and his reliance on me to be there outweighs his doubt. If this is love, then it's as simple as it gets.

The bus driver comes down the aisle to do a final count and I lean back in my seat. His footsteps remind me of old, stern Mrs. Rolnik back in Texas, her dignified walk in my direction along the row of desks. *Do something with your life, Griselda.* The rich feel of the ribbon in my hand when she placed it there, like a promise of things to come. Back then, there was so much hope. Back then, I loved nothing more than the brown newsprint where I tallied numbers and blocked out letters, the cool feel of the desktop when I rested my head in the afternoon as she calmly read to us for fifteen minutes. The bus backs out of the station; nothing will stop its determination to bring us back home. Ay, the cool feel of resting my head on the desktop. Fifteen minutes. Just enough time to dream. Timoteo is already fast asleep, his head against the window, and I would do anything to rest my head against his shoulder, to nestle there. Ahead of me, the other women and their men face forward, together and stoic, all of them alert to the city streets, to what's passing by and what's coming. It's still love, the back of their heads seem to say to me. Not one woman is resting her head on her man's shoulder, so I sit upright and look straight out into the distance.

Russell Banks

A Permanent Member of the Family

I'M NOT SURE I want to tell this story on myself, not now, some thirty-five years after it happened. But it has more or less become a family legend and consequently has been much revised and, if I may say, since I'm not merely a witness to the crime but its presumed perpetrator, much distorted as well. It has been told around by people who are virtual strangers, people who heard it from one of my daughters, my son-in-law, or my granddaughter, all of whom enjoy telling it because it paints the old man, that's me, in a somewhat humiliating light, or maybe humbling light is a better way to put it. Apparently, humbling the old man still gives pleasure, even to people who don't know him personally. I half expect to see a version of the story appear, drained of all sadness and significance, in a situation comedy on TV written by some kid who was in a college writing workshop with my grand-daughter.

My main impulse here is merely to set the record straight, get the story told truthfully once and for all, even if it does in a vague way reflect badly on me. Not on my character so much as on my inability to anticipate bad things and thus on my inability to protect my children when they were very young from those bad things. I'm also trying to reclaim the story, to take it back and make it mine again. If that sounds selfish of me, remember that for thirty-five years it has belonged to everyone else.

It was the winter following the summer I separated from Louise, the mother of my three younger daughters, the woman who for fourteen turbulent years had been my wife. It took place in a shabbily quaint village in southern New Hampshire where I was teaching literature at a small liberal arts college. The divorce had not yet kicked in, but the separation was complete, an irreversible fact of life, my life and Louise's and the lives of our three girls, Anthea, Caitlin, and Sasha, who were six, nine, and thirteen years old. A fourth daughter, Vickie, from my first marriage, was then eighteen and living with me, having run away from her mother and stepfather's home in North Carolina. She was enrolled as a freshman at the college where I taught and was temporarily housed in a studio I built for her above the garage. All of us were fissioned atoms spun off at least three different nuclear families, seeking new, recombinant nuclei.

I had left Louise in August and bought a small abandoned house with an attached garage a quarter of a mile away that felt and looked like the gatehouse to Louise's much larger, elaborately groomed Victorian manse on the hill just beyond. Following my departure, her social life, always more intense and open-ended than mine, continued unabated and even intensified, as if for years my presence had acted as a party killer. On weekends especially, cars rumbled back and forth along the unpaved lane between my cottage and her house at all hours of the day and night. Some of the cars I recognized as belonging to our formerly shared friends; some of them were new to me and bore out-of-state plates.

We were each financially independent of the other, she through a trust set up by her grandparents, I by virtue of my teaching position. There was, therefore, no alimony for our lawyers to fight for or against. Since our one jointly owned asset of consequence, that rather grandiose Victorian manse, had been purchased with her family's money, I signed my half of it over to her without argument. It had always seemed pretentiously bourgeois to me, a bit of an embarrassment, frankly, and I was glad to be rid of it.

Regarding the children, the plan was that my ex-wife, as I was already thinking of her, and I would practice "joint custody," a Solomonic solution to the rending of family fabric. At the time, the late 1970s, this was seen as a progressive, although mostly untried, way of doling out parental responsibilities in a divorce. Three and a half days a week the girls would reside with me and their half sister, Vickie, and three and a half days a week with their mother. They would alternate three nights at my house one week with four nights the next, so that for every fourteen nights they would have slept seven at the home of each parent. Half their clothing and personal possessions would be at my place, where I had carved two tiny, low-ceilinged bedrooms out of the attic, and half would be at their mother's, where each child had her own large, high-windowed bedroom and walk-in closet. It was an easy, safe stroll between the two houses, and on transitional days, the school bus could pick them up in the morning at one parent's house and drop them off that afternoon at the other. We agreed to handle the holidays and vacations on an ad hoc basis—postponing the problem, in other words.

That left only the cat, a large black Maine coon cat named Scooter, and the family dog, a white part-poodle mutt we'd rescued from a pound twelve years earlier when I was in graduate school. A spayed female unaccountably named Sarge, she was an adult dog of indeterminate age when we got her but was now very old. She was arthritic, half blind, and partially deaf. And devoted to everyone in the family. We were her pack.

Louise and I agreed that Scooter and Sarge, unlike our daughters, could not adapt to joint custody and therefore would have to live full-time in one place or the other. I made a preemptive bid for Sarge, who was viewed as belonging not to either parent alone, but to the three girls, who were very protective of her, as if she were a mentally and physically challenged sibling. Despite her frailty, she was the perfect family dog: sweetly placid, utterly dependent, and demonstrably grateful for any form of human kindness.

Scooter, on the other hand, was a loner and often out all night prowling the neighborhood for sex. We had neglected to neuter him until he was nearly three, and evidently he still thought he was obliged to endure mortal combat with other male cats for the sexual favors of females, even though he was no longer capable of enjoying those favors. He had long been regarded by Louise and the girls and by himself as my cat, probably because I was an early riser and fed him when he showed up at the back door at dawn looking like a boxer who needed a good cutman. And though neither of us overtly acknowledged it, he and I were the only males in the family. He ended up at my gatehouse down the lane not because I particularly wanted him there, but more or less by default.

In keeping with the principle of dividing custodial responsibilities equally between ex-husband and ex-wife, since the ex-husband had been claimed by the cat, it was decided that the dog would stay at the home of the ex-wife. She insisted on it. There was no discussion or negotiation. I balked at first, but then backed off. Keeping Sarge at her house was an important point of pride for Louise, I saw, the one small tilt in her favor in an otherwise equitable division of property, personal possessions, and domestic responsibility. It was a small victory over me in a potentially much more destructive contest that we were both determined to avoid, and I didn't mind handing it to her. Choose your battles, I reminded myself. Also, claiming Sarge as her own and not mine was a not-so-subtle though probably unconscious way for Louise to claim our daughters as more hers than mine. I didn't mind giving that to her either, as long as I knew it was an illusion. It made me feel more magnanimous and wise than I really was.

Back then there were many differences between me and Louise as to reality and illusion, truth and falsity, and a frequent confusion of the causes of the breakdown of the marriage with the symptoms of an already broken marriage. But I'd rather not go into them here, because this story is not concerned with those differences and that confusion, which now these many years later have dwindled to irrelevance. Besides, both Louise and I have been happily remarried to new spouses for decades, and our children are practically middle-aged and have children of their own. One daughter is herself twice divorced. Like her dad.

At first the arrangement went as smoothly as Louise and I had hoped. The girls, bless their hearts, once the initial shock of the separation wore off, seemed to embrace the metronomic movement back and forth between their old familiar family home, now owned and operated solely by their mother, and the new, rough-hewn home operated by their father a few hundred yards down the lane. With a swing set and slide from Sears, I turned the backyard into a suburban playground. It was a mild autumn with a long Indian summer, I recall, and I pitched a surplus army tent among the maples by the brook and let the girls grill hot dogs and toast marshmallows and sleep out there in sleeping bags on warm nights when there was no school the next day. Back in June, when I knew I'd soon be parenting and housekeeping on my own, I had scheduled my fall term classes and conferences for early in the day so that I could be home waiting for the girls when they stepped down from the bus and came into the house. With Vickie living over the garage—although only sleeping there irregularly, as she now had a boyfriend at school who had his own apartment in town—my place that fall was like an after-school summer camp for girls.

The one unanticipated complication arose when Sarge, the beloved old family dog, trotted arthritically along behind the girls as best she could whenever they came from their mother's house to mine. This in itself was not a problem, except that, when the girls returned to their mother's at the end of their three or four scheduled nights with me, Sarge refused to follow. She stayed with me and Scooter. Her preference was clear, although her reasons were not. She even resisted being leashed and went limp like an antiwar demonstrator arrested for trespass and could not be made to stand and walk.

Within an hour of the girls' departure, Louise would telephone and insist that I drive the dog "home," as she put it. "Sarge lives with me," she said. "Me and the girls."

Custody of Sarge was a victory over Louise that I had not sought. I had never thought of her as "my" dog, but as the family dog, by which I meant belonging to the children. I tried explaining that it appeared to be Sarge's decision to stay with me and assured her that I had done nothing to coerce the dog into staying and nothing to hinder her in any way from following the girls up the lane when they left. Quite the opposite.

But Louise would have none of it. "Just bring the damn dog back. Now," she said, and hung up. Her voice and her distinctive Virginia Tidewater accent echo in my ears these many years later.

I was driving a Ford station wagon then, and because of her arthritis poor old Sarge couldn't get into the back on her own, so I had to lift her up carefully and lay her in, and when I arrived at Louise's house, I had to open the tailgate and scoop the dog up in my arms and set her down on the driveway like an offering— a peace offering, I suppose, though it felt more like a propitiation.

This happened every week. Despite all Louise's efforts to keep Sarge a permanent resident of her house, the dog always managed to slip out, arriving at my door just behind the girls, or else she came down the lane, increasingly, on her own, even when the girls were in their mother's custody. So it wasn't Anthea, Caitlin, and Sasha that the dog was following, it was me. I began to see that in her canine mind I was her pack leader, and since I had moved to a new den, so had she. If she didn't follow me there, she'd be without a pack and a proper den.

There was nothing that Louise and I could do to show Sarge how wrong she was. She wasn't wrong, of course; she was a dog. After about a month, Louise gave up, although she never announced her capitulation. Simply, there came a time when my ex-wife no longer called me with orders to deliver our family dog to her doorstep.

Everyone—me, Sarge, the girls, I think even Louise—was relieved. We all knew on some level that a major battle, one with a likelihood of causing considerable collateral damage, had been narrowly avoided. Yet, despite my relief, I felt a buzzing, low-grade anxiety about having gained sole custody of Sarge. I wasn't aware of it then, but looking back now I see that Sarge, as long as she was neither exclusively mine nor Louise's, functioned in our newly disassembled family as the last remaining link to our pre-separation, prelapsarian past, to a time of relative innocence, when all of us, but especially the girls, still believed in the permanence of our family unit, our pack.

If Sarge had only agreed to traipse up and down the lane behind the girls, if she had agreed to accept joint custody, then my having left my wife that summer and fall could have been seen by all of us as an eccentric, impulsive, possibly even temporary, sleeping arrangement, and for the girls it could have been a bit like going on a continuous series of neighborhood camping trips with Dad. I would not have felt quite so guilty, and Louise would not have been so hurt and angry. The whole abandonment issue would have been ameliorated somewhat. The children would not have been so traumatized, their lives, as they see them today, would not have been permanently disfigured, and neither Louise nor I might have gone looking so quickly for replacement spouses.

That's a lot of weight to put on a family dog, I know. We all lose our innocence soon enough; it's inescapable. Most of us aren't emotionally or intellectually ready for it until our thirties or even later, however. So when one loses it prematurely, in childhood and adolescence, through divorce or the sudden early death of a parent or, more usually, war, it can leave one fixated on that loss for a lifetime. Because it's premature, it feels unnatural, violent, and unnecessary, a permanent, gratuitous wounding, and it leaves one angry at the world, and to provide one's unfocused anger with a proper target, one looks for someone to blame.

No one blamed Sarge, of course, for rejecting joint custody and thereby breaking up our family. Not consciously, anyhow. In fact, back then, at the beginning of the breakup of the family, none of us knew how much we depended on Sarge to preserve our ignorance of the fragility, the very impermanence, of the family. None of us knew that she was helping us postpone our anger and need for blame—blame for the separation and divorce, for the destruction of the family unit, for our lost innocence.

Whenever the girls stepped down from the school bus for their three or four nights' stay at my house, they were clearly, profoundly comforted to see Sarge—her wide grin; her wet, black eyes glazed by cataracts; her floppy tail and slipshod, slanted, arthritic gait as she trailed them from the bus stop to the house. Wherever the girls settled in the yard or the house, as long as she didn't have to climb the narrow attic stairs to be with them, Sarge lay watchfully beside them, as if guarding them from a danger whose existence Louise and I had not yet acknowledged.

Vickie wasn't around all that much, but Sarge was not attached to her in the same intense way as to the three younger girls. Sarge pretty much ignored Vickie. From the dog's perspective, I think, she was a late-arriving, auxiliary member of the pack, which I hate to admit is how the three younger girls saw her too, despite my best efforts to integrate all four daughters into a single family unit. No one admitted this, of course, but even then, that early in the game, I saw that I was failing to build a recombinant nuclear family. Vickie was a free radical and, sadly, would remain one.

Mostly, when the children were at school or up at their mother's, Sarge slept through her days. Her only waking diversion, in the absence of the girls, was going for rides in my car, and I took her everywhere I went, even to my office at the college, where she slept under my desk while I met my classes. From dawn to dusk, when the weather turned wintry and snow was falling, if I was at home and my car parked in the driveway, Sarge's habit, so as not to miss an opportunity for a ride, was to crawl under the vehicle and sleep there until I came out. When I got into the car I'd

start the engine and, if the girls were with me, count off the seconds aloud until, fifteen or twenty seconds into my count, Sarge
appeared at the driver's side window. Then I'd step out, flip open
the tailgate, and lift her into the back. If the girls weren't there
I still counted, but silently. I never got as high as thirty before
Sarge was waiting by the car door.

I don't remember now where we were headed, but this time all
four daughters were in the car together, Vickie in the front passenger's seat, Anthea, Caitlin, and Sasha in back. I remember it
as a daytime drive, even though, because of Vickie's classes and
the younger girls' school hours, it was unusual for all four to be in
the car at the same time during the day. Maybe it was a Saturday
or Sunday; maybe we were going ice-skating at one of the local
ponds. It was a bright, cloudless, cold afternoon, I remember that,
and there was no snow on the ground just then, which suggests a
deep freeze following the usual January thaw. We must have been
five or six months into the separation and divorce, which would
not be final until the following August.

Piling into the car, all four of the girls were in a silly mood,
playing with the words of a popular Bee Gees disco song, "More
Than a Woman," singing in perfect mocking harmony and
substituting lines like "bald-headed woman" for "more than a
woman," and breaking each other up, even the youngest, Anthea,
who would have just turned seven then. I can't say I was distracted. I was simply happy, happy to see my daughters goofing
off together, and was grinning at the four of them as they sang,
my gaze turning from one bright face to another, when I realized
that I had counted all the way to sixty and was still counting.
That far into it, I didn't make the connection between the count
and lifting Sarge into the back of the station wagon. I simply
stopped counting, put the car in reverse, and started to back out
of the driveway.

There was a thump and a bump. The girls stopped singing. No
one said a word. I hit the brake, put the car in park, and shut off
the motor. I placed my forehead against the steering-wheel rim.

All four daughters began to wail. It was a primeval, keening, utterly female wail. Their voices rose in pitch and volume and became almost operatic, as if for years they had been waiting for this moment to arrive, when they could at last give voice together to a lifetime's accumulated pain and suffering. A terrible, almost unthinkable thing had happened. Their father had murdered the beloved animal. Their father had slain a permanent member of the family. We all knew it the second we heard the thump and felt the bump. But the girls knew something more. Instinctively, they understood the linkage between this moment, with Sarge dead beneath the wheels of my car, and my decision the previous summer to leave my wife. My reasons for that decision, my particular forms of pain and suffering, my years of humiliation and sense of having been too compromised in too many ways ever to respect myself again unless I left my wife, none of that mattered to my daughters, even to Vickie, who, as much as the other three, needed the original primal family unit with two loving parents in residence together, needed it to remain intact and to continue into her adult life, holding and sustaining her and her sisters, nurturing them, and more than anything else, protecting them from bad things.

When the wailing finally subsided and came to a gradual end, and I had apologized so sincerely and often that the girls had begun to comfort me instead of letting me comfort them, telling me that Sarge must have died before I hit her with the car or she would have come out from under it in plenty of time, we left the car and wrapped Sarge's body in an old blanket. I carried her body and the girls carried several of her favorite toys and her food dish to the far corner of the backyard and laid her and her favorite things down beneath a leafless old maple tree. I told the girls that they could always come to this tree and stand over Sarge's grave and remember her love for them and their love for her.

While I went to the garage for a shovel and pick, the girls stood over Sarge's body as if to protect it from desecration. When I returned, Vickie said, "The ground's frozen, you know, Dad."

"That's why I brought the pick," I said, but the truth is I had forgotten that the ground was hard as pavement, and she knew it. They all knew it. I was practically weeping by now, confused and frightened by the tidal welter of emotions rising in my chest and taking me completely over. As the girls calmed and seemed to grow increasingly focused on the task at hand, burying Sarge, I spun out of control. I threw the shovel down beneath the maple tree and started slamming the pick against the ground, whacking the sere, rock-hard sod with fury. The blade clanged in the cold morning air and bounced off the ground, and the girls, frightened by my wild, gasping swings, backed away from me, as if watching their father avenge a crime they had not witnessed, delivering a punishment that exceeded the crime to a terrible degree.

I only glimpsed this and was further maddened by it and turned my back to them so I couldn't see their fear and disapproval, and I slammed the steel against the ground with increasing force, again and again, until finally I was out of breath and the nerves of my hands were vibrating painfully from the blows. I stopped attacking the ground at last, and as my head cleared, I remembered the girls and slowly turned to say something to them, something that would somehow gather them in and dilute their grief-stricken fears. I didn't know what to say, but something would come to me; it always did.

But the girls were gone. I looked across the yard, past the rusting swing set toward the house, and saw the four of them disappear one by one between the house and the garage, Vickie in the lead, then Sasha holding Anthea's hand, and Caitlin. A few seconds later, they reappeared on the far side of the house, walking up the lane toward the home of my ex-wife. Now Vickie was holding Anthea's hand in one of hers and Caitlin's in the other, and Sasha, the eldest of my ex-wife's three daughters, was in the lead.

That's more or less the whole story, except to mention that when the girls were finally out of sight, Scooter, my black cat, strolled from the bushes alongside the brook that marked the edge of the yard, where he had probably been hunting voles and ground-feeding chickadees. He made his way across the yard to where I stood, passed by me, and sat next to Sarge's stiffening body. The blanket around her body had been blown back by the breeze. The cold wind riffled her dense white fur. Her sightless eyes were dry and opaque, and her gray tongue lolled from her open mouth as if stopped in the middle of a yawn. She looked like game, a wild animal killed for her coat or her flesh, and not a permanent member of the family.

I carried the body of the dog to the veterinarian, where she was cremated, and brought the ashes in a ceramic jar back to my house and placed the jar on the fireplace mantel, thinking that in the spring, when the ground thawed, the girls and I would bury the ashes down by the maple tree by the brook. But that never happened. The girls did not want to talk about Sarge. They did not spend as much time at my house anymore as they had before Sarge died. Vickie moved in with her boyfriend in town. By spring the other girls were staying overnight at my house every other weekend, and by summer, when they went off to summer camp in the White Mountains, not at all, and I saw them that summer only when I drove up to Camp Abenaki on Parents' Weekend. I emptied the jar with Sarge's ashes into the brook alone one afternoon in May. The following year I was offered a tenure-track position at a major university in New Jersey, and given my age and stage of career, I felt obliged to accept it. I sold my little house down the lane from my ex-wife's home. From then on the girls visited me and their old cat, Scooter, when they could, which was once a month for a weekend during the school year and for the week before summer camp began.

Dina Nayeri

A Ride Out of Phrao

IN HER LAST WEEK in America, Shirin sells or gives away all her possessions, returning to the same small parcel she carried when she first arrived—a purse full of dried fruit and extra underwear. She feels thirty again.

She is happy to be leaving Cedar Rapids—a place that, in fifteen years, never grew to fit her strange edges—and to be sent closer to home. She is moving to a village somewhere in northern Thailand. Iran isn't on the list of Peace Corps countries, after all, and this is a comfort. She has been away for too long and is a stranger now. Why go back and ruin the beautiful image her Tehrani relatives have of her? Still, she misses the East. She writes a letter about it to cousins in Tehran, emphasizing that the Peace Corps is a great honor, leaving out any hint of her lack of options. Months later, she suspects she misspelled the name—*Peace Core*, she remembers writing, a place that carries peace at its core. Is that not the meaning?

She often reminds herself that to be accepted to the program you have to be American. As a citizen, she qualifies, though now and then it feels like a deception. Sometimes she repeats every detail of her application to herself. Was any of it a lie? No, no, it was not. At first there was some question about her age, but the man on the phone said that she had the enthusiasm of the young and that many older people volunteer every year. To this she replied that she was only forty-five. *Yes, of course,* the man said, which made her dislike him and look down on his so-called peacekeeping organization. But, for Shirin Khalilipour-Anderson, the Peace Corps is a solid, respectable way out of town. No one will have to know about the bankruptcy, the loss of her house, or the series of demeaning bureaucratic jobs for which she was overqualified and whose titles she often changes for her Iranian friends. *Doctor of New Research*, she calls the last one, in which she was paid slightly above minimum wage to sit beside three bleary-eyed researchers, filing their work according to a needlessly convoluted system.

She was fired for doing too many "extra" things: for making suggestions to the other employees; bringing *baghlava* for everyone; tuning out when the boy who hired her spoke. The boy called it downsizing, apologized, then made a backhanded recommendation that she seek work someplace that would appreciate her special kind of initiative. At the next meeting of her church's widows group—an organization she joined despite the very alive state of both her ex-husbands—Shirin told the other ladies that she had quit her job because of exhaustion. She added that she had spent a week training her replacement—which wasn't strictly true, but she would have done it, if they had asked.

After a short training program in Washington, DC, she travels to Phrao, a village two hours outside the big city of Chiang Mai. She lives alone. There are no other Peace Corps volunteers in this poverty-stricken town of barely two thousand. She chafes against her new living standards—a hut, no furniture except a small table and a sleeping mat. No air-conditioning. She works under two young Thai bureaucrats, offering medical services in a one-room clinic. Soon she will begin a second job teaching children a few words of English a day. She begins to relish the rigors of it. The Thai people are strange, their every custom a struggle, but Shirin enjoys their company. They seem cold at first. She learns that they aren't naturally effusive to strangers, as Iranians are. To Persians, a dramatic show of unearned love—hugs and kisses and empty offers—aren't falsehoods so much as necessary illusions of warmth and community. Privately, Shirin finds it tiresome, though she would never betray her native culture by saying so. Besides, there are the good parts; the face-saving parts—Iranians give each other room to pretend. (Yes, I have a second home in Shiraz. Yes, my son has a PhD. Yes, yes, yes.)

Thai people are restrained. No hugs. They bow and bow.

American, she says when introducing herself to her new neighbors, and they nod, easily accepting this. They ask, *New York?* She smiles and says yes. It's close enough; her daughter lives there. She misses Leila, twenty now and studying psychology in the world's top city. It's a shame none of their Tehrani relatives can see the woman Leila has become, her beauty and charm, her ability to relate to Americans, to make them love her so easily. Leila has many men, and Shirin overlooks this, though it is a sin. The girl is just like her father, so addicted to being adored that he stayed in Tehran among his many lovers rather than risk exile, knowing that a new land would spit him out.

Oh, but Leila . . . she succeeded at becoming American in less than one year. What a thing to have done! Fifteen years and Shirin has yet to complete this task. And so she wants to show Thailand to her New York daughter—here she seems to have clicked into place somehow. She has written her daughter several times, inviting her to visit. Leila has never written back, and in truth, she hasn't spoken to Shirin in a year. But that isn't important— they've had a fight, that's all. Leila often overreacts when Shirin doesn't spell out every detail in a way that Leila considers "candid." Now Shirin doesn't even remember what she is supposed to have lied about—something small like the value of her house, or how many credit cards she had before the bankruptcy. At least a small part of it was over the decision to move to Thailand. *Running away,* Leila called it.

Young people often travel to Thailand—maybe she will come. Shirin wants Leila to notice that the villagers don't hear her accent, and, at work, her bosses defer to her because she is older. And if she makes suggestions, they make a show of complying. She marvels at this. How could it be so easy? Later, when her Thai is better, her neighbor, a tiny speckle-faced woman, asks her about her history and she mentions having been a doctor in Iran, then a housewife in America, and then a *Manager of Advanced Research*. From then on her neighbor calls her "Dr. Rin," which is a wonder for so many reasons.

The name catches on, and she lets it.

Her early days are spent gradually acquiring this and that. Pots and pans. Sanitary pads. Proper spoons. Conditioner. Toothpaste without salt. (Salt in toothpaste. What a repulsive thing!) A rice cooker is easy to find. She adapts easily to the Thai style of eating rice, happily slicing mango in her bare hands, letting the sticky yellow juice flow through her fingers as she relishes the strange new taste of consuming dry rice, no butter, with fruit. She wipes her hands on her Thai clothes, cheap cotton tunics made for soiling.

She surprises herself each time her sticky hand reaches for her shirt hem as it would a dishrag. At her widows' group meetings she often wore her nicest silk blouse, a lavender Chanel piece that she had preserved for ten years, ironing it for fifteen minutes after every hand wash. The blouse had an ugly seam just above the hip, an imperfection she took great care to hide, tucking and re-tucking it into her skirt every so often.

Never let your seams show, she used to tell her daughter when she was young.

At church functions, she turned down every good appetizer for fear of soiling that blouse. Now she thinks that this is the greatest sign that she was a stranger there. *They're not your people until you share a meal with some ease.* She has never been comfortable eating with Americans. In Iran friends and neighbors ate together on a cloth on the floor, spending hours in one another's company. They interacted with food and with each other in the most basic and intimate ways.

She finds that Thai stores have all her Persian spices and utensils. Barely any bread, though. When she asks people where to find bread, they say, eyes full of sympathy, "Don't you have rice to eat?" This makes her chuckle. She answers in clunky Thai, "Just my strange American tastes."

Her house stands just off the ground, on short stilts hidden here and there by patches of shrubbery. It has a roof shaped like a straw hat, so that from far away, the hut looks like a squatting woman, head down so that her hat falls over her eyes, her skirt of shrubs lifted, exposing her bare legs in two or three places. The image amuses her. It seems to signal the house's greatest difficulty—the toilet is a hole in the ground, like in Iran. But her bladder is American now and so it takes an hour of squatting to squeeze a few drops. Afterward she's elated with herself, adapting like a young person.

Most of the meat here is pork. She's no Muslim, but don't the Thai people realize that this vile animal eats the flesh of its own species? Evil. A lot of things in Thailand carry the sensation of evil. She doesn't like the Buddha shelf in her house. She considers Buddhism idol worship. And every morning she wakes up under her mosquito net, eye-to-eye with a new kind of enormous lizard. On the first night she killed one. Its guts are still on her bedroom wall. Each night she scrubs it, in a strange ritualistic way that is starting to feel like penance, and so she has come to a kind of truce with the creatures. The Thai people often talk of demons. Maybe her pretty new house has spirits and they visit her in an endless line of lizards. Now one is dead and the others mourn it, a reptile community, arriving every night to that same spot, flicking their wretched tongues, taunting her. *You asked for this, didn't you?*

"Filthy little beasts," she answers when she is alone and sleepy and she wants to hear the music of Farsi words, even the ugly ones, spoken aloud.

. . .

On the morning she begins her job at the local school, a hot rain soaks the village and she glimpses her neighbors eating a wordless morning meal on the floor. Their window is barely three feet from hers, so that she can examine their food, hear some of their whispers, breathe in the sharp scent of their incense. The rain blurs the lines of their faces and bodies, and their movements become dreamlike. They remind her of her parents, the way they broke fast quietly, always on the floor, and as a teenager she often gave them fifteen minutes before she joined with her cup of tea.

She eats breakfast alone, black tea and purple sticky rice with mango and banana. She adds some coconut milk and mung beans, thinking, *How authentic it seems.* She has allotted too much time for breakfast, so she peels rambutan and mangosteen, not because she's hungry, but for the pleasure of peeling. She is enthralled by the strange, sensuous fruits of this country. When you peel a mangosteen, for example, it is impossible to stay clean because there are inner membranes to remove. If you cut it sloppily, you will get a mouthful of the foul along with the sweet. In almost all her favorite fruits, a sticky seam divides the best from the worst. It reminds her of the persimmons of Iran, with their four watery petals tucked inside a bitter stinging jelly, the thin skin between them the difference between an exquisite flavor and a repellent one. Separating the two parts is an art, requiring a steady hand and a tiny spoon.

In early mornings when she misses Iran and the knowledge of a long-impending loneliness hits, like a brick suddenly falling into both arms, she forces herself to think of her early years in Cedar Rapids. She was married then—to this man who gifted her with *Anderson*—for only six months when she was a new immigrant, thirty and lonely and clueless about how to relate to an American husband. *Why did he marry me,* she wonders, thinking of herself in those days, how hopeless she seemed with her five-year-old daughter and her damaged hair and her ragged tote full of dried fruit and extra underwear in case at any moment she should need to flee the country again. *What did he want with such a mess of a woman?* After a while, she always dismisses this question and gathers her backpack of Peace Corps essentials. She was very beautiful then—of course.

The schoolroom is stifling and ripe with a sour milk smell. Rows of eight-year-olds with greasy, bluish black hair giggle and stare at Shirin, overwhelmed by her foreignness. She has been told that the Thai people are suspicious of strangers and that it is important to answer all their questions, even if they seem nosey. Often as she bikes through rice fields, wearing her straw hat and wraparound fisherman pants to blend in, fellow bicyclists stop her and ask strange things. *What is your name? How old are you? What have you eaten today?* Though at first she thought she had misunderstood, now she presses her hands together as in prayer, greeting them with a *sawat-dee-kha* before answering simply, *I am Shirin. Forty-five. Much rice today. All is well.*

She doesn't lie about her age—this is how they decide how much respect to show.

The schoolchildren ask the same intimate questions as their parents. *How old are you? Where did you come from? How much was your tunic?* In the weeks that follow, she teaches them English words by talking about Leila, showing photos of her life in New York and describing each item: Woman. Books. City. Man with glasses. Man with yellow hair. Man in jeans. The children love Leila's photos, fighting over them as if she were a starlet.

One child, Boonmee, always lingers by the wall. He has a sleepy expression, his eyes so small they are obstructed on both ends by fleshy cheeks and heavy eyelids. His thick rosebud lips seem ever swollen, as if he is constantly having an allergic reaction. He rarely smiles. He sits in a corner by himself, saying nothing. When he laughs, it is always in strange moments, as if at his own thoughts, his eyes opening suddenly just a crack like an oyster shell so that she can see the dark glimmer inside. Shirin comes to like him best.

Each morning she asks in English, "Boonmee, how are you?"

He never answers, so to illustrate, she answers herself, "Fine, thank you."

One day, Shirin finally hears Boonmee's voice. When a new child points at Shirin, and shouts, "*Farang!*" the Thai word for foreigners, Boonmee looks up from his corner and speaks for the first time: "That is no *farang*. That is Dr. Rin!"

She imagines this is the beginning of a secret understanding between them. Somehow, this boy knows that foreignness is her burden.

"Thank you, Boonmee," she says in Thai. He shrugs and looks away.

In her fourth week of teaching, Boonmee is absent twice. Then, on the third day, he shows up hand-in-hand with the regular schoolteacher, Sawat, the only person in town who can speak decent English. He hangs his head, his chin tucked so that she can only see the black of his hair and the outline of his cheeks. He refuses to look up, his gaze fixed on his sandals. "What's wrong?" Shirin asks.

Sawat kneels beside Boonmee and says something in Thai. The boy doesn't look up from his feet. Then Sawat wipes her thick bangs from her forehead, smiles at Shirin in that deferential way, and—never taking her hands off Boonmee's shoulders—says, "All fine. Let's learning English?"

All through class Shirin can't keep from glancing in Boonmee's direction. He seems to be hiding something, slumped and folded over himself, his right side turned toward the wall. His breathing is strange, his stomach contracting and expanding in a sad tempo. When she can no longer tolerate the mystery, Shirin tells the class to practice copying letters from the board and goes over to him. She tries to turn his face, but his body goes rigid and he pushes against the wall. A strange noise, like a chirp or a high-pitched howl, escapes his throat. Sawat gets up from her chair, whispers in Thai, "Let's go outside." She takes Boonmee's hand and leads him away from Shirin. This annoys her, angers her, like Sawat has just taken her own child from her arms.

She follows them into the half-covered walkway outside where the rain has soaked the orchids, blending the sweet scent with the stench of a nearby aloe tree. Something about the way Sawat kneels beside the boy, the condescension in the act, reminds Shirin of her own parents, who never knelt but always sat. So she drops down onto her haunches on the concrete, cross-legged as if ready for a night with the water pipe. She tries again to turn Boonmee's face toward her. She can see that whatever he is hiding is shameful to him, in front of the foreign *doctor*. "It's okay," she says. "Let me see." When he finally looks up, his rosebud mouth is quivering and a yellowish bruise covers half his right cheek and his upper neck.

Sawat whispers, "His father has a demon."

Yes, there are demons here. There are crafty lizards and Buddha shelves, and everything is a lie. You are told every day to smile, even if you have no joy in your heart.

Sawat says the man's name, Khunpol, and Shirin thinks she has seen him in the village. He has an outdoor restaurant—three plastic tables and a pot of noodles—that she often visits. Khunpol is a smallish man, with a hard-set face, yellow teeth, high cheekbones like a woman's, and two missing fingers. He makes a very good *pad see ew*. He has no wife. Does this boy, then, have no mother?

In Thailand, there are rules about greeting strangers, rules about touching, about older and younger. Hands together, bowing. But Shirin pulls the boy into her arms and presses him hard against her chest, so that she can easily feel his tiny pulse speeding up, fast and faint, like the heartbeat of a bird in the hand.

She holds him there for a moment and his body loosens. Sawat shifts around uncomfortably. Then Shirin feels something strange. In her arms, the boy is squirming, readjusting his body somehow. She feels his hand wriggle free and she loosens her grip but doesn't let go, thinking that this boy must be starving for affection. She whispers, "It's okay," rubs his back and drones on and on in the soothing way she once used with Leila, as if to teach him her Western ways, *this is how we say everything will be fine* . . . in Iran or America or somewhere. In the universal language you may one day learn.

Then she feels his small hand on her breast, resting there, the way her daughter used to do when Shirin held her close. The boy breathes warmly on her neck, and he reminds her so much of a helpless infant, a tired baby falling asleep. But just as she is about to revisit that old motherly wound, his hand moves and she is gripped by a wicked thought. It must be wicked, because who can think such a thing of a harmless boy? It must be the evil in her mind, the influence of the Buddha shelf or whatever strange spirits live in this country. Could it be that this child is willfully touching her breast—?

She pulls away quickly, so that some hurt registers in the boy's expression.

She looks at Sawat, who only smiles. It seems she missed these small movements. She considers asking Sawat if such an action is normal, but does not. It seems shameful.

For days she obsesses over the incident. Was it the evil in her own heart that caused her to hurt a fragile boy only wanting a moment of maternal affection? Or was the child acting out of some ugly preadolescent curiosity? Was it her demon or his? Maybe he was confused. Surely she did nothing wrong in hugging the boy. Though in the end, her guilt seems always to rest upon that moment of hurt in his sleepy eyes, when she pulled away and he looked up like a child whose spoon has been pulled out of his mouth. Does Boonmee ever get hugged in his house? Was it wrong to push him away when he was grabbing for a substitute mother?

At bedtime, she puts on Iranian music. A sad melody by Googoosh called "Nafas," which means "breath." Googoosh's life reminds her that even if you are beautiful and beloved by the world, even if you've conquered every mundane worry, what you do suffer you suffer alone. She makes herself a plate of fruits for dinner, saying the names out loud so that when she talks of them later, she will use the right words. There is the spiky red one, the one that looks like a baby armadillo, the one that smells like feet. She likes peeling back the thin inner lining that separates the flesh from the rough skins of almost all of them. She imagines that even the richest people on earth don't eat better than the fruits of Thailand—God's bounty on a plate.

At mealtimes alone, she has a habit of retreating deep into her own imagination, usually dreaming up what she will say in her next conversation with Leila, whenever that may be. If they were to talk today, she thinks, she would seek advice about Boonmee. They would discuss him at length, because Leila is a student of psychology. She would tell her daughter about the poverty here, the stifling heat of her house, the neighbors she can see through her window who never talk to each other. *Leila* joon, she would say, *you don't know what they suffer here.*

The question of the boy consumes her. After dinner, she sits up with a cup of tea and wonders why she has only ever e-mailed her daughter. Obviously the girl doesn't check her university account. She sends four expensive text messages to Leila's phone before her ancient mobile comes to life at three a.m.—Leila must have forgotten the eleven-hour time difference. In her rush to answer, she almost trips out of bed, forgetting about the mosquito net. A lizard sticks its ugly tongue out at her. "Evil thing," she whispers.

"Leila *joon*?" she answers, already breathless.

"What's wrong?" Leila asks, and Shirin realizes that if the matter is not urgent, Leila will be angry. They are, after all, in the middle of a cold war. Still, Leila's voice warms her through, like weighty palms pressed to a sore back.

"Oh nothing," says Shirin, "I'm just a little sick. I shouldn't have bothered you."

"No, no," says Leila, her voice tentative but concerned. "How are you?"

It seems that Leila is opening the door to a conversation and so Shirin tiptoes through. She mentions the hot weather, the watery fruits, and the Thai people's obsession with demons, how they are tied to more than just sin—"They're everywhere, Leila *joon*!"

Soon they fall into natural conversation and Leila tells her about school. She uses words and phrases that, after fifteen years in America, Shirin understands but will never appreciate. Leila's new boyfriend, it seems, is turning out to be *a colossal dick*, and she is thinking of *phoning in* some paper on Carl Jung. She throws psychology words into her everyday speech. Somebody has a *Napoleon complex*. Somebody else is engaging in *serious transference*. Shirin listens and waits for the chance to discuss Boonmee. What part of his psyche made him do this strange thing? Her daughter will have theories.

Finally, Leila starts to say that she has to leave and Shirin blurts it out, "One of the children at school grabbed for my breast. Is that normal?"

There is a moment of silence, and then Leila laughs, her sweet young laugh. "Oh Maman *joon*," she says, amused but on the verge of distraction. "It's just instinct."

For a moment Shirin forgets her concerns. She tells the story only to entertain, and Leila rewards her with gasps and giggles and clever American jokes. Then she says, as if just thinking of it, "I'm going to Tokyo for a week during break. What if I visit?"

Something moves in Shirin's chest, a flutter, like when Leila was a child and they were friends. "Are you serious?" she says. "You can take the time off?"

"I *just* said it's break," says Leila. "I'm Googling Chiang Mai right now. What street's your apartment on?" She reads the websites aloud, thrilled by the city's many restaurants and elephant reserves and massage parlors.

Shirin waits for a moment. Before she can think through the consequences of the lie, and her daily promises to God and to herself, she has already blurted, "Right in the center, Leila *joon*. It's very modern. Very, very nice. You'll love it."

Sometimes the villagers offer her gifts, watery lychee and pungent durian, heavenly fruits that she knows to accept. In Iran, accepting is impolite, and it is customary to refuse three times. In Iran one must show no need, no suffering. One must always be above it. Here, it is better, simpler, to share your troubles so that the community can help. This feels so natural that soon Shirin forgets the old ways. She puts away the last of her American clothes, deciding that the fisherman pants are far more appropriate. On the twentieth of the month, when she usually colors her hair, she tells herself that she is too busy and as the weeks pass she continues to skip it, preferring to show her true age. Her neighbors' bows grow deeper with each *sawat-dee-kha*.

Two weeks before her daughter's visit, she considers coloring her hair for Leila's sake, but decides against it.

Leila is scheduled to arrive on a Saturday morning. Shirin spends a week preparing, cooking Iranian dishes, washing the floors of her hut, finding a flowerpot for the Buddha shelf. She thinks of what she will say to Leila. *Leila* joon, *did you know there are water monitors here as big as a small car? Did you know that the durian is a fruit that you can only eat after it rots, its best value coming in its most decrepit state? Leila* joon, *let me tell you about Boonmee. I think he might have a demon, or some other kind of strangeness you might explain.* She lays out a number of pungent herbs that are supposed to ward off the lizards. They don't work. She has arranged a ride from Phrao to Chiang Mai Airport in a weekly van bound for the night market. She is the first one inside, and the rest trickle in. Most of the other passengers are food vendors. In the stuffy, humid van, the smell of fish and meat on their bodies becomes a toxic vapor that nauseates her. She spots Boonmee's father, Khunpol, sitting in front, and she wants so much to confront him on the boy's behalf. Instead she glares at the back of his neck and wishes for all the fattest lizards in Thailand to visit him in the night.

She rechecks the bus schedule, their transportation back to the village. On the return trip, she will be with Leila—the thought fills her with anticipation. At the airport lounge, she waits with a fragrant jasmine necklace that she has made. After an hour, she sees a familiar figure in the distance, her exhausted daughter, long and shapely in jeans and a T-shirt. She can barely contain her joy as she flings the necklace around Leila's neck. Leila laughs. "I missed you, Maman *joon*," she whispers into Shirin's shoulder.

The trouble starts on the bus, but Shirin is sure she can manage it. "It's just a short ride," she says, to a visibly annoyed Leila, who promptly falls asleep on her shoulder. She wakes up two hours later and asks how long it's been. "Fifteen minutes," says Shirin.

Leila checks her watch and frowns. "So you *don't* live in Chiang Mai?" She says this in that way she has, always accusing. Her stare pierces Shirin and she is forced to look at her lap. "You didn't have to do it again," Leila whispers, as if she's already a licensed psychologist. "I would've come either way." They've talked about the lying before, and Shirin has tried to explain. *It's not lying. In Iran everyone knows a real lie from these everyday things. You just don't know your own culture.*

As soon as they arrive Leila falls asleep on a mat on the floor. Shirin thinks this is a good sign. She prepares some food and checks the bicycles for their evening ride. When she wakes an hour later, Leila looks around and groans, scratching her bare arm where she has been bitten several times. *So much fuss,* Shirin thinks. "Maman," Leila says calmly, "we need to talk about this situation."

Shirin ignores her and suggests they go for a walk. *What situation?* Her daughter has become too American for her own good, always alluding to later discussions. Just say it or don't say it. Though, a minute later when Leila meanders to the bathroom, Shirin thinks maybe she has raised a true Persian daughter, after all. Iranians may be good liars, but they're even better at drama. There is a phrase in Farsi, *putting the whole house on your head.* It's used to describe the moment when someone goes so crazy, so uncontrollably bonkers, as Americans would say, that they explode into a thousand sizzling pieces, their anger like shrapnel, piercing everything.

This is what happens when Leila sees the toilet.

A boycott ensues. "I will *not* even attempt to go in that hole," Leila says. "Maman *joon*, you *said* Chiang Mai. Why would you not give me time to plan for this?"

Leila falls asleep again, this time under the mosquito net (which, thank God, she finds charming), and Shirin sits up worrying about her daughter's colon and bladder—all the digestive problems she could develop, holding it in after twenty hours of flying. For a second she allows herself the realization that she should have anticipated this. Leila is a city girl, an American. She has always been weak in her body. Should she forgive this?

No . . . She prepares a speech about gratitude and authenticity, about Boonmee. She wants to tell her daughter that she is letting her seams show, an ugly thing. She chops watermelon with a machete. She cleans the toilet, which, to be fair, isn't a hole. It's lined with porcelain, and that makes it a *style*, not a lesser thing. She imagines that she will win over her stubborn, city-spoiled daughter with lessons and beautiful words about strength of will and true beauty. Then she will teach Leila how to use this toilet and they will laugh at the silliness of it, remembering the last time she taught Leila this very skill, when Leila was two and they were in Iran, in a bathroom exactly like this one.

When Leila wakes, she is crying softly into the pillow. "I can't sleep. It's so hot," she whispers. Shirin brings her the watermelon.

"Don't you remember Iran?" Shirin says. "The villages we used to visit?"

"No," says Leila, putting on that professional stare again.

"How about a ride in the rice fields," Shirin offers. "I borrowed a bike for you."

"Okay," Leila says, and takes one bite of the watermelon, then winces. She whispers, "Maman *joon*, you lied so so much. Why can't you stop? Why do it with *me*?"

Shirin ignores this. "Get dressed. Let's go."

For the rest of the weekend they follow Shirin's schedule: biking through rice fields, walking through the village, visiting each and every one of her acquaintances. She can see that Leila is suffering through it for her sake. On Sunday, Leila says fewer words, though it's a joy that as the hours pass, the words she does speak are mostly Farsi.

When there is little to say, they laugh at small things. "What the hell is that?" says Leila on Monday morning, as she crawls out from under the mosquito net they share.

"Don't try to kill it," says Shirin, wanting to annoy her daughter, "too much guts."

Leila rolls her eyes and suppresses a smile. Then she surprises Shirin by touching the evil creature, letting the lizard crawl onto her hand. "Hello there, little guy," she says.

After breakfast, Leila visits Shirin's school, sits in the back and listens as Shirin gives the lesson with twice her usual energy. The children sense the cause of this and flock to Leila. Later over noodles under a straw awning, Leila says, "Maman *joon*, that boy has a touch of autism . . ." She pauses. "I'll send you some books to read. Maybe if his family understood it better . . ." They discuss this for an hour, as they might do in a café in New York. Later, Shirin notices that Boonmee is the only topic they spoke about as friends, two adults without a bitter history or any foreignness at all.

Now and then, mostly in the hours when Leila's jet lag is strong, they suffer each other with much huffing. On the third day of the visit, the hottest yet, Leila steps outside, into the half-covered area between Shirin's house and the quiet couple next door, wearing tiny shorts and a tank top. Shirin rushes to her, hoping to get her back inside before the neighbors see. "You can't dress like that here," she says.

"It's a hundred degrees. What else am I gonna wear?" says Leila as she takes her sunglasses out from between her breasts. Shirin can see that her daughter is on edge, and that her patience is running out, but she persists. When Shirin presents her with a pair of fisherman pants—a light rose pair she picked out at the last Sunday market—Leila laughs. "I'm comfortable as is. I'll just go out by myself today. You rest here."

"Leila," says Shirin, growing angry. "Stop this. People here won't respect you in those clothes. How will I go on living here if my daughter behaves like a total *farang*?"

"Respect me? Are you serious?" Leila snaps, wiping the sweat from her arms, her skin now covered with the bites of a hundred mosquitoes.

Shirin sighs. "How did I raise such willful daughter? New York has ruined you."

Leila laughs. Then she just smirks for a moment. "You really care *that* much . . . ? Maman, they're all strangers." She says this word slowly, as if Shirin doesn't know the meaning. "Nobody gives a flying fuck what I—" Leila is raising her voice now and they are only a few feet from the neighbor's window. Shirin pulls her daughter inside, where Leila proceeds not just to put the whole house on her head, but possibly the entire village.

Shirin hurries to the kitchen window, to see if they are watching. The couple is sitting on the floor, having tea, neither of them looking up from their cups. She can see from their profiles that they are absolutely listening—such an impolite daughter, only the wickedest woman must deserve such offspring. What has the foreign woman, this *farang*, done in her life to earn such a curse, they will wonder.

Shirin too wonders things. How much face has she lost in this one exchange? Will the villagers still call her doctor? Will they listen raptly to her every word?

Mother and daughter don't speak for the rest of the day. It's as if all the tension of the last three days has struck them dumb and lame in each other's presence. Finally, just as Shirin gets up to warm some dinner, Leila meanders barefoot into the long corridor that serves as a living room. Shirin used to be so charmed by this small space, its bright blue walls and cozy shape. She was proud of it, but now it is as if the gauze has been removed from her eyes. Now, looking through Leila's eyes, it is just a walkway to connect the shameful toilet, meager kitchen, and stifling bedroom under one roof. Leila drops to the floor, presses her face against the cool, cherry-red tiles. She moans a little.

"Mommy *joon*, I tried," she whispers to the tiles, "I really, really tried. But I can't stay here longer. I haven't taken a shit in three days. I'll die."

Shirin raises an eyebrow. "What have you been doing in the bathroom then?"

Leila shrugs. "I'll die," she repeats.

Oh, what drama, my Persian girl. "Whatever you want," says Shirin, thinking of all the imagined conversations with her daughter, over the ten days they were supposed to have together. So far they've only conversed once, and even that about somebody's strange boy. "I'll find you a ride to Chiang Mai." The weekly van isn't due for four days.

"You come too," says Leila. "We can travel around together. Stay in hotels."

Shirin has already thought of this. It's impossible, and why should she give in to Leila's whims? "I'm needed here," she says. "I won't follow you around Thailand."

"Don't be stubborn," says Leila. "Isn't there a teacher that can cover for you?"

"That's not the point," Shirin snaps. "I work at the clinic too. You go. It's fine."

"They have midwives," mutters Leila, because she is trying to be cruel.

Her daughter believes that Shirin has lied about being a doctor in Tehran. She believes that Shirin was actually a midwife. Shirin has tried to have her credentials sent to America, but has failed to locate them. They were left behind in a hurry when she escaped the Islamic Republic. Likely they were lost or destroyed in the ensuing government lootings of her office. It is the only true thing that Shirin wishes known about herself: that she was a top doctor in Tehran. This is the truth: She once attended the best college in a big city, as Leila is now doing. She was a doctor, a very good one. But what's the point? Her daughter believes she is a liar, and is desperate to get away. In Iran and in Thailand, children never leave their parents, not even bad ones like Khunpol.

They spend the early evening walking in silence through the tiny village—three unpaved roads snaking out of a central fish market—knocking on every door. Shirin cringes each time she has to explain to a neighbor that her daughter is sick and that they need a ride into Chiang Mai tonight. No, it can't wait, she says. Yes, she is a doctor herself but she is ill-equipped here. No, she doesn't have a better explanation.

"Tonight?" the first neighbor, a young seamstress with a browning half tooth, asks. "Really so urgent?" She doesn't have a car, but she offers to call a friend who does.

As she goes inside her hut to find her mobile, Shirin catches the eye of the girl's mother, sitting cross-legged on the floor just inside the screen door, facing outside. It is a strange place to sit, and the old woman smiles perpetually, never closing her mouth. Shirin smiles back. Leila looks baffled. She swats flies from her legs and leans against a tree stump a few feet away from the grinning mother, whose mouth just opens wider. The two stare at each other wordlessly. It's exhausting for Shirin to watch them.

Finally, the woman asks in Thai, "How old is she?"

Shirin responds, also in Thai, "Twenty."

"Ohhhh," says the old woman. "She looks much younger."

"She says you look young," Shirin mutters to her daughter. "It's a compliment."

Leila thanks the old woman, in Thai, pressing her palms together in an elegant *wai*. Shirin stares at her daughter, unable to keep her eyebrows from creeping upward. *"What?"* says Leila, crossing her arms. "I read the guidebook on the plane."

The young seamstress returns, carrying a bunch of bananas. She offers them to Leila, who, though confused, accepts with both hands, bowing a little. Shirin feels a tingle of pride at her worldly daughter, but she fights it back. Because isn't the girl forcing Shirin to go door to door, to give up all the respect she's gained, just because she's hot and needs a *farang* toilet? The seamstress motions for them to follow her to the next house, where a man in traditional Thai clothes and an old American-style cap answers. After a short exchange, Shirin thinks maybe they've found a ride. The man is coming outside. Maybe he has a truck behind the house. But soon it becomes clear that his only intention is to follow and observe as the seamstress leads them to a third house.

Half an hour later, they stand sweaty and furious, in front of the eighth house, with the occupants of all seven previous houses in a whispering cluster behind them. Their errand has become an *event*. "This isn't happening," says Leila. "Fucking unreal."

"Please don't speak," says Shirin.

For the eighth time, someone asks, "You need to go to Chiang Mai tonight? Why tonight? Is everything okay?" then shakes their head and says, "Impossible!"

Maybe this won't work, thinks Shirin. Maybe Leila will have to stay another night, and then her jet lag will be fully gone and she can see that things aren't so bad here, that her house is quaint and charming, a window into a new world. Maybe they can bike far past the rice fields and she can tell Leila about the time she was chased by a water monitor, a lizard so big and fast, it outran her even though she was cycling. But then, how can she take Leila around the village again, after tonight? How can she present her, knowing that everyone will whisper? Dr. Rin's spoiled daughter. The girl who yelled at her own mother in the front yard. The daughter who needs air-conditioning to survive.

Each time they go from one house to the next, an act that feels very much like begging, the crowd behind them grows by the inhabitants of the last house. People ask her daughter's name, her age and occupation. They ask if she's had rice today. After a while, Leila seems to recognize these questions and answers on her own behalf. She loves the one about rice. They marvel at her answers.

Shirin focuses on a point on her fisherman pants. There's a tear there, on the knee. Has it been there all day? She tries to push away that sickening humiliation that worsens with each door and every knock—her frayed seams showing clearer and clearer. Someone touches her arm. She has been so exhausted that she has stopped noticing the individual people joining the expedition, which they are now calling "Dr. Rin's Mission." Sawat, the schoolteacher, is smiling beside her. "You need a ride, Dr. Rin?" she asks.

"Sawat," she whispers, because what's the use of holding back this one last favor she needs? They already know all her business. "How do I get them all to go home?"

"Why go home?" says Sawat, surprised. "They want to see what happen!"

Shirin stares dumbfounded. "I think it's a lost cause," she mutters.

Sawat's thin eyebrows gather. She doesn't seem to know the expression, so Shirin elaborates: "I think we failed at the mission."

Sawat laughs. "This *Dr. Rin's* mission . . . it is Phrao that succeed or fail."

Absurd, thinks Shirin, then chastises herself, her bitter heart, for scoffing at such a lovely sentiment. These people love her. In an hour and a half of knocking on doors, she and Leila have no ride but they are weighed down with fruits. Leila, whose fatigue seems to go in and out, is peeling lychee in a happy cluster of women her age. This too angers Shirin and she thinks maybe she's growing old and cynical. She looks back at the swelling crowd and wishes she were in her bed beside the lizards.

"I know who we ask," says Sawat suddenly. She gives a quick bow good-bye and rushes off down the road, the only direction from here.

"Let's just go home," whispers Leila in accented Farsi.

"I have to wait for Sawat," Shirin says coldly. "You can't just treat people like they're your servants, then dismiss them when you're done."

"Fine," says Leila in English, as if her Farsi has been rejected. "Just saying . . ."

Ten minutes later Sawat returns, a male figure lumbering behind her. Khunpol is strutting quickly, his head down as if he is counting his own steps. His walk conjures in Shirin's mind the memory of Boonmee in the school courtyard, his head hanging, and her anger flares. How could Sawat bring this man here? When the crowd sees the keys dangling from his hand, they whisper and cheer. A ride has been found, they say, Khunpol is a good man, a reliable man—lies for which Shirin blames Leila.

She tries to calculate how much this day has cost her and, unable to do so, she decides she is finished. Her peace is gone. When Khunpol motions to the next street, where his truck is parked, and indicates that he will do the job for 1,300 baht, Shirin accepts. She wonders who will watch Boonmee while his father is out.

They load Leila's suitcase into the back of the truck, but it has only two seats, so Shirin says good-bye at the door. She feels sick to her stomach, every now and then thinking that she should stop Leila. But the entire town has gone to so much trouble to find a ride. They have let it escalate too far to turn back. What a marvel, she thinks, the distance that can grow between a mother and daughter, two creatures who once shared a body. Did she give birth to this American stranger who needs to get far away from her for a peaceful breath? For a second she considers Khunpol's temper, the demon Sawat mentioned. But there is no reason to worry. This is a small community, and she a well-respected member of it. Leila is as safe with this man as with any of them.

She pays Khunpol, says good-bye to her daughter. There is no question of her visiting again. "Maman *joon*," says Leila in Farsi, as she settles in the front seat. "I'm sorry about that midwife crack earlier. I know how it was in Iran."

"No mention," says Shirin, reverting to Iranian pleasantries but using English words, maybe to show that she's still angry. "It was a really nice time having you here."

She almost apologizes for having lied about Chiang Mai, but she doesn't—though she plans to later. She promises herself that she will, as soon as she has found elegant enough words, about Iran and homesickness and children and her own sinful heart. There are secrets she has yet to confess, painful half-truths about Leila's father and her days in Tehran. Maybe she will, slowly, not now. The next day Leila calls to say she plans to spend the rest of her vacation in Bangkok, and this seems reasonable to Shirin.

After the truck has pulled away, Shirin passes by Khunpol's house. She peeks into the window. Boonmee is in the front garden, picking leaves off a tree, trying to blow bubbles from the sap. His rosebud mouth and sleepy eyes cheer her. And she thinks, *What a thing I thought of the poor boy who, after all, just wanted a mother's love. It was my own wickedness.* She goes to say hello and the boy bursts into unexpected laughter, his strange habit, conversing with himself. Maybe he does have a demon, and maybe that's not such a bad affliction. A demon is just another foreign thing that needs its space. When he lifts his arms toward her, a thing he would never have done at school, she wraps him up in a warm hug. Again his hand creeps toward her breast. She pulls back, searches his face for malice. She says in broken Thai, "This is how we touch mothers." She puts a hand on each of his cheeks. His small eyes widen and eagerly he mirrors the gesture, his warm palms on her face reminding her of childhood and isolation and the thin line of nature, like the skin inside a spiny fruit, that separates the sweet from the foul.

Emily Ruskovich

Owl

W̱HEN THE DOCTOR LEFT, I fed the cats their cornmeal. For Jane's sake. My wife. Two bullets taken from her body and still she remembered the hunger of our sickly, mewing clowder; still she had the strength to recite her whole tiresome routine to me. *Let it cool first*, she whispered, holding out her hand, and when I took her hand, *Let it cool first*, she said again. Well, twelve years prior, I had not let it cool first. I had thought the bastards would have the sense to wait till the cornmeal wasn't boiling. But they stuck their faces in and ate. One or two got badly splattered, and after that the white scalds on their eyeballs kept them in the dark. Twelve years ago. Those cats long dead, the offspring of their offspring prowl our land. It happened once. How many times had I seen her feed the cats since then? How many thousands of times had the cornmeal cooled? And yet, recovering from her wounds, she called out to me through all those layers of ether, wrapped up in all those layers of gauze, called out to me in an urgent whisper to *let it cool first*, as if I would not hear it, as if I could forget the blind cats pawing around in their idiot darkness, as if what she sensed at my very core, when her delirium peeled off all the rest, was a thick and hot and yellow-colored cruelty.

Well, I forgave her that. I went outside. The dust hung in the air from the retreat of the doctor's wagon. I pumped the water 'til the bucket was half full. Then I went on into the house to boil it.

I was thirty then, Jane twenty-seven, and we had lived on the land by Bonner's Ferry for twelve years. I arrived in spring of 1890, the year I married Jane, the year my father died. It had been his land before that. The undiluted offspring of his cats were all that was left of him. Skeletal, startled, brainless, they purred when they were scared. Each generation had larger heads than the one before. "Skulls," I called them, never cats.

But in spite of my daily protests against feeding the inbred beasts at all, in spite of all the work there was to do, and of this being my first moment alone in three long days, and in spite of my preoccupation with the question in my mind concerning the face of my young wife's *shooter*—I let the cornmeal cool first. And while it cooled, I went back upstairs. Julie Bennett, the minister's daughter, had nursed Jane for three days. Before she left for good that afternoon, assuring me that time was all we needed, she had washed the hair of my crippled wife in vinegar, sitting on the bed with a bowl in her lap and Jane's head tilted over the lip of it. She pulled twigs from the knots. Why so many twigs so badly tangled up? Because my wife lay on the ground after they shot her. She moved her head from side to side in the broken weeds as if to say, *This isn't so.*

Her hair, damp and dark and spread out on her pillow in the light, dried as she slept and I could smell it drying. The smell mingled in my body with the onset of something like sickness, which it took me a moment to realize was relief. Relief soon had me shaking, had me down weak-kneed on the chair beside her bed, clasping hard, in spite of my desire to let her sleep, her still and lovely hand. She woke, briefly, and was gone again.

All this while the cornmeal cooled, the cats still hungry outside.

After a moment, I recovered from my state. The shaking ceased. I calmed my mind enough to consider.

There were four of them, the boys that shot her, all boys I knew by sight and by their fathers' names, except for one. The one who held the gun—his name I knew. Peter. Three years before, when I made the journey north to Sandpoint to see to the arrangements of my only cousin's burial, I hired the boy without having met him, on the recommendation of a fellow trapper who assured me that the child, then fourteen years old, would be able to check my traps and look after the chores that Jane could not. I was gone five days. The boy, Peter, slept in the barn, where my young wife, now crippled by his gun, brought him plates of eggs and hot venison sausage at sunrise. She stood over him, in the barn, and watched him eat.

I know because she told me. She told me as soon as I arrived home, before I could even unsaddle my horse. First she asked in a hurried, distracted way about my journey, and after a vague answer that should not have satisfied her, she began to tell me about the boy in the barn eating his sausage, as if there was any- thing at all unusual about this. I could not see—I still cannot— why she was compelled to narrate to me so mundane a detail of their predictable routine, and this so soon after my return, when there was a great deal else to say.

"He was like a little starved dog," she said. "He cupped his hand over the sausage as if I was going to steal it." She laughed and there was pity mixed up in that laughter, but also something else, something private and unseemly, and even as I dismissed it as female sentimentality over having played mother to a little boy for five days, even then it struck me.

And sitting in my chair, as the cornmeal cooled, it struck me again. I closed my eyes and tried to picture the boy—at fourteen when he ate the sausage, at seventeen when he shot my wife—but all I could see was the bleary darkness beneath his distinct cap of windy hair.

Shouts coming from that darkness. Scared, excited shouts.

It bothered me. Why could I not see his face, when I had seen it so clearly the night he shot my Jane? She stood at the edge of the woods and they, the four boys, waited just inside the shadows of the trees. The house, where I was, was behind her.

An accident. Well, of course.

Then there was the smell of ether in the sunny room, stirred up in the sheets from her movement. She turned onto her good side so that the light that had just been in her hair now fell on the bandage on her shoulder. Her hand twitched in mine, then left it.

"Jane," I said, because it occurred to me in this newfound calm that there was something I had not asked, what with the doctor there and the minister's daughter fumbling with the gauze and my own mind staggering around with the basic fact of so very little blood. To my surprise, the boys had stayed to help. They obeyed my every order; while I carried her up into bed, two rode into town, on my horse, to get the doctor and the sheriff. There seemed to be no fear of punishment, only the shock—and was it joy?—of having been a part of so supreme an accident.

But why was she out there in the first place in the middle of the night? What was she looking for that she wouldn't ask me first to go and see? This was the question that occurred to me in those quiet moments by her bed, and I said her name again, to ask it.

But she didn't wake. I ran my fingers over the bandage on her shoulder. I touched the tiny circle of blood that had traveled so far up through the gauze that it was not like blood any longer but like the faded pink of a wild rose.

There was another bandage on the lower part of her leg, but it was hidden by the sheet.

"Jane," I said.

But several loud knocks on the door downstairs startled me out of the chair. As I got up, my foot bumped the washbowl beneath the bed. It splashed dirty vinegar and twigs onto the floor. I went to the top of the stairs and I looked down.

There, on the porch, behind the screen door, three boys. They were knocking, all of them—on the door frame and on the side of the house. They stopped when they saw me there, except the red-haired boy, the youngest one, who was looking off to the side. His knock came quietly and then, when he realized he was the only one, not at all.

I came down the stairs and opened the screen door. I did not mind taking my time before I spoke. They understood they were to wait until I did. The red-haired boy, about twelve, had no shirt on. I could see the shirt, though, stuffed into the pocket of his trousers, as if to make a show of his good intentions, as if admitting that he had a shirt was the same as putting one on. Against his body, he held a pie covered in cloth. His neck was very white like it was recently scrubbed. By contrast, his freckle-splattered face looked filthy, as if underneath a film of orange dust.

The other two were brothers. Both had dark, curly hair. The younger one, who looked a little older than the red-haired boy, wore a straw hat and held a basket of corn bread already cut. The older brother, about sixteen, stood with his head hung back a little, so that it seemed he was looking at me not with his eyes but with his slightly open, bored-looking mouth. He held, awkwardly, a bowl of cherries, at such a precarious slant that with one small movement of his wrist, the cherries would come pouring out.

I said, looking at this older brother, "You can leave those things on the porch and thank your mothers."

But he spoke back to me. "We came to see her." I was so startled by his audacity that I did not respond.

The younger brother, in the straw hat, in a softer voice, said, "We brought her some things."

"It was an accident," said the red-haired child.

Then again, from the older brother: "Where is she?"

"No," was all I said.

One of the skulls appeared then, uncharacteristically unafraid. It rubbed against the leg of the red-haired child, who held the pie against himself. The boy looked down at the cat with what seemed, inexplicably, to be longing. As startling as it was that someone other than my wife could look at the beasts with anything other than disgust, I saw in the boy's eyes a yearning to touch it and I myself was touched by that. It was respectful the way he stood so still, knowing this was not the time to pet a cat, even such a friendly, stupid one, and that show of self-restraint softened me a little. Tired as I was, I began to feel like I owed something to these boys. Some gesture of forgiveness. So I said, as gently as I could manage, "You can bring those to the table."

They came in all at once. Suddenly there was movement everywhere and I felt dizzy. I had not slept since the accident three nights before, and I was beginning to realize, as the breeze outside caught the smell of the food, that I had not eaten in that time either. I was so overcome with my exhaustion right then that I had to put my hand on the rail to steady myself. But the boys didn't notice. They bumped into one another, looking around the entryway, at the coats hanging on their hooks and the shoes lined up below them.

"Those are hers," whispered the red-haired one, pointing at Jane's boots.

"Is she up there?" This from the oldest. The sunlight he'd stepped into revealed a single, white, glossy hair on his Adam's apple. He was standing right in front of me, looking over my shoulder, up the stairs, at the bedroom door.

By this time, I'd got a handle on myself. "No," I said. "She isn't." He looked right at me, and shifted the bowl of cherries from one hand to another. "You can put that on the table over there," I said, forcing some pleasantry into my voice for Jane's sake, in case she could hear me. She was sentimental about boys. She would want me to forgive them. Even so, it came out harsh, so I added, "Smells good," but that too was in a strange voice not like my own.

They filed into the kitchen and I followed them. The house felt cramped and oppressive with the boys inside. They had a smell to them, a mix of soap and filth. They laid their dishes on the table where the boiled cat food was cooling in the pan. A few flies had landed and gotten stuck on the grainy skin forming on top of the cornmeal. The red-haired boy was watching them. He had a bright red mark on his bare side from having held the pie so tightly against himself.

"It's good of you," I said. "You didn't have to do that, but it's good of you."

"Why can't we see her?" asked the oldest one. He was holding his head back once more, with his lips parted, waiting for my answer. He rolled a cherry pit against his teeth with his tongue.

"I said 'No.' "

I felt on the verge of losing my temper. Even the sight of that cherry pit annoyed me. He had brought those for my wife. He had brought those to make an apology. And yet he thought it fine to help himself along the way.

I was tired of looking at them, so I lifted the cloth off the top of the pie and I looked at that instead. There were slits cut into the crust and thick yellow juice had leaked up through them and was hardening on the top now, shining.

The boys were shifting, delaying their departure. I might have yelled, I felt so fed up by that point. But instead I said something that surprised me. "The one who shot her"—and the spoken admission that this was who they were felt vulgar, even to me. "The one who shot her," I went on, "we understand it was an accident. I'm not coming for him. You can pass that on."

But when I caught the glance that moved among them, I felt for the first time the presence of the boy in question, the boy who fired the gun, there in the kitchen among the rest. Of course, it wasn't so. But he seemed to emerge on their faces. Why else did they look at me like that? As if they knew what I was searching for, and wanted to harden their faces against my recognition? They each wore an expression of an almost bored obedience, their eyes glazed over, even the little one. Underneath that expression was something else, some twitch of disrespect. Any other day I would have hit the oldest on the side of his head to make an example of him. But standing there in the kitchen something came over me and I did not have the strength to raise my hand. I couldn't speak.

All I could do, looking at them, was strain my mind to picture the boy who shot her, the fourth boy, the one not there. The boy who ate the sausage in the barn. Peter.

But again, just his body and his hair, just that clothed darkness. The gun lying in the weeds beside my wife.

I realized then that the boys were waiting for my dismissal. They were standing in a half circle around the table, their mouths firmly shut. And I remembered then the way they stood in a half circle around Jane that night. At first it had been a full circle, all around her. At first all I had seen from the doorway were the backs of their bodies, bent over her, shoving each other. I knew, without seeing, that she lay at their feet, like the center of a flower or the pupil of an eye. They turned their heads when they heard me come out the door. They stepped away from her.

The rifle in the grass, fallen like an eyelash.

"Go home, then," I said, this time with anger. Their bodies jumped to life. They went past me without another word. All the awkwardness was gone. They were freed of their dishes and their careful displays of their acceptance of blame, and they moved like boys again. They jammed their fists into the screen door to keep it open for each other.

That same skull meowed as they went past and this time the red-haired boy stopped to pet her. I stood at the doorway for a long time after they left and finally heard shouting by the river. Their voices faded, then became loud again, and I could picture them crossing the water to the other side of the woods.

My hunger struck me then suddenly and sharply. I could not wait a second longer. I grabbed a fork and gouged out a bite of pie. Before I had time to swallow, I stuffed my mouth with bread, and I ate so fast I tasted nothing. Then I went outside and set the cornmeal down and I watched the skulls eat too.

It had taken a long time for the boys to admit what they'd been hunting. They had spoken of it as if it was something complicated, something they could not put into words. That first night, with the doctor and Julie Bennett bent over Jane in her bed, bickering, and Jane crying for help even as they gave it, I found myself standing by the window, looking out. There was nothing else for me to do. The window was open. A warm night. The sheriff was down in the yard with the boys. Though the cool room blocked their bodies from my view, I could hear their voices clearly.

"But what?" the sheriff kept asking them. "What did you think she was?"

In the end they answered, and though I could not see the boy who said it, I can still hear the answer spoken flatly and with a shrug. "An owl." None of the other boys protested this or tried to add anything to it, but there had been—I noticed it even then, in the midst of everything—an air of disappointment and disbelief that that was all it ever was.

The day after the boys visited, Jane again gave elaborate instructions for her cats, in greater detail than she had the day before. She told me the time of day that I should feed them; she described the placement of the pan; she said to mix in bacon grease, to make them want it more; she insisted the two scared ones had to be fed from a separate bowl, in a separate place.

"For God's sake," I said to her. Shell-shocked in our bed, she took this as my refusal. She turned away and wept.

"Jane, stop, of course I'll do it right," I said.

And so I fed the skulls. I sat and watched. It made my stomach turn, the way their demented bodies jerked, as if throwing up the food instead of eating it. It was against every one of my instincts to waste our cornmeal sustaining so perverse a race. But even so I did it. They all got fed, including the scared two. A separate bowl. A separate place. For Christ's sake, I did it.

And afterward I went up to report it all to Jane.

"The scared ones ate?" She was skeptical.

"They're bloated and asleep."

She smiled. "Skulls," she said. She held my hand awhile. Her wounds were healing; the blood from both wounds had stopped traveling through the gauze, the muted stains remained as they had been, no larger, no deeper of color. She fell asleep and so did I, hunched there in my chair. For the first time in a while, a bit of peace. Except for the fact of the fourth boy. The absence of his face took on a sort of presence in my dream, a darkness in the edges.

I woke up to Jane's fingernails digging in my hand. She moaned, and put her free hand over her eyes. It took a while for me to understand that a terrible headache had seized her.

"It's the shock," I said.

She cried with fury. There was nothing I could do. It lasted through the rest of that day and into the night. The following morning, when she still had had no relief, I decided then to do as the doctor had directed me if such a case arose, which was to go into town for medicine.

In the misery of those long hours before I decided to go, there had been moments of relief for my poor wife, sudden clearings in her pain from which she looked out at the world as if she'd been a long time gone from it. The moment before I left for town was one of them. I was standing at the top of the stairs, about to go down. From lack of sleep, I felt shaky, not myself. I felt the darkness of that fourth boy's face growing larger and larger in my mind. I stood at the top of the stairs, trying to blink it away, to get back the energy I needed to go into town for help.

Then I heard her voice. Very faint, as if from very far away. "This is a nice house," she said.

I am not a sentimental man, but in that moment I was deeply touched, so much that I could not even turn around to face her. I have thought of this many times since. Why, of all the moments in my life, is that the only one that when I think back on it now, I can still feel the ache that I felt then? As if no time has passed at all, I can still feel that rail beneath my hand. I can still feel the way that pervasive darkness, my secret question, seemed to soften at its edges then, seemed to dim at the sound of her voice. I can even still see the light that fell across my feet, which I stared down at when I might have turned to her.

"I'll be back in a few hours," I said. I hoped the tone of my voice, and the fact I could not face her, conveyed to my dear wife that her quiet admission was not lost on me, that this was, of all the moments of my life, the main one.

I knew Jane's father before I knew Jane. He was a sheep farmer in Helena. When I came to him for work, I was eighteen years old, South Dakota raised, the son of a lazy man. The one-room house of my childhood had finally fallen down, just months after my mother lost her battle with the dust.

The floors of my mother's house were made of dirt. My father had built the pitiful place on a piece of over-farmed soil. The more we beat it down with our feet, the finer the dirt became. The dust rose with every step, with every gust, with every turn in the night of our bodies in our beds. It settled in our sheets, on our clothes, in our hair, and finally in my mother's lungs, where it lingered for years before it turned into the infection that turned her, with a bit of time, into dust herself. Sometimes, I think, a little bit of lumber could have saved her. A few boards. Well. Phrases come from somewhere and "dirt-poor" came from a life like ours, one you couldn't afford to put a board over. Around the time the infection set in, my mother discovered coffee grounds.

She spread them wet across the dirt. It was the only thing that ever worked to keep the dust down, her one triumph in all those years as housewife in a house without floors, and she began to drink so much coffee, as a side effect of using it on the floor, that deep down I wonder if it wasn't her lungs that let her down but her heart. Just before I closed the lid of her coffin, which I did alone, my father having long since left, I smelled the coffee that had replaced the dust on her body and her clothes, and I thought what a shame it was to bury someone whose essence was still so much alive.

I think of that often, even still, the coffee smell of my mother's corpse. I was thinking of it then, a few months later, when I met Jane's father and saw what a good man he was, what nice floorboards he provided even me, in the dim little shed where I slept.

In the weeks that I worked shearing on his farm, I became close to him, though I saw nothing of his family. I barely knew that they were there, somewhere inside that looming house. A wife and two daughters.

Until one day a letter came. It informed me that in the time since he'd left my mother and me, with nothing in his pockets but a barely weaned kitten, my lazy, sentimental father had pulled himself together enough to own some land in the northern part of what just that year became the state of Idaho. The land, the letter said, was mine. My father had passed on.

I left a note at Jane's father's door, letting him know of my inheritance. I let him know that I planned to leave, that that night was my last in Helena.

And it was. But in the middle of the night, very late, a knock on the door woke me up. I opened it. There they all stood: the man, his wife, a girl of maybe ten, all still dressed, all with their hands on the older daughter.

"Please," the good man begged. They had been up all night discussing it. He put both his hands on Jane's shoulders, and he shook her at me, as if my eyes weren't bound to land there on their own. That was the first time I saw her. Stunned-looking, red-faced Jane. She was fifteen years old.

We stood facing each other, she and I, in a nearly empty church the following morning.

"You don't have to if you really don't want to," I said, interrupting the reverend.

"It's not your fault," she wept.

And there, at the altar, I took her chilly hands in mine. It was the first time we ever touched.

The boy whose child she carried was not from Helena. He had cut across her father's property one night and she had seen him from her window. Inexplicably, she went outside. They spoke for a few minutes, and then she helped him catch a piglet so that he could steal it. He came back the following night for another one, and on the third night what she gave him was herself. Willingly, knowingly, and with—she spat at her father the following morning—all her love. He was fifteen too. She promised to kill herself if they kept him away.

But as it happened, her boy stabbed another boy. Her boy was beaten, then arrested for murder, then taken to jail.

Even Jane's young sister pleaded with me that final night. "You have to take her now. It's the only thing to do."

Well, I guess it was. I didn't have time to give it much thought.

She was polite to me, my Jane. She thanked me in the church through her tears. But when it was time to get into the buggy her father provided us, Jane fought him like a child. She kicked and screamed so hard that her father, a man I respected, had to tie her wrists behind her back to get her in. Then he gave me a startling amount of money that he pulled clumsily out of his pockets, some of which fell from his shaking hands. He said thank you, and added, after what seemed to be a very panicked moment, "Son."

I drove in a state of shock, the money fallen at my feet. After several miles, I looked over at my new wife, slumped in her seat, her hands tied behind her, her head bobbing to the rhythm of the horse's hooves, her eyes cast out at the prairies.

I stopped the buggy. I untied her wrists. She smiled at me, weakly.

She did not speak until we reached Bonner's Ferry two very long days later. What she said then, when I told her we were nearly there, was that if it had to be anyone but the father of her child who took her away, then she was glad that it was me. Well, all right. I took her into my father's house. One room. Dirt floors. She slept there and I in the barn. I carved her a tiny swaddled baby out of wood, but she lost the real baby early on in her pregnancy, and in some unspoken way that felt more like the start of a marriage than our wedding had been. We shared a bed after that. Soon I had built a good, sturdy house, with boards across the floor. She tended to the twenty, thirty cats that inhabited the land, at first, I think, as a way of teasing me, and later as the task she took most seriously of her daily chores. Early on, when she got pneumonia, and I was scared to death of losing her, I went outside and I fed the little beasts myself. Calling to them in a tender, desperate way I cannot have meant, reaching to pet their coarse fur. I was still a boy more or less. I had not been struck so hard by anything as I was by the thought of losing her.

That was the time I didn't know to let the cornmeal cool, and of course that's all she remembers of the whole hellish thing.

What I felt for her, easily enough, was love.

Though sometimes, when I think back on it, I start to wonder if what I felt more than my own love was the presence of her patience. It wore on me a little, her feminine resolve. Her endless glances out of windows. I felt, even as I moved inside of her, that her submission to me was so deep that there was no way of ever reaching who she really was, so far down inside. I tried and tried to reach her that way, and I wonder now if the reason we never could conceive had to do with the fact I never made it far enough.

But enough time passed—years and years—that this patient woman became not only who she really was, but who she had always been. I began to think that the intensity I saw in her when we first met was nothing more than the phase of a spoiled child, a brief period of adolescent insanity that would have passed no matter what, with or without me or my father's land.

She never contacted her own father again, but every six months or so, she went into town alone to send, she said, a letter to her sister, that ten-year-old child I had seen only once. She always came back from these town trips looking refreshed and satisfied, with packages under her arms of dress material or other much-needed feminine things. But her satisfaction seemed to have little to do with the letter she sent, and more to do with a day in town. I say this because only once did she mention her sister writing back. I did not see the letter in her hand, but saw from our window that she was holding something close to her as she led the horse into the barn, and that she remained in the barn a long time, presumably to be alone with this piece of home a little while longer. I remember wondering what the child could possibly have to say to her sister, whom she had known only for that brief time in her life that all of us eventually forget. It made me sad for Jane, I remember, thinking of the way she cherished it. When she came out of the barn finally, there was no letter at all, only a certain warmth that she carried inside the house afterward. "She must have written back," I said to her, and at first she looked startled, but then she smiled. "Yes," she said, "she did."

But I don't remember Jane having any more correspondence after that. I don't remember her sending any other letters at all.

When I came back from Bonner's Ferry with the medicine, the door to the house was open. I saw it from the tree where I tied my horse. Carefully, I set the medicine down, then I loaded my gun, and I went closer. I stopped and listened.

There was a sound that rang out like something new—laughter. Jane's. When I stepped inside, there was another sound that was actually the silencing of many sounds I didn't realize I'd been hearing. A stillness in the room upstairs.

My heart racing, I went up. Our bedroom door was half open and I opened it all the way with the barrel of my gun.

The three boys. Sitting around her bed in chairs brought up from the kitchen. Jane was propped up against her pillows.

I shouted. What, I don't remember, but I pointed my rifle at the oldest boy.

But Jane cried out. *Please, please!* All three boys, terrified to silence. The red-haired boy, the brothers with their dark and reeking curls. The fear for my wife that I had felt at seeing the open door was replaced by a rage I didn't recognize in myself, one that took all of my effort to control.

"They brought me flowers," said Jane, her voice shaking, and with her good arm motioned to the skunk flowers in the vase of greenish water on the windowsill.

Skunk flowers. Well. I didn't lower my gun.

More meekly, she said, "They want me to get well."

"They should not have shot you, then," was what I said, and, turning to the boys, "You don't come into a woman's room. What the hell is wrong with you?"

"Please," whimpered Jane, in a voice I'd never heard from her. I looked at her, startled. Did she think I was going to shoot them? Is that what she thought of me?

The tears rolled down her cheeks. I was taken aback. "I asked them to tell me," she cried. "They were telling me about Peter." She looked at them. "He was the one who said I was an owl."

I admit that my conviction faltered. The prospect of learning anything at all about that boy whose face I couldn't see outweighed at that moment my anger. It had been five days since Jane was shot and still I had not been able to recall the boy at all. The darkness pounded in my head. I lowered the gun and I looked right into their faces, giving them permission to speak.

"We're sorry, sir," said the red-haired boy.

"What do you have to say about the other one?" I said.

"Just that he's sorry, sir. We're all very sorry, sir."

The oldest stood, and then his brother. And then the red-haired one.

"You like us to take these chairs down?" The older of the brothers, no longer afraid.

"Leave them," I said.

They went past me one by one, and down the stairs. I stared hard at Jane's face while we listened to their footsteps.

She stared hard back at me. When I heard the screen door bang shut against the house, I went to the window and watched the boys disappear into the woods.

"Your head is better," I said to her, as an accusation.

But she only sighed. Her body was still trembling. "It is. It's much better."

"I don't want them coming back."

"They won't." Her certainty startled me.

"What do you mean?" I asked her.

She was lying down again.

"How could they?" she said, then she turned her head away from me, and gazed for a long time out the window.

The days went on and I kept busy. In addition to setting and checking traps, and preparing the pelts for sale, there were Jane's chores for me to do too—milking, collecting eggs, washing our clothes in the river, and of course the boiling and cooling of the cornmeal. Some nights I was up so late catching up on my work that I did not want to disturb her by getting into bed; I unfolded the blankets in the barn and spread them out over the hay. I woke almost daily to the puking of a skull, somewhere down by my feet. It purred defensively when it saw me see it, though it heaved still, above its slick and grainy, undigested little pile.

Which always, by the afternoon, was gone.

Very early one morning, I watched the light open into the barn. It was the earliest light; it spread on the ground with a sort of wetness, and like wetness it seemed to soak into the leather of my boot, dampening with warmth my sock and skin, so that I felt a heaviness in that foot—the other foot in shadow—and did not know, for an instant, if I could ever lift so great a weight.

And then, anchored there by the greatness of that warmth, unable to move, I saw in that light, that melted light, a vision of my wife. The expression on her face was half-amused and half-appalled, wide-eyed but only slightly smiling. She was somewhere she shouldn't be, and I sensed in her a strange delight. What was she watching? What was she waiting for? She stood there, looking down, holding, inexplicably, a glass of milk.

Then a white plate was handed up to her, through the light,

and seemingly—though I did not sit up or move my hands—from me. She took the plate, then handed down the glass of milk, which, the closer it came to me, became a glass of light, a liquid white light that made me flinch my eyes. Then I woke fully, and out of breath. What disturbed me right away was the fact I was disturbed, that the image of my wife with a glass of milk, standing in that golden light, feeding breakfast to a child, could cause my heart such panic. I could not help but throw the blankets off myself, so filled was I with loathing for the thought of that boy, Peter, sleeping here in this hay, beneath these same blankets.

I had to get out of the barn. I had to see her.

But I still felt the heaviness in my foot. With my hand, I moved it out of the light, and it wasn't warmth it was heavy with; it was a deadness. My heel had fallen into a hole beneath the hay, and its cramped position the whole night had left it numb. When I pulled, the dead boot caught on a small board.

At first I tossed this board aside but then, seeing the deep and crudely dug hole it was meant to cover, I picked it up again. I held this board in my hand, to consider. Then I examined the hole it had hidden, about six inches deep, and wide enough to hold—what? What had he hidden there?

I got up. I went inside. I found Jane already sitting up in bed, looking out the window.

"Are you missing anything?" I demanded.

"Good morning," she said, not looking at me.

"I need to know. Not recently, but a long time ago. Did anything of yours go missing?"

She looked at me, finally, her expression blank. "What are you asking?"

It took a moment to decide to articulate the ugliness of what I had in mind. As overcome as I was that morning, I did not want to put into her mind anything she wasn't ready for, anything that could offend her femininity or her frail health.

Still, the image had grown more clearly, even in the moment

since she turned her head, and what I saw down in that hole was a bit of thin female cotton, stale and filthy, rolled around in the sickness of the night between fourteen-year-old fingers still dirty from the digging.

"Underthings," I managed, barely a whisper.

Jane gave a laugh of shock.

But then—inexplicably—before I even let her answer, I thought of something else. It made no sense, much less sense than underthings—that smell of her body, a secret worthy of the little hole and the sly board that covered it—and yet I could not get this other thing out of my mind. Before I meant to, I said it aloud, to my own bewilderment: "The baby."

I saw in her then a flash of what I had not seen since she was placed, thrashing, in my buggy, her father's money sticking to her damp and dirty feet as she kicked and screamed for her release. I saw in her face shock at my audacity at having so suddenly crossed that line into her past. "Not the real baby," I qualified quickly, so startled was I by her expression. "The wooden one I carved you. Where is it?"

At first I thought the shock on her face was born out of my insane idea that a fourteen-year-old boy would find any meaning at all in the theft and subsequent hoarding of an effigy of a never-born child. But it wasn't that—I remembered in the same instant I had not yet told her of the hole. What it was instead was shock at my having divined, for the first time since she came into my bed, her secret. Because, to my astonishment—and to her own—my wife Jane opened up her hand and I saw the little swaddled bit of blank-faced wood, which I had not seen since the day I carved it, shining from the sweat of her palm.

We did not speak of it again. None of it. Not ever. The baby in her hand was a kind of admission I could not bear, of what she still held on to. I never mentioned the hole in the barn, which I filled immediately with soil. She did not ask what I had meant about her underthings.

The only signs that the boys were ever in our lives were the wounds on her shoulder and leg, which, following that queer morning, she began to keep covered, hidden—from me. As if the sight of the wounds was embarrassing to us, vulgar, a reminder of what I had not yet found the courage to ask.

A strangeness grew between my wife and me from that morning on. Though we were not cold to one another, we hardly spoke, even after she healed and was outside again. I saw her once from the edge of the woods, as the empty traps hung over my shoulder. She was scraping cornmeal out of the pan and beckoning, with a smile that always disappeared when she sensed I had seen it, the scared skulls toward their separate bowls, lined up in the dust near the barn.

We never discussed the moment she opened up her hand and revealed to me the very object that had come into my mind. Such a coincidence unsettled me—the baby in her hand, at the very moment I should ask for it, after all those years of forgetting it was there. It unsettled me so deeply that I took to bed for a day, once Jane was well and I could allow myself, sweating out what must have been a fever but felt, truly, like something else, like some presence or knowledge I wanted to wring from myself like a rag of blood.

At any rate, what had been a drowsy, warm summer turned into a hot, dry one. The river ran low; the sun baked the hides of the cattle. Jane recovered fully, though she walked a little different, and I noticed a habit she developed whenever she was deep in thought, of resting her hand on the shoulder of the same side, the one that had been hurt. I often saw her standing that way in her garden, looking down at the dry rows, considering.

At some point, she washed the pie pan and the other dishes that held the food the boys had brought, and she set them out on the porch in case they ever returned. The dishes remained on the porch the rest of the summer. I got so used to seeing them there that I stopped seeing them at all. Soon they held no associations; they collected the same dust as everything else.

Then one evening, early in the fall, I came home from a hunt just after sunset and saw that the dishes were gone.

"Jane," I called, as I opened the door, "did they come for their dishes?" But she didn't answer. I went inside, where there was a fresh vase of flowers on the table. "Jane," I called again. The house felt very peaceful. There was a fresh smell, like cold weeds carried in on someone's hair.

I went upstairs, but our bedroom was empty, our bed made, some linens folded on the top of the dresser. On the night table, I saw one of her novels, opened facedown, beside a plate with a half-eaten piece of toast, shining with butter. The window was open.

Looking out that window briefly, I felt for an instant what my wife must have felt all these years—that someone was standing just inside those trees, standing and waiting. And at that moment, I became aware of the heavy emptiness of the room and also of a presence. How can I possibly describe it? It was almost as if someone else had left his shadow there.

I got my gun and I went outside to search the barn. Jane's horse was tied up and eating. The cats, cold grains of cornmeal stuck in their nostrils and the corners of their eyes, followed me at a distance, blinking back the grains.

I checked the garden. I checked the fields. Thinking it likely she had gone into the woods, maybe after a wounded skull, I followed our usual trail down, calling out her name.

But there was no Jane.

I will admit what came into my mind, standing down there by the river: That the boys had come back to finish what they started. To kill my wife, to shoot her down. But I knew it was not possible; I knew it had to be dismissed. I kept reminding myself of the skunk flowers. You don't bring a woman skunk flowers if you plan to shoot her down. You don't point at her shoes in the entryway and say with awe, "Those must be hers." If anything, they had seemed to love my wife; there had seemed a sort of reverence among them, almost a possessiveness for having been part of something I was not—for having seen her fall at the sound of the gun, just she and they, alone.

This knowledge carried with it its own suspicion. Not that they had shot her—but that they took her. That they put her down in some crudely dug hole in some secret, decrepit shed, to keep, and feed, and touch, and love.

Dear God, there was that feeling. That old pneumonia feeling. The one I could not face.

I stumbled down the shallow river, against the current, my own dread getting the better of me. It occurred to me they would have been waiting a long time for me to leave. They would have been waiting inside the trees just at the edge of the woods, watching and waiting, like they had been the night they shot her.

Did she hear something from her bed, through that open window, as she had before? Did she put down her book, her piece of toast, and go outside to see?

It was as if she was expecting them all along, all those years she lay waiting beside me in our bed.

I staggered through the woods, and as the woods got darker, so too did the edges of my mind, where the empty face of the fourth boy, which had abated somewhat the last few weeks, was pressing against my vision now with all its force. I could barely think. I stopped and leaned my hand against a tree, as if some secret door might open and reveal her.

"Think," I said aloud. "Dear God, please think."

The closest house belonged to a fellow trapper, Clyde Moor, a short red-haired drunk prone to cruelty and theft. On two occasions I had found several of the traps I had set on my land empty and bloody, and I knew, from the difference in our methods— Clyde Moor's and mine—that they'd been sprung and reset, the pelt and all the rest of it, stolen.

I had passed onto his land. I was careful only to walk in the water, for in my panic I had neglected to bring a lantern, and thus would not be able to detect, as I would in daylight, his traps set beneath the leaves.

He was the father of the red-haired boy, the young one, who pet the skull and held the pie tight against himself. It was a long way to his house, as no road connected our properties. They had no association with town. Only the boy brought the pelts to sell. I had seen his father only once. We had met on the line between our lands.

Soon I saw the light in the window of the trapper's house. Out of breath, I paused and looked inside, where husband, wife, son, and baby ate a late dinner of potatoes and broth. Their dirt floor was nearly black with what looked to be coffee grounds.

I knocked. And when they did not answer, I opened the door. "I'm looking for my wife," I said. Clyde Moor, drunk, jumped up from the table, ready to fight.

"She isn't here," he said.

"Ask your boy if she is," I said to him, then both of us looked at the child, who at that moment set down his spoon and widened his eyes beneath that cap of blazing hair.

"What's he got to do with it," said Clyde, coming toward me.

I stood my ground. "Ask him," I said, and to my surprise, that's what Clyde did.

"What have you got to do with this man's wife?"

The boy shook his head. "Nothing!"

"Except that you shot her," I said.

"Peter shot her!"

Then the wife, as if shaken from a daze, cried out, her voice trembling, "He gave you the pie, didn't he?"

"Please," the red-haired child began to cry. "I don't know where she is."

"Didn't you give him the pie?" screamed the mother at the child, so that the infant in her arms began to wail.

"Tell him to show me," I said to Clyde. "Tell him to show me every little hiding place."

Clyde grunted at the boy, who stood at this order. Clyde, looking dizzy and defeated, sat back down. He seemed relieved ultimately that my business was with his son, and not with him. The wife sat down too and cooed at the screaming baby.

The boy led me through three tiny rooms. He opened up the cellar door when I told him to, then I told him to pry open the door to the rotten shed and he did. I moved the hay away with my foot, and stamped the ground to check for any sign of softness, an echo. None. He opened the lids of four barrels filled with water. He tore down the boards over the window of a henhouse.

"Where the owl killed our hens," said the boy, nervously. He held the lantern up. "See, the glass is broken. That's why we were hunting it. They're not just my family's chickens. They're all of ours."

"Show me under there," I said, and motioned to a large mound covered with burlap. The boy threw the burlap off. Underneath was only branches.

"Which is Peter's house?" I asked.

"I don't know where she is," he said.

"Is Peter's the house to the north?"

"He doesn't know either," said the boy.

"Where does he live?"

The boy pointed north.

"Go inside now," I said. "It's all right."

But first I took his lantern.

A dog barked in the distance. I followed the sound. I approached the house from the back way, near a barn. I looked in through a window at a few cows and sheep. The sheep had gray, matted wool and knocked their heads against the boards of their pens, trying to turn around and look at me.

I heard boys' voices.

As I got closer, I could see their bodies through the crack in the barn door. Three boys, their backs to me. The two brothers sitting on a gate, and Peter—his posture I knew, though I could not see his face. He leaned against a post, talking to the brothers on their gate, the three of them laughing brightly, so hard that Peter's shoulders shook.

And then, as if pulling herself up from the floor, I saw rising suddenly in the window the back of a woman. Jane. She wore a dress I didn't recognize, loose over her shoulders. Her dark hair fell dully down her back.

I kicked the door open, but stumbled as I came inside, over a crate of tools. As I tried to pick myself up, I heard one boy yell to another to run. I heard them stumbling and I heard Jane scream. In a moment I was there behind her, as she was trying desperately to climb up over the gate. I grabbed her shoulders. I turned her toward me. I shook her in my hands with my relief.

A girl. Fifteen or so. She had a dirty face and her dress was falling down over her shoulder. I let go of her suddenly, shocked.

The two brothers were both standing in front of the gate now. Peter was gone.

"Where is she?" I asked them.

"Who?" said the older one with a smirk.

"Jane," I yelled at them.

I grabbed the older brother by the collar of his shirt and threw him back against the gate. But then, from behind me, came the girl's slurred voice. "I'm Jane, here I am," and when I turned to her she waved at me while her tongue flickered against her teeth. She laughed, looking at the boys for them to laugh too, which they did not. She looked back at me, her eyes shining.

"Hey," said this dirty-faced girl, and as she said this she came up very close to my face and tilted her head to see me better. Her dark hair curled around her pretty, filthy face. She smiled at me with her glassy eyes. She put her finger into her mouth, then drew it out. This did make the boys laugh, meanly and unafraid. The younger one tossed his hat at her.

"They tied me up," she said, as the hat hit her body. She held her wrists up in front of my face to show me her rope-burned skin. She giggled at my surprise, and when she moved her wrist even closer to my face, I grabbed it and moved her away roughly.

"Hey," said the girl, turning back to the two boys. "Which one of you is gonna marry me?" She went up to the older brother, and pushed him in the shoulder, then drew her hand back.

"Stop it," he spat at her.

"Come on," she said, but she was stumbling now. She put her hand on the back of a sheep to keep her balance. "Come on."

"Stop it," he said again.

"Peter," I said to the boys, "where did he go? Is he back there?" There was a corral behind the gate that the brothers seemed to be trying to block from my view.

"What did Peter do?" said the drunken girl.

"Shut up," mumbled the younger brother.

The girl looked at him in protest. "But I'm Jane." Then she started to cry, clutching my arm. Her fingernails dug through the sleeve of my coat. She leaned in close to me. I looked at her face as if for the first time. Her drunken eyes, the bruise on her cheekbone. Her foul breath. And yet there was something familiar, as if somewhere inside of her was the girl I took away.

"They tied you up?" I asked. I could only manage a whisper.

"They tied me up," she cried, "they put me here." But after one long moment in which she looked into my eyes, her mouth open, she started to giggle again. Her face became something different, belonged to someone I didn't know. I shoved her out of the way. I grabbed the older boy by his shirt and I slung him down. "Where is Peter?" I said.

He rubbed his arm. He pointed behind the gate. "He's in there."

I opened it and squinted to see. The space was deep and dark. I could hear the boy breathing, a coward crouched in the hay. I half-expected him to plunge a knife into my leg. But instead I heard him whimper.

"I'm so sorry." He sniffled. "I really am."

I reached down and grabbed his arms. I threw him out of the corral and into the light, facedown at the feet of the girl and the brothers. I turned him over with my boot.

But the face I looked upon in that moment, the awkward face of a scared young man, did not fill up the darkness of my memory the way I thought it would. I do not mean this was not the boy who shot Jane. He was. I recognized him plainly from the awful night that he and the others stepped away from her, when she lay down in the grass, moving her head back and forth in the weeds. His eyes were as wide then as they had been the other night. There was no doubt of who he was.

And yet there was no relief. There was only the pressing darkness in my head.

"Hold still," I yelled, because I needed to see. I needed to know.

But he wouldn't stop shaking his head, and there was no way to stop him except by the weight of my boot on his chest. His head stopped moving but his eyes flinched shut.

"Open your eyes."

The tears ran out of them, closed.

"Open your eyes!" But he opened his mouth instead. And so I put my rifle in. His eyes shot open then. Blue, wet. I didn't take the rifle out. His eyes shone at me and I stared back. And so I knew. I knew for certain then. I felt, as I stared at this face that meant nothing to me, the tremors of the darkness in my head, and within that darkness, Jane. Running, running into it. All those years of looking out the window—! The weight of all that patience settled on my life like dust. I understood then her willingness, at any sign of movement in those trees—especially the sound of a young boy's voice—to set down her book, turn her back on me, and run outside to meet him.

Only not him, but other boys, hunting other things.

Did she think he'd look like this, like them, after all these years had passed?

The crudely dug hole, the secret board. A letter in the dirt.

"Oh, oh, please," the girl behind me managed. I could hear her body trembling in her voice.

I took my rifle from Peter's mouth. He rolled over onto his side. Holding himself like a small boy, he wept. The other three ran out of the barn, the older brother grasping the girl's hand, and the girl crying so hard it sounded like joy.

The skulls haven't been around in years. It wasn't that I stopped with the cornmeal—I didn't. I called to them like she had done. I'm not saying that I'm proud of that, but I was lonely.

Then a few years back, one of the sheriff's hounds had pups, and he offered me one, and I took it. A bluetick hound. The mother was one of the dogs the sheriff had looking for Jane. The search had ended, but the dog had looked a long time, so long I imagine that Jane's smell is still moving through that body, carried in her dog blood and her dreams, and that each time she drank from the river she would breathe above the surface of the water first, looking for a trace of her footsteps—and his. That smell will remain in her long after it's gone from the clothes in Jane's drawers, which I never open, for fear it is already.

But the little dog I've got now has no search in him, no hunt at all. He was very good about the skulls. He never chased them. But they got spooked anyway. Maybe it was the last hint of instinct the inbred beasts had left: They didn't like his smell.

And so they wandered off, and, I suspect, were killed off quickly, by coyotes or owls or—in one case that I admit was very hard—the traps of men.

Becky Hagenston
The Upside-Down World

"TAKE OFF YOUR SHOES," says Gertrude. "So we can say we dipped our feet in."

Jim has no desire to dip his feet in. It's late August, and the rocky beach along the Promenade des Anglais is scattered with sunbathers at ten in the morning; a light breeze is whiffling the surface of the Mediterranean. He has been thinking of all the ways he and Gertrude are out of place here, in the South of France: They aren't rich, tan, or beautiful; they can't speak or understand French; they are neither honeymooners nor retirees. They are middle-aged siblings, with matching potbellies and thinning gray-brown hair, and Jim has come to rescue his sister from . . . from what, exactly? He's not entirely sure. Jeannie, his wife, was the one who'd answered the phone in the middle of the night to Gertrude babbling. When Jim got on the line, she'd said, in strangely calm tones, "Jimmy boy. I just took a seven-hundred-euro taxi ride to Monte Carlo in my nightgown. Do you think I'm losing it again?"

He rubbed his temples. "Fine," he said. "I'll get a flight to Nice."

"'Fine, I'll get a flight to *Nice*'?" his wife said, and rolled over in a huff. "As if there are direct flights to *Nice*."

Gertrude has gained at least thirty pounds since the last time he saw her, three Christmases ago. The weight has made her seem younger, less pinched, but he isn't sure how to say this in a way that sounds flattering. She's now pulling off her sneakers and socks. "Come on!" She has thrown off her canvas purse and is making her way, wincing, over the rocks, toward the water.

When they were children vacationing in Ocean City, she was always swimming out too far and needing to be hauled to shore by lifeguards. "Keep an eye on Gertrude" was pretty much the theme of their vacations. There are no lifeguards here that Jim can see, just some teenagers, topless old women, and men with their bellies hanging over their Speedos. Would she actually start swimming in her clothes? There's no telling.

Jim kicks off his loafers and pulls off his socks, and he and Gertrude slip over the rocks together, the shifting smoothness of the pebbles giving way and almost tumbling him on his behind; Gertrude grabs his hand and they have a rare moment of triumphant camaraderie, holding on to each other as the surprisingly cold water laps their shins, until Gertrude turns around and says, "Oh, shit—my purse is gone."

It's all right there in the guidebook: Do not leave your valuables unattended, and absolutely do not take valuables, passports, or more cash than you need to the beach. Right there, under Security and Health. Elodie reads this out loud to Ted in their hotel room. She knows he likes it when she mispronounces things.

"*Health* with an *H*," he says. "And it's *beach*, not *bitch*." He grabs the book from her hands. "What else is in the bag?"

She sorts through the stuff she's poured out on the bed: an ancient flip-phone, a small leather wallet (Visa, American Express, Maryland driver's license featuring a scowling, round, forty-five-year-old face, seventy-six euros), a L'Oréal lipstick (not Elodie's color, but it's new so she pockets it), a spatula-shaped plastic room key with a 2 on it but no hotel name, a half-empty packet of Kleenex, and a tube of fruit Mentos.

"I don't condone this sort of behavior," Ted says, shaking his finger at her. Elodie knows he not only condones the behavior, he enjoys it. Ted is American, and she met him last week at the Gare Routière. He looks about thirty, and she told him she's nineteen, adding two years. He sleeps on the far side of the bed, telling her he's "a churchgoing man" in an accent from an old cowboy movie, but he has quick sex with her while she pretends to be asleep.

"It is *très utile* to have a guidebook," she says, flipping through the photos. "Perhaps we will learn some things." Then she smiles at Ted to let him know she's joking, that she already knows all she needs to.

At the hotel, the German proprietress shakes her head and says, "That was very stupid, to leave your valuables on the beach."

"No kidding," says Jim. Gertrude just laughs. She refused to report the theft to the police, and now she says, "So what? What have I lost? Some cash and a guidebook and some credit cards I can just cancel. You have your phone and credit card, our passports are safe, I already paid for my room, and the plane tickets are electronic. So what's the big whoop?"

Jim feels neck sweat dripping down the back of his shirt. She's right, it could have been worse, but her caution-to-the-wind attitude is disturbing. Also he didn't bring any credit cards—just five hundred dollars which he then exchanged for a little over three hundred euros. Jeannie had insisted that he leave the credit cards at home in case he got pickpocketed, "and it would be such a hassle to get that straightened out."

"And if my money gets pickpocketed?"

"Let your sister take care of you," Jeannie said. "For once."

So much for that.

"You're going to take me to lunch now," Gertrude announces. "And we can pour our hearts out to each other and talk about old times." Then she starts laughing so hard that the proprietress rushes forward in alarm.

"She does that sometimes," Jim says by way of apology. Then he digs out a hundred euros from his wallet and says, "I'll pay for my room now, before anything else gets stolen. We won't need the Continental breakfast tomorrow."

Gertrude stops laughing long enough to punch him in the arm and say, "Yes, we will," so he peels off another ten euros.

Elodie was sixteen when her mother killed herself last winter, and in the spring she took the bus from Aix-en-Provence to Cannes, where she met a dreadlocked Australian named Davey who told her she had eyes like sharks, lips like coral. He was a scuba diver. He was fifty-one but in no way reminded Elodie of her father, who is white-haired and chain-smokes and never goes barefoot, ever. In a small hotel room on the Rue Félix Faure she told Davey about her family's apartment on the Cours Mirabeau, and her father's business dealings with shady Corsicans, and how she was supposed to go to a grande école but had disappointed everyone by flunking out of the lycée. Then, more to her shock than Davey's (who seemed to be expecting an opportunity to get her out of her clothes), she broke down sobbing; he pulled her shirt over her head and nudged her arm gently with a cold can of Kronenbourg. She stayed with him in his hotel for almost a week, but Cannes depressed her, so one night she stole two hundred euros from his wallet and took a train to Paris, where she lived for a few weeks with a Belgian in a depressing *banlieue* full of concrete towers.

In the months since then, she has been as far north as Normandy, but she knows she is a warm-blooded girl who belongs in the south, so three weeks ago she came to Nice, for the sun and the tourists. She had been staying in a dingy hotel near the train station and was at the Gare Routière to steal cash from more sunburned, khaki-pantsed Americans. Her hand was almost in Ted's fanny pack when he grabbed her wrist and said in his deep, John Wayne voice, "Now just hold on there."

"I wasn't doing anything," she said, pulling away, but he had a tight grip.

"You were robbin' me," he said. He smiled. "Come on, let me buy you a nice meal." She knew the price for the meal—besides sex—would be a story about her life. Not the real story, of course, but the one she made up, the one she had practiced, featuring more elaborate and interesting tragedies than her own.

Lunch is getting expensive (Gertrude is on her third beer), they still have to get the bus to the airport tomorrow, and what about dinner? Maybe Gertrude is planning to stuff herself full enough to last until tomorrow. They are sitting outside at a small round table crammed up against other small round tables on the Place Masséna, a pedestrian mall, but they might as well be in Miami, with all the loud Americans shouting and laughing and clinking glasses. He and Jeannie went to Miami once early in their marriage—a present from her parents—and ate shrimp cocktail and argued at the pool, then made up in the dim white hotel room. They not only made up, they also made Claudia, and thinking of his lovely nine-year-old daughter now makes him feel as if he's failed her, or is going to fail her, in ways he can't even imagine.

It occurs to him that this feeling of sharp anxiety is not unfamiliar in the least, which means he can't blame it on Gertrude. It's been lurking in his chest for years, a dull buzzing just below his skin, like the vibration from a distant chain saw. It's almost a relief to feel the wind of it on the back of his neck.

"And so, like a fool, I went off my medication," Gertrude is saying. "You know how they say that when you start to feel better, that's a sign the meds are working?"

"Sure," says Jim, even though he hasn't been on antidepressants for years and they never seemed to work for him anyway.

"Well, I thought, I'm obviously cured, so I don't need to take them at all! Brilliant, wasn't I?"

"You're on them now, right?"

"Sure," she says. Then, when he relaxes: "No, you idiot! I'm drinking heavily, I'm ranting like a lunatic—but a happy lunatic, mind you. No, I did not start taking my meds again."

"Yet," he says, the chain saw whizzing closer. "Right?"

She doesn't seem to have heard him. "I quit my job. That's a big surprise, isn't it?" The last Jim knew, she had some office job in Baltimore that sounded so dull he could never remember what exactly it entailed. "What would you be doing tonight if you were at home? Grading spelling tests? How are the little sixth-grade cretins?"

"Seventh grade," he says. "They're fine. And tonight I'll be missing an aldermen meeting." He was hoping to impress her with this, but she smirks and raises an eyebrow. The main item on the agenda is whether a law should be passed requiring cats to wear leashes, but he doesn't mention this. "And Jeannie is taking Claudia to judo. She's an orange belt."

"That's it?" says Gertrude. "I would've thought at least green by now."

He's wondering if he should remind her about California, about what happened the last time she went off her meds—or at least, the last time he had to rescue her because she went off her meds—but something has occurred to him. "You said you had a guidebook in your purse."

She nods.

"You had a *guidebook*. You *planned* to have a nervous break-down in the South of France! Because if you're going to have a nervous breakdown, that's certainly the place to do it!"

"I planned to go on vacation in the South of France," she says. "But I got to Marseille and then I just couldn't stop crying. I was staying in this nice hotel and I just had to get the hell away, but where? I went downstairs and told them to call a taxi, and then I got in, crying, in my pajamas, and said, 'Take me to Monte Carlo!' I obviously didn't think it would cost seven hundred euros. I put it on my credit card, so I'm thinking when I report it stolen, I can say it was stolen that night. Then I don't have to pay it." She smiles, showing her small, perfect teeth.

"I gave you my phone to call the credit-card company. You haven't done it yet?"

She shrugs. "Let whoever has it have a little fun. I'll just say, 'Whoops, I didn't realize it was missing, my bad.'"

Gertrude waves her hand in the air as if swatting insects. After a few uncomfortable moments of this (Jim briefly wonders if she's having some kind of fit), the waiter appears: long nose, scowling face, white apron. "Encore!" Gertrude says, holding up her half-empty glass of beer, and the waiter scowls, a little more heartily, and goes away.

Jim is picking at his lunch; they both ordered *moules frites*, which have turned out to be mussels and French fries. The black shells clatter unappetizingly in the bowl; the mussels are surprisingly shriveled and dry, even with the white-wine sauce. Everything seems parched and dried out, especially him. He takes a sip of the sparkling water he ordered by accident—he'd meant to just get water-water, but when he said, "Water?" this is what the waiter brought him: a huge green bottle of Perrier which is probably going to cost as much as Gertrude's beer. A fool and his money, he thinks, should not go to France.

The meals cost eleven euros each, the beers six, the Perrier six. Jim peels away euros and tries to ignore the panic in his chest. More clichés occur to him: *fish out of water*, is that what he and Gertrude are? Or maybe, he thinks—as Gertrude downs the last of her fourth beer and wipes her chin with the back of her hand—*out of the frying pan, into the fire*. That might apply, too.

Ted wants to go sightseeing after all. "There's a Russian Orthodox church," he says, studying the guidebook. "And a Chagall museum. And what about Old Town?"

"It's full of pickpockets," she says. "We should go there." They are sitting at a café in the Place Masséna, and even though she isn't particularly fond of tuna, Elodie has ordered the *salade niçoise* because she's in Nice and Ted is paying. She pokes at an anchovy.

"We should go because you look innocent and I look . . . what?"

She regards him, his chubby, ruddy face; his cheap cowboy boots. "You look like a fool," she says, and he grins as if she's just told him he looks like a movie star. American men like to be insulted, she has realized; it makes them want to impress you. French men would never stand for being called a fool; her father would have slapped her mother for saying such a thing.

Ted takes out the foldout map and regards it, frowning. "We'll take the bus to the Chagall museum. Whaddya say?"

It's so hot that everything—her water glass, the sky, the tourists with their shopping bags, Ted's face—looks coated with grease, thick and shimmery. "Fine," she says. *"Pourquoi pas? Allons-y,"* she adds, because he likes it when she says things he can't understand.

"Nice used to be Italy," Gertrude says. "And I used to be sane."

They are walking through Old Town, where the street signs are in both French and Italian. The buildings seem aglow with inner fires of yellow, pink, sepia, ochre—colors from an ancient palette. The air smells of sausage and spices; the cafés are crowded with people eating *moules frites* (why do the French like those so much?) and drinking white wine. Gertrude rushes ahead and Jim thinks of a toddler he saw in the Philadelphia airport, straining against her fuzzy leash while her mother cried, "Slow down, Tasha!" After a moment he sees his sister, her face buried in a bouquet of sunflowers while a frowning woman in a green apron looks on.

"Do you want to go back to Johns Hopkins?" Jim says to Gertrude, who still has her face buried in the flowers. The green-apron woman is saying something that sounds very insistent, so Jim grabs Gertrude's arm and she turns to him, her face flushed. She looks almost beautiful. "Do you want me to take you there when you get back, so you can sign yourself in? Do you want me to sign you in?" She spent six months there many years ago and came out looking as if she'd been slapped, her eyes too wide and bright, saying, "I think that did me a lot of good."

Now she regards him with an expression he can't identify, a kind of confused joy. Then she's gone, plowing into the crowded alleys, heading in between the pink and yellow buildings.

Keep an eye on Gertrude, he thinks, and jogs after her.

The huge paintings in the Musée Marc Chagall are like the fever dreams of sick children: women with flowers for bodies, flying through the air, bare breasted, under swan wings; crimson horses curled up with violet goats and golden birds; elongated men and women tilting their heads, smiling; big-eyed, long-lashed horse-people; humans and beasts in red and violet, floating through an indigo sky.

When Elodie was seven, her mother presented her with a copy of *Through the Looking-Glass, and What Alice Found There*, and Elodie smudged all the mirrors in their house with her nose and fingers, trying to push her way through to that other world. Now she is standing just as close to one of the paintings. She feels certain someone will stop her, but no one does.

Her mother was Irish and Catholic; what would she think of these angels and saints and pits of fire? She would love them. When they went to the Louvre all those years ago, her mother grabbed Elodie's hand so hard the bones had cracked. They were staring at *The Raft of the Medusa*, a wall-sized painting of roiling sea and what seemed to Elodie (once she knew the story behind the painting) pretty healthy-looking castaways starving to death on the raft. "It's so beautiful," her mother said. "Or maybe not beautiful. Moving." She didn't mention that the castaways were going to become cannibals. Years later, when Elodie learned this gruesome historical fact, she was oddly delighted.

This museum is nothing at all like the Louvre. The walls are white and sunlight seems to pour in from everywhere to cast a glow upon the huge paintings: no morbid sea-grays here, no sallow browns. There are no crowds of schoolchildren or rucksacked teenagers, either; just a few other tourists—a Japanese couple, a stout German family—moving silently through the bright, open rooms.

She finds Ted in the stained-glass auditorium, standing in the glowing indigo light with his head cast down in a way that makes it seem, at first, as if he's praying. There are three windows, decreasing in size, all dark blue with swirls and diagonals of red, green, gold. She can make out what looks like a tiny goat in the second window, a gold-headed angel in the third.

"Are these all from the Bible?" she says to Ted, who is reading about the windows in the guidebook instead of actually looking at them.

"Yep," he says without looking up. "Out there is Old Testament. In here is supposed to be the Creation of the World. So what does this mean?" He points to a brochure that's written in French. "Sense dessousse?"

"*Sens dessus dessous. Le monde renversé de Chagall,*" she reads. "The upside-down world of Chagall. Topsy-turvy."

"Huh," he says.

The Japanese couple has come in, openmouthed and reverent, and are staring at the glowing panels and murmuring to each other. Elodie is glad she doesn't know what they're saying. She can imagine it's: *Let's float away on a cloud of fire, my goat-faced man, my winged, flower-bodied woman. . . .*

Of course, they're probably just asking each other where they want to eat dinner, or if they changed enough money.

Ted has taken off his left boot and sock and is rubbing his foot.

"What are you doing?" she hisses.

"My feet ache," he says. "What?"

"Nothing," she says.

Later, in the gift shop, she manages to sneak a magnet into her pocket. As she does so she feels a strange twinge that she first identifies as fear—the shop lady just looked her way—and then realizes is actually shame.

Outside the sky has clouded and the air is cooler. At the bus stop the Japanese couple is staring into a laminated map. "Here," Elodie says, tossing the magnet in the air for Ted to catch.

There was one summer at the beach with Gertrude, when Claudia was a baby: Jeannie carrying Claudia, the diaper bag slung over her shoulder, her tank top askew, hair falling out of its clip. Jim was laden with beach towels, a shovel—though Claudia was too young for shoveling—suntan lotion, beach ball. He and Jeannie were sniping at each other, hot and tired, the sand too warm and deep, each step an effort. And Gertrude far behind them. She called, "Wait up, please." She was walking slowly, her sandals in her hand, wearing a black sundress, her hair in a bun, looking so . . . *empty* was the thought that came to Jim. *Unburdened*, though not in a good way.

He had thought, *Good, she's okay.* He'd said this later to Jeannie, when they were having lunch at a picnic table, their feet freshly rinsed in the cold water fountains lining the beach. "She seems fine, doesn't she?" he'd said. Gertrude had gone to the restroom, Jeannie was holding Claudia on her lap. Jeannie was sunburned, her freckles glowing across her cheeks.

"She's good with Claudia," Jeannie said, but then she frowned when Jim suggested leaving Claudia with Gertrude in the hotel so that they could go out dancing that night. "Never mind," he said quickly, and leaned over to kiss his wife on the mouth, his daughter on her warm forehead. He wondered if he should have ever told his wife about what had happened all those years ago in California, Gertrude living on the streets of Long Beach. How when he found her after a month of searching, she didn't remember his name.

Less than a year after the day at the beach, Gertrude was in the Johns Hopkins psych unit: She'd been almost hit by a car, wandering a dark stretch of road. She'd told the cop who stopped for her that she was running from aliens.

At least there are no aliens this time, thank God, Jim thinks, following his sister through the crowded alleys of Old Nice, clotted with gift shops: the T-shirt stands (PARIS in sparkles: Claudia would love that), the shops selling lavender soap, ceramic cicadas squawking in windows, postcards, pottery, linens. Gertrude is standing in front of an orange-and-red cicada the size of a small cat and is waving her hand over it to make it squawk.

Souvenir, he thinks: One of the few French words he knows. Jim's cell phone vibrates in his pocket: a text message from Jeannie. *Good news. leash ordnce passed. Taking C to judo tonight. Mkg slpy jos. Miss you.*

Cat leashes, sloppy joes, spelling tests to grade: A foreign jail would certainly cure him of ennui (another French word!), but he knows this won't happen, that he won't get caught. He is sharp-witted, fast, clear-headed, adrenaline a clarifying tonic, his blood on fire. *A stranger in a strange land,* he thinks, and tucks a burlap sack of lavender into his pocket.

Elodie's parents met in Nice, her mother on vacation with her parents and her father there on business; they were all staying at the Hotel Negresco and, according to Elodie's mother, kept making eyes at each other over dinner at the Chantecler restaurant. Jacques was thirty-two and Maura was nineteen, heading to nursing school in Dublin, having left a lovesick boyfriend behind in Killarney. There were secret, late-night meetings in the hotel bar, kisses under the chandelier in the salon and on benches along the Promenade. Letters and phone calls were exchanged, and four months later they were married (a civil ceremony in the *mairie* in Aix-en-Provence) and living in the apartment on the Cours Mirabeau.

On her first night with Ted, Elodie informed him that she had a brother who had drowned, a father involved in the Corsican Mafia, a mother who threw herself in front of a train. She stole this last part from a book, but Ted apparently hadn't read it. She told him she'd run away because she had witnessed a murder, but she didn't have to make up anything about that because Ted didn't ask. He didn't seem impressed by any of it, even the part about the Corsican Mafia—the part which, according to Elodie's mother, was true. Elodie supposed that was more interesting than a husband who had grown tired of you and preferred the young girls he met on business trips.

Maura had never been warm-blooded, never learned much French, and never had the courage to leave a man who didn't love her—except in that very final way. Two of Jacques's girlfriends had come to the funeral. "I'm so sorry for your loss," one of them said to Elodie in a thick Italian accent, and the look on her face made Elodie realize that her father had told the girl that Elodie had been the one to find her mother hanging. It hadn't occurred to Elodie to leave until then, but two days later she was hitchhiking on the *boulevard extérieur*.

Sometimes she still thinks: *If he wanted to find me, he would have by now.*

Sometimes she wonders what would happen if her father turned around and saw her vanishing in a crowd, slapping the empty place where his wallet used to be.

"Old Town?" Ted says now. "For the pickpocketing?"

"Let's go in the Negresco," Elodie says. "The salon is supposed to be nice."

"We'll pretend we're tourists," Ted says, and grabs her hand.

"What would we do in Nice," Jim asks Gertrude as·they walk back along the palm-lined streets, "if we were rich?"

A silver train whooshes past, nearly silent; a fountain erupts in a square. High above them stand smooth blue-white statues of men kneeling, arms at their sides. They are passing what seems to be a horseshoe, a hundred feet tall. This town is like a hallucination. Jim fingers the bag of lavender in his pocket and wonders if this is what it's like for Gertrude: a temporary madness you want to cling to, just a little longer.

"How rich?" she asks.

"Movie-star rich."

"We'd stay at the Negresco, we'd go out on a yacht. We'd probably drink champagne that costs more than your house."

"The Negresco," he says. "It sounds like a cookie."

"One of the fanciest cookies in the world," she says. "We'll be lucky if they let us in the front door."

"We can try," he says.

Elodie can't actually imagine her parents standing under the crystal dome of the salon, staring up at the chandelier—that is, until Ted informs her, reading from the guidebook, that the chandelier was commissioned for Tsar Nicholas II. "You know," he says, "the one who got shot during the Russian Revolution. So he never got his chandelier." They stand side by side, gazing up, and Elodie finds herself wondering if her teenage mother knew the chandelier was a gift for doomed royalty.

But of course she knew: Jacques would have told her; he loved a tragic story and so did she, and that was probably why she first let him kiss her, half-hoping the crystals would come crashing down around them because that would be so romantic.

A middle-aged couple, both wearing T-shirts, shorts, and flip-flops, has entered the salon and is staring at a life-size sculpture of a shiny yellow woman with her arms in the air and her one leg kicked out behind her. Maybe she's supposed to be dancing, but to Elodie she looks as if she's teetering on the edge of something, trying not to fall. The middle-aged woman pantomimes the sculpture: her arms in the air, one leg behind her, and sure enough she does teeter a little, until her husband grabs her by the arm—a little forcefully, it seems to Elodie—and says something that makes the woman burst out laughing.

"The bedspreads here are mink," Elodie says to Ted, suddenly remembering something her mother had mentioned long ago. But Ted has wandered off; he's already halfway around the circle of the salon, past the pillars and the red brocade wall hangings, the paintings of thin-lipped men in shiny waistcoats posing before their horses; their ladies wear big bonnets with pastel ribbons caught in an invisible wind. He pauses near the man and woman—who are now also staring up at the chandelier—then catches Elodie's eye and makes a face. She has no idea what this is supposed to mean.

The middle-aged woman says, "Damn, that's impressive. If I was rich, I'd definitely get one of those."

The man has wandered back toward the yellow statue. "Claudia would like this," he says. "Don't you think?"

It's sweet, Elodie thinks, the way they talk about these things as if they can actually have them. And then she feels a pang of jealousy of this drab American couple, who are probably celebrating their twenty-fifth anniversary. First trip abroad, buying lots of lavender soap and postcards for everyone back home. Just as quick, the pang is gone.

Ted is standing behind her, holding her shoulders. He leans down and says, "When do you want to rob this silly couple?" The silly couple has left the salon and they're walking toward the lobby, where the uniformed bellmen give them appraising looks but don't stop them as they head toward the bar.

Elodie feels like an actress auditioning for a role in a play she has neither seen nor read. She imagines her mother saying to her father, "Buy me a drink, but make sure my parents don't find out," and this is what she tells Ted, who smiles at her with wide-eyed delight, as if she's just told him again how foolish he is.

Yes, this must be what it's like for Gertrude: like breathing underwater, then surfacing to find the air bright with electricity. Then diving again, floating. The bar is dim, with red curtains and white pillars, and in the watery light he and his sister could be any age at all. What on earth are they doing here, in this impossible place? They are sitting on pink velvet bar stools, that's what. The bartender says, in accented English, "Yes, what can I get for you?" and Jim looks at the menu and orders a thirty-nine-euro whiskey.

"Champagne," says Gertrude. Thirty euros.

The small room is nearly empty. A small blonde woman in a black dress is at the other end of the bar, feeding rice crackers to a Pomeranian. A young couple comes in, sits down in a far corner, and begins nuzzling over a guidebook. The stereo is playing "I Shot the Sheriff" very softly.

The bartender looks about eighteen. He brings them their drinks, sets a ceramic bowl of rice crackers in front of them, and then goes to take the order of the nuzzling couple. Jim catches the girl's eyes, and she smiles at him and lifts an imaginary glass.

"Are you okay?" Gertrude says, touching his hand. This is a strange question, coming from her.

He stares at his whiskey and then takes a sip. It doesn't taste any different than it does back home, where it costs twenty-five dollars a bottle. "Sure," he says. "Cheers." Still, her question seems impossibly complicated. In less than two days he will be back in Pennsylvania with the two people he loves most in the world; he will teach seventh graders the parts of speech, he will fight hard to improve the quality of life in small ways in his small town. His chest is full of fire; he takes another sip of whiskey. He considers telling Gertrude: *I think I know what it's like for you, a little. I never want to feel this way again, but what a tragedy if I can never find my way back to it!*

"Because I'm starting to get tired of all this," Gertrude is saying. "I'm starting to want to feel normal again. Thanks for the champagne, though." She downs it in one gulp.

"I wish we were staying longer," Jim says.

"No, you don't," says Gertrude.

When the bartender is busy pouring a complicated drink that seems to require four bottles and several cherries, Jim says, "Quick and quiet. We're drinking and dashing." Gertrude gives no indication that she has heard him, but she's already standing up. She links her arm in his and then they're gliding out to the lobby. *"Bonne journée,"* the red-capped concierge calls after them, and they smile at him and keep walking.

. . .

Elodie had wanted to stay for her drink, but Ted is shoving at her, saying, "Hurry, come on, let's go." The middle-aged man and his wife have risen from their bar chairs and are walking, arms linked, toward the lobby. As they glide past, Elodie is struck by their faces, how the years have padded and worn them in the same way, making them look startlingly alike. Is this what happens when you spend twenty, thirty years with the same person? And yet—the woman is staring straight ahead as if she's seeing something bright and wonderful: a girl flying with a bouquet of violet flowers, perhaps, or a red horse in the sky. The man's brow is furrowed as if he's seeing the same thing but doesn't want to be heading toward it.

"Bonne journée." The concierge swoops out from behind a marble counter to bow a little, and the middle-aged woman nods as a bellhop pulls the doors open and she and her husband step out into the late afternoon, Elodie and Ted close behind. The noise and the brightness of the Promenade des Anglais seem to swallow the couple for a moment—Ted is pulling Elodie by the elbow, like a hostage—and it occurs to Elodie that the woman isn't carrying a purse. The man must have all the money in his wallet, so that means a quick shove, a distraction. It all suddenly seems like too much trouble.

"Stop it, wait." Elodie pulls away from Ted. "Just stop."

"Come on. It's fun, isn't it?" He looks like a child, his eyes bright and vacant. He shrugs and takes off running.

And then the sirens begin, blaring through the blue sky. The noise lifts over the sound of the waves and the traffic, answering a panic Elodie hadn't been fully aware of until now. She pushes her way through the slowing pedestrians, and when she catches up to Ted, he says, "Don't go any closer."

Traffic has clotted on the boulevard, and motorcycle policemen are swarming in figure eights. The middle-aged couple has slowed down; the woman seems to be straining against her husband's grip. Then Elodie sees the tiny white Renault with its front window smashed, the glass buckling in the center. There's a woman's shoe lying in the road. A black high heel.

"Don't gawk," says Ted. "I don't think we want to see what's on the other side of that car."

"Maybe she's okay," says Elodie.

"You don't smash a car windshield like that and end up okay," he says.

A death, Elodie thinks. A death. But she is also thinking, as her heart sparks with an electric hum, that the cruise ships in the bay are oblivious, and the joggers are barely stopping, and now even the older couple—the woman with her hand covering her mouth—is moving on. The sky is the blue of a Chagall angel, the sun a yellow goat floating. Tonight, she knows, she'll steal what she finds in Ted's wallet and leave their hotel, go back to the Gare Routière and take a bus to Avignon or Arles, a place where the tourists come for the history instead of the sun. Maybe that's what she needs, too, a thoughtful stroll through the Palais des Papes; a drink at a café in the shadow of the Roman amphitheater.

Some of the beachgoers are coming up slowly from the Bay of Angels, blinking like sleepwalkers at the spectacle. The sirens are turning the sky into glass. "Let's see what they left for us," Elodie says to Ted, and they dodge traffic and head toward the water.

Lynn Freed
The Way Things Are Going

GWEN WAS THE ONE who had insisted that Ma and I move to America. Sooner or later, she'd said, it would happen again, it was only a matter of time. And I suppose she was right. But really it was all my fault; I should have known better than to let them in. I did know better. How many times had I read of people tied up, beaten, robbed, raped, or killed by men pretending to be the police? Or by the real police? What was the difference, once they were tying you up? And what stupidity had had me sliding off the door chain if not my infuriating habit of consideration for others?

So if anything were to blame, it was that—the manners we'd been saddled with right from the start. Even on the plane, with the aging pharmacist talking me through the history of the national parks of America, and me nodding—oh yes? oh really?—wishing him struck down right there by a stroke, even then I was thinking, *I'll never be free of this, never.*

And now here we were, Ma and I—she settled into Gwen's guest room, and me with the washing machine and the dryer on the glassed-in upstairs porch, her snoring thundering through the glass door between us.

I pushed my hair off the scar across my forehead, a new habit.

It still throbbed when I was tired, a sort of memento mori, or memento stupiditi more like it, because they had told me not to look at them, told me to keep my head down or they'd shoot me right there, and still I'd looked up to ask—well, what? What was there anyone could ask of such people on behalf of one's own life?

So that's when the gun had come down across my forehead, slamming my face back to the floor. They'd laughed, and one squatted over me and began fingering under my skirt, considering, no doubt, whether I'd be worth the trouble of a rape. And even so, lying on the cloakroom tiles, the blood pooling under my face, I'd whispered, *Please—please don't!*

And then suddenly the fingers were withdrawn and a hand grasped the back of my neck, banged my head hard, once, twice, on the tiles.

"Combeenayshin, beetch! Geev me the combeenayshin or I shoot you now!"

And so I did, hearing the numbers bubble out low and warped into the pool of blood—two left, eight right, six left—as if a giant bell had settled over me as I lay there in the damp echoing darkness of the cloakroom, with the smell of rubber raincoats and the faint barking of the Moffits' dogs, waiting for death to come.

And only then did I remember Ma. What had they done to her up there? I'd heard the stories, horrible, ugly, monstrous stories of what they did to old women. I could hear them up there now, smashing things, grunting, banging. One was in the dining room, kicking at the liquor cabinet, and I tried to say, *The key's in my bag*, because who knew what they'd do if they couldn't get at the liquor? I did say it, but they seemed to have broken in already, I could hear the bottles clinking. *Please,* I prayed, *please let the Moffits hear them and call the real police before they get so drunk that they rape and kill us both.*

How many of them were there? Three? Four? I couldn't tell. And when one came to stand over me and I saw his policeman's boot, felt the urine running in a warm, stinking stream through my hair and over the gash, I wondered, in the calm way of the doomed, whether he was the fingerer, and if he was whether he had AIDS. Most of them had AIDS, people said. Most of them were high on drugs as well.

And just then the phone rang, silencing everything for a moment. The answering machine clicked on and Gwen's voice came through. "Hey, Jo," she said, "it's me. You there? Gladys? Gladys, would you pick up the phone please? Hmm. Look, Jo, I'll try again in ten minutes. If you're not there, I'll phone the Moffits."

That's when they began to quarrel, hissing and spitting at each other. One threw the phone to the floor, kicked it. They even seemed to have forgotten me as they ran here, then there, dragging things, heaving things, until at last the front door opened, letting in a draft of warm night air. And a car started up. And they were gone.

So, here we were now, drinking tea out of mugs around Gwen's kitchen table.

"You girls should do what I did," Ma said brightly. "Take in the odd man of an afternoon."

Gwen snatched up the scones and held them out. "Here, Ma," she said. "Sonia made them."

"Sonia? Who's Sonia?"

Sonia rolled her eyes. She was a charmless girl, sneering and sarcastic. Gwen said they were all this way, American teenagers, because right from the start they'd been fed a diet of praise and false encouragement. And look what it produced—joylessness, confusion, discontent.

"I just followed the recipe," Sonia mumbled.

Ma twisted around to take her in. Soon she wasn't going to be able to see at all, Dr. Slatkin had warned me, nothing to be done about it. "Couldn't you find a girl who speaks English?" she said.

I saw Gwen stiffen. "Let it go," I whispered. "She's just enjoying herself."

But Gwen could never let a thing go, certainly not when it

came to Sonia. She might have theories about American teenagers, send the girl to her father's when she'd had enough of her rudeness, because really she was just like him, she said, vicious, unprincipled, aggressive—she might long for the day when the girl would be out of her hair and away at college—but when it came to Ma, all she wanted was to have Sonia properly loved.

"That's Sonia, Ma!" she said, starting the whole rigmarole again. "And we don't have a 'girl' here, only a cleaning woman, who, as a matter of fact, doesn't speak a word of English. This 'girl' is your granddaughter. And she certainly speaks English! American English! Because she's an American!"

Ma shrugged. "Well, whoever she is, there's no reason even an American can't make use of her afternoons. Mark my words, my dear, it would go a long way toward helping with the petty cash."

Sonia launched herself from her chair and stamped out of the kitchen. Hers was a different world from ours, Gwen had explained, and there was nothing you could do to bring such teenagers around to the sort of compunctions under which we ourselves would have had to labor if an aunt and a grandmother suddenly descended into our lives.

"Oh, Ma!" Gwen said. "She's only fifteen, for God's sake!"

But Ma just gave her a cagey look. "Fifteen? You could always try marrying her off, you know. If she'd stand up straight and do something with that hair, some man might find it in him to take her off your hands."

Somehow, Gwen said, the whole thing must have got through to Ma, even subliminally, didn't I think so? All this business about *belles de jour* and so forth?

I shrugged. As far as anyone could tell, they'd overlooked Ma completely. Pure luck, people said, that phone call. And maybe Gladys was the one who'd tipped them off. Why else would she have come back so late from church? And then gone into such an aria of shrieks before she'd even seen me on the cloakroom floor?

Still, it was her shrieking that had alerted the Moffits, John

Moffit, who had untied me, and Aileen, who had run upstairs to find Ma. And, yes, there she was, fast asleep and snoring.

"I mean, she must have heard you talking about it," Gwen said, "not to mention giving evidence to the police and so forth."

We had always thought in different directions, Gwen and I, but I could never quite bring myself to point this out to her. So if she wanted to believe that Ma fancied herself a *belle de jour* because one of the intruders had considered raping me, or that Ma loved me best because I had never had a chance, as Gwen put it, "to threaten her primacy" with my father—if it comforted her to think life ran in those directions, fine with me.

"Perhaps I should look into some sort of therapist for her," Gwen said, "someone versed in this sort of delusion." She took out her notebook and jotted something down.

Next to my bed was a plastic folder full of her notes, all printed up, with headings and page numbers. This was how to use the washing machine, that the alarm system, and to set it every time I went out, regardless, and if I did happen to set it off by mistake, to phone this number within three minutes or the police would come and there'd be a hefty charge.

The gash on my forehead began to throb. We'd been at Gwen's for thirteen days, and even before we'd landed I'd been considering a polite way to free myself. But when I suggested a little flat of my own somewhere, even a room, she just reminded me that we were living on rands here, Ma and I, not dollars, and did I realize how far rands would go in a place like California? Surely it would be more sensible for us all just to bung in together? Share the burden? Didn't I agree?

And so, of course, I did agree. But every night I lay awake, feeling myself slide down so far into what I always became when I was with Gwen that soon there would be nothing to grasp onto to pull myself back up. And if I went on agreeing with her like this, one day I'd forget how to know what I thought or felt, and would find myself heaping scorn on the sort of people I'd always loved, people she considered "full of nonsense," because I'd have forgotten how full of nonsense I was myself, so bewitched would I be back into childhood, with Gwen wielding all the authority of ten years between us.

I switched on the bedside light. 11:57. At home it would be Sunday morning already, hadadas on the lawn and the sea silver in the morning light. That Sunday morning, as I'd driven down to the beach, hill after hill, I'd been thinking of Ma waking to the thought of another day without a future to look forward to. She'd be asking for me, I thought, and Gladys will have to remind her that it's Sunday, my day for the beach. And then, feeling forsaken, she'd start casting about, looking for someone to blame.

And that would be Gwen, never mind that she lived on the other side of the world. I'd tried to explain to Gwen that Ma was rudderless without her sight, couldn't even see herself in the mirror anymore or read without some sort of headgear that she refused to wear. If I were going blind like this, I'd say, if I'd lost my looks and the life that went with them, I'd also be full of blame.

"Life?" Gwen cried, full of blame herself. "What life? Anyway, you're blind already! Can't you see what you're doing? Won't you at least promise that you'll consider your own future?"

And so, of course, I did promise. But walking out along the pier that morning, I thought that the future was, perhaps, the whole point of a married man. Without a future, there was just this—the pier, the sea, the beach, and him sitting, as usual, among the Indian fishermen, quite unaware that his presence there might spoil their morning's fishing. He was selfish in this way, greedy for what pleased him. Standing behind him, with the sun on my skin, the sting of the salt, the bucket of dying fish, I realized quite suddenly that this had been part of it all along—his selfishness, his greed. And that even as I stood there, longing for him to turn, and for the smell of his sweat, the taste of his skin, it was as if a cloud, cool and sweet, had been passing over us all the years we had known each other, and when it passed, as it was passing already, everything would be different, exposed in a glare of light.

You're early, he said, not turning around. It was a trick of his, knowing I was there while pretending not to. He was glossy, like the fish he'd just caught, and, for once, I was glad it was Gladys's Sunday off and I couldn't go up the coast with him for the afternoon.

Gladys would be waiting for me to come home, dressed already in her severe Sunday clothes. She was a sour, taciturn woman, with a way of clicking her tongue when she was displeased that had always unsettled me. If Ma upbraided her for this or for anything else, she just stood there, sullen, silent, until she'd been given the usual warning and sent back to the kitchen.

When I began to take over the running of the house, I thought that at last I'd be able to replace her with someone more tractable. But it was too late. Ma would consider no one but Gladys to help her out of the bath, or to know how she liked her eggs, or which dress she meant when she couldn't find the words to describe it.

And so we were stuck, Gladys and I, with our mutual dislike. We both knew that the ease Ma and I enjoyed was due in large part to her. I knew too that in the long history of leisurely societies ours was young and fragile, and would not last. And if I didn't know this already, there were the Moffits to remind me. One need only consider the way things are going in the country these days, James had said that morning, handing me the blueprints for a new security wall, new gates. And before you balk at the price, he'd added, just consider Aileen—voting for all the right things all these years, and now, three afternoons a week, learning to use a gun.

John and Aileen lived in the other half of what had once been her grandfather's house. It was they who had divided the old place into two maisonettes, each with its own garden, they who had sold our half to my father a few months before he died. He'd wanted somewhere up on the ridge to lodge his pregnant mistress and her daughter. And Ma was proud of having been the mistress, proud of what he'd done for the three of us, for Gwen too, who wasn't his, and who'd never uttered a civil word to him, not even on his deathbed.

Ma had always understood by what means she'd risen to that life of orders given, orders taken, and a bell in every room to summon the servants. Every now and then she'd reminded us of this, Gwen and me, and if Gwen didn't want to hear it, well who did she think she was, Ma said. Her father was a Scottish soldier Ma had married during the war. Or thought she'd married. Only after he'd got himself killed did she find out that the real widow lived in Glasgow and had a Gwen of her own, both of them named after his sainted mother, also living in Glasgow.

Still, Gwen couldn't help herself. At the mention of my father, she would draw her lips into a tight line, which had the same effect on me as Gladys's tongue clicking. I longed to tell her that if she couldn't change her attitude she could start looking for another job.

I did tell her this, but she didn't find it funny.

I was thinking all this as I settled myself onto the couch that evening with John Moffit's blueprints. Gwen was lonely with the future she'd made for herself in America, I thought, lonelier than she'd been in the life she'd left behind her. And just as I was considering whether to tell her this when she phoned, to say that Ma, too, was lonely without her old roué and the life that went with him—just as it occurred to me that once you have been happy, it is hard not to expect to be happy always—just then the doorbell shrilled, and I walked through to the hall and peered through the jeweled glass of the front door.

A black policeman was standing there, maybe two or three more just out of the light. "Police," he said softly, respectfully. And thinking something must have gone wrong in the servants' quarters—thinking that to question him through a locked door might seem like an affront, the way things were these days—I said, *Just a minute, please*, and slid off the chain to find out what the matter was.

Brenda Peynado

The History of Happiness

This was the night I reached the end of my traveling money, and I had to move on from the Prince Edward Hostel and the sleazy backpackers who called to me, *baby, querida, nushka*. I thought of setting up tent on the East Coast beach of Singapore, the side of the island pointing toward Indonesia. I also thought of lifting a wallet or two, ignoring the fact that the previous year an American was caned for just spray-painting. I imagined the punishment for stealing would be cutting off my hands or something equally as drastic. I had been robbed before myself, when my boyfriend and I were still together, but that didn't stop me from feeling some sort of karmic retribution was in order. I was angry at the boyfriend, for leaving me while we were in India, during an existential crisis that drove him to join the Hindu monks. I was angry at myself and doing things like couch surfing with strangers, stealing wallets, and lifting bank account passwords from Internet café computers, and I dared some terrible consequence to happen.

It was October, the month that Diwali—the Indian festival of lights—and the Chinese full-moon festival happened at once, so the Indian side and the Chinese side of Singapore bargained over streamer space. That month the harvests were over and farmers down in Indonesia burned hundreds of acres of the Borneo rain forest for new land because it was cheaper than reconditioning already-tilled soil. The winds blew the smoke from the burning jungles over Singapore, and it hung like curtains between the skyscrapers and tinfoil decorations.

I followed an American couple. They were in well-cut suits, the woman a blonde with downturned eyes, the man bald and stout, and they were not affectionate with each other. They wore white hospital masks to breathe through. I guessed they were traveling on business, so their company would reimburse them if I lifted a purse or a wallet or two. It was already dusk in the mall district down Orchard Road, so it was easy for me to hide in all the streamers and decorations and parades as I followed them.

The American couple stepped around a corner, right into the Hard Rock Cafe on Orchard Road. I took a seat at the bar to wait for an opening, for my hand to slip into the woman's purse hanging from her chair. Two Indian men sat across the bar from me. A dark man dressed in women's clothing and high heels emerged through the billowing smog and introduced himself as the bartender.

I ordered a drink called Potent Love, which the bartender told me was very strong. I brushed him off. It was my last few Sing dollars, and I wanted it to count. Onstage, a Mohawked Chinese teenager was finishing the last chords of "Tangled Up in Blue." Across the bar, the two Indian men looked my way. I looked beautiful and I knew it. That night, I had dressed in green and I had done up my eyes, and I did this to cover the fact that I couldn't feel anything anymore. I tried to remember what it felt like back in high school when I'd watched *Great Expectations* and first fell in love with falling in love. I tried to remember what I felt like the first time I'd been robbed, found my emergency phone, wallet, passport gone. But no feeling swooped in to overtake me as I remembered. A sweet voice crooned "Rocket Man" with a Singapore accent—the dropped *K*s, the short Chinese vowels, the British words—crooning these normal American songs with me so far from home. The American couple sipped their drinks, fiddled with their utensils, ordered dinner. Another foreign couple held hands, laughed, looked straight into each other's eyes, and I thought, what right did they have to happiness? The Borneo smog curled down into my throat, and I felt the buzz. I felt like I had reached the end of the world. The end of my money, the end of a previous life.

The two Indian men from across the bar still stared at me. The first: taller, stronger, with a face harsh and all angles and planes, the one who continued to stare after I caught them looking. The second could barely lean over his elbows on the bar he was so short, with a tiny belly, saucer eyes, full lips. I looked away.

I had debated earlier that week with a fellow backpacker why women looked away when men looked them down. I'd said, if you stared back at men, it was like you owed them something then, for looking; they hung around you and they wouldn't let you go home. It was like looking into the abyss and the abyss stared back. And how could anyone know the difference between a good man and a bad man; when you fall into a well, does it end in a bucket of water or the abyss?

I pulled out my journal, my favorite trick for looking busy and unavailable. Dear Jake, I wrote, Hard Rock Cafe in Singapore. Smog. Two men are looking at me and I am thinking of you. I hope you're happy. You're a coward. You sound like a mystical idiot. How are the monks?

At the time, when he had said he wanted to stay in India and find himself, what I had said was, what the hell did you think this trip was for? We were both computer science majors and once we got a job we would spend the rest of our lives in a five-by-five box controlling machines and we wanted to see the real, human world. Instead, we witnessed hostel after hostel of these backpackers on their own strange quests of self, throwing around terms like *happiness* and *freedom* in these hushed, self-important voices. I'd said I didn't know who I was either. He had shrugged and looked toward the Himalayas like he was already gone.

The tall Indian, the one who was all harsh planes, tapped me on the shoulder and introduced himself. Satik.

Hi, I said, and turned back to my journal.

What are you writing there in your book?

A letter to my first love, I lied. I swiveled my stool to turn my back to him.

Satik tapped me again. Come dance, he said.

No, I don't dance, I said. I glanced back at the American couple, and I thought I might miss my chance if this Satik kept his eye on me.

You don't dance?

No, I said. The woman was finishing her food, but the man was still going.

I bet you can dance the Bhangra, Satik said.

I don't even know what that is, I said.

Hey, Anil, why don't you show her?

Satik's friend, the shorter one with the full lips, appeared behind Satik. He grinned. He said, point one finger up in the air and lift your other foot. He did this and then jumped on one leg. His belly flopped up and down. He yelled Balé, Balé, as he danced.

You've got to be joking, I said.

Satik smirked. That's the Bhangra, he said. Now you jump.

No, I said. I don't dance like that. That doesn't even look like fun.

The American man was almost done with his steak and the woman picked up her purse to go to the bathroom, and I knew my chance was over. I wanted to punch Satik and Anil.

I looked at Anil and his full lips as he ordered me another drink and signed his bill.

What the hell, I thought. I downed the drink. I moved toward the exit. I danced the Bhangra like I was stomping the ground. I jumped up and down. My hair flayed my back, and I fell out of the bar's hazy lights, all the way into the din of Orchard Road and the sudden soft darkness. I felt like a fool, and I was angry.

That's it? I said.

Oh, yes, Anil said. Much better than American dancing.

Satik shook his head. They were haloed in pools of street-lights. Most of the people walking to the bar were wearing surgical masks for the smoke, but we weren't and I could see Anil and Satik smiling, and they looked like grinning angels. We're going to the beach, they said.

That must be nice.

Come with us. They grinned like idiots, like angels, like angel sharks, and I knew then that I'd try to rob them instead.

It's Diwali, Anil said, and he raised his arms, pointed his fingers up to the sky, and jumped the Bhangra.

Come celebrate, Satik said, and I said yes, and I thought they'd be the ones to regret it.

We lay on the picnic sheet far enough back from the lapping waves that the crabs couldn't get to us. Mosquitoes pierced my bare soles. I had undone my heels in the sand, in case I had to run after I did the deed. The shores in either direction sweltered under the orange smog glow from skyscrapers, the premature dawn encircling the island like an uneasy smile. A little bit away, Chinese twentysomethings in hospital masks waved their cell phones as flashlights, barbecued barefoot, and ate mooncakes stamped with the Chinese characters for harmony and longevity. Their tents bloomed like little mushrooms in the dark. The moon, half empty, clung to the sky.

I had one hand behind my head, the other hand on the wine bottle they'd bought at the beach's convenience store. The bottle lay close to Anil's pockets. Anil talked about Hinduism and Happiness. His English was good but not that good. He worked for DHL, head of the delivery receipt department. Satik worked under him. They were speaking English for my sake.

Happiness? Satik said. He looked at me with the crook of my left elbow cradling the bottle and sneaking off to the left.

You are not happy, Satik said.

I am plenty happy, I said.

Happiness is making expecting low low and reality matches, Anil said. Lower expecting.

No one of us is Buddhist, Satik said, looking by the sneer of his lip like he was mildly angry.

Fah, I said loudly, gesticulating wildly, hand inching inside Anil's pocket. I said, It's our lack of damn love for the world, not our expectations of it, that's at fault.

It is a pride of the backpacking class to be deceitful while talking deeply. It's a pride of humankind. It's the very nature of talking deeply, and I had perfected the skill. I let the bottle roll to its side then, jumped back away from it with the wallet in my hand, and put it underneath me. Both Anil and Satik jumped away from the rolling bottle. Satik picked it up.

I hope it didn't spill, I said. I patted the blanket with my now empty hand.

No, nothing, Anil said.

Satik lay back down, this time resting his head on my feet, watching me with dark eyes. I stared him down, hoping he would become uncomfortable and move, but it was like looking into the abyss and the abyss staring back, his dark shadow blocking the hazy orange glow of the skyscrapers near the horizon. I would have to wait until Satik moved before I could inch the wallet out from under me.

Anil brought out his harmonica and butchered Indian songs in between sentences. Anil said that he had grown up in Punjab tending cucumbers, stealing the cool, spice-ridding tastes of them when it rained and the fruit got so heavy and fat that the stems gave way in his hands. While he was growing up, he had never seen the ocean. He had never learned to swim.

Satik remembered when he was seven, a family trip during a hot July day in Chandigarh, his whole family on one motorcycle, behind him his mother holding the baby in her arm, her right arm reaching over him to hold on to his father's worn white, wind-billowing shirt. He held on to his father's shirt against the black tar ground tempting him, just as dust, mosquitoes, mouth-fuls of his mother's sari, her hair, and the song he was trying to sing rushed back into his throat to force him to breathe. The dark, gunmetal allure of the furious, hurtling motorcycle. That night, his father would teach him to whirl a chicken around by its neck to kill it.

They told me all of this in their crazy English. Anil and all the brilliant things in the wavering of his lips and his breath trembling over the harmonica reeds. Believe it or not, I was having a good time. I got a little drunk off their wine. I hadn't forgotten about the wallet underneath me.

Just wait you get older, Satik said, like us. Then you will know unhappy. Trust us. He put his hand on my elbow, on the arm palming the wallet underneath me.

I moved my arm. I don't trust anyone, I said.

Interesting, Satik said. You don't trust the person you love?

Anil shifted next to me, turned to watch the waves. The sky was beginning to purple as rain clouds crawled in under the night. I don't love anyone, I said. I told them I had been to India before coming to Singapore, but not to Chandigarh or the Punjab area. I told them about that night in Rishikesh when Jake and I walked across a bridge over the Ganges, and he told me he wanted to go to the night prayers at the monastery. We were there at sunset. The monks in their orange robes, some of them looking only ten years old like orange-swaddled babies, began swinging great layered trays of fire and singing to the river their thanks. We crouched over the cold, clear water trying to send downriver our little bowls of flowers couching tiny sparklers. As the night bled into the mountain, thousands of sparklers from all the pilgrims on the river drifted like stars slipping away from us in the black. This was the last time I was to feel alive for years. It was when a white woman, probably on drugs, danced her way through the procession, her wrists and her hands blending and flapping and swimming up to the sky, this was when Jake, Jake with his face angled and orange and smoky from the trays of fire the monks swung around us, told me that he'd be staying there in Rishikesh with the monks. He wouldn't be moving on with me, he said softly, like he was entranced. He said he didn't need anything else but that stillness. He didn't need me, he implied. I rode a train to Delhi the very next morning.

Well, Anil said, you have to trust someone. For example, I scuba dive with a buddy out there. He pointed toward Malaysia.

I thought you never learned to swim? I said. While I said this, I finally managed to tuck the wallet all the way into the back waistband of my jeans underneath me.

Satik shifted, and I froze for a second, but it was just to put his hands behind his head.

Anil said, Well, I don't really know how to swim.

You mean you don't snorkel?

He said, I never saw the ocean in India. I dream of swimming. I dream, I dream, I dream. So when DHL sends me to Singapore, I take scuba diving lessons. And the test, I was supposed to be swimming, so I walked on bottom in the shallows and flapped my arms. I swim like fish.

He got up in the sand and flapped his arms around us. I laughed, thought of him as a ridiculous angel, one sent to help me keep on moving.

Anil continued to play the harmonica. I suddenly felt tired. I looked away from the deep purple sky threatening to rain. I turned my face toward the sea, arm over me to hide from the mosquitoes and from Satik's intent gaze. The skyscrapers' stacked pinpricks of neon blended into more lights across the ocean horizon, like a string of Christmas lights hovering under the moon. I thought it must be Malaysia, land, the opposite shore. I thought I might be moving on there the next day, taking the subway ride off the island to Kuala Lumpur. I thought, no twinkling lights like that could mean anything but good coming my way.

I need to use the restroom, I said, nudging Satik with my foot and sitting up. Anil began another song on his harmonica. Satik rolled over toward the bathroom and the teenagers still bobbing the lights of their cell phones and laughing. I could feel Satik's dark eyes on my back, but I knew my shirt covered the bulge behind me as I hiked through the sand.

Two girls laughed in the bathroom, a part of the group camping and barbecuing for the full-moon festival. My bare feet in the gritty pools of bathroom water. A small, neat sign said, No durian, no washing of clothes, no bathing of pets. I thought the two girls might be tourists, because they chattered only in Chinese, or that they had switched specifically from Singlish so I wouldn't understand them. I caught a look at myself in the mirror and realized what they might have been talking about. I looked crazed, a little drunk, and sleepless with bloodshot eyes. There was sand in my hair, and my braid reached large fingers of hair out to the humidity. I looked like someone to stay away from. Then I hoped there was enough money in the wallet to get me to the next place.

I went into a stall and blew my nose loudly, snot black from smog on the toilet paper. I dug through the wallet. A photograph of Anil with a woman and a toddler, staring at the camera intensely; his Singaporean ID, his Indian ID, smiling in each; a credit card, useless because he could cancel it the instant he realized it was missing; and three Sing dollars. Nothing I could use. Nothing to keep me moving forward.

I wedged the wallet in the waistband of my jeans. I smiled thinly at the two girls. I walked back between the mushroom tents and crab tracks. The rain had crusted the sand into small craters. The waves kept beat with the crunching of my steps. Satik spoke rapidly to Anil in Hindi, but they got quiet when I approached.

My wallet is not here, Anil said.

Oh? I said. Panic wrapped me in a hot blanket. I froze. Is it in the sand? I asked.

Satik lifted himself up on his hands. Through the heat that

rushed over me despite the cool rain, I didn't even think of running. I felt like my knees would give out in the sand. I had never been caught before, not even close.

Anil put his hand on Satik's arm and used it to stand up. Yes yes, Anil said. I think I have let it drop.

Because no one would be foolish enough to steal anything in Singapore, Satik said.

I let my breath out in a rush. The rain deposited cool coins of water on my face. I didn't even know exactly the consequences in Singapore. I guessed the worst. I reminded myself that I liked having two feeling, working hands. I was immediately sober. I said, We'd better start looking then.

Anil picked up the blanket and Satik grabbed the trash. We retraced our steps to the beach. I tried to dislodge the wallet from the waistband of my jeans and drop it without them noticing anything. Anil kept reaching into his pockets and pulling them back out again, like he thought any moment the wallet might reappear in them. Satik kept his eye trained on me. He didn't seem to be looking for the wallet at all. I, however, was looking very intensely at the ground. Every strand of seaweed, every piece of trash discarded, every rain crater, every grain of sand, which, Jake had said in one of his stupid mystical e-mails, can hold all the world's happiness or none of it.

When we reached the gutter to the street, I'd managed to get enough ahead of them that they couldn't see me too well through the rain. I yelled that I'd found it, bringing my left hand down to the gravel, then up to grab the wallet from my right hand, and up above my head. I shook it a little bit for good measure.

How like fortune! Anil said.

I handed the wallet to him with all the satisfaction of actually finding it. He opened it. He let out a deep sigh of disappointment. The picture must have fallen out, he said.

The picture isn't there? I said. I looked at the ground, but I didn't see anything except wet street. I bent over just to be sure, and as I curled I felt the photograph still tucked in my waistband.

It's the only photograph he brought, Satik said.

This is terrible, I said. What was the photograph of?

Anil had a wife and son. The picture was of the three of them. They're still in India, he said, in Chandigarh. It was good, that they stayed. I loved my son too much, he said. I loved him so much that every night I would talk to my son on the couch in front of the TV, I would whisper to him all things. I would give him baths, and then one night when it was dark and the lights from the TV flickered across the room, the concrete and the carpet, my son grabs my face, and I turn away so that he will not catch my eye, and there is my wife in the doorway, with her look of anguish, her loss of both of us, our exclusion of her.

He told me all of this in broken English, with the rain pounding in our eyes. It was just before dawn at this point, I could see the sky turning gray and green at the edges. The rain was pricking us like a million thorns. The twentysomethings had already zipped themselves up in their tents, although they were still awake. I could see the two girls from the bathroom playing cards through their tent window. Satik tried to smooth back his hair, but it kept streaming down his face with the rain and getting in his eyes.

We can keep looking, I said.

Anil said, Look, come to my apartment. It's just next to the beach. We can walk. It is morning, and the rain continues. We will sleep.

Let's keep looking, I said.

With this rain, that picture is already ruined, Satik said.

Come sleep, Anil said.

I said, I just met you.

A guest bedroom for you. I make Satik sleep on the couch, Anil said. We've already talked so much.

Satik said, We won't hurt you. Just sleeping. I had planned on sleeping on the beach, but I had left my backpack and tent at the train station, and although I could curl on the beach between dunes, not with that rain. We had already talked for so long. I wanted to trust them. I wanted to return the photograph. Maybe I was still just the slightest bit drunk.

I said yes. I would leave the photograph somewhere in his apartment where he'd think it had slipped out before he'd even left. They grinned. We picked our way through the puddles and stumbled like those who'd been awake for too long to Anil's apartment a few blocks away. The sky sent up its colors at the edges like a curtain rising. The tiny elevator smelled like things that had been wet too long. The closeness of Anil and Satik's two bodies, the strange smog glow tingeing the hallway green where a little light came in.

The apartment was small but clean. Satik went to the hallway closet for sheets to make up the couch, like he was barely a guest. Anil got me a glass of water to take into the guest bedroom that doubled as his office. I smelled like wet beach and seaweed. While they were busy, I used the bathroom sink to wash my face and my finger with a glob of toothpaste on it to brush my teeth. I left the photograph, wet and bubbling in spots, on top of the magazine rack where Anil would surely find it.

Lying down on the bed felt like a giant sigh. I didn't even bother to get under the covers. At first I kept jumping if I heard a noise because I thought it was the doorknob turning, but then the buzzing tiredness I felt won over. Just before I fell asleep, I thought about how maybe I could love Anil, but it's one of those things; when you're moving quickly through places, you love everyone because you don't have to keep them.

I woke to the sound of ship horns, the air conditioner humming its furious song. I inhaled wet musk and docks and burning wood. Between the black bars on the window, the sun was white and dim with smog. The lights on the horizon the previous night had been so dense I had thought they must be land, buildings, something solid. But that morning, what I had thought to be the lights of Malaysia had transformed into black ships packed tightly on the horizon like frozen ants. The tiny ships, stark and black, settled into the gray Borneo haze. The place I was moving on to and the way to get there had dissolved overnight.

I sat down at the computer desk to collect myself. I thought I might cry, but instead I felt a deep hollowness inside me, and no matter how hard I sucked in breath, I felt myself filling with only the wet Borneo smoke. I hadn't cried since Rishikesh. I saw my future before me: I would set up camp on the beaches of Singapore, begging leftovers from trash cans until I could scrounge up a few wallets from the backpacks left outside the tents, and that is the way I would see the world. And then eventually I would get home when I'd had enough, and then I would get a job in IT, and every day I would manipulate data, program commands and black box methods, but I would look into this heart of the machine and it would be as incomprehensible to me as I had found the human world. I felt like Anil's wife, staring at my own exclusion, everywhere people approaching happiness, and I grasped toward it with empty hands.

The dark face of the computer in front of me reflected a blur of my image. I turned on the computer. I hoped that Jake had sent me an e-mail, one of his many saturnine messages that would end with promises of more to come. But more never did come, only the cryptic one-liners he had learned from the monks, or a one-sentence description of the Himalayas or the temple. I opened the browser, checked my e-mail. More spam from someone in Nigeria asking for Ponzi-scheme money. Nothing from my parents, who had disapproved of the trip and had sworn not to send one cent, even if it was to get me home. Nothing from Jake. His last e-mail had been accusatory, and I had yet to compose a good comeback for it. You don't want happiness, he said. You want to blame all your tragedies on the world. Everything is maya. Your suffering is illusion; your happiness is illusion.

I sat back in the chair. I could hear Anil or Satik clattering pots in the kitchen, presumably making breakfast. The clatters of pots were like the melody of the present, empty moments banging against each other to move toward the future. My eyes burned from the smog. And then I noticed it. A glaring, neon yellow Post-it note stuck to the computer screen with the word: *swimlikeafish85624*.

I snapped out of all that longing and remembered what had brought me to that tiny apartment in the first place. I remembered the credit card in his wallet had worn the logo of an Indian bank, and I guessed that someone un-savvy enough to stick a password to his screen would be similarly naive in other ways; when I visited the bank's website, his username was saved and automatically popped up. The only thing I needed to enter his bank account was his password. I typed in *swimlikeafish85624*. He had a credit card and a savings account with about five hundred thousand rupees, about ten thousand dollars. Surely, I thought, that was enough for him. Afterward I would wonder what is ever enough—enough places to visit, enough experiences, enough to understand, to be satiated, to be happy. I wired four hundred dollars to myself. It wasn't enough to get me home, but it was enough to keep moving; to Malaysia, Kuala Lumpur. By the time Anil would check his account, maybe some days from then, I would be across the bay and long gone.

When I came out of the room, Anil was frying something that looked like pancakes. Satik snored on the couch.

I should be going, I said.

You must stay, Anil said. Today is a good day. I found the photograph. Have paratha!

He flipped the pancake-looking paratha in the pan.

I promised some friends I would meet them for one of the full-moon parades, I said.

He didn't know I had no one. I backed away toward the door. The knowledge of the stolen money burned in my brain like sunsets. I felt something hard underfoot, and then I was on my back with a loud crash.

A plastic, red-white-and-blue tricycle rolled away from me into the living room. Satik startled and sat up on the couch.

It's for my son, Anil said. My wife and son are moving here soon. Just until we're sure we can pay for it.

I'm not too hungry, I said, picking myself off the floor. Thank you for the night.

Satik leaned against the doorway to the kitchen behind me, his harsh frame hunched against the wood.

Good morning, Anil said. I found the picture.

How coincidental, Satik said.

What a high vocabulary, I said.

I looked over at Anil to see if he'd understood Satik's code. Anil rounded the kitchen bar and came at me with his arms outstretched. I thought, this is it, this is when everything comes down. But it wouldn't be then. I flinched when his arms wrapped my chest and took my breath away. His small paunch of a belly jiggled with mirth. He was hugging me.

I said, Please, no need for hugs.

Anil said, What a night. First time we have made a friend. Right, Satik? Stop by again if you're still in Singapore.

I smiled through my relief and said, I will. Good luck with your family.

As I was shutting the door, I heard Satik saying his good-byes to Anil, that he had work to catch up on, boss.

The hallway grayed with veils of smog. The open window's tinsel decorations fluttered in a hollow breeze. A ship's horn bellowed and another ship howled back. Just outside the window, seagulls screamed their bodies down to the littered ground. I pressed the button to the elevator. Behind me I heard, Wait! As I entered the elevator, no matter that I punched the close door button, Satik ran and shoved his hand in the shrinking space between the doors.

He pushed into the elevator. His cheek's harsh angles framed his dark eyes. It was a dark and deep abyss.

And what did I think would happen then? That I, finally, would be punished, that he would be the bad guy, that the story of an innocent girl taken in by two men, strangers, would be played out the way those stories go? Satik's hand in the elevator gripping my braid and pulling me down to the mildewed floor. I thought I could take happiness by force, but I wanted the world to punish me for my excess. I glared at him, I dared him, I gripped the elevator walls as we plummeted into the lower stories, I thought, here we go.

He put his hand on my shoulder. I didn't even bother pushing it away. A cry caught in my throat.

Do you want a ride? Satik said.

What? I said. I drowned in the abyss in his eyes.

A lift? Satik said. I can take you to your hotel.

No, I said. I choked out a thank-you. Then we reached the ground floor and he walked outside through doors gaping open, mouths wide, and I saw that the hunger of the abyss was my own hunger.

I stayed for a long time on a bench by the sea. The seagulls plummeted like dying jets and came back up with fish. Each breath was the acrid smell of burning jungles sliding off the waves. Seagulls screamed into the surf. I burned with shame. I began my last letter to Jake while I looked out at that false other shore that had disintegrated into ships waiting in the harbor to approach. I felt like I'd dove underwater without knowing how to swim, hovering between kicks, I sucked in a breath, the cool rush of air into my lungs, the sudden but slow hiss from the intake valve in my mouth, the pressure of a million years of water like an anchor, the whole false world above, and I can't return.

Dear Jake, I began, I know about happiness.

Naira Kuzmich

The Kingsley Drive Chorus

On the corner of Kingsley and De Longpre, we lived our
lives pressed against the glass. Our husbands—carpenters,
jewelers, mechanics, and laborers—spent their days without us.
When they came home in the evenings, they were quiet and so we
were quiet, too. Our girls retreated into schoolbooks with words
beyond our knowing and our boys spilled onto the winding
streets of Los Angeles. We had done what we could, all the things
we told ourselves we could have done. We resigned ourselves to
our windows. We wiped down the glass. We waved.

The first time Carmen Oganesyan's son, Zaven, called her
from jail, she did what any of us would do: She blamed his
friends. She told us she had a feeling when he first introduced
Robert and Vardan to her, all those years ago. They were Mariam's boys. They lived in #3. Robert and Vardan were a little too
skinny in the arms, as if they hadn't lifted a single weight in their
entire lives. Their hair was spiked. Robert, fifteen at the time,
was a tall boy who tried hard not to be. He wore oversized sweaters and pants that added bulk to his thin frame and he slouched
when he walked. We all thought he'd have back troubles by the
time he was thirty, but he found himself with bigger problems
much earlier. Vardan was a quiet child, then thirteen, Zaven's

age. Vardan's quietness made us uncomfortable. You'd say hello as you passed him in the garden and he'd glance down at your heavy grocery bags and say absolutely nothing. These were not the kind of boys Carmen wanted her Zaven to befriend, but she had been glad that he was at least making an attempt to fit in; she and her husband had pulled him out of his happy life in Yerevan just months before.

When Zaven called, Carmen was in the kitchen, preparing her famous *kyoftas*. Just imagine little eggs of beef, filled with more beef. They taste great with a squeeze of lemon. New Year's Eve was approaching, and we were all busy making the same food, each of us hoping ours would taste different, better than everyone else's. But no one could make *kyoftas* like Carmen. She had beautiful hands. After dipping her long fingers into the bowl of cold water, she'd mold the ground mixture into a shell, thumbing the beef and bulgur into place. The shells were thin, but never broke, and she'd stuff them with filling before closing them, always leaving an exaggerated tip that hardened after cooking. Everyone broke off that piece first. She'd joke that to make the perfect *kyofta* you had to pretend you were washing a child's head. You had to be careful, certainly, but more than that, you had to do it with love. The egg always knows, she said.

Only eighteen, Zaven was out on bail the next day. Carmen was a proud woman, but not enough to let him stay in jail. She asked us for loans, a hundred dollars here, a hundred there. Some of us helped; most couldn't. All of us, even those without sons, sympathized. Our boys don't adapt well here. Something doesn't translate. We don't worry much about the girls because they're beautiful and smart and quick to assimilate. Like Armineh's daughter, Sona, who's at Berkeley now, a good enough reason to leave her mother alone with a finicky husband all year long. Or Sofia, Ruzan's oldest. We hear she's married and has a kid, a beachfront house in San Diego, a white husband. We don't have many success stories here that star our boys.

Carmen always said her son would be different. But we told

her that sons become not their fathers, or even their grandfathers, but something altogether terrible. And we can't help but love them because they are ours, though it is hard to do. Carmen said that this was the problem, that our love stopped being easy, and what is a boy to turn into but a monster if his mother does not see in him a god?

It was drugs. Zaven was found smoking marijuana in the bathroom stalls of the community college with Robert and Vardan. Vardan, just months shy of being legal, got away with a reprimand. Robert and Zaven were charged and then released after a few hours, due to overcrowding. Carmen met her son outside the jail. Mariam wasn't there, so Carmen hugged Robert, too.

We never went to Mariam's for coffee or *gata*. We were polite to her, but Mariam flaunted her sons' failures as proof of America's shortcomings, more proud of being right than of anything good or kind her boys had ever done for her. She hadn't wanted to move to Los Angeles. Unlike us, she had lived well in Armenia, but her husband wanted to live even better. Carmen and Mariam were never friends, but Carmen was the nicest of us: a fault, really, that goodness. Her husband tried to beat it out of her. But she was even better than that, and he knew it, so he stopped once Zaven got to be his size. We still don't know if Zaven ever protected his mother, if he ever placed his hand against his father's chest and pushed back. We hope so, but we suspect not.

After the drug incident, Carmen told Zaven to stop spending time with Mariam's sons. They're trouble, she said, and they're bringing it into her house.

"Home," Zaven corrected her. "We don't have a house."

"Don't speak to me like that," Carmen replied, raising a finger. They were on the couch, he sprawled on one end, flipping through channels on the TV, his wife-beater tucked into his tracksuit pants. Carmen sat rigidly on the other, peeling a grapefruit, dieting in preparation for the holidays.

"And lower your voice." Carmen put down her hand. "Don't let your father hear you say something stupid like that."

"He's not *home*," he said, raising his eyebrows. "See what I did there, Ma?"

"Zaven."

Zaven jumped from his seat and grabbed his mother's shoulders. Shook them—with love, Carmen would tell us pointedly—and said, "You're really something, Ma." He kissed her on the forehead and went to his room. He put on Armenian rap, which Carmen hated even more than black people's rap because she understood every single word. She heard him shut the door and was momentarily flattered by his thoughtfulness, but those lyrics only felt more dangerous now, seeping through the cracks in his door.

Carmen would say hello whenever she ran into Mariam in the basement laundry, or in the cement backyard where we all hung our linens, not trusting the cranky machines the manager installed because of a complaint to city council (he found the cheapest washer at Sears out of spite, and we kept to our bathroom sinks and tubs). Whenever Mariam's sheets were dry but still on the line, Carmen would fold them, put them in her own basket, and return them to her, knocking softly on the door. Mariam took them in with a quick nod, biting onto her cigarette so she could use both hands. Mariam was not very womanly, no. She was skinny, but not fashionably, her legs so straight that they looked like arms, and she, this strange, hungry creature, was always puffing on something. No hips on her, either, not even a hint. Who knew how she gave birth—if she did at all. We used to talk of adoption. Mariam spent all her time in malls, trying on designer dress after designer dress, pretending she could still buy them.

Carmen didn't fault this in Mariam; she, too, sometimes wished she was someone else. We believed the problem with Mariam was that she didn't just stop there, with wishing. She didn't live here with the rest of us, but rather in her head, with her sad grandeur and delusions of the past. Carmen was nice, she was polite, but she was no friend to Mariam.

Robert and Vardan were just babies when they got to our building. We remember pink, wet lips and fat cheeks, games of tag with older boys who left their mothers hurting as soon as they learned to drive. Then—suddenly, it seemed—they were seven and nine, going to elementary school at Ramona. The first few weeks Mariam walked the mile to school with them, to and from, and we all sighed, remembering ourselves. But it was not long before Mariam let the kids go by themselves. When they returned home, they returned with bags of chips, with orange fingers, or with crumbs stuck in their teeth or spotting their white uniforms.

Carmen did her best following that first arrest to break the boys up, and we were all very impressed by her efforts. She would hide Zaven's cell phone, the charger, and his wallet, and he'd be so frustrated by the time he found them that he didn't even try to go out. She feigned headaches and strange stomach pains, guilted him into staying home. And whenever Robert and Vardan knocked on her door for Zaven, Carmen made sure to get there first, to tell them he was already out, doing whatever it was that young men do. "I'm sure he meant to invite you two," she'd sometimes whisper. "I'm sure you'll run into him somewhere." But there are only so many times a woman can open the door first, anxious and eager. When Carmen explained herself to her suspicious husband, she was met with laughter, a wave of the hand, a "let the boys be boys." But her son was no longer a boy. She couldn't remember the moment he stopped being one, but Carmen knew that only a man could break his mother's heart like that, getting arrested, in a school, no less.

"Even if he is your son," we told her over coffee, "he's no longer your child."

We'd see them together, Zaven, Robert, and Vardan. Smoking in front of the 99 Cent Store on Sunset, or the nearby Water Station, at the Shell, smoking as they washed Robert's Camry every other day during summer, making use of the quarters their mothers were supposed to be using for the washer; we'd see them smoking by the main door of the apartment building, huddled in their leather jackets zipped up to their chins. Everywhere we looked, there they were, the three of them, so much dark smoke hanging like an omen above their heads.

On August 14, 1999, just hours before she saw her son on television, his head being pushed down into the back of a police car, Carmen was listening to Céline Dion and doing laundry. We all knew whenever she and her husband fought because Dion's songs would reach our ears before a word came from her own mouth. She was the prettiest of us, but where we come from, pretty faces are as useless as our husbands' vows of loyalty.

Carmen's hair fell across her chest as she bent down to pick up her son's wet T-shirt from the basket and draped it over the line. Her hair was long and thick, a cascade of dark waves past her waist, thinning out at the edges over her hips. Her husband had married her for her hair, she once said: "I kept it in two long braids as a girl and when he first saw me, he just knew he wanted to pull apart those braids, comb them through with his own fingers." It was hard to imagine Ruben having such a romantic notion. He was a factory man, tall, with wide, strong shoulders and a thick neck, built to be a laborer. When he came home from work, he still glowed from the heat he faced all day, forging metal into iron. His skin was freckled as if burned by years walking against the wind. Carmen's description. She really loved him, poor girl, but when has love ever saved anyone?

Carmen's jeans were of a faded blue and they were loose around her stomach, the pouch of lost fat wrinkling unattractively under her top as she bent down to grab another shirt. She had been dieting again, which meant our building smelled for days entirely of cabbage. Carmen was an optimist, a master negotiator. It was an art, the way she tried to appease her husband and keep her son on the right path. She did so many things very well. She had learned, she said, to adapt.

She knew just how much salt to put into lentil soup, what shoes Ruben wore most and needed the most shining, when she could wear a skirt and when not. "It's what four years of engineering school teaches you," she told us. "There is always a solution to the problem." Carmen had graduated from the Civil Engineering Institute of Vanadzor and married Ruben three weeks later because that's what you did.

Unlike his mother, Zaven was a poor student. Disinterested, his mother would clarify, definitely not dumb. He was still going to LACC—*going*, a relative term. Carmen would add, But I know he wants to go to UCLA. He can only take night classes right now because of work. *Work*, another funny word: Our children thought that sitting in front of a computer and finding cheap auto parts on eBay and selling them to local shops was work. But work was what their fathers did, coming home with soot under their nails, sweat under their arms, and money in their pockets. We never saw any of our children's earnings. None of their earnings fed us, put new linens under our bodies, bought towels that did not leave their pink and blue threads on our damp skins. "As long as Zaven takes care of his expenses, I'm happy," Carmen claimed. We knew otherwise. We knew Carmen wondered just exactly what those expenses were. We certainly did. What does a twenty-one-year-old without a car, without rent, have to pay off?

Carmen was clipping her wash down when Mariam approached with her own basket. We watched from our living room windows as she put it down by her feet, reached into her dress pocket for a lighter. Carmen's shoulders must have tensed. Since that first arrest three years prior, Carmen had begun to reconsider some of her kindness to Mariam.

We watched as Mariam leaned against the stone wall that blocked in the building's backyard and began taking long drags of her cigarette. Carmen moved her basket slightly to the left and continued her work. She threw a white bedsheet across the line and pulled it straight. As she bent to pick up the clothespins, she could smell Mariam's cigarette. We saw the face she made from the third floor and we knew that she wouldn't be able to hold it in much longer.

"Mariam, please."

"What?" Mariam moved her cigarette away from her face and tapped it in the air. "What?"

Carmen pointed at the cigarette. "The sheets, Mariam."

"Excuse me?"

Carmen shook her head and again kicked her plastic basket to the left, a little harder this time. It scraped against the concrete and stopped by the trunk of the tired fig tree. Our only source of joy sometimes, this, peeling away the sticky skin for a taste of home.

"Do you not understand why I don't want smoke on my sheets?"

"Don't be dramatic. It's one little cigarette. I'm not doing a goddamn barbecue."

"That's the problem with you, Mariam. One cigarette is enough to stain a whole load."

"Problem with me?" Mariam put the cigarette in her mouth and began pulling the wash out of her basket, throwing it on the line, one thing on top of the other, until the line dragged, slumping in the middle with the weight.

Carmen didn't say anything as she reached to grab the towel that was hanging dangerously low. She threw it over her shoulder and continued removing the rest of her wash, a pair of jeans, a few shirts and pillowcases. We shivered thinking about the cold she was bound to get, the wet clothes sinking through the flimsy fabric of her dress and into her bones. She had been complaining about her hands recently, how sometimes she could not make a fist. We told her it was the weather but we knew it as a sign of aging. We told her to dress more warmly.

"Don't worry. God won't let your sheets get dirty. The whole world might end." Mariam laughed and spread the wash across the line, balancing the weight. She didn't look at Carmen, so we did. She seemed so small under all those clothes, her head a little fixture, dimming against the rising whiteness on her shoulders. Carmen lifted her elbow and placed her palm on top of the left pile, bending with her knees to grab the half-empty basket and put it against her hip. Walking slowly, quietly, she moved past Mariam, and Mariam turned her head to watch her neighbor disappear into the building. Then she spit out the cigarette and stomped on it. She lit another and we watched her smoke it for a while.

When she got home, Carmen decided to take a bath. She told us later that she had draped the wash over her furniture, scattering it all around, though she left the undergarments for her bedroom, as they were private business, even if it meant she had to dampen the bed. Ruben liked a clean bed, no frills, just white sheets, good quality, and a pillow for each, but apparently that day he had complained about the breakfast she had made him, that the eggs were too runny, and so she draped her clammy panties and his briefs all over the covers in punishment. She described the scene to us as a little absurd. Sexy, too, a little, she admitted, and we wondered when she had last performed her wifely duties. It made her blush as she looked at her work—we could picture this so clearly, her rosy cheeks, the color bruising her neck, too. Sometimes Carmen's passion was stronger than her sense of decency, but we knew God would forgive her for that. It wasn't often.

When she returned to the bathroom, she said the heat warmed her bones with promise. In Yerevan where they had lived, the water came on at two in the morning and the Russians shut off the gas five minutes before that. (Our friends, the Russians. How dreadful to admire someone so fiercely and have them hate you in return.) Each day, each night, they had water for exactly fifteen minutes. Some of us remember this, sitting in our darkened living rooms, waiting to hear the deep rumbling of water course through our brick walls and pulse below our feet. We'd hurry to the bathroom to pick up the pots and pitchers stacked on the floor and fill them from the faucet, filling as much as we could before it all stopped.

The day the Soviet Union fell, Ruben started planning their

way out and Carmen was grateful. America meant one thing for her: that Zaven would not have to bathe at night, in freezing temperatures, with buckets of water. That she wouldn't have to look down at Zaven sleeping on his stomach, his feet digging into the mattress, the sheets pooled under his chest, and shake him awake. If Carmen was awake now in the middle of night, it was not because she had work to do, water to collect. It was because she wanted to look at Zaven asleep, see his face soften, his eyebrows, slightly touching in the middle, unfurrowed. Carmen used to imagine taking a razor to the hairs in the soft area between his eyes, pushing down the blade against his skin quickly in his sleep, so as not to wake him, so as not to let him know that he was not perfect.

After Carmen rinsed herself and stepped out of the bathroom, she was surprised to hear sirens blaring. She wrapped the robe closely around her as she moved to the kitchen window. She craned her head over the sink, her forehead pushing against the thin screen. Police cars weren't rare on Kingsley Drive, but they weren't common in the afternoon. At night, we knew things happened, that people got hurt, did things they regretted in the morning.

Carmen couldn't see much, but when she heard the helicopter, so close that the palm trees on our street trembled and whistled in the air, she felt as if she, too, was fluttering away. She hurried to her door and locked it. She clutched at her robe, then dropped her hands to her sides, scolding herself. She walked toward the home phone, taking measured breaths. When she dialed his number, she didn't expect Zaven to pick up. Like us, she always had to try her son several times so he would know she was serious, that it was not just another motherly call, a how are you doing or where are you now? She clicked the red button and dialed again, punching in the numbers one by one instead of pressing redial. "To give him time," she explained. At the third attempt, she moved toward the window again and saw all of us making our way toward the main building gate, walking slow and talking fast. She saw us trying to get a closer look. Later when she asked us what we thought we'd see out there, why we left our apartments, why we weren't afraid, we told her the truth: because our sons had either picked up their phones or were already in jail. When you know that your children are safe—even there, even there they can be safe, safer—you grow bold. Relief makes you do foolish things.

Carmen turned away from the window. She moved the damp T-shirts from the couch and took a seat on the cold leather. She picked up the television remote, hoping for something funny. But there, on Channel 7, breaking news, her little boy, looking not very little at all, taking up the backseat of a police car, his face filling, it seemed, the whole window. He was looking straight at her with the kind of expression Carmen always tried to convince herself was learned, something he had picked up from his angry friends, something not natural to his face. Carmen took one of the wet shirts beside her, brought it to her face, and screamed.

The Armenian channel did a special broadcast a week later. We all watched. Mr. Levon Hagopyan sat behind his fancy desk, hands clasped as if in church, and talked into the camera and our living rooms. "Women," he said. "Women, you need to do something. We have had enough. Enough of these shipwrecked boys, losing their way in Los Angeles. They're in prisons, in unhappy marriages, in motel bathrooms by the 101 highway, shooting up. They're your sons. Just what are you going to do about it?" We watched him shaking his head in disgust and we nodded along. It pains us to admit this, to remember.

After the arrest, the only time we saw Carmen was in the back-yard, hanging her wash, the snap of the line as she jerked her linens off. We'd glance out of our windows from time to time and she appeared to us smaller than ever, smaller than before, much smaller still.

Mr. Levon Hagopyan told us that police had responded to an anonymous phone call. The caller noticed three men entering a house on Kentwood from the back, dressed in dark clothes and wearing sunglasses. The house belonged to an elderly Armenian couple and they were home when they weren't supposed to be. They were tied with masking tape. The Sulemanyans sat with hands behind their backs on their maroon couches, waiting, watching, as three boys who looked like they could one day marry their granddaughters ransacked their house. When they heard the sirens, the boys ran to the car. Robert drove, his brother beside him, Zaven in the back. Robert drove for three miles before he nicked a sedan with two children and a mother inside. "The police report tells us," Mr. Levon Hagopyan said, "that the sedan spun twice and then slammed into an oncoming Nissan. The youngest broke his arm and the mother now wears a scar on her forehead." On Western, the Camry scraped a parked truck, and the police cars behind the boys multiplied. The helicopter caught up. The boys thought to make a run for it, in the daytime, with the helicopter above them and the police behind. They decided to run home. They were running to us. In front of our very steps, on Kingsley Drive, the police got them. Vardan and Robert were brought down together because they were running just inches apart. Zaven met the pavement by himself. The cameraman captured the moment. As she waited for her husband to come home, Carmen watched the news, all of it. She took one of Ruben's taped movies and recorded over it, a good fifteen minutes. Always of the same scene, that second when Zaven looks behind him, twisting his neck, and the officers press their palms into his face and push him down onto the gravel. And the moment after, when Zaven looks out of the police-car window, the cameras flashing him a ghastly white.

We don't know where Mariam was when her boys got taken away, if she was hiding in her apartment, or hiding from herself, but we saw her the next day, sitting on the low stoop in front of her place. Her head was wrapped in a towel, and a tattered robe revealed her purple-veined legs. She was smoking, head tilted back, breathing in the same smoke she breathed out. There was a plate of chocolate cake next to her, a gold-plated fork stabbed into its center. But the cake appeared untouched. When she saw us notice it, she picked it up with her free hand and waved it in our faces.

"You want it? Take it."

We shook our heads.

"Take it. I'm not going to eat it. I thought I might, but I'm not hungry."

"Mariam," we said.

"Fuck you. I said take it. You want my fucking cake? Take it and don't feel bad about it. Take it home and share it."

"Mariam," we pleaded. But she blew smoke in our faces and we turned away as if slapped. When we caught her eyes once more, she was chewing wildly, her whole face contorted, cheeks puffed out and nose flaring, brown smearing her upper lip.

A month later, Carmen and Mariam had a talk. We tried not to listen in, not to open our windows just a crack, because we understood how easy it was to destroy the illusion of dignity between broken women. We did it anyway because we were hurting, too. We had rooted for Carmen, for her boy, for ourselves. Even when we stopped—we like to tell ourselves now—we didn't. Mariam had just taken out the trash when Carmen turned the corner with her basket. The women stopped short of running into each other, but the space between them was like no space at all. They stood there for a second before Carmen moved the basket from her hip to her stomach and Mariam took a step back.

"Yes, yes, that's right. You do that. You keep going, Mariam. And don't stop until you're miles away from here."

Mariam laughed and we cringed. Her laugh could be a bitter thing, as if it scraped her throat as it rose from her belly.

"Don't be silly, Carmen. It's not very becoming. What would your husband say if he saw that ugly expression on your face?"

Carmen put down her basket, bending slowly in front of Mariam, and for a moment we worried that Mariam would push her down, shove Carmen into that plastic container that seemed to be forever attached these days to her thinning shape. But it was Carmen who made us gasp as she took a wet blouse from the basket and flung it at Mariam's face. Mariam whipped her head back, but the shirt seemed to fix itself around her, wrapping its sleeves around her ears. Mariam pulled it off with the tips of her fingers, dropping it to her side like it was a dirty diaper.

"You're pathetic." Mariam said it so softly we thought we misheard, and we pushed our heads closer against our windows. Carmen pulled her arm back but she didn't strike. Mariam only tilted her head to the side and looked at her.

"Can't you see what you've done?"

Mariam looked behind herself, then turned back. She placed a hand over her chest. "Me?"

Upstairs we wanted to nod along. We wanted to point. Now the whole world knew what we knew, what we learned here. That we loved our sons not because of who they were, but because of what they were to us.

Carmen lowered her arm, both hands now rigid at her sides. She looked like a soldier. "How can you just stand there? How can you pretend none of this has happened? How can—"

"All you do is ask questions, Carmen. Questions, questions, questions. 'Why me?' Well, why the hell not?"

"Why were you never at the court for the hearings?"

Mariam put her hands over her face and groaned. But then her groan turned into strained, muffled laughter, as if she were convulsing. Carmen frowned, took a step forward.

When Mariam removed her hands, her teeth showed. "Because I know what my boys are. I don't need the court to tell me."

"And what are they, Mariam?"

"They're worthless."

The slap stunned us. The suddenness of Carmen's movement, the loudness of the flat thud. We jerked away from the windows, out of breath, and just as quickly, returned to look. Mariam very slowly righted her neck. She licked her lips and we shook our heads. From above, we mouthed a plea: Stay silent.

"They're criminals."

Carmen slapped her again, her palm hitting the same side of Mariam's face. An audible sigh escaped Mariam's mouth. We began to pound on the glass. Carmen kept her hand in the air. Neither woman looked up.

"I wish they weren't mine."

There are a few things we remember of that moment. The sound Carmen's knees made as she hit the ground, like the logs our fathers would axe in the mornings during the summer months, when they were split open and fell on opposite sides. The way Mariam looked down at Carmen, the gentle shake of the head, and the way, leaning back, she finally saw us, her hands brushing the hair from her face, eyes unblinking. How she stepped over Carmen's outstretched arms. Carmen, there on the ground, bent forward like a Turk, wailing. And when we averted our eyes, resting them on our empty couches, we had the feeling we used to get when we were young girls, our backs opening once a month, that gnawing sensation all over, like little kernels pushing against the skin, ready to puff up, ready to burst, but never gathering enough heat, enough steam, always missing the opportunity to become something beautiful.

In the following weeks, Carmen seemed to return to her former self. She smiled when we saw her outside, checking the mail; she winked when we caught her cutting the basil that grew by her stoop—our landlord forbade it, said the smell hid other smells—pocketing it swiftly in the money pouch she wore around her waist when she was gardening. She came over for coffee, for stories. We tried not to pry but Carmen appeared comfortable sharing with us the details of what she was feeling. We weren't too surprised; we were like that, too, finding comfort in the telling. It saddened us, disappointed us, but her acceptance of the situation was of great solace, too. She was not any better than us.

Of course, some things we knew we could never ask. What Ruben thought about all this. What Zaven had to say, how he was doing. Some questions are not so much questions as they are accusations. When Zaven was convicted in November, we learned about it through the *Armenian Daily*. We were careful. We couldn't help it. We had our friend Carmen back and we tried to forget about Mariam, the way she looked up at us that day, all-knowing and unapologetic. Carmen never mentioned her name.

The holidays were approaching and we went to work. We buttered our filo doughs and ground our walnuts. We chopped up our carrots, pickles, and potatoes and put them in the back of the refrigerators. We took out the beef to thaw and rinsed out the bulgur. We unearthed our fine china and the Italian-made tablecloths left over from our dowries.

When we first came to America, our children tried to force us to celebrate Christmas on the twenty-fifth, like their classmates did. But ever since we could remember, we had exchanged presents and drunken kisses and plates of *kyofta* on New Year's Eve. It was a Soviet leftover, one that we tried very hard to get our kids to understand. Celebrating a fresh beginning, where the past didn't matter, where the past was just that, past: That still had great meaning for us, especially as immigrants. So the twenty-fifth came and went, and we hurried to the department stores to do our "Christmas" shopping, taking advantage of all the sales on clothing and ornaments, shirts and shoes, and dancing Santas.

Carmen cut down the laundry line on the morning of the thirtieth. She just took a scissor close to the two poles and snapped it right off. The thin rope fell to the ground and Carmen bent down and began rolling it loosely around her wrist, like it was merely yarn for the knitting. When she was finished, she looked up at us and we waved from our windows. She smiled and waved back. It was her normal smile, wide, no teeth showing—she was always embarrassed about her teeth. But did the smile reach her eyes? We women always wash our windows on the thirty-first, so we can welcome the New Year with light unobstructed, our glass spotless and vision the most clear. On the thirtieth, we couldn't see as closely.

It was Mariam who found her. Mariam who stood up on the

stool that Carmen had used to loop a noose from the drainage pipe in our laundry room. Mariam who wrapped one arm around Carmen's waist as she cut down the rope ripping into our friend's skin. Mariam who fell under Carmen's body on the dirty concrete floor next to the washing machines. Skinny old Mariam. It was then that she cried out, when Carmen's body fell on her chest, Carmen's head gently sloping over her pounding heart, then that Mariam let out a howl so terrible, so strange, so loud, that we stopped in our kitchens, in our living rooms, and ran downstairs. When we reached the laundry room, Mariam was sitting with her legs spread open, Carmen between them, Carmen with her head falling back over Mariam's shoulder, Mariam rocking back and forth, Mariam *shh shh shh*–ing, as if it was a child in her lap, as if Carmen was still alive and only hurting.

Ruben didn't tell Zaven that his mother was dead until after the funeral. Zaven served six years; he was out early on good behavior. He married quickly, began driving a truck, bought a small one-bedroom condo a few miles from here. As for Robert and Vardan, we don't know much. Mariam tells us that they are free to live their own lives and that her main concern has always been to do the same. Now she says Los Angeles is not such a bad place to grow old in. She waters the fig tree in the backyard and plants a new batch of basil every spring. She takes cooking classes at the community college and invites us over for dessert. Before she takes the first sip of her *surj*, Mariam raises the cup in a toast. To all those we have lost, she says.

And knowing what we know now and seeing what we have seen, we can't help but nod. We bring the demitasse cups to our lips and sip soundlessly. But the taste of Mariam's coffee is always bitter. At night, when we return to our apartments, when we put our heads to the pillow, when we lie beside our husbands, we still can't help but wonder: If all it took was for them to see us dead, we too would've done it ourselves.

Emma Törzs

Word of Mouth

I HAD A JOB, FINALLY, at a new restaurant called the Whole Hog, though no one ever came because the owner didn't believe in advertising. "Word of mouth," he kept saying, but didn't seem to understand that there had to be a first mouth to speak the first word. The Hog was off Highway 200, thirty minutes out of town—twenty if you drove the speed limit, which I never did, because this was Montana and the limit was astronomical. The roads were mountain-cut and followed high above the seething river, and there were white wooden crosses planted alongside the sharpest curves, as tribute to the ones who'd zoomed beyond the sound barrier forever.

I'd been out west and unemployed for six months, ever since my grandmother had passed away and left me all her money, though in a sense she'd been supporting me for over a year; throughout my junior year of college I'd been living with her as her caretaker, paid from her social security pension. Her money in my bank account felt greasy, fingerprinted with guilt, and I was glad to begin receiving paychecks from the restaurant, paychecks that had nothing to do with her. I'd dropped out of college soon after her death ("a hiatus," hoped my mother), and I was glad, too, to feel responsible for something again, even a barbecue joint with no patrons.

As for employees, so far it was just me and the cook, so I tried my best to get friendly with him even though I didn't smoke weed anymore and that seemed to be his only passion. His name was Holt, and he was older than I was, maybe thirty, with well-set eyes but the mouth of an idiot, his clumsy lips always wet like earthworms. Afternoons we went out onto the porch to sit at one of the picnic tables and I watched him pack a bowl, tamping it down with the butt of his lighter—not how I'd done it, back in my high-school smoking days. I'd preferred it loose.

"That's what she said," said Holt.

It was four o'clock and the sun was still golden in the sky, skimming the sharp points of the mountains and playing angel with the smoke, and I could hear the river through the trees although I couldn't see it. The restaurant was set back from the highway, camouflaged by branches and its own tree-colored walls, and I said, "If we don't get some kind of sign out there, this place is doomed."

Just then a Subaru turned sharply off the road and came jouncing up the drive, dust rising in a cloud.

"Finally," I said, and stood, but Holt waved me back down. His dog was barking from where she was tied up around back, her voice high and strained from the rope around her neck.

"It's not a customer," Holt said. "It's this poor fuck keeps coming around asking about his wife."

The car stopped on the gravel lot in front of our patio and a man got out, pushed his sunglasses up to the receding line of his hair. He was sunburned and clean-shaven, with a pad of softness around his cleft chin like a cartoon dad.

"Hi," he said, and climbed the first stair. The dog was still barking.

"Hi again," Holt said over the noise. "Still no word."

"Can I give you a couple flyers to pass out to your customers?"

"No one comes in here, man," Holt said.

"Just two or three."

He didn't seem like he was going to come any further up the stairs, and Holt didn't move, so I stood and went over to him and took a flyer. Front-and-center was a photo of a woman, and she wasn't young, wasn't lovely the way I expected missing girls to be; she was what the old books would call handsome. A striking, bottom-heavy face, take-no-bullshit lines around her mouth, lots of coarsely dyed blonde hair.

"We came out from New Hampshire," said her husband, a fixed mindlessness to his tone. "I wanted to learn how to fly-fish. We were on the Blackfoot together just two nights, and when I woke a week ago, she was gone from our camper. Her shoes, too. Her favorite sweater. She must have left for a walk and got lost? I'm out of my mind thinking of her alone in these mountains."

"I'm so sorry," I said. "We'll keep our eyes out." Though I didn't want to be the one who came across her. This was bear country. This was whitewater, crumbling-bluff, stray-bullet country; there were many different ways a woman could expire, and I'd had my fill of finding people dead.

"Haven't seen you here before," the husband said, like an accusation or a come-on.

"This is my third day," I said.

"Where are you from?"

I got this question no matter where I was, though it proved more common in the great white West. My father was half black and on me this registered as something vaguely foreign, a suspicious curl to my dark hair, a permanence about my tan. He died when I was ten and I'd always wished I looked more like him. "Also from out east," I said. "New Jersey."

"I'm Brian," he said.

"Jenny," I said. "And Holt."

"Well, if you see my wife," Brian said, a hand on his heart, "she answers to Peggy."

He got back in his car and Holt said, "*Answers* to Peggy?"

"It says Patricia on the flyer," I said. "He was telling us her nickname."

"Dogs *answer to*," Holt said. "Women are just *named*. I think he killed her himself."

I'd been thinking along the same lines—spooked by his monochromatic voice, the spinning blankness of his eyes, how very on-vacation he appeared—but felt the need to offer Brian at least a token defense.

"It's true he seems a little sketchy," I said. "But people get strange when bad things are happening to them."

Case in point: my landlady. I was renting a house with a German girl named Emily, a quiet grad student in wildlife biology, and we'd signed a sublease that was supposed to take us through December while the owner was in Thailand for a year with her girlfriend. But in June she'd called to say they were coming home early because she had ovarian cancer and needed treatment. We could stay in the house, she'd promised, which was generous considering the circumstances, but meanwhile they were living two blocks away at her girlfriend's house and had taken to showing up unexpectedly. "Don't mind us," they'd chirp, letting themselves in, and my roommate and I would listen to them bicker in the kitchen.

"Is this our mug or theirs?"

"It says 89.1. Did you donate to Public Radio last year?"

"Don't remember—we may as well just take it."

When I got home from work that night, the landlady, Miranda, was sitting in our living room with Emily, eating pizza barefoot and in a too-tight wifebeater. She hadn't started chemo yet and still looked healthy and overweight, though she'd buzzed her gray head as soon as she was diagnosed and now liked to refer to herself as "GI Jane." This evening she was on the couch talking loudly about her new iPhone.

"I was always in the less-is-more camp, just wanted a nice, retro flip-phone, but sometimes you don't realize you need something until you have it; like it creates its own need. It's manipulative and horrible and now I can't live without it."

Emily was at her desk, eyes fixed on her biology textbook, chewing pizza in staccato, I'm-not-listening Morse code. When I came in she looked up at me with begging eyes.

"Hey," said Miranda, "if it isn't Miss Whole Hog herself. Any customers yet?"

I hovered in the doorway to the kitchen and tried to look exhausted beyond conversation. "Not yet," I said. "You and Amy should come out sometime."

"For the coleslaw? No thanks. Get some veggie dogs, then we'll talk."

"Well," I said, and backed away.

"Jenny," Emily said, very loudly. "Come and have some pizza."

Emily rarely raised her voice. Rarely spoke at all, except in Skype conversations with her German boyfriend late at night, so I couldn't deny her. I edged back into the living room and sat on the flowered couch beside Miranda.

"Where's Amy?" I said.

"Sulking," said Miranda. "We're in a fight." She rolled her eyes. "We'll be over it by tomorrow, you know how it goes. How was your day?"

"There's a woman who's gone missing in Potomac," I said. "Her husband stopped by with flyers. Weird guy."

"Weird how?"

"I don't know. Just . . . something about him."

Miranda reached for another piece of pizza. "So you think she ran away?"

"Oh—no. I mean, I hadn't thought of that. I was thinking he might've killed her, actually."

"Well, Montana's a good place to disappear," Miranda said. "If she's gone on purpose. Though of course you can't always tell from looking at someone."

"If they're running?" I said.

"If they're cruel to their partner," she said. "I had a boyfriend who treated me like a black-and-white starlet when we were in public—opening doors for me, kissing my hand, paying me these witty compliments—but when we were alone he liked to slap me around. You have that problem less with lesbians, I think. It's different between two women. The power thing is different."

I thought that sounded true. Though I'd never been in love with a girl, at twenty-two my defining relationships had so far all been with women: my mother, my best friend, various roommates, and most recently my grandmother, whose tissue-lidded cirrus eyes still chased me into sleep at night. The year I'd lived with her, she'd never raised a hand to me, and even if she had, she'd have been too weak to even leave a bruise . . . yet there had been no question in my mind that I was subjugated to her. Her power over me was not physical. At the level of the body, the control was mine. Each morning I waded through the swampy, florid air of her bedroom to help her rise from her pillows, holding her up by her birch-limb arms (skinny and pale with dark splotches), leading her to the bathroom in breath-measured steps. After her shower, while I guided her ankles through the holes of her terrible underwear, she said things like "This is the best job you'll ever hope to get" and "I can see the nigger in you when you kneel like that."

If she hadn't gotten sick, I'd've had no dealings with her. I thought about that often, listening to her breathe over the baby monitor by my bed, the constant static of her lungs; I wished her well, or dead.

That night, after Miranda had gone, I took the flyer into bed with me and Googled Patricia ("answers-to-Peggy") Cataluno. She worked for the Providence historical society, and was the kind of woman who made the same face in every photograph. There she was, steel-eyed in front of an old farmhouse; there she was, steel-eyed in front of an old mill. There she was, steel-eyed at a Christmas party with her husband's arm wrapped around her, the man I'd met just that morning. Brian. He was grinning, relaxed, but when I enlarged the photograph I thought I could see the indentation of his fingers on the skin of her bare shoulder, and his knuckles seemed pale, like he was gripping very hard. Maybe he'd known she'd soon slip away. There was a set to her chin that made her look difficult, cruel even, a certain telltale crease between her eyebrows, and I felt a sudden muddled lean toward sympathy for Brian—if he had killed her, I guessed it had been accidental.

"You think *I* care about fly-fishing?" Peggy might have shouted. They'd have been inside their camper, a bright enclosed bullet surrounded by darkness. "You think I give a shit about your pathetic last-ditch urge to be a man? You can't know how stupid you looked in that life vest. Like a big fat baby in a snowsuit. I can't believe I ever let you touch me! Just the thought makes me sick to my stomach."

Standing so close. His fingers fisting shut without his say-so. A blinding howl building up inside.

When my grandmother called for me over the monitor, panicked, four a.m., the night she died, that same howl kept me lying in my bed. She'd never said my name with any semblance of affection or respect, but now she was gasping for me with a desperate yearning: "Jenny! Jenny! Jenny, please!" I only wanted to listen to her need me, take a moment's power for myself, but instead I'd listened to her die. I'd doomed myself to an eternity of my own name raising goose bumps in my soul.

And Brian, too, would suffer. I couldn't pity a murderer, but I had sympathy for that pivot moment right before. Action: inaction. Sometimes the only difference was the "in": what we spun ourselves into.

The next afternoon we had a customer. A family of them—two moppy-headed sons and their athletic parents, fresh from a morning of fishing at Johnsrud. They were pure Missoula, with their strong calves and even tans and the way the mother lowered her voice and said, sickly-sweet, "Tell the lady what you want, honey. Come on, tell her."

I didn't like being called "the lady."

"A pulled-pork sandwich," said one of the boys. "Please."

"Except tell her you don't want a pickle," the mother prompted. "And tell her you can't have any bread, just the pork." She looked up at me. "He can't have bread."

"Got it," I said.

"Jesus Christ," Holt said, squinting at the ticket. "What *didn't* they order?"

"Just be glad they're here," I said.

"It's better with no customers," he said. "That way it's not even like a job."

"You know how else it's not like a job?" I said, and rubbed my thumb and fingers together.

"Gotta holla for the dolla," Holt said, resigned.

The mom and dad were tucking napkins into their kids' T-shirts, and the dad tried to tuck one into the mom's neckline, too, but she batted him away with an open hand and laughed. He pushed her aside and went for the neck again.

They were finishing their meal, all of them merrily smeared in rusty barbecue sauce, when Holt's dog started barking. She was a sharp-toothed heeler with the erratic territorialism of a cokehead landlord, so Holt always kept her on a run out back, but she'd gotten into the habit of stationing herself at the rear door and barking straight into the restaurant. Now the place filled with the sound of her, drowning out the jingle of the bells as the front door swung open.

It was Miranda. She looked sweaty and expectant, grinning when she saw me behind the counter.

"I came!" she said.

"Wow!" I said. "Welcome. Can I get you a table?"

"Nah," she said, "I'm not here to eat. Just wanted to take a look around the place." She leaned on the countertop to pluck a napkin from the holder beside the register, and swiped at her damp brow. "It's so pretty out here. Long drive without A/C, though."

Behind her, the mother of the family caught my eye and mouthed *check*.

"Just one minute," I said, and Miranda granted me time with a queenly nod. She sat at the counter on one of the high-backed wooden stools and watched me bring the check, box the leftovers, run the credit card. She was bright-eyed in the way of a feverish child, breathing with her mouth open, and I remembered that she was sick—a fact usually overshadowed by my irritation with her.

"Can you get a break?" she asked as the family traipsed out the door. "Show me around?"

I wanted to say no, wanted to say, This is my *job*, I have to *work*, but anyone could see that I did not. I glanced at Holt, hoping he'd interfere, and he must have misunderstood my big, pleading eyes, because he said, "Do I look like I give a shit? Just keep your eye on the driveway and hustle back if someone shows."

"Not such a bad gig, huh?" Miranda said, leading me down the steps. "Can we get to the river from here?"

"Through the trees," I said. "It's kind of a steep climb down, though."

"Give me a challenge while I'm still up to it," she said. "Sooner or later I won't be good for much except puking my guts out from all the chemicals they're feeding me."

I thought of my grandmother's vomit smeared across tissues in my hand, the proud way she stared me down when I wiped her face. "How's that going?" I said, trying to be delicate.

"Cancer?" Miranda said, and snorted.

We walked through the dry grass surrounding the restaurant, still flattened from the winter's snows and pressed against the ground in swirls. Around us the mountains stretched their jagged edges to the unpierceable blue sky. The sun was hot on my neck and I could feel myself start to sweat through the black Whole Hog tank top I was forced to wear, but it felt good after the beef stench I'd been soaking in for the past three hours. At the tree line we picked our way down the rocky slope toward the water, its rushing mechanical voice growing louder as we approached.

"Do people fish this part of the river?" Miranda asked.

I cast my eyes like a line across its clear bed, the white froth and the moss-slick rocks below, shining from the constant hand of the water. "I know next to nothing about this place," I said. "I just work here."

She leaned to unlace her shoes and reveal her pale, well-formed feet, the toenails painted a cheerfully ugly orange. Wading out, she stopped when the water was just above her ankles, and clasped her hands behind her back, head down. I'd been raised in the city, where beauty was the greening crumble of an old foundation, or a sunset blooming on the mirrored faces of the skyscrapers, and I still couldn't believe I was allowed to live here among healthy streams and molting birches and the constant upsurge of rocky earth. The land made me feel blindly cared for.

Behind us, up the bank, a stick cracked and someone said, "Hey down there."

I turned, shading my eyes against the tree-rippled sun. It was the husband, scrambling toward us. Miranda had turned, too, reaching for her shoes as if she didn't want to be caught barefoot by a stranger.

"I've been walking all over these grounds," he said as he reached us, breathless, ruddy-faced. "I feel like *I'm* supposed to find her. You know when you feel something deep in your gut? It's got to be *me*."

"This is Brian. He's looking for his wife," I said to Miranda—unnecessarily, since her eyes were already bright with interested comprehension.

"I heard about that," Miranda said. "I've been thinking about both of you."

"Thank you," he said. "Thoughts can't hurt."

"Well," she said, "they *can*. But."

"I can't believe this is my life," he said. He threaded his hands through his thinning hair and squeezed his eyes shut, lips clamped. There was a smudge of dirt on one puffy cheek.

"I assume you called the cops," Miranda said. "The forest service. I assume there's been a search party?"

Brian opened his eyes again. "They won't take me seriously," he said. "They looked for two days, then bam. Left me on my own."

"Did she have her money with her?" Miranda said, crossing her arms. "Her wallet? Her passport, maybe?"

"Yes," Brian said, and his ruddy face grew even ruddier, flushed and petulant. He poked his sunglasses down onto his nose. "I know what you're thinking," he said. "That's what the cops are thinking, too. But Peggy wouldn't just leave me like this, out in the middle of nowhere. She's the one who always deals with our plane tickets. I mean, they're in her e-mail box, not mine. She wouldn't just leave me here without a ticket home."

He was talking loudly, almost yelling, to be heard over the chatter of the water. From beyond the riverbank came the sound of a car, followed by the frantic yapping of Holt's dog, and I began to back toward the restaurant. "I'm sorry," I said, "but I need to get back to work."

I glanced at Miranda, expecting her to follow me, but her eyes were fixed on Brian.

"I'll help you look," she said.

Emily was deep in Skype with her boyfriend when I got back to the house that night, her crispy German vowels coming strong through the door of her room. Miranda'd left the restaurant just before the sun set, and I'd seen her embrace Brian on the porch, reaching up to pat his cheek with force, a gesture caught between chastisement and affection. After her car had battered down the driveway, he came in to eat a chicken sandwich at the counter. Holt watched him with bloodhound eyes and flared nostrils, like he was catching some elusive scent. "One thing that always tastes good," Brian had said, swiping his finger through a trail of sauce, "is food."

I exchanged my Whole Hog tank top for a red T-shirt, then stared into the chilly maw of the fridge until the freezer-burned reek of old food began to sicken me. Finally I ate a cherry tomato and took a bottle of beer and went outside into the hot night. The air was dry, rich with the smell of flowers and forest fires, and as I settled myself onto the porch steps I could hear strains of music from the houses of my neighbors: Kanye, country.

Miranda came by in the middle of my beer, and before I could check myself, *don't encourage her!*, I smiled. She was wearing a long, loose dress, and when she sat beside me on the step I felt the heat coming off her body. "You just get home?" she said.

"Little bit ago." I didn't stand. She wasn't quite a guest. "Want a beer?"

"I'm not supposed to drink," she said. "But if I may, I'd take a tiny sip of yours."

I passed her the bottle.

"That poor man," she said. "Brian."

"Yeah?" I said. "Are you still certain Peggy left him?"

"Oh, he knows too," she said. "He's in denial, but he may as well have told me outright. Her backpack was gone, not just her shoes, not just her favorite sweater. Most all her clothes. They've been unhappy for a while. Still, it's not a nice thing to do, to leave someone in unknown territory." She passed my beer back to me.

"How long do you think he'll stay?" I asked.

She shrugged. "How long does it take to give up on someone? An idea of someone, anyway. An idea of yourself."

"So he's sticking around?"

"We didn't talk about it." In the porch light her face was waxy as a leaf. "If I were him, I wouldn't want to go home any time soon. That's when shit gets real. At home. That's when reality sets in. So you know, in some ways I think it's good for me, to live at Amy's while I'm going through this business." She gestured to her midsection. "If I still lived here, in my own familiar house, I'd be more likely to fall victim to self-pity. Like when a little kid falls down and feels okay until their mother shows them sympathy. Then they bust out crying even though deep down, they're not too badly hurt."

"I really thought Brian might've killed her," I said. "I was sure of it."

"Who's to say he wouldn't have?" Miranda said, and laughed. "From what he told me, Peggy's not a simple lady. Maybe she got out right in time."

"That takes guts," I said, thinking of myself, and my own cowardice. "To up and go."

"Sure," Miranda said, and was quiet, staring out into the arid street. I looked at her, her open, farmwife face, and remembered all the times I hadn't met her eyes, had ignored her questions or given her one-word answers in the hopes she'd take the hint and leave me be.

"I guess there's some things you'd like to get away from," I said.

For a moment she didn't respond, then she sighed and propped her chin up on her hand. "No," she said. "Actually, I want to *face* this thing. Being sick. Right now it's like we're in the preliminaries. I know the awfulness is still to come, and I'm a sitting duck for it. Give me something to fight! Or at least complain about." She grinned.

I only knew Miranda as she was now: bald, intrusive, overtalkative, ill. And she only knew my current incarnation, a taciturn waitress who lived in her house and refused to meet her halfway. The difference was, I had never asked to be known, because I didn't plan to be this me for long.

But here I was.

"You can complain to me anytime," I said, and impulsively I reached over to take her hand. Her palm turned up and opened to me like a morning glory. It had been a while since I'd touched another person with tenderness; since my grandmother, maybe.

Even when I hated her the most, I had to be gentle with her: running soap across her bony shoulders, tilting her head back to hook oxygen to her nose, fastening the buttons on her blue dress. All that gentleness . . . it was bound to sometimes feel like love.

"Right back atcha," Miranda said, and squeezed my fingers for a long moment. Then she stood to go. Not home; but somewhere like it.

Back in the house, Emily was still talking to her boyfriend. I paused outside her door and listened to her muffled, foreign words, and the tinny crackle of his voice coming back at her through cheap computer speakers. I tried to guess by the rise and fall of her language what they were saying, but everything sounded like *Where are you, I'm sorry, good-bye.*

Christopher Merkner

Cabins

1.

PRESUMING HE WAS STILL well married, I told one of my
friends I could not imagine living near my wife in divorce.
I've always imagined, I said, that if I got divorced I would live
alone in the wilderness. I have a cabin. I have a boat. I can see my
little cabin from where I sit in the boat. The water is slapping the
boat. I'm on an elevated chair whipping lures that race across the
surface of the water as I reel them back in. My wife is not nearby.
In my cabin, as in my entire life in divorce, she's not anywhere to
be found or heard or smelled.

And I miss her. I am morose and I am broken without her in
my cabin. If I cannot have her, I can have no one and nothing
except my cabin and my boat. The idea of having her part-time,
it's unthinkable. It is the galling grotesque of sitcom television.
I walk and drink a lot. Sometimes I walk drunk down the road
to the bar just to get more drunk. Sometimes the local girls at
the bar hit on me, but I've been there long enough, rejected their
advances so often and so sadly, that they mostly just stand back
at the bar and call me by the name they've made up for me, Deer
Eyes, which I for years believe is actually Dear Eyes, and they

feel for me as one tends to feel for roadkill. I stumble back to my cabin drunk, I cry, I sleep, I fish. Where I get the money I live off I have no idea.

I'm sorry, I said to my friend, I'm just making this shit up.

2.

A different friend had called me shortly before this and invited me to a part of town I'd never even considered visiting. That night, cruising in the right lane, I spotted through the passenger window the address he'd given me. It was a hookah bar. I pulled over and went inside. He was sitting in a booth by himself. I slid in across from him.

I have news, he said.

You're dying, I said.

A little, he said.

This is a nice place, I said.

He looked around the room. He said, Yeah, man. Then he said that going to places like this was part of his new life philosophy. He put a black rubber hose in his mouth. He inhaled, I waited, he coughed. He handed me the hose. I just held it. I looked around while he cleared his lungs. I had not seen so many young people in the same room since college. I felt very old, very ridiculous holding my hose. I gave it back to my friend. He said he was divorcing. Then he put the hose in his mouth again and closed his eyes.

I fought the urge to call my wife. I had my hand on my phone. Instead, I got up and ordered a festive piece of cake. My wife and I had talked about these two a lot. They were not a pleasant couple to be friends with. We desired to be rid of them. They seemed to love each other in a way that nauseated us. He always told her what to do; she always told him to fuck himself. And then they would laugh. We assumed they'd be together forever like this.

I returned to the table and watched my cake ooze lard. My friend detailed his wife's affair, or what he called the pin that had popped their balloon. His wife had apparently known this other man for decades. They were friends in grade school. They had not spoken in years and then, for reasons that no one but God could understand, they "ran into their souls" at a nearby car dealership on a Saturday evening. After decades of each having been married to another person, my friend told me, his wife and this guy bumped into each other?

Not their "soul mates," he clarified. Their "souls."

Ah, I said.

Anyway, he added, pulling his mouth away from the hose just as he'd brought it to his lips, you just hope for this kind of thing for everyone. Then he inhaled, released, and coughed.

I said, Okay.

He went on to explain that his wife and her new man had each thought often of the other over the years. They did not realize they'd lived in the same city all this time. Apparently, my friend said, straight-faced, the guy made a birthday cake for my wife every year to commemorate her birthday—and then he'd go and dump it in a fire pit in his garden and burn it.

What about your daughters? I asked.

My folks are divorced, he answered.

I nodded. So you've told them about all this?

They know.

I nodded again. He took another long drag from his hose and looked up at me.

Single parent, he said, short of air. There's a lot of street cred in that these days.

You are kind of blowing my mind right now, I said.

He exhaled. Yeah, he said. He didn't cough. He began studying the hookah, like he hadn't realized this artifact had been there between us the whole time. Well, he said, I basically just want to kill myself.

3.

I took him to my car. I acted cool. I called my car a name. He laughed. He seemed fine. In the car, however, as I drove through his neighborhood, he began knocking his head against the passenger window. I studied him from my periphery. I began talking about my heart attack the previous fall. He said he had heard about it. He was sorry. He was obviously not interested, but it seemed right to continue talking about myself. I believed I was offering us both some greater context for our rather narrow sorrow. I told him in detail what I could remember about the catheter. When I pulled up to his house, I extended my hand. Thanks, I said.

He didn't move. He didn't take my hand. He just stared straight ahead.

You still living together? I asked.

He nodded.

That hurts, I said.

You would think so, he said. Then he invited me in. He said he had some beer in the fridge.

I said I needed to call my wife first.

He clicked his teeth. Ah, he said. He wagged his finger in my face.

I know, I said, I know. I forced a light laugh. I looked at my phone.

He didn't move.

I'll be up there in just a minute, I said. You can leave the door open.

I don't want to be left in that house alone with her anymore.

I dialed my wife. She did not pick up. The machine came through. I left a vague message about being "on my way" and withheld the expression of love I would have ordinarily voiced, were there not a divorced friend of mine sitting right beside me.

We walked up to his house and went inside. It was dark.

I can't see anything, I said.

She's in here somewhere, he said.

4.

In bed the night I made the remarks on my divorce cabin, I rolled over to look at my wife. She was reading a book on the history of crochet and needlework. I said, If we divorce, who gets the baby?

5.

The next morning, I played basketball with a third friend I'd presumed married. I told him about my recently discovered divorced friends. I told him that I could not understand people divorcing. It seemed, I said, an incredible amount of work. Then I shot a lay-up.

My friend was silent until he told me that he'd always believed marriage was for the brainwashed dickheads of a Hallmark psychological takeover. I passed him the ball and said, I think Maya Angelou's cards are actually pretty cool.

That's because you are gay, he said.

I let this slide. He had not gone to school, this particular friend. I had always thought him to be a rough but decent sort of person—a simple man with values and priorities that approximated my own. But I didn't really know this to be true. I said, Aren't we all?

He drained a left-hander from the short corner and looked at me. He shook his head. No, he said.

I bet your wife loves your marriage, I said.

Not unless she's fucking it, he said. Then he said, We tanked it last year.

No way, I said. He was dribbling the ball between his legs. I was like Helen Keller on drugs in that marriage, he said. I beat the shit out of everything in that house. That marriage was costing us both a fortune. I broke like ten thousand dollars in walls.

He drove the lane. I did not contest this. He rolled the ball over the rim. I'd met this guy at that same gym about the time of my heart attack. The first time we shot together, he brought beer to the court and made me try to finish the case with him. We might have pulled it off, had he not broken his leg trying to grab a rebound before it went into the small set of aluminum bleachers near the emergency exits. I had to drive him to the hospital. Both of us were drunk. For a while I sat there in the waiting room with his wife, a cool woman. Then I fell asleep. When I woke up, she was gone. I was just sitting alone and I was in the hospital lobby. I thought she had perhaps gone off for coffee. I sat there for two hours. I checked the nurses' station. My friend had already been released.

I shot from about six feet. The ball hit the rim and came right back to me. I shot again. What do you do now? I asked my friend. Are you dating?

He told me he was doing my mother. He snapped the ball off the glass and ran the length of the court. He ran back. He stood in front of me. He told me to take that look off my face. He told me I made him sick. Marriage, he said, made him sick. Then he walked off the court, taking the ball with him.

6.

It's a good cabin. I think about it a lot. I go there a lot. When I'm there, I live off berries and perch. In the winter, however, the average temperature is ten. I eat very little, but I drink a lot. I work on insulating the walls of the cabin while drinking. Sometimes I will fall asleep with a tool in my chopper mitten. I do not dream. I often get up and have another drink, and then I leave the cabin to walk to the bar in town. I talk to no one there. Sometimes, people talk to me and suggest I shower. Also, that I have my cheeks and nose looked at by a professional, since the frostbite seems to be blackening my exposed flesh. Have you insulated that place, they say, and that's usually when I return to the cabin, where a Nordic woman is washing the kitchen counter with a white cloth. The room is glowing in candlelight. She has made a fire in a fireplace I have no memory of building into the planked walls. She has decorated the cabin with lovely red and blue fabrics and floral tapestries. She has an apron on. She wears a scarf on her head from which long blonde hair spills. She brings me a cup of hot cocoa. She says she is the Swiss Miss girl all grown up and has come from the hills to be my wife and make ruddy children. She is in love with me, she knows it's sudden. She says, Oh, Dear Eyes, and she kisses my eyes, and though the planks of the cabin have caught on fire and are burning down around us, I say nothing because inside my body I am so, so cold.

7.

The fourth well-married friend I discovered divorced was my former neighbor. He was driving by his old house, as he often did, and he'd seen me weeding in my front yard and pulled his car over. He rolled down his window. He told me he was on his way to the state penitentiary. He told me he had started a therapy group for inmates who were, had been, or feared they would soon be divorced by their partners or spouses. He said, You should come.

I went over to his car. I laughed. I said, You are the fourth person to talk to me about divorce in the past few days. What is up with that?

You should come with me, he said.

Why would I do that? I said.

Empathy, he said.

My friend is not a therapist. He is a veterinary surgeon with a specialty in genetic eye diseases. He and his wife were our neighbors for several years. They divorced just before they moved out. They were extraordinarily public about their divorce. They fought brutally in their house with the windows open, and they made love brutally in their house with the windows open. Even the discreetest neighbors in the area talked about them. They often shouted the word *divorce* at each other. You could hear that word on the wind so often it became a sort of third party in their arguments and lovemaking sessions.

Listen, I said. When did you guys know it was time to get divorced? When we first got married, he answered.

8.

That night, I tell my wife about all my friends who are suddenly divorcing. I tell her about our former neighbors and the afternoon I spent at the state penitentiary. I tell her about the dude at the gym. I have my head in her lap. I look up at her, and she is sleeping.

She is very pregnant. She is deep into our pregnancy. She is sleeping even when she is not asleep. I keep talking. I tell her about the first guy to tell me he was soon to be divorcing, and how he was still living with his wife. I tell her that the first thing I wanted to do, when I heard this, was to tell her. I tell her that I didn't know, at first, what to say to a person in his position. I tell her that I didn't realize so many people were divorcing in the world. I tell her I do not know what I would do if we were divorced.

I let these remarks flitter away into the silence of our living room, and I look up again at my wife. She is a pretty sleeper. Anyway, I say, I tried to call you. You didn't pick up. So I went with him into his house. He asked me to follow him into the kitchen to get a beer. And I did. I asked him if I should take my shoes off. He laughed. I asked if we should turn on the lights. We went into the kitchen and stood across from each other at his center island. We kept the lights off. The moonlight from outside lit his face. He just stared at me, or he seemed to. You all right? I asked.

Sad, he said.

Then he turned around, flung open the moon-bright refrigerator, took out a bottle of beer, and wrenched it open with his hands. He drank back on it and then slid it over to me. I looked at it. He said, You want one of your own. He went back to the fridge, pulled out another beer, palmed the bottle, then stopped and stood stock-still.

I said, What?

He whispered, Listen.

I said, I hear the house fan.

I hear her breathing, he said.

I said, Okay.

I hear her breath, he said.

Then I heard something too. I heard footfalls on the staircase. At first they were quiet, and then his daughters pattered into the kitchen. Suddenly it became very noisy. We flung on a light. There were his girls, beaming. They looked at me and talked to him. They were so happy he was home. They were so happy that they could have breakfast in the dark. They asked him why we smelled like smoke.

9.

I got into his car. I asked him how he got hooked up with this therapy group, and he told me he'd decided to do it all on his own. He said he was just driving past the prison one day shortly after he and his wife had ended their marriage and had thought, You know, there are probably a lot of single guys in there feeling just like me. He told me he went up to the front gate and asked to see the warden, and, when the warden appeared, asked if he thought anyone inside might be interested in getting together to talk informally about love and its absences. The warden laughed and said that he doubted it, but that my friend could get a day pass and sit down in the field during a thirty-minute outdoor lunch to see if anyone came over.

And now guess who joins my little group of forty-five inmates every week?

The warden?

That fucker, my friend said. He looked wistful. I love that fat fucker.

We were sitting in his car, staring at our houses. He had stopped talking. I had nothing more to say. It was interesting to just sit and look at the houses, actually. I took a deep breath.

You like the new owners? he asked me.

They're fine, I said.

They'll disappoint you, he said. That's the way it is with neighbors.

We had very little in common, in fact, aside from our property lines. We drove in silence and when we arrived at the penitentiary I learned that its parking lot is a vast—just absolutely sweeping—dirt desert that goes out beyond view for miles. From any particular spot in this desert, you have to walk about a quarter mile before getting to the prison's tiny entryway, which is surrounded by barbed-wire fencing. When they let you in, you pass through a maze of hallways of windowless cinder block, and you are patted down and scanned at every steel-barred gate, of which there are more than five between the entry and the open field where selected inmates can take a thirty-minute outdoor lunch. My friend and I went every step of the way through this in silence.

Out on the lawn, many of the guys had already gathered, waiting for my friend and former neighbor. They were sitting folded-leg style in the grass. They eyed me as we approached. I sat down. My friend went to the front of them and stood. He lifted his hands and, when they'd quieted down completely, he thanked them for coming and for their willingness to "see the world beyond love."

The men were nodding. My friend continued. He spoke for some time on "the intrinsic colossal disaster of seeing love that isn't actually there," and he used an example of two blind dogs he'd come to love when he was interning at a veterinarian clinic in North Carolina. The dogs had died. He'd discovered them dead one morning. Just gone, he said, his voice beginning to tremble. He snapped his fingers. He cleared his throat. He said he was devastated. He said he has never known devastation like this. No devastation has ever compared, he said. He said he imagined we knew what he was talking about.

The sun was exceptionally warm. I looked around again. One thing was clear from the expressions on the faces of the men in that group: It was not a good idea to talk about dead dogs. They did not like that. Some of the men got up. This agitated one of those still sitting. My neighbor continued talking as though the exchanges occurring among these men were trivial, subdued. Dead dogs, he said, were only a metaphor. But they were not. One man stood up, shoved another one from behind, and called him a bitch: The warden shifted and rolled up to his feet. I was trying to stand when three or four other men pushed me back down and jumped the warden and the guy who'd called the other man a bitch. They kicked him in the head. I saw the man's head moving in horrible angles. Three or four men kicking a head is a gruesome thing. Then the shots came and the yard was filled with weaponry and shouting. I was on my stomach, pinned. I could see others pinned to the ground also.

10.

I look up at my wife. She's still sound asleep. The baby is coming in the next few weeks, and she is sleeping so hard, for such short periods of time, in such odd contorted positions, I am amazed to see the way serenity can sometimes play across her face. We have been married six years. We have planned everything carefully, strategically, my anomalous heart attack and double bypass last year notwithstanding. We were ready, I had been thinking until this spate of divorces, to have this baby. I tell her that it makes me uneasy that everyone is getting divorced. It's crazy, I say. What are divorces, anyway?

11.

Eventually my friend turned on a few more of the house lights and seemed to loosen up. He told silly stories to his girls, and I drank a second beer. The television was switched on. His daughters described their favorite late-night television show to me. They said Jimmy Kimmel was "kank," but he was also a little bit "smunt." Neither could have been more than six. My friend looked at me and shrugged.

Then I noticed that my friend's wife had materialized in the kitchen, in a blue robe. She was holding a beer. She stood at the edge of the kitchen, just where the kitchen met the living room. She asked what time we'd gotten home. My friend didn't answer, so I told her. I told her it was nice to see her again.

Yeah? she said.

Then she asked me about my wife. I asked her about her lawn. I complained about the housing market. She said she knew it was strange but she loved crabgrass. We went on like this for a few minutes, talking small, my friend playing with his daughters by the television. She had come over to me and sat on the arm of my chair. She seemed entirely easy. She only looked in her husband's direction a few times.

Well, I said. I stood up to leave.

She looked surprised. Oh, she said. You don't have to go anywhere.

No, I said.

Have another beer, she said.

She got up and went to the fridge, even as I was saying I shouldn't drink any more, and she opened that beer, twisting the cap off with her bare hands, and brought it back to me. Then she went back to the fridge, opened another bottle, and gave it to her husband. Then she told her husband, my friend, to sit on the sofa.

And he did. He got up from the floor and threw himself onto the sofa. She sat on his lap. What else is new? she asked me.

I hear you're getting divorced, I wanted to say.

Very little, I said.

My wife is still sleeping as I tell her this. I tell her that when I looked up again, I saw the two of them—my friend and his wife—kissing on the sofa and I presumed, at first, it was a quick and conciliatory kind of thing. I looked at their girls, who were also looking at my friend and his wife.

They kept kissing. I looked again at the girls. The TV went on commercial. I saw my friend's wife's tongue, and his hand slipped inside her robe. They were both still holding their beers. As soon as he dropped his beer on the carpet, I stood up. I patted the girls on the head. They took this as a sort of signal. They left the room with me, as if they were going to walk me to the door. Instead they went straight up the stairs to their bedrooms. Good night, I whispered to them, and they turned around.

12.

My cardiologist took particular care of me during my heart attack and subsequent surgery. He visited my room often. He said little, but he checked my stats with a sort of earnest determination, flipping papers, hammering things into his computer. The night before my surgery, after everyone had left, he came to my room and closed the door. He sat on the edge of my bed. He said, You know what you need?

A hug?

He looked at his watch. I find most heart patients, he said, need someone to scare the shit out of them.

Okay, I said.

If you are not going to change your lifestyle, he said. He looked at me, and then he produced a plastic model of the human heart from his coat pocket, and he stuck his fingers into the model and started pulling it apart. He scattered the rubber pieces across my bedsheets and left.

13.

C'mon, the older daughter said. She summoned me up. I followed. At the top of the stairs, we turned to the right and went into a room lit only by candles. Inside, the walls were lined with mounted game. I stared at a zebra head. Jesus, I said. The older daughter told me the zebra's name was Beverly. The fox was Lenny, the pheasant Jennifer. And the wild turkey had no name at all, because they had just killed it that morning.

14.

I take my head off my wife's lap and I sit up. I upset the sofa cushions a bit, bounce a little, so that she will wake up. I touch her shoulder. She wakes up. She smiles. She wipes her face. She reaches into a stretch, and she brings her hands to her stomach, to our bursting child inside there. She tells me she feels like hell, and I say I know what she means. She rolls her eyes. Take me upstairs, she says. I consider this. I consider carrying her. I consider her weight. C'mon, she says. I put my arm under her legs. I support her back. I lift her. Her eyes close. Her mouth sags. It's chilly. The gravel path is lit only by dull moonlight. There's a breeze. The crickets are calling. I hear the waves lapping at the shore. I hear my boat rubbing the wooden pier. The rope moorings are aching. The cabin is dark. I put my wife down on our creaking bed. I stand upright and look at her form. It's no easy journey getting her here. I wish we lived closer.

Molly Antopol

My Grandmother Tells Me This Story

Some say the story begins in Europe, and your mother would no doubt interrupt and say it begins in New York, but that's just because she can't imagine the world before she entered it. And yes, I know you think it begins specifically in Belarus, because that's what your grandfather tells you. I've heard him describing those black sedans speeding down Pinsker Street. I've been married to the man almost sixty years and know how he is with you—he makes every word sound like a secret. But he wasn't even there. He was with his youth group by then and even though I *was* there I don't remember being scared. Even when they knocked on our door, I didn't know what was happening. Even when they dragged us outside with our overstuffed suitcases spilling into the street, shouting through megaphones to walk in the road with the livestock, I still didn't know. I was thirteen.

The story really starts in the sewers. Everybody in the uniform factory whispered about them, and everybody had a different theory. Some said they were an escape route a plumber had spent years charting, an underground system of tunnels running from Poland to Belarus to Lithuania. Others said they were an impossible maze with no way out. But when my mother pulled me aside after only six days in the factory and whispered that she'd worked out a plan for me—smuggled vodka for the guards, a shoulder bared (my poor father, a lifetime of loving a woman who knew just how to spark another man's sympathy)—I simply stood there, taking notes in my head. After dinner, she said, I'd slip past the guards and down the street, around two corners and up a road where I'd see the slats of a sewer. The grate would slide off easily, she said, and she and my father would find me soon. I had no reason not to believe that was true, no way of knowing the sewers would lead me to the forest. That night all I knew, as I climbed inside the manhole and down the metal ladder, was that it smelled worse than anything I'd imagined, of shit and piss and garbage all together.

It was black in there, and dank and cool, the ceiling so low I sank to my knees and crawled. I just kept following the crowd of voices speaking in Yiddish, which was both comforting and horrible, hearing that language forbidden in the factory. Then there was a rumble, and water rushed in and knocked me down. I gasped and tried to wade forward. The sewer started filling up, and I felt around in the slimy water for the person in front of me. But everybody seemed far ahead, and it took me a minute to realize dinner must have been ending aboveground, everybody washing dishes and taking baths and pouring water down the drain all at once.

Soon I had no sense of how long I'd been underground. My eyes grew accustomed to the darkness, and I saw the shapes around me: The woman up ahead, the hunched slope of her back. The walls of the sewer. The shadow of a rat before it ran across my arm. Then my whole body started to shake, and I knew I wouldn't make it through a wave of morning dishwashing, so when I saw lines of light through the grate, I stopped.

Keep going, the woman behind me whispered.

But I couldn't. I waited for the group to pass, and when I heard nothing above, I slowly lifted the grate and climbed onto the streets of a village that looked as if it had been completely passed over by the war. I wasn't used to the sun after an entire night in the sewers—it was just rolling up over the houses, and the forest beyond was so bright it looked painted. Dirt, barns, sky—everything stunned me. That the wooden cottages lining the road were still intact, that people were feeding their horses and selling vegetables and sweeping leaves into the gutter.

A man passed with his young daughter and she stared. The father took one look at me, yanked her arm, and hurried down the road. I knew then not to spend another minute standing there in the daylight, so I crossed the road and entered the forest. It was cold and dim, and when I leaned against a tree trunk, exhaustion came right at me.

I wasn't sure how long I'd been asleep when I heard footsteps. I opened my eyes and stared up—into the barrel of a gun. I swallowed, hard, refusing to make eye contact. That much I knew to do. I looked at the sticks and pinecones littering the forest floor and thought up a story. I was lost, searching for mushrooms, and could he help me find my way back? But how to explain the smell, or my work uniform, and before I opened my mouth, the boy put down the gun and said my name.

How odd that the first word I heard in that forest was my own name, and for a minute I wondered if that night in the sewers had made me crazy. Then I looked at him. I know how you see your grandfather, sweet and smiling, always insisting that we put on a movie after dinner and then dozing on the sofa halfway through. Your chess partner, your theater date, the man who checks out the minute your mother and I start up. You wouldn't have recognized him. His long, bony face splotchy and pink from the sun, his light brown beard growing in sparse, threadbare patches—he was only fifteen—and his straight hair obviously hacked off with a knife. But even with that terrible haircut, even with a rifle over one shoulder and paper sacks swinging from the other, he still looked like the same Leon Moscowitz I'd grown up with.

It was one of the great miracles of my life, finding someone from home, right there, in the middle of the woods. But I won't lie and say he was the person I'd wanted to see. I barely knew him back in our village. He was two grades above me and had struck me as bigheaded and bossy, one of those boys who always raised his hand in class. I hadn't been the shining student he was but had been a good girl, a rule-follower. Your grandfather had not only seemed the opposite—it was like he saw anyone *not* challenging every point made in class as a weakling. His whole family was like that. His father had been a professor, and the one time I'd gone to his house to make a delivery from my parents' tailor shop, I remember how dark and dusty it was: books pulled from the shelves and strewn on the floor in a way that must have made his family feel intellectual but to me just looked sloppy, brown drapes so thick you immediately forgot about the sun outside. That past year your grandfather had stopped coming to school one day, but I wasn't surprised—so many were fleeing by then that I hadn't spent much time wondering where the Moscowitzes had gone to hide.

You look like shit, Raya, he told me then.

I know, I said.

No, he said, eyeing me more closely. You have actual shit on you.

I came from the sewers, I said.

He nodded, as if I wasn't the first he knew who had, then said, And your family?

Back home. In the uniform factory.

Your grandfather nodded again. He reached into a paper sack, and when he handed me a loaf of bread, it was so heavy I almost dropped it.

When's the last time you ate? he said. I had no idea. I didn't know what time it was, or even where I was. As I followed your grandfather through the forest, he talked. His family had escaped to a city in the North that past winter, he said—this was all happening in September—where he and his three younger brothers had trained with a youth group. The entire family had gone from there to Palestine, but he had met a plumber, Yosef Zanivyer, who'd seen something special in him (I couldn't help but roll my eyes that even then, in those silent, deserted woods, your grandfather had to let me know how fabulous he was) and asked him to stay. Yosef was the plumber who'd engineered the sewer route I'd just come through, he said. For the past few months, your grandfather and his group had been roaming a labyrinth of tunnels, committing them to memory for an evacuation and supply route they'd use to smuggle weapons and food into the forest.

He led me in a zigzag through uncleared scrub and over so many marshes and creeks I couldn't count, until finally we reached the densest part, a cluster of trees so tall and thick it suddenly felt like evening—an area protected sufficiently by branches, he told me, that no military plane could spot us from the air. He took my hand, and we elbowed our way around trees and bushes until an entire village emerged. There were blanket tents held up by logs, what looked like an infirmary, a makeshift kitchen surrounding a fire pit. About forty people, all teenagers, almost all boys, unbathed and bedraggled, were at work in different stations. Everybody was speaking Yiddish, and the whole scene was so stunning I didn't know what to look at first. But your grandfather just kept leading me forward, as nonchalant as if he were giving a tour of our school back home.

This is Yussel, he said, pointing to a squat, suntanned boy. He was a medical student and runs the infirmary here. And this is the kitchen—here he handed me a potato, still hot from the fire—and this is where we run drills after dinner. He waved to a bigger kid, this one fifteen or sixteen, oafish and freckled with red flyaway hair, the parts of a gun spread out on his lap. That's Isaac from Antopol, he told me.

Isaac, your grandfather said, meet Raya. We grew up together.

I'm trying to concentrate, Isaac grunted without even shooting me a sideways look, and your grandfather shrugged and said, He'll grow on you.

Then your grandfather stopped. Can you cook?

Not really. My mother cooks. I could barely say it.

What can you do, then?

I thought about it. I can do ballet, I said. I can play the flute.

That was when your grandfather started laughing. Wow, he said, throwing his hands in the air, thank God you're here, and I wanted to smack him. But your parents are tailors, right? he said. So I'm guessing you can sew, and I can't tell you how much it meant to me right then that there, in the middle of the forest, someone knew this basic fact about my family.

Yeah, I can sew.

Good, he said. We already have a tailor, but if you're quick with your fingers, you can go in the armory.

So that afternoon I went to work, learning how to repair broken rifles and pistols, mending cracked stocks and replacing worn parts. He was right: All my years helping my parents sew on buttons and rip out seams made the job come easy. I was grateful I was good at it, and for many hours I sat alone, a little relieved I didn't have to talk to grumpy Isaac. Your grandfather was running around, stopping at every station. It seemed obvious he was the leader, which I learned for certain that night at dinner, when five new boys arrived at the campfire.

They were young, your grandfather's age, and had just come back from a mission. Your grandfather crouched beside me and explained. Everyone here was part of a brigade, he said, called the Yiddish Underground. He'd started it back with his youth group, doing combat training in basements around the city. In the beginning, they'd slipped into nearby villages and robbed peasants for food and tools and weapons. But every day the war seemed to be getting worse, he said, and now the brigade was traveling farther to carry out attacks. They torched cottages and stole guns. When they ran out of bullets, they sneaked into cities with empty shotguns and long, straight branches, which, from a distance, could pass as rifles. They chopped down telephone poles, attacked supply depots, burned bridges to disrupt military routes—and that night, the five boys at the campfire had just returned from dislodging two hundred meters of rail line.

And? your grandfather said then, turning to one of the boys.

And the conductor stopped the train, the boy said, spearing a sausage from the fire. And I walked right on and shot four soldiers in the dining car. They didn't even have time to put down their forks.

Your grandfather clapped the boy's shoulder like a proud parent, and I just sat there swallowing.

I told the other passengers to tell the police the Yiddish Underground was responsible, the boy continued, and your grandfather nodded. Everyone on the train was so scared, the boy said, and I just kept saying it as I walked through the cars. I took all of this, he said, gesturing at the suitcases and sacks of vegetables and bread by his feet.

Perfect, your grandfather said, and when he flicked on his radio, everyone put down their food to listen. He tuned through static until an announcer came on with word of the day's casualties. But when the announcer described the ambush, he said it was the work of Russian guerrilla fighters, Communists camping out in the woods. The Yiddish Underground wasn't mentioned at all. All around us were these kids, huddled together in stolen coats, waiting for their commander to speak. Your grandfather cleared his throat. He looked his age for that second, wide-eyed and serious and more than a little frightened, and I had a flash of that same boy in the schoolyard, the market, walking his younger brothers down Pinsker Street. I knew that whatever he said, inside he felt as lost as every one of his fighters. But he stood up. He switched off the radio and said the only way they couldn't ignore us was to plan bigger. We have to let them know, he said, that there's a secret army they can't touch, soldiers fighting back with weapons taken from them, then retreating deep into the forest to plan their next attack.

This is the part of the story where I know you want to hear how we fell in love. I understand—don't think I haven't noticed how you're always free to visit your grandfather and me, even on Saturday nights. How five years out of college you're still living like a student, still alone in that shoebox studio. Even when you were little, it was your favorite part of every story. It used to kill me when I'd overhear you asking your mother those kinds of questions about your father, this young chubby you with long blond braids and a dreamy expression. As if with your eyes half-closed you could envision a time when your parents weren't sneaking around your living room at night, scribbling their names into each other's books, or storming after each other outside your old apartment, fighting over who got to keep this ceramic, fish-shaped platter your mother said she made at summer camp but that your father claimed he made at an adult ed class at the Y—a fish, he yelled, that held his nachos just right.

And I remember after he left, you and your mother piled all of your possessions into a taxi and headed over the bridge to our apartment in Queens, where the two of you moved into her childhood bedroom, sleeping side by side on her trundle bed, surrounded by her spelling ribbons and stuffed-animal collection, as though you were living in an exhibit in the museum of her life. And I remember all the dates she'd bring back—Philip and Hugh and the one who wore his sunglasses inside—how she'd parade those men into my home with the same defiance she had in high school, only she was thirty-six then with a four-year-old daughter in the next room eating dinner with her grandparents. From the kitchen the three of us would listen to her carrying on, her voice high and clear and always drowning out the other person's, which probably made her a good teacher during rowdy assemblies but not such a hit on those dates. There were so many nights when I'd watch her crawl into bed beside you after her date had left, her back to the wall, her bare feet wrapped around yours, holding on to your stomach so tightly it was like she feared the distance you might fall was so much greater than from the bed to the carpet.

I want to tell you mine was a great love affair, but the truth was that the only reason your grandfather started coming into my tent at night was to protect me. There were so many things to be afraid of in the forest. Not just the soldiers but bears and snakes and wolves. Russian Communists who lived in other parts of the woods, coming by our camp, offering bullets for a night with one of the girls, sometimes taking one even if refused—men who disliked your grandfather but respected him enough, even as a boy, not to touch the one he was with. Anyway, it was almost winter—I will always remember that as the coldest season imaginable, the winter I watched hot tea freeze in a cup—and when your grandfather climbed in one night and lay beneath my blanket, his hands roaming up my shirt and into my pants long before he thought to kiss me, it didn't feel romantic—more like a basic physical need that had little to do with me.

We'd already seen each other naked, anyway—we all bathed around one another, there was no other choice—and even though I was thirteen years old and he was my first kiss, I wasn't so naive as to believe your grandfather was in love with me, though for a lot of my life I did believe our relationship wasn't so bad. We had no one but each other when we first arrived in the States, and a big part of me wondered if I had another option, if there were any other Jewish men left. We never even talked about marrying—we just did it. I think your grandfather and I both wanted to forget everything that had happened and try to be as normal as all our neighbors on Dinsmore Avenue. It was only years later when you and your mother were living with us that I had to listen to her opinions on how I would never be normal, my fuse was just too short, she'd never met a person who could go from zero to sixty so quickly. From the beginning, though, it was like that with your mother and me—even in the womb I think she was kicking me on purpose. Whenever we argued, your grandfather would walk out the door and around the block, as if your mother and I had taken up all the air in the apartment. But you would always stay. It used to drive me crazy, watching you watch *us*, as if our fight were being transcribed and filed away in the card catalog of your mind. But the truth was that there were moments when I'd look at you—you always resembled me more than your mother, especially when you were young, with your light hair and cheeks that went red no matter the weather—and think that you reminded me of another version of myself.

I too might have lived in my head if, when I was a girl, I'd had a school to spend my days in and an apartment for my nights, rather than a tent and a bed of pine needles that I shared with your grandfather. But to his credit, he never once tried to pretend ours was some sweeping romance. At fifteen, he'd already had a life separate from our village, a life of organizing and combat training and falling in love with Chaya Salavsky, whom he called the most brilliant thinker from his youth group and promised to reunite with one day in Palestine, where she'd gone with his two younger brothers and most of their brigade. After the war, he said, he'd join his brothers on the collective they'd started, and every day he'd swim in the sea and eat grapefruits and lemons that grew wild from trees. You can come with me, he'd say, always an afterthought. But during those talks I'd be lying quietly beneath the blanket, trying to convince myself that if anyone in a uniform factory was going to stay alive, it was tailors like my parents. I'd heard reports on the radio that the soldiers were finding themselves ill equipped for the Russians, and since winter was coming, they'd put more people to work sewing uniforms and fixing weapons and equipment. I held on to the belief that my parents were safe for as long as I could—it would be another eight months until I knew for sure they were not.

When your grandfather wasn't talking about Palestine, he was talking about the war. The rules were changing every day, he said—soldiers patrolling nearby villages in grimy work clothes, passing as farmers; military planes flying so low we'd hear their engines rumbling. And the day before, Isaac had been on watch when he found a teenage boy wandering the woods, claiming he was looking for blackberries, when anyone from the area knew they weren't growing so late in the year. It was halfway through November—I'd been in the forest two months by then. Your grandfather felt it was time to move, to scout another location in the woods to set up camp, but first he wanted to plan one more mission, and he wanted me to come. With my light hair and green eyes I could easily pass as a gentile—and anyway, your grandfather said, who would expect a girl so young?

I didn't want to go. In those two months I'd found a routine that made me feel almost safe: cleaning barrels and collecting spent shells from the forest floor, going to target practice after helping the other girls clean up dinner, or working with Yussel in the infirmary, where he was always concocting a new treatment out of herbs and pig fat and other loot the fighters brought back. But the forest had become home to me, the brigade a kind of family, and—I know this will make you uncomfortable, so I'll say it very quickly—in many ways your grandfather was beginning to feel more and more like an older brother than a boyfriend, even those nights together in the tent. I think that, at thirteen, I still needed to be taken care of, to have a hand guiding me through the forest, and if your grandfather felt I was ready for a mission, I believed him. So I sat and listened the following night as he and Isaac strung together the plan in the dugout beside the kitchen, where they always held their meetings.

The train, your grandfather told me, would carry sixty-four soldiers and two cars' worth of supplies. At nine fifteen the following night, it would stop in Haradziec, where I'd have already laid out explosives.

It's a stupid idea, Isaac said, crouching low in the dugout—I was the only one short enough to stand up straight under the ceiling of blankets. Maybe she'll go unnoticed, he said, but she'll slow us down.

Secretly I agreed with Isaac, but your grandfather ignored him. He had a way of dismissing people without starting an argument simply by pretending he hadn't heard them to begin with. It's a trait I now can't stand (sometimes I feel like he's walking around the apartment wearing earplugs), but on that night I admired it, watching him roll out a map on the dirt floor, the yellow light of the lantern flickering across his face, which was getting thinner every day. It was an old map, one I remembered from school, from when my village was still part of Belarus. Right then I didn't know what was what. I stared at the names of towns, trying to will them to memory as your grandfather dragged a finger along our route.

We won't have to worry about snakes in this weather, but watch for bears, he said, passing out pistols and bullets to Isaac and me.

I'd never pointed a gun at anyone. I'd held plenty—in the armory workshop and at target practice. Back home my father had a rifle above the fireplace, but I'd never seen him load it. I touched the slide of this one now, feeling my way to the trigger.

A pistol's entirely different, Isaac said, and I sensed he was right: I'd been using shotguns during practice, but these would be easier to hide. You know how to push your weight against a shotgun, remember? he continued. With this, it'll be twice as hard to have the same accuracy.

I wrapped my hands around the grip. Even before Isaac could criticize me, I knew my stance was wrong. My shoulders were hunched, my arms stiff. I hated the way your grandfather looked at me then, as if he suddenly recognized every risk in bringing me and was embarrassed for thinking up the plan at all.

But he just sat beside me and said, Push the magazine all the way up until you hear a click, then pull back the slide to chamber a round—that's the only way to know it's loaded for sure. You probably won't need it anyway since you'll be with us. And remember that if you *do* hear something, don't shoot. It might just be an animal.

I nodded. I knew the rules. They'd been hammered into me since my first day there, your grandfather reciting them around the campfire every night: Don't get cocky with your weapon. Remember what happened to three of our fighters who were loud and overconfident on a raid and were gunned down from a window (their stupidity was already forest legend by the time I'd arrived). If you kill an animal, make sure the carcass doesn't drip blood as you carry it back to camp. Don't forget that many of the

242 / MOLLY ANTOPOL

peasants in the surrounding villages are good people, suffering as well, some even risking their own safety to protect us. If you have to rob them, take only what you absolutely need. These rules were important to your grandfather. To Isaac and some of the others, not so much, though they always did what he said.

I didn't know if Isaac had always been gruff or if the war had made him that way. I knew he'd seen things I hadn't, that when he'd heard soldiers coming into his village, he'd been quick to scramble behind a barn and from there had submerged himself in a pond to hide, and that when he crawled out hours later, he found himself completely alone. It was like Isaac was running on adrenaline to stay alive, whereas with your grandfather it was something different. Even that night in the dugout, I knew he was considering morals only partly out of decency—in his heart of hearts he saw himself as a boy with a legacy. A boy who, after the war was over, would be written about in textbooks, talked about in reverent tones: Leon Moscowitz, whose rebel army not only changed the course of the war but did so ethically.

I had never met a person so aware of his own voice, carefully stringing together sentences with the hope they would be quoted later, even as he told me to cup my hands as he passed out explosives. First a grenade, then six long sticks of dynamite.

This part's easy, your grandfather said. Lay the sticks flat on the tracks.

And then what? I said.

For God's sake, Isaac said.

Just before the train comes, your grandfather said calmly, hold the spoon of the grenade down with your thumb. Then twist off the pin with your other hand, and the moment you throw it, start sprinting toward the woods.

This is ridiculous, Isaac said. She'll get us killed. Why not stay back in the armory?

Your grandfather stood up, as if secretly grateful Isaac was running his mouth so he had a reason to lecture. Just this week a statement went out all over the country, he said, offering farmers

two sacks of grain for every one of us killed. Do you think anyone else is wasting their time with these concerns, pondering the
differences between kids and teenagers, boys and girls? His eyes
flicked around the dugout as though his audience was much bigger than Isaac and me.

Then he turned to me. If anyone stops you, he said, you have
to remember, even if you're terrified, to keep the Yiddish out of
your accent. Okay?

Okay, I said.

You could be a Dina, he said then, looking at me.

Or maybe Henia, Isaac said. Henia from the North, visiting
her family?

He handed me a stack of clothes, all from a previous raid.
Folded on top was a knit brown hat, which I slipped over my
head. Your grandfather pushed it back, scrutinized my face, and
said, There. Already she looks like a different girl.

Yeah? I said, fingering the hat. What about Sonya? Sonya Gor-
ski, I said, sounding it out, almost beginning to enjoy our game.
It was like the dress-up I used to play back home, my best friend,
Blanka, and me playing around in my parents' tailor shop, darting between the tall spools of fabric and draping the scraps around
each other, pretending we were classy society ladies, dressing for
the opera where our handsome, imaginary boyfriends would be
waiting outside on the marble steps in suits.

The following day I got ready for Haradziec. A gray wool dress
and coat, leather boots, and thick brown stockings. The boots
were too large but everything else fit so snugly it was as if I'd
picked out the clothes myself. In my pocketbook were my pistol
and a case of bullets. I clutched it under an arm as I followed
your grandfather and Isaac down the dark path. These woods
I knew—it was where we foraged for shells and mushrooms.
We were quiet walking through, your grandfather brushing the
ground with a stick to cover every footprint. Then Isaac called
out to me, If the police stop you while you're casing the station—

I'm Henia Sawicki. Staying with my grandparents nearby.

And if they ask what you're doing on the tracks?

Looking for my ring. It slipped off somewhere.

These lies, I knew, were the easy part. But really, the entire plan was simple. We'd walk along the edge of the forest—far enough in the woods to go unnoticed, close enough to glimpse the villages through the trees. In Haradziec, I'd slip out and cross the tracks, set the explosives down, run back into the forest. Your grandfather had made it sound so effortless in the dugout, but here I worried about keeping it straight in my mind. If one wary soldier saw through my lie, that was it—I'd be shot, your grandfather and Isaac probably next, or maybe tortured until they led the soldiers to the brigade. So I was trying to remember the plan—Henia, the ring, the grandmother—while clonking along in my too-big boots, and that was when I tripped on a rock and fell to the ground, twisting my ankle so hard I couldn't stand up. There I was, splayed in the dirt with my ankle throbbing, and even before your grandfather helped me to my feet, Isaac was already moaning about how he knew something like this would happen.

Twenty minutes out, he said, and your grandfather snapped, Tell me, Isaac, one of us couldn't have fallen?

Before your grandfather could hoist himself back onto his soapbox, I started hobbling along the route, and all they could do was follow.

Don't be stupid, Isaac called.

He's right, your grandfather said, catching up with me.

I was suddenly so angry—with your grandfather for always acting like he knew what was best, with Isaac for being so hard on me, with myself for botching the attack. For the first time since the sewers, I felt utterly hopeless and alone. I had no idea what to do, or who to ask what to do, because—and this was the first time it really became clear to me—I had no one left. The only people I had in the world were these two boys I barely knew at all, who looked so unbelievably confused right then, walking in their oversized coats, Isaac breathless and jittery, your grandfather's cap falling over his eyes. Up ahead, through a gap in the trees, I saw brown fields, the jagged steeple of a church. I kept limping down the path, and when a village came into view, I slipped out of the forest. We were still two hours from Haradziec. My ankle was swelling, my clothes covered in dirt. I pushed through town, not even sure what I was looking for. The streets were empty and so eerily quiet it was as if something terrible had happened the second before we'd arrived.

Your grandfather and Isaac hurried behind me, whispering to get back in the forest. But I kept on, and that was when I realized this was the town I'd crawled into from the sewers. Huddled along the road were the same houses, the same barns and mill and school, only now the buildings were deserted and destroyed: broken windows, piles of bricks, rats darting up stairways leading nowhere. The war, it seemed, had finally arrived here. A few cottages were still smoldering. A man, hard-faced and dirty, dragged a skinny horse past without even looking up. This time, I knew, I was no more shit-stained than anybody else.

Along the strip of shops was a bakery. The door was open, and when I walked inside, I saw the glass cases were smashed, the shelves bare, only half the tables standing. But as I kept on, through the kitchen and up the stairs, I saw shadows flash beneath a door. I pulled out my gun, pushed the door open with my shoulder, and strolled inside.

The room was small enough to take in all at once: just two wooden chairs facing the fireplace with a bed and dresser in the corner, a stove, sink, and table against the wall. A mother washed dishes. She had a cinched little mouth like a balloon knot and dark hair twisted tight at her neck. A boy, eight or nine, bent over homework at the wooden table. The mother glanced at me and at my gun, and put down the pot she was drying. The boy stared. My hands wobbled as I aimed at them.

I need something to wrap up my ankle, I told the mother. It

was the first time I'd spoken, and my words sounded loose and heavy in the silent room. And boots and a coat and your warmest hat and scarf. And gloves, I added greedily as she sifted through drawers.

She handed over the clothes, and I peeled off my dirty ones. I didn't even have my tights off when the mother yanked the boy's head toward her chest, and it took me a second to realize I'd gotten so used to bathing around everyone in the forest that it hadn't seemed strange to strip down in front of this family.

Henia, Isaac hissed from the doorway, where he and your grandfather were standing. Let's go.

But I couldn't, not yet. As I sat at the table and tied a clean sock around my ankle, bruised and puffy but possibly only sprained, I looked at the math problems the boy had printed out neatly on lined white paper and imagined, for just a second, what it would be like to have homework again. Not that I'd even liked math—it had been my worst subject, the one my father had to spend close to an hour correcting every evening. But to be at a table again with my mother, to have class work and meals and chores—I had wished for my family every day in the forest, but never before had what I'd lost been flaunted so vividly in front of me. I was filled with a sudden rage at this boy. This kid who had so little, whose father could be dead or at war or just not around, whose school was certainly shut down, and whose mother was probably trying to keep up some semblance of routine by making him practice math in the middle of this chaos—at that moment I resented them both.

What was for dinner? I asked them.

Soup, the mother said.

What kind?

Potato.

Fill three bowls for me.

It's gone, the mother said. She held up the empty pot she'd just dried.

What *do* you have? I said.

She handed over a potato and three turnips.

I pocketed the food as I walked the length of the room, opening cupboards, rifling through drawers, feeling under sweaters and pants for a hidden stash of *something*.

I need your money, I said.

We don't have any, the mother said.

Why should I believe you? I opened their closet, overturned pillows, shook out blankets.

I promise you, the mother said, looking at me pleadingly. It was already stolen—everything was.

You'll be sorry, I said, if you don't give me your money. It took me two tries to pull back the slide, but it didn't matter, I realized, when I was the only one holding a weapon. I grabbed the boy, circled an arm around him, and pressed the gun to his cheek. He was shaking, and his fine brown hair was damp with sweat. He felt like such a *child* next to me, his skinny arms tight at his sides, his breath coming out in short, hot gasps.

The mother was blinking quickly, and she kept looking at her son, then back at me. A sound came out of the boy's throat, squeaky and remote, and I pressed the pistol more firmly against his skin. The mother closed her eyes. Then she crawled under the bed, ran her hand along the bottom of the mattress, and pulled out a thin stack of bills. It was a small amount, enough for maybe two weeks of food.

Give it to me, I said.

We'll starve, she said. Leave us something. Please.

Give it to me, I said again, and when she did, I let go of the boy. I waited for him to run to his mother's arms, but it was like his feet were nailed to the floor. The room was so quiet I could hear a horse's hooves clicking by outside. I walked backward with the pistol still cocked, out to the stairs, where Isaac and your grandfather were waiting.

They wouldn't talk to me as we made our way through the

bakery and out the door, where the cold air chilled me through my new coat. We were halfway down the road when your grandfather said, That family did nothing to you.

He grabbed my shoulders and shook me, like a box my voice might fall out of.

How could you take everything they had?

But I kept walking. I don't know how to explain it except that a haziness washed over me where I could hear his words but they suddenly meant nothing to me. I will always mark that as the moment I stopped listening to your grandfather, and also as the day Isaac started looking at me with a curious, cautious respect. We were back in town, the same route we took in, and as we passed that row of gutted shops, I caught my reflection in a broken window. There I was, thirteen years old and stumbling around in someone else's boots, looking more hideous than I could have imagined. I hadn't been in front of a mirror since back home with my parents, I realized, and in that time I had become an ugly girl. My hair was greasy and knotted and so beaten by the elements it had turned a shade lighter. Black circles rimmed my eyes, scabs dotted my chin and forehead and lips, my teeth had gone as rotten and brown as tree roots. In only a couple months I had become a medusa, a monster, a creature from the forests of a fairy tale.

I still see glimpses of that ugliness now. At the salon, when the hairdresser finishes my blowout and spins me around to face the mirror. Or sometimes on the subway, when the person across from me gets up, and I'm shocked to see that same terrifying beast staring back at me in the scratched, blurred glass.

But I want you to know it wasn't that way for everyone. Your grandfather did the same things, lost the same things, watched that same boy doing math at the table—and responded by patiently sitting with your mother the entire time she was growing up, helping her with algebra and history and even with spelling, though it pained him to sound out words in a language he barely knew. I'd watch the two of them hunched over her homework at the kitchen table and wish I was the kind of person who could be grateful I was still in the world to join them, rather than always standing a few feet from everybody else, slouched in a doorway.

Your grandfather, once the biggest loudmouth I knew, became a quiet, almost invisible man in America, stumbling over his English, bashful in public, shy to ask directions on the street after hearing some teenagers singsonging his accent. He was rejected for every job he tried to get—an immigrant without even a junior high school education. I was the one who found work first—in a clothing factory, if you can believe it, back in a hot room sewing in seams and zippers. Your grandfather was humiliated that he could provide for the brigade but not for his own family, humiliated when he finally *did* find a job, making deliveries for a beer distributor, just another tired man dozing on his subway ride to work.

Still, he found small parts of his life to genuinely appreciate: growing tomatoes on the patio, listening to the radio after dinner, taking the train to the city on weekends. And yet none of those things I could ever teach myself to love. Your mother and I may not have the easiest time together, but I'll admit when she's right. And though it pains me to say it, she told me something once that I know is true: I never stopped thinking people wanted to hurt me, even when they no longer did, and that rage would rumble through me during even the nicest times: Walking in the park with your grandfather on the first real day of spring, eating at a good restaurant on our honeymoon in Atlantic City. On vacation in Israel, almost forty years ago, when we could finally afford to go. Finally your mother met that side of her family, finally your grandfather visited his parents' graves, finally he saw his brothers, middle-aged by then, with wives and children and grandchildren. I remember sitting in your great-uncle Natan's backyard in Ramat Gan, drinking orange soda and eating cashews, and right away your grandfather started asking about Chaya Salavsky.

I hadn't heard his voice climb so high since his speeches in the dugout. Did they still see her, what was she up to? He assumed after all these years she'd married?

His mouth quivered on that last word, and when his brother said she'd died a couple years ago, rather than taking my husband's hand and murmuring condolences while he blinked back tears, I started chewing on my lip the way I always did before saying something risky.

How dare you ask about her with me right beside you! I yelled, in front of all my new in-laws, in the backyard surrounded by the grapefruit and lemon trees your grandfather had dreamed about for so long. Get over yourself, I continued, though I wasn't actually angry, or jealous of a dead woman I'd never met, a woman he hadn't seen since he was a boy. I was simply filled with an urge to fight, so electric and immediate I felt my face flush. So I carried on, even as your grandfather cleared his throat and looked at his shoes and rattled the ice in his empty glass.

And no, I won't tell you the rest. You can guess. You can go to the library and read about the sixty-four soldiers killed that night in Haradziec, in a train explosion engineered by an unknown anarchist group. You can waste full days in the research room, ruining your eyes scrolling through microfilm. You can read about the attacks that followed—eight more before the war ended—about how your grandfather and I missed the quota to Palestine and were loaded instead on a boat to the States, not an option either of us had ever considered. The place didn't feel real even as we docked at the immigration port and saw Manhattan glittering in front of us. You can even find stories about Isaac, killed a year after we left for New York when his homemade bomb went off prematurely, still on his way to some unknown mission—one of those kids who couldn't imagine living anywhere but Europe even once we were allowed to leave. Maybe because he was addicted to the fighting, maybe because he could finally go home but no one was there. Search for his story in the library—for that and everything else. But you won't learn what happened to that mother and son I robbed, because believe me, I've looked and looked and there's just no way to find out whether those people survived the coldest year of their lives.

I don't understand you. All your life you've been like this, pulling someone into a corner at every family party, asking so many questions it's no wonder you've always had a difficult time making friends. It's a beautiful day. Your grandfather's on the patio grilling hamburgers, your mother's new boyfriend is already loud off beer, she's hooked up the speakers and is playing her terrible records. Why don't you go out in the sun and enjoy yourself for once, rather than sitting inside, scratching at ugly things that have nothing to do with you? These horrible things that happened before you were born.

Lynne Sharon Schwartz

The Golden Rule

IT STARTED INNOCENTLY ENOUGH. Could Amanda pick up a few groceries—it was raining so hard. Mail a letter (addressed in such light pencil that Amanda doubted it would ever arrive)? Program Maria's new alarm clock—digital, baffling—for the hours of her medication? Amanda thought nothing of it. It was the sort of thing you do for a frail old neighbor. They lived on the same floor of a solid downtown building where Maria, it seemed, had occupied her apartment since the dawn of time. The other neighbors were newer, young families, everyone running off to work and school, the building left to nannies and maids. How could she refuse?

Over the last month or two, though, the phone calls had become more frequent, their tone more pressing. Would Amanda fetch a prescription at the drugstore, have something copied at the local shop? In mid-October, Maria opened her door as Amanda was coming in—she'd taken a rare half-day off to do some shopping—and handed her a set of keys to her apartment. Just in case, she said, her voice obsequious, petulant. "And do you have a minute to come in and call the doctor for me? I can't cope with his new phone system, pressing all those buttons, and in the end you don't even get a real person."

"Sure, I'll just get rid of these packages and be right back."

When Amanda and Jack moved in twenty years ago, Maria had been the age Amanda was now, and quite able to manage her own errands as well as attend the nearby church most mornings. Even then she was tiny, birdlike, a bird without feathers or song, who spoke in whispers as if she feared eavesdroppers. She had an unlisted phone number, she'd told Amanda, in a tone that suggested lurking menace. She always wore a navy-blue kerchief tied under her chin—Amanda would rather have died than be seen in such a thing—and white Peter Pan–collared blouses, dark skirts and stockings, oxford shoes. Slacks, never, even in the coldest weather. Over the years her costume had remained the same, but her voice had grown weaker, though no less tinged with complaint.

Amanda had never been in Maria's apartment before. Its gloom was startling: moss-colored drapes on the windows, massive dark furniture, and a stale, sequestered smell, reminding her of grottos she'd visited in Italy long ago. Bits of paper littered the dining room table, jotted notes in a prim, upright handwriting, like a convent schoolgirl's. The doctor's phone number, when Maria finally located the scrap of paper, was written in that maddening number four pencil, so faint that Amanda had to read it under one of the fringed lamps.

Returning home was like coming out of an afternoon movie to the stun of brightness. Amanda's own apartment was splashed with color, open to the light. After Jack's death five years ago, she had immersed herself in redecorating projects. She'd also made sure to keep her clothes in order, get her hair cut regularly, not let things go. It had been disheartening, at first, to look at her face in the mirror: It wasn't so much the minuscule lines or the no-longer-glowing skin—she was familiar with the concoctions to remedy those. It was the somber resignation in the eyes, the slackening of the profile, the downward slant of the mouth that suggested disappointment and an unappealing severity. She felt herself in a permanent battle with time and nature, and though in the end she would lose, as everyone does, she resolved to fight valiantly to the death. She had the means and the will.

Several weeks later Maria called at six in the morning to say she had terrible pains in her stomach.

Ben, who'd slept over because of a thunderstorm, rolled over and grunted irritably, so Amanda took the phone into the living room. "Did you call the doctor?"

"It's too early. They're not in yet. Anyway, he's out of town and I don't like the substitutes."

"But even so . . . Do you want me to call?"

"No, I told you." Maria's voice was becoming a whimper. "I didn't get any sleep all night, the pain was so bad."

The emergency room, Amanda declared. She'd get dressed and take her.

"No, no emergency room. They make you wait for hours, and you have to sit with all kinds of people."

"I'll call an ambulance, then. They'll take you right away." This she knew from Jack's heart attack. Arrive in an ambulance and you get first-class treatment.

No, those doctors were just students. She didn't trust them. And no, she didn't want Amanda to come over.

"Well, I don't know what else I can do." She struggled to keep her voice even, her impatience in check. "I'll phone you later from work. If it gets any worse, call 911."

"Her again?" Ben muttered, throwing an arm over Amanda. And after she explained, "So if she won't let you help, then why'd she call?"

"Not to be alone with it, I guess." She knew what that felt like. She'd often been tempted to call friends at the slightest change in Jack's condition, simply not to bear the information alone, as if she were in a narrow space with a large package and needed help carrying it—not that it was so heavy, only very hard to maneuver.

She'd given in to the urge, though it hadn't helped much. Her daughter, Jessica, had phoned daily—she was in Spain then, with a new baby. She'd flown back in time for the funeral. "Tell her you can't be her personal assistant—you have a business to run." He couldn't see why Amanda capitulated: She should do what was convenient and refuse the rest. Ben, a vigorous sixty-eight, was ten years older than Amanda and prided himself on not being "needy"—he liked to show he was up on current buzzwords. Of course he wasn't needy, Amanda thought: He had a housekeeper and a secretary. But she knew better than to say that. He was easy and compliant. Best of all, he was firmly settled in his own place uptown and busy with his accounting practice, leaving her free to spend long hours at the shop. Jack, whom she had loved to distraction, hadn't been easy in any way, especially near the end. But he'd never talked smugly about neediness. He would have understood why she gave in to Maria, would even have been amused. Always into self-improvement, he used to tease. Is that so bad? she asked. Not bad, he said, just a whole lot of work. He would have understood Maria's strategy, too: the cunning tyranny of the weak. And grasped that in Amanda, so clearly strong—large, firm-voiced, competent, occupying space with the authority of ownership—Maria had found the perfect foil.

"She probably just has gas pains," Ben said, and rolled over. Was that what he'd say if she woke up one morning in agony? Kindness, Amanda thought, but didn't care to explain to him at six fifteen in the morning, shouldn't depend on convenience, or even affection. If it did, it couldn't be called kindness. She was following the Golden Rule, after all, doing unto others . . .

Did Maria follow the Golden Rule? Not very likely. She was mean-spirited, bigoted. She whispered carping comments about the neighbors, and the things she said about their West Indian cleaning women made Amanda shudder. Everything about her was scant and pinched, plus she hardly ate—a refusal of life that irked Amanda—and her clothes were dreadful, though this,

Amanda knew, was hardly relevant; she noted it in her inventory only because she thought about clothes all the time—she owned a selective upscale boutique and chose every item herself.

Of course none of this should matter. Charity need not be deserved, nor should it be offered grudgingly, in bad faith. Her objections, Amanda knew, were more than uncharitable. They were suspect, rising as they did from the pit of her own dread.

She couldn't sleep anymore—the call had left her jittery. She moved closer to Ben and asked, "Do you still think I'm beautiful? Or am I becoming an old lady?"

"Of course you're beautiful. Why do you even ask?"

"It's good to hear it once in a while."

"You're beautiful. This part is beautiful, and this, and this." At first he sounded tired, mechanical, but as he went on his voice gathered enthusiasm. He moved his hands down her body, enu-merating, making it a game. "I can't get anywhere below the knee from this position, and I'm too comfortable to move."

"Never mind. That's enough."

"You know what's especially beautiful?"

"What?"

"Here. The hipbone. I like the way it pokes out."

"Don't talk about bones, please."

"Well, I like what's around them. Your wrists are very nice too. And your hands. The fingers are really long. Look, I'll show you what they can do."

Was this, what he wanted of her now, also a species of kind-ness? She had brought it on herself, asking if she was beautiful. She'd never asked before and now wished she hadn't; beautiful or not, she was tired.

Afterward, she lay in his arms and ran through the teenagers in the building, the ones Maria found so offensive, their scant mumbled greetings, their boisterous ways, their door slamming. Which ones would she be calling someday, asking them to pick up a quart of low-fat milk and a loaf of bread?

No, what was she thinking? When that day came, twenty

years from now—if she was lucky—those teenagers would be off on their own. It was their parents she should be considering. They'd be just the right age by then—past full-time parenthood, old enough to have subsided into compassion, yet still competent. Maybe she should start cultivating them now. Who else would there be? Jessica would be full of concern, but would she fly in from halfway across the globe to tend to her? Right now she was in Prague. Her husband was in the diplomatic corps; she'd always be far away. When they spoke once a week, the old closeness returned—a sheltering warmth of knowing and being known, a loosening of every taut cell—but when Amanda put the phone down, the warmth dissipated as if she'd shed a fur coat.

As for Ben, most likely any helping would be the other way around. That was the price for having a lover at her age: Eventually the woman had to manage the decline. She'd thought of it when they first met two years ago and fell immediately into bed. Did she really want to risk going through all that again? Yes. So far she didn't regret her decision, even though bed was not quite what it had been at the start. A man a decade younger rather than older would be preferable, but that opportunity came up very rarely.

The shop was bustling that day. There was a convention of psychotherapists in a nearby hotel and the women came in groups, chattering, going through the racks and taking turns in the dressing rooms. Her two assistants were overwhelmed, and Amanda had to help at the register. The neighborhood was buzzing with the rumor that the landlord was planning to raise the rent: It was only a matter of time before the independent shops would be forced out. This Amanda refused to think about. She telephoned Maria the first chance she got. No change. The pains were still terrible.

"You must call the doctor immediately."

As soon as Amanda got home, the phone rang. Maria must

have watched from the peephole or listened for her key in the door.

"The doctor said I have to call an ambulance and go to the hospital as soon as I can."

"So? It's nearly eight o'clock. What are you waiting for?"

"I have to have my dinner first."

"Dinner? With all that pain?"

"I can't go on an empty stomach."

"I'm coming over in half an hour to call the ambulance. Be ready."

Several of the teenagers were standing outside the building as she saw Maria into the ambulance. They nodded and looked appropriately sober; one boy offered to help Amanda with Maria's overnight bag, which was hardly necessary. They probably thought she and Maria were of the same generation—to teenagers everyone over forty looks alike.

Maria had emergency surgery to remove her appendix. Amanda veered between sympathy and rage. If the appendix had burst and been fatal, she would have been the one to find the body when she went in to check. A vague guilt, barely averted this time, hovered nearby.

She visited the hospital every few days on the way home from work, summoning the required good cheer. It was like putting on an old dress she'd never much liked but was right for certain occasions—a funeral dress, a job interview dress. Hospital visits to Jack had been easier after he lost consciousness—at least she didn't have to pretend optimism. Maria's progress was slow, the nurses said, not because of the operation, which was successful, but because she wouldn't eat. She sat in a wheelchair and whined about the poor food. She was down to eighty-five pounds, she told Amanda with a perverse pride.

Fortunately there was a social worker in charge now. This was Amanda's busiest time. Christmas wasn't far off: The gift items had to be displayed, and meanwhile she had to go around looking at the designers' spring fashions. She needed to do some shopping for herself as well. It wouldn't do to appear shabby—not that she ever approached shabbiness, but her standards were high.

Nevertheless, when Maria told the social worker that the one thing she enjoyed eating was soup, Amanda made a vegetable soup to welcome her home. The next day Maria reported the soup was "too much," so she'd put it in the freezer. Amanda seethed. What did too much mean, anyway? Quantity? She needn't eat it all at once. Too thick? Add water. She was sorry now that she hadn't kept any for herself.

Fine, she thought, once you finish starving yourself to death I'll defrost it and have a memorial meal.

December was unusually dark and bleak. The first ring of the phone didn't quite wake her but transformed into a dream: Jack was calling from the hospital, his voice surprisingly strong and deep, as it was when they first met. He asked her to bring him a book about World War II that he'd been reading before his heart attack and wanted to finish before he died. She tried to remember where in the apartment she'd last seen the book: in the freezer, it seemed, but that didn't make any sense. The phone kept ringing, the dream slid away, and Amanda leaped up, thinking how odd it was that anyone, especially Jack, should want to die with war on his mind. Her hand on the receiver was shaking—she half-expected to hear his voice when she picked up. Instead it was the familiar plaintive whisper.

"I'm sorry to call so early but could you come over right away?"

"Maria? What's wrong? Are you sick?"

"No. I can't tell you over the phone. Could you just come over?"

Her whisper was like the rustle of a mouse. Amanda had to strain to hear. "Do you realize what time it is?" She glanced at the clock. "Five fifty-four. Isn't the aide with you?" Since the surgery, there were aides around the clock.

"She's sleeping. If you could just please come over? And close your door very quietly."

Amanda put on a robe, drank a glass of water, and smoothed down her hair, glancing in the mirror as if something might have changed while she slept. But there was that face again, the face she couldn't believe was her own: tense and ashy without makeup, ringed by hair that was lusterless and awry, a face that warned of things to come. She grabbed her keys, and, like a helpless child seeking small ways to show power, didn't close the door quietly as instructed.

Maria's door opened a crack and she motioned Amanda to sidle around the edge. The dim hall smelled like old cooking—dark root vegetables, eggplants, turnips, squash. In the wan light, Maria's bony face was gray-green, the hollows in her cheeks tinged beige. Besides the kerchief tied under her chin, she wore a short filmy garment that reminded Amanda of Indian holy men with their begging bowls. She had on the black oxford shoes and white stockings, dotted with holes, that went from her ankles to her knees like dancers' leg warmers; between the stockings and the nightgown was a bare strip of desiccated bluish thigh. Her legs were so narrow that Amanda could have ringed them with her hands. She tried not to stare.

The aides couldn't be trusted, Maria whispered. Things were missing.

"What things?"

"Things. I want you to take something for safekeeping. Come." She shuffled into a small room crammed with ancient furniture and pointed to a two-foot-long metal box on the floor, labeled with her name. "This is my good silver and some other things. I want you to hold it for me."

"Oh, come on. No one's going to make off with that. It must be heavy." She lifted it; it was very heavy. At this hour, for this absurd caprice, patience deserted her. "I was sleeping. Did you really have to wake me for this?" The call from the hospital when Jack died had come at 4:17—she remembered the green numbers on the clock. That was in June, the sky already lightening, and she wasn't sleeping well anyway.

"I'm sorry," said Maria. "Don't talk so loud. Will you take it, please?"

"Maria." Ridiculous, this whispering in the dark like conspirators. "You know I'd help you with anything reasonable, but this—this is . . ."

"Will you take it?" she pleaded.

"All right. But if you keep thinking this way, next thing you'll be accusing me of stealing it. Have you been eating?"

"I'm okay," Maria murmured. "Just a little weak."

"From now on, don't call at this hour unless it's an emergency." Amanda lugged the box across the hall and stowed it under the bed in Jessica's old room. She didn't want it in sight, reminding her of that cringing imperiousness, those dreadful stockings, the Tinkertoy legs, the whining voice. This must not continue, she thought, as she climbed back into bed, her insides trembling. Later she'd call the social worker and tell her about the growing paranoia.

But she never did manage to call. The day turned out hectic. An order of cashmere scarves was delayed, one of the assistants was out sick, and a longtime customer made a fuss about returning a suede coat that had obviously been worn. The rumors about the landlord continued, becoming more credible. Just when Amanda thought she might catch her breath, a new customer entered, young, impeccably turned out, flaunting her beauty, and so much like Jessica—the glossy chestnut hair with its nonchalant swing, the broad shoulders and narrow hips and small breasts—that for a mad instant Amanda thought she'd come on a surprise visit and almost dashed over to embrace her. Luckily she caught herself in time. The young woman's fingers flicked swiftly through the clothes on the rack as she frowned in concentration. Clarissa, one of the assistants, greeted her and began the usual routine. Instead of working at her desk in back as usual, Amanda lingered nearby until the woman went into the dressing room with three suits. Later she asked Clarissa if she'd bought anything. No. "I don't think she was really serious. Probably just passing the time before a lunch date." Amanda was so rattled that she had to do the accounts over again; she'd forgotten to save her work on the computer.

She didn't get home till almost nine. The janitor was polishing the brass in the lobby.

"She's gone, your neighbor," he said in greeting. At her puzzled look, he added, "The skinny lady opposite you? An ambulance came at five. Big scene. That's why I'm so late doing this."

"Gone? You mean back to the hospital?"

"Gone like dead."

Amanda's heart thumped, and then came a small ping of relief: Thank goodness she hadn't had to deal with it.

"She looked dead already when they loaded her on. Can't nobody live, that thin. I knew when I saw her after the operation. It was only a matter of time."

Isn't it always? she thought. "She's been here for ages, hasn't she?"

"Fifty years. Longest tenant in the building. The super next door, Freddy? He remembers her husband."

"She had a husband?" This was incredible. What could he have been like? Cringing and fearful like her? Or overbearing, a hawk to her sparrow? Immediately she envisioned sex: not possible. Maria being caressed, penetrated? Maria under a man, or sitting on top, bouncing up and down? The chirping sounds she'd manage to squeeze out? The vision was grotesque.

"Yeah, he died maybe thirty years ago," Freddy said. "In a wheelchair by the end. She must've lost her will after that. You need will to go on in this life."

She preferred the super's bluntness to the professional tones of the nurse who'd called about Jack: "We're terribly sorry to tell you Mr. Green has passed on." She could still hear the creamy voice. Four seventeen, a promising June day.

No more crack-of-dawn phone calls. Well, she would hardly

miss those. In fact she wouldn't miss anything about Maria, not even the chance to exercise her own virtue.

And yet Maria would not be quite gone. There was still the box. Upstairs, Amanda dragged it out from under Jessica's bed. The label was written in a spotty ballpoint pen, a marginal improvement on the number four pencils. She had no desire to open it, no curiosity, only distaste. Probably she wasn't supposed to open it. There must be a lawyer involved, maybe a distant heir. There'd been a husband; could there be children, grandchildren? Maria had never mentioned any family and seemed never to have visitors. What was it like to pass through life leaving no one, nothing? Would anyone turn up to arrange a funeral service? Someone from the church, maybe. Maria had managed to get there now and then until her appendicitis.

The box could wait. She shoved it back out of sight, then lay down on Jessica's bed as if she too were waiting. Shouldn't she be feeling something? Her own callousness distressed her. She hadn't always been this way. When had she changed? In an effort to induce a respectable response, to pierce the numbness surrounding her like a bubble, she tried to picture Maria's last hours, alone except for the aide she distrusted. Pain, maybe. Fear, certainly. She was sorry Maria had had to endure them. But it was a generic sorrow, what she might feel for any living creature. There was nothing that reached inside the bubble, no grief, no loss. Perhaps Maria had drifted off in her sleep. Or had she reached for the phone to call Amanda? She checked the machine again: no messages.

It was useless trying to conjure emotion out of nothing; she need not add hypocrisy to detachment. She changed into a pair of sweatpants, turned on the TV in the kitchen to catch the news, and got busy making a salad.

Two days later, at the shop, she got a call from a lawyer who informed her that she was the heir to the contents of Maria's apartment.

"I assure you, you're the designated heir. It's in the will."

"The will? But what am I supposed to do with all that stuff? I mean, I don't know what to say. I had no idea she planned to . . ."

"There are places that deal with unwanted items. Auctions, that sort of thing. I can send you some information when I send a messenger with the keys."

"I have her keys. She gave them to me weeks ago."

"I still have to give you the set of keys in my possession."

She told the lawyer about the box. "What am I supposed to do with it? Silver, I think she said. There must be someone . . ."

"There's no one else mentioned in the will. I'm afraid everything she had is now yours." He had a rueful, ironic tone that appealed to her. He understood—he must have known Maria. She wondered what he was like, how old he was.

"What about . . . will there be a funeral?" Surely this could not fall to her too.

He seemed to read her mind. "Yes, not to worry. The church is handling that."

The conversation was over before she could learn anything about him. They arranged for the messenger and he gave her his phone number in case she had any questions.

Now she could repossess her rejected soup. Ben would enjoy it. But at the thought of the soup a wave of nausea skimmed through her. She wouldn't go so far as to think Maria poisoned it—though the notion did flash by—but she imagined the soup might have soured simply by languishing in the freezer of that unwholesome apartment.

The next day she opened the box. She found an excellent set of silver, service for eight, in an austere, old-fashioned pattern; it needed a good scrubbing and a dose of silver polish. Wrapped in a bit of flannel were a strand of pearls, a plain gold bracelet, and two pairs of earrings, small glittering studs. They looked like costume jewelry, but she would have them appraised, to be sure. If they turned out to be worth anything, she'd give the money away; she did not wish to profit from her inheritance. She didn't deserve to profit, because there had been no love. Only kindness. No, even less, acquiescence. She rather liked the silver, but would not use it. It felt . . . tainted. The word that sprang to mind surprised her. Tainted by what? By solitude, by isolation, and those would not wash off.

She delayed entering the apartment for several days, dreading her task. At last, on a Sunday morning, she unlocked the door and turned on every light. She ripped the drapes from the windows and they settled on the floor in a cloud of dust. Daylight came oozing in, strained by the film of dust coating the windows. She was overcome with desolation. Why had all of this been given to her? Possessing it seemed to taint her with dust as well, with a musty odor of loneliness and decline. It was given to her because there was no one else. Because Maria had appreciated her help. Or perhaps the opposite: a slap in the face, paying back the false kindness in kind. Or was there an even more subtle motive for the bequest, an ironic, taunting message: You too, someday . . .

Whatever the motive, Amanda resolved to do the minimum— the dead don't need kindness. Any papers that looked important, she'd give to the lawyer, then call one of the places he'd suggested and have it carted away. She could pay the janitor to empty the refrigerator. It was the landlord's job to have the place cleaned for the next tenant. Someone else in her position, she knew, might be eager to go through Maria's things, construct a plausible history or unearth surprising adventures, to understand how a person could come to such a solitary end. But she had no curiosity; she had had none before, and death had not altered her indifference. No matter what she might discover of Maria's past, it had evaporated. Now there was only emptiness.

She stood at the window looking out at the park across the street; the bare branches shook in the winter wind. She rubbed at a small area on the pane to see more clearly, but though her fingers got sticky with dust, the view stayed filmy: too much grime on the outside. Her own past—Jack, Jessica as a child, the beauty that had sustained her—felt like something she had once dreamed. She still had the shop—though maybe not for long if the rumors about the landlord were true—and she had Ben, yet they felt meager compared to what was gone. Insubstantial some-how, like polyester clothes.

One day Jessica would stand gazing out at the same trees, won-dering what to do with her mother's possessions. The clothes, the books, the furniture would seem a burden. Though maybe she'd want some of the clothes, all so finely made and carefully chosen. Jessica was more or less the same size, at least when Amanda last saw her. She might have gained weight with the second baby. Later she would phone Jessica. Maria's apartment was chilly; she needed to feel warmth. Love. Not so much Jessica's love—that was dependable, if distant—but her own. Love of the world. She needed her daughter's voice to rouse her into feeling.

Joan Silber

About My Aunt

THIS HAPPENS A LOT—people travel and they find places
they like so much they think they've risen to their best selves
just by being there. They feel distant from everyone at home who
can't begin to understand. If they're young, they take up with
beautiful locals of the opposite sex; they settle in; they get used to
how everything works; they make homes. But usually not forever.

I had an aunt who was such a person. She went to Istanbul
when she was in her twenties. She met a good-looking carpet
seller from Cappadocia. She'd been a classics major in college and
had many questions to ask him, many observations to offer. He
was a gentle and intelligent man who spent his days talking to
travelers. He'd come to think he no longer knew what to say to
Turkish girls, and he loved my aunt's airy conversation. When her
girlfriends went back to Greece, she stayed behind and moved in
with him. This was in 1970.

His shop was in Sultanahmet, a well-touristed part of the
city, and he lived in Fener, an old and jumbled neighborhood.
Kiki, my aunt, liked having people over, and their apartment
was always filled with men from her husband's region and expats
of various ages. She was happy to cook big semi-Turkish meals
and make up the couch for anyone passing through. She helped

out in the store, explained carpet motifs to anyone who walked in—those were stars for happiness, scorpion designs to keep real scorpions away. In her letters home, she sounded enormously pleased with herself—she dropped Turkish phrases into her sentences, reported days spent sipping *çay* and *kahve*. She sent home to Brooklyn a carpet she said was Kurdish.

Then Kiki's boyfriend's business took a turn for the worse. There was a flood in the basement of his store and a bill someone never paid and a new shop nearby that was getting all the business. Or something. The store had to close. Her family thought this meant that Kiki was coming home at last. But, no. Osman, her guy, had decided to move back to his village, to help his father, who raised pumpkins for their seed oil, as well as tomatoes, green squash, and eggplant. Kiki was up for the move; she wanted to see the real Turkey. Istanbul was really so Western now. Cappadocia was very ancient and she couldn't wait to see the volcanic rock. She was getting married! Her family in Brooklyn was surprised about that part. Were they invited to the wedding? Apparently not. In fact, it had probably happened already by the time they got the letter. "Wearing a beaded hat and a glitzy head scarf, the whole shebang," Kiki wrote. "I still can't believe it."

Neither could any of her relatives. But they sent presents, once they had an address. A microwave oven, a Mr. Coffee, an electric blanket for the cold mountains. They were a practical and liberal family; they wanted to be helpful. "I know it's hard for you to imagine," Kiki wrote, "but we do very well without electricity here. Every morning I make a wood fire in the stove. Very good-smelling smoke. I make a little fire in the bottom of the water heater too."

Kiki built fires? No one could imagine her as the pioneer wife. Her brother, Alan (who later became my father), was always hoping to visit. Kiki said not a word about making any visits home. No one nagged her; she'd been a touchy teenager, given to sullen outbursts, and everyone was afraid of that Kiki appearing again.

She stayed for eight years. Her letters said, "My husband

thinks I sew as well as his sisters" and "I'm rereading my copy of Ovid in Latin. It's not bad!" and "Winter sooo long this year, I hate it. Osman has already taught me all he knows about the stars." No one could make sense of who she was now. There were no children and no pregnancies that anyone heard about, and the family avoided asking.

Her brother was just about to finally get himself over for a visit when Kiki wrote to say, "Guess what? I'm coming back at last. For good." No, the husband was not coming with her. "My life here has reached its natural conclusion," Kiki wrote. "Osman will be my dear friend forever but we've come to the end of our road."

"So who ran around on who?" the relatives kept asking. "She'll never say, will she?"

Everybody wondered what she would look like when she returned. Would she be sun-dried and weather-beaten, would she wear billowing silk trousers like a belly dancer's, would the newer buildings of New York amaze her? None of the above. She looked like the same old Kiki, thirty-one with very good skin, and she was wearing jeans and a turtleneck, possibly the same ones she'd left home with.

Her luggage was a mess, woven plastic valises baled up with string, very third world, and there were a lot of them. She had brought back nine carpets! What was she thinking? She intended to sell them.

Her brother always remembered that when they ate their first meal together, Kiki held her knife and fork like a European. She laughed at things lightly, as if the absurdity of it all wasn't worth shrieking over. She teased Alan about his eyeglasses ("you look like a genius in them") and his large appetite ("has not changed since you were eight"). She certainly sounded like herself.

Before very long, she moved in with someone named Marcy she'd known at Brooklyn College. Marcy's mother bought the biggest of the rugs, and Kiki used the proceeds to rent a storefront in the East Village, where she displayed her carpets and other items she had brought back—a brass tea set and turquoise beads and cotton pants with tucked hems that she herself had once worn.

The store stayed afloat for a while. Her brother wondered if she was dealing drugs—hashish was all over Istanbul in the movie *Midnight Express*, which had come out just before her return. Kiki refused to see such a film, with its lurid scenes of mean Turkish prisons. "Who has *nice* prisons?" she said. "Name one single country in the world. Just one."

When her store began to fail and she had to give it up, Kiki supported herself by cleaning houses. She evidently did this with a good spirit; the family was much more embarrassed about it than she was. "People here don't know how to clean their houses," she would say. "It's sort of remarkable, isn't it?"

By the time I was a little kid, Kiki had become the assistant director of a small agency that booked housekeepers and nannies. She was the one you got on the phone, the one who didn't take any nonsense from clients or workers either. She was friendly but strict and kept people on point.

As a child I was a teeny bit afraid of her. She could be very withering if I was acting up and getting crazy and knocking over chairs. But when my parents took me to visit, Kiki had special cookies for me (I loved Mallomars) and for a while she had a boyfriend named Hernando who would play airplane with me and go buzzing around the room with me on his back. I loved visiting her.

My father told me later that Hernando had wanted to marry Kiki. "But she wasn't made for marriage," he said. "It's not all roses, you know." He and my mother had a history of having, as they say, their differences.

"Kiki was always like a bird," my father said. "Flying here and there." What a corny thing to say.

I grew up outside Boston, in a small suburban town whose leafy safety I spurned once I was old enough for hip disdain. I moved to New York as soon as I finished high school, which I barely did. My parents and I were not on good terms in my early years in the city, but Kiki made a point of keeping in touch. She'd call on the phone and say, "I'm thirsty, let's go have a drink. Okay?" At first I was up in Inwood, as far north in Manhattan as you can get, so it was a long subway ride to see her in the East Village, but once I moved to Harlem it wasn't quite so bad. When my son was born, four years ago, Kiki brought me the most useful baby stuff, things a person couldn't even know she needed. Oliver would calm down and sleep when she walked him around. He grew up calling her "Aunt Great Kiki."

The two of us lived in a housing project, but one of the nicer ones, in an apartment illegally passed on to me by an ex-boyfriend. It was a decent size, with good light, and I liked my neighbors. That fall the TV started telling us to get prepared for Hurricane Sandy, and Oliver had a great time flicking the flashlight on and off (a really annoying game) and watching me tape giant Xs on the window glass. All the kids on our floor were hyped up and excited, running around and shrieking. We kept looking out the windows as the sky turned a sepia tint. When the rains broke and began to come down hard, we could hear the moaning of the winds and things clattering and banging in the night, awnings and trees getting the hell beaten out of them. I kept switching to different channels on the TV so we wouldn't miss any of it. The television had better coverage than my view out the window. A newscaster in a suit told us the Con Ed transformer on Fourteenth Street had exploded! The lights in the bottom of Manhattan had gone out! I made efforts to explain electricity to Oliver, as if I knew. Never, never put your finger in a socket. Oliver wanted to watch a better program.

At nine thirty my father called to say, "Your aunt Kiki doesn't have power, you know. She's probably sitting in the dark." I had forgotten about her entirely. She was on East Fifth Street, in the no-electricity zone. I promised I'd check on Kiki in the morning.

"I might have to walk there," I said. "It's like a hundred and twenty blocks. You're not going to ask about my neighborhood? It's fine."

"Don't forget about her, okay? Promise me that."

"I just told you," I said.

The next day the weather was shockingly pleasant, mild, with a white sky. We walked for a half hour, which Oliver really did not like, past some downed trees and tossed branches, and then a cab miraculously stopped and we shared it with an old guy all the way downtown. No traffic lights working, no stores open—how strange the streets were. In Kiki's building, I led Oliver up four flights of dark tenement stairs while he drove me nuts flicking the flashlight on and off.

When Kiki opened the door onto her pitch-black hallway, she said, "Reyna! What are you doing here?"

Kiki, of course, was fine. She had plenty of vegetables and canned food and rice—who needed a fridge?—and she could light the stove with a match. She had daylight now and candles for later. She had pots of water she could boil to wash with. She had filled the tub the night before. How was I? "Oliver, isn't this fun?" she said.

Oh, New Yorkers were making such a big fuss, she thought. She had a transistor radio so the fussing came through. "I myself am enjoying the day off from work," she said. She was rereading *The Greek Way* by Edith Hamilton—had I ever read it? I didn't read much, did I?—and she planned to finish it tonight by candlelight.

"Come stay with us," I said. "Wouldn't you like that, Oliver?"

Oliver crowed on cue.

Kiki said she always preferred being in her own home. "Oliver, I bet you would like some of the chocolate ice cream that's turning into a lovely milkshake."

We followed her into the kitchen, with its painted cabinets and old linoleum. When I took off my jacket to settle in, Kiki said, "Oh, no. Did you get a new tattoo?"

"No. You always ask that. You're phobic about my arms."

"I'll never get used to them." I had a dove and a sparrow and a tiger lily and a branch with leaves and some small older ones. They all stood for things. The dove was to settle a fight; the sparrow was the true New York bird; the tiger lily meant boldness; and the branch was an olive tree in honor of Oliver. I used to try to tell Kiki that they were no different from the patterns on rugs. "Are you a floor?" she said. She accused my tattoos of being forms of mutilation as well as forms of deception over my natural skin. According to what? "Well, Islamic teaching, for one thing," she said.

Kiki had never been a practicing Muslim but she liked a lot about Islam. I may have been the only one in the family who knew how into it she'd once been. She used to try to get me to read Averroës, she thought he was great, and Avicenna. Only my aunt would believe that someone like me could just dip into eleventh-century philosophy if I felt like it. She saw no reason why not.

"Oliver, my man," she was saying now, "you don't have to finish if you're full."

"Dad's worried about you," I told Kiki.

"I already called him," she said. It turned out her phone still worked because she had an old landline, nothing digital or bundled.

She'd been outside earlier in the day. Some people on her block had water but she didn't. Oliver was entranced when Kiki showed him how she flushed the toilet by throwing down a potful of water.

"It's magic," I said.

When we left, Kiki called after us, "I'm always glad to see you, you know that." She could have given us more credit for getting all the way there, I thought.

"You might change your mind about staying with us," I called back, before we went out into the dark hall.

.   .   .

I had an extra reason for wanting her to stay. Not to be one of those mothers who was always desperate for babysitting, but I needed a babysitter.

My boyfriend, Boyd, was spending three months at Rikers Island. He was there for selling five ounces of weed (who thinks that should even be a crime?). For all of October I'd gone to see him once a week, and it made a big difference to him. I planned to go that week, once the subways were running and buses were going over the bridge again. But it was hard bringing Oliver, who wasn't his kid and who needed a lot of attention during those toyless visits.

I loved Boyd but I wouldn't have said I loved him more than the others I'd been with. Fortunately no one asked. Not even Boyd. There was no need for people to keep mouthing off about how much they felt, in his view. Some degree of real interest, some persistence in showing up, was enough. Every week I saw him sitting in that visitors' room in his stupid jumpsuit. The sight of him—heavy faced, wary, waiting to smile slightly—always got to me, and when I hugged him (light hugs were permitted), I'd think, *It's still Boyd, it's Boyd here.*

Oliver could be a nuisance. Sometimes he was very, very whiny after standing in so many different lines, or he was incensed that he couldn't bring in his giant plastic dinosaur. Or he got over-stimulated and had to nestle up to Boyd and complain at length about some kid who threw sand in the park. "You having adventures, right?" Boyd said. Meanwhile, I was trying to ask Boyd if he'd had an okay week and why not. I had an hour to give him the joys of my conversation. Dealing with those two at once was not the easiest.

I got a phone call from Aunt Kiki on the second day after the hurricane. "How would you feel about my coming over after work to take a hot shower?" she said. "I can bring a towel, I've got piles of towels."

"Our shower is dying to see you," I said. "And Oliver will lend you his ducky."

"Kiki Kiki Kiki Kiki Kiki!" Oliver yelled when she came through the door. Maybe I'd worked him up too much in advance. We'd gotten the place very clean.

As soon as my aunt emerged from the bathroom, dressed again in her slacks and sweater and with a steamed-pink face under the turban of her towel, I handed her a glass of red wine. "A person without heat or water needs alcohol," I said. We sat down to meat loaf, which I was good at, and mashed potatoes with garlic, which Oliver had learned to eat.

"This is a feast," she said. "Did you know the sultans had feasts that went on for two weeks?"

Oliver was impressed. "This one could go on longer," I said. "You should stay over. Or come back tomorrow. I mean it."

Tomorrow was what I needed—it was the visiting night for inmates with last names from *M* to *Z*.

"Maybe the power will be back on by then," Kiki said. "Maybe maybe."

At Rikers, Boyd and the other inmates had spent the hurricane under lockdown, no wandering off into the torrent. Rikers had its own generator, and the buildings were in the center of the island, too high up to wash away. It was never meant to be a place you might swim from.

"You know I have this boyfriend, Boyd," I said.

Kiki was looking at her plate while I told her, as much as I could in front of Oliver, the situation about the weekly visits. "Oh, shit," she said. She had to finish chewing to say, "Okay, sure, okay, I'll come right from work."

When I leaned over to embrace her, she seemed embarrassed. "Oh, please," she said. "No big deal."

· · ·

What a mystery Kiki was. What could I ever say to her that would throw her for a loop? Best not to push it, of course. And maybe she had a boyfriend of her own that I didn't even know about. She wasn't someone who told you everything. She wasn't showering with him, wherever he was. Maybe he was married. A man that age. Oh, where was I going with this?

When Kiki turned up the next night, she was forty-five minutes later than she'd said she'd be, and I had given up on her several times over. She bustled through the door saying, "Don't ask me how the subways are running. Go, go. Get out of here, go."

She looked younger, all flushed like that. What a babe she must've once been. Or at least a hippie sweetheart. Oliver clambered all over her. "Will you hurry up and get out of here?" she said to me.

The subway (which had only started running that day) was indeed slow to arrive and very crowded, but the bus near Queens Plaza that went to Rikers was the same as ever. After the first few stops, all the white people except me emptied out. I read *People* magazine while we inched our way to the bridge to the island; love was making a mess of the lives of a number of celebrities. And look at that teenage girl across the aisle in the bus, combing her hair, checking it in a mirror, pulling some strands across her face to make it hang right. *Girl,* I wanted to say, *he fucked up bad enough to get himself where he is, and you're still worried he won't like your hair?*

Of course, I was all moussed and lipsticked myself. I had standards. But you couldn't wear anything too revealing—no rips or see-through fabrics—they had rules. *Visitors must wear undergarments.*

After I stood in a line and put my coat and purse in a locker and showed my ID to the guards and got searched and stood in a line for one of Rikers's own buses and got searched again, I sat in a room to wait for Boyd. It was odd being there without Oliver.

The wait went on so long, and it wasn't like you could bring a book. And then I heard Boyd's name read from the list.

Those jumpsuits didn't flatter anyone. But when we hugged, he smelled of soap and Boyd, and I was sorry for myself to have him away so long. "Hey there," he said.

"Didn't mean to get here so late," I said.

Boyd wanted to hear about the hurricane and who got hit the worst. Aunt Kiki became my material: "Oh, she had her candles and her pots of water and her cans of soup and her bags of rice, she couldn't see why everybody was so upset."

"Can't keep 'em down, old people like that," he said. "Good for her. That's the best thing I've heard all week."

I went on about Kiki's gameness. How she'd taught me the right way to climb trees when I was young, when my mother only worried I'd fall on my head.

"I didn't know you were a climber. Have to tell Claude."

His friend Claude, much more of an athlete than Boyd, had recently discovered the climbing wall at some gym. Boyd himself was a couch potato, but a lean and lanky one. People told him he looked like LeBron James, only skinnier. Was he getting puffy now? A little.

"Claude's a monster on that wall. Got Lynnette doing it too." Lynnette was Claude's sister. And Boyd's girlfriend before me. "Girls can do that stuff fine, he says."

"When did he say that?"

"They came by last week. The whole gang."

What gang? Only three visitors allowed. "Lynnette was here?"

"And Maxwell. They came to show support. I appreciated it, you know?"

I'll bet you did, I thought. I was trying not to leap to any conclusions. It wasn't as if she could've crept into the corner with him for a quickie, though you heard rumors of such things. Urban myths.

"Does Claude still have that stringy haircut?"

"He does. Looks like a root vegetable. Man should go to my barber." The Rikers barber had given Boyd an onion look, if you were citing vegetables.

"They're coming again Saturday. You're not coming Saturday, right?" I never came on Saturdays. I cut him a look.

"Because if you are," he said, "I'll tell them not to come."

You couldn't blame a man who had nothing for wanting everything he could get his hands on. This was pretty much what I thought on the bus ride back to the subway.

Oh, I could blame him. I was spending an hour and a half to get there every week and an hour and a half to get back so he could entertain his ex? I was torn between being pissed off and my principles about being a good sport. Why had Boyd told me? The guy could keep his mouth shut when he needed to.

Because he didn't think he needed to. Because I was a good sport. What surprised me even more was how painful this was starting to be. I could imagine Boyd greeting Lynnette, in his offhand, Mr. Cool way. "Can I believe my eyes?" Lynnette silky and tough, telling him it had been too long. But what was so great about Boyd that I should twist in torment from what I was seeing too clearly in my head?

I was on the bus during this anguish. I wanted Boyd to comfort me. He had a talent for that. If you were insulted because some asshole at day care said your kid's shoes were unsuitable, if you splurged on a nice TV and then realized you'd overpaid, if you got fired from your job because you used up sick days and it wasn't your fault, Boyd could make it seem hilarious. He could remind you it was part of the ever-expanding joke of human trouble. Not just you.

When I got back to the apartment, Oliver was actually asleep in his bed—had Kiki drugged him?—and Kiki was in the living room watching the Cooking Channel on TV.

"You watch this crap?" I said.

"How was the visit?"

"Medium. Who's winning on *Chopped*?"

"The wrong guy. But I have a thing for Marcus Samuelsson."
He was the judge who had a restaurant right in Harlem, a chef
born in Ethiopia, tall and rangy and very good-looking. *So,* I
wanted to ask Kiki and I almost did, *is the whole fucking world
about men?*

"Oliver spilled a lot of yogurt on the floor but we got it cleaned
up," she said.

I wanted a drink, I wanted a joint. What was in the house? I
found a very old bottle of Beaujolais in the kitchen and poured
glasses for us both.

"When does he get out?" Kiki asked.

"They say January. He's holding up okay."

"He has you."

"You don't have to tell me if you don't want to, but when you
got divorced," I said, "was it because one of you had been messing
around with someone else?"

"Whooa," Kiki said, "where did that come from?"

"Someone named Lynnette has been visiting Boyd."

Kiki considered this. "Could be nothing."

"So when you left Turkey, why did you leave?"

"It was time."

I admired Kiki's way of deciding what was none of your business, but it made you think there was business there.

It was my bad luck that Con Ed got its act together the very next
evening, so electricity flowed in the walls of Kiki's home to give
her light and refrigeration and to pump her water and the gur-
gling steam in her radiators. I called her to say Happy Normal.

"Normal is overrated," she said. "I'll be so busy next week."

"Me too," I said.

Oliver hardly ever had sitters. He was in day care while I went
off to my unglamorous employment as a part-time receptionist
at a veterinarian's office (it paid lousy but the dogs were usually

nice) and at night I took him with me if I went to see friends or Boyd, when I used to stay with Boyd. Sometimes Boyd had a cousin who watched him.

"Oliver wants to say hi," I told my aunt.

"I *love* you, Great Kiki!" Oliver said.

This didn't move her to volunteer to sit for him another time, and I thought it was better not to ask again so soon.

Oliver wasn't bad at all on the next visit to Rikers. The weather was colder and he got to wear his favorite Spider-Man sweater, which Boyd said was very sharp.

"Your mom's looking good too," Boyd said to Oliver.

"Better than Lynnette?"

I hadn't meant to say any such whiny-bitch thing; it leaped out of me. I was horrified. I wasn't as good as I thought I was, was I?

"Not in your league," Boyd said. "Girl's nowhere near." He said this slowly and soberly. He shook his onion head for emphasis.

The rest of the visit went very well. Boyd suggested that Oliver now had the superpower to spin webs from the ceiling—"You going to float above us all, land right on all the bad guys"—and Oliver was so tickled he had to be stopped from shrieking with glee at top volume.

"Know what I miss?" Boyd said. "Well, that, of course. Don't look at me that way. But also I miss when we used to go ice-skating."

We had gone exactly twice, renting skates in Central Park, falling on our asses. I almost crushed Oliver one time I went down. "You telling everyone you're the next big hockey star?" I said.

"I hope there's still ice when I get out," he said.

"There will be," I said. "It's soon. Before you know it."

Kiki had now started to worry about me; she called more often than I was used to. She'd say, "You think Obama's going to get this Congress in line? And how's Boyd doing?"

I let her know we were still an item, which was what she wanted to know. Why in God's name would I ever think of splitting up with Boyd before I could at least get him back home and in bed again? What was the point of all these bus rides if I was going to skip that part?

"You wouldn't want me to desert him at a time like this," I said.

"Be careful," she said.

"He's not much of a criminal," I said. "He was just a bartender selling on the side, not any big-time guy." I didn't have to tell her not to mention this to my father.

"Anybody can be in jail, I know that," Kiki said. "Hikmet was in jail for thirteen years in Turkey."

I thought she meant an old flame of hers but it turned out she meant a famous poet who was dead before she even got there. A famous Communist poet. She'd read all his prison poems.

Boyd wasn't in jail for politics, although some people claimed the war on drugs was a race war, and they had a point. My mom and dad were known to smoke dope every now and then, and was any cop stop-and-frisking them on the streets of Brookline?

"So can I ask you," I said, "were there drugs around when you were in Turkey?" What a blurter I was these days. "Were people selling hash or anything?"

"Not in our circles. I hate that movie, you've seen that movie. But there was smuggling. I mean in antiquities, bits from ancient sites. People went across to the eastern parts, brought stuff back. Or they got it over the border from Iran. Beautiful things, really."

"It's amazing what people get money for."

"If Osman had wanted to do that," she said, "he wouldn't have become a farmer. It was the farming that made me leave, by the way."

I was very pleased that she told me.

"And he left off farming five years later," she said. "Isn't that ironic?"

"It is," I said.

"I still write to Osman. He's a great letter writer." This was news. Did she have all the letters; how hot were they; did he e-mail too? Of course, I was thinking: *Maybe you two should get back together*. It's a human impulse, isn't it, to want to set the world into couples.

"The wife he has now is much younger," Kiki said.

By December I'd gotten a new tattoo in honor of Boyd's impending release. It was quite beautiful—a birdcage with the door open and a line of tiny birds going toward my wrist. Some people design their body art so it all fits together, but I did mine piecemeal, like my life, and it looked fine.

Kiki noticed it when it was a week old and still swollen. She had just made supper for us (overcooked hamburgers but Oliver liked them) and I was doing the dishes, keeping that arm out of the water. Soaking too soon was bad for it.

"And when Boyd is out of the picture," Kiki said, "you'll be stuck with this ink that won't go away."

"It's my history," I said. "My arm is an album."

"What if Boyd doesn't like it?"

"It's for me," I said. "All of these are mine."

"Don't be a carpet," she said.

"You don't really know very much about this," I said, "if you don't mind my saying."

Why would I take advice from a woman who slept every night alone in her bed, cuddling up with some copy of Aristotle? What could she possibly tell me that I could use? And she was getting older by the minute, with her squinty eyes and her short hair cut too close to her head.

It was snowing the day Boyd got released from Rikers. I was home with Oliver when Claude went to pick him up. He didn't want me and Oliver seeing him then, with his bag of items, with his humbling paperwork, with the guards leaning over every detail. By the time I got to view Boyd he was in our local coffee shop with Claude, eating a cheeseburger, looking happy and greasy. Oliver went berserk, leaping all over him, smearing his snowy boots all over Boyd's pants. I leaped a little too. "Don't knock me over," Boyd said. "Nah, knock me over. Go ahead."

"Show him no mercy," Claude said.

Already Boyd looked vastly better than he had in jail, and he'd been out only an hour. "Can't believe it," he said. "Can't believe I was ever there." He fed French fries to Oliver, who pretended to be a dog. Boyd had his other hand on my knee. We could do that now. "Hey, girl," he said. The snow outside the window gave everything a lunar brightness.

The first night he stayed with me, after it took forever to get Oliver asleep in the other room, I was madly eager when we made our way to each other at last. How did it go, this dream—did we still know how to do this? We knew just fine, though there were fumbles and pauses, little laughing hesitations. I had imagined Boyd would be hungry and even rough, but, no, he was careful; he looped around and circled back and took some sweet byways before settling on his goal. He was trying, it seemed to me, to make this first contact very particular, trying to recognize me. I hadn't expected this from him, which showed what I knew.

At my job in the vet's office my fellow workers teased me about being sleepy at the desk. They all knew my boyfriend had returned after a long trip. Any yawn brought on group hilarity. "Look how she walks, she hobbles," one of the techs said. What a raunchy office I worked in. All I said was, "Laugh away, you're green with envy."

I was distracted, full of wayward thoughts—Boyd and I starting a restaurant together, Boyd and I running off to Thailand, Boyd and I having another kid, maybe a girl, what would we name her, Oliver would like this—or would he? I lost focus while I was doing my tasks at the computer and had to put up with everyone saying how sleepy I was.

. . .

Jail doesn't always change people in good ways, but in Boyd's case it made him quieter and less apt to throw his weight around. He had to find a new job (no alcohol). I was proud of him when he started as a waiter in a diner just north of our neighborhood, a big challenge to his stylish self. This was definitely a step down for him, which he bore grudgingly but not bitterly. After work his hair smelled of frying oil and broiler smoke. His home was not exactly with me—he was officially living at his cousin's, since he no longer had his apartment—but he spent a lot of nights at my place. I liked the cousin (it was Maxwell, who had once babysat for Oliver) but he had a tendency to drag Boyd out to clubs at night. In my younger days I liked to go clubbing same as anyone, but once I had Oliver it pretty much lost its appeal. I had reason to imagine girls in teensy outfits throwing themselves at Boyd in these clubs, but it turned out that wasn't the problem. The problem was that Maxwell had a scheme for increasing Boyd's admittedly paltry income. It had to do with smuggling cigarettes from Virginia to New York, of all idiotic ways to make a profit. Just to cash in on the tax difference. "Are you out of your fucking mind?" I said. "You want to violate probation?"

"Don't shout," Boyd said.

"Crossing state lines. Are you crazy?"

"That's it," Boyd said. "No more talking. You always have opinions. Topic closed. Forget I said a word."

I didn't take well to being shushed. I snapped at him and he got stony and went home early that night. "A man needs peace, is that too much to ask?"

"You think I give a fuck?" I said.

I was with Kiki the next day, having lunch near my office. She was checking up on me these days as much as she could, which included treating me to a falafel plate. I told her about the dog I'd met at my job who knew three languages. It could sit, lie down, and beg in English, Spanish, and ASL. "A pit bull mix. They're smart."

"You know what I think?" Kiki said. "I think you should go live somewhere where you'd learn another language. Everyone should, really."

"Someday," I said.

"I still have a friend in Istanbul. I bet you and Oliver could go camp out at her place. For a little while. It's a very kid-friendly culture."

"I don't think so. My life is here."

"It doesn't have to be Istanbul, that was my place, it's not everyone's. There are other places. I'd stake you with some cash if you wanted to take off for a while."

I wasn't even tempted.

"It's very good of you," I said.

"You'll be sorry later if you don't do it," she said.

She wanted to get me away from Boyd, which might happen on its own, anyway. I was touched and insulted both at once. And then I was trying to imagine myself in a new city. Taking Oliver to a park in Rome. Having interesting chats with the locals while I sat on a bench. Laughing away in Italian.

My phone interrupted us with the ping that meant I was getting a text. "Sorry," I said to Kiki. "I just need to check." It was Boyd, and I was so excited that I said, "Oh! From Boyd!" out loud. *Sorry, baby* was in the message, and some other things that I certainly wasn't reading to Kiki. But I chuckled in joy, tickled to death—I could feel myself getting flushed. How funny he could be when he wanted. That Boyd.

"Excuse me," I said. "I just have to answer fast."

"Go ahead," Kiki said, not pleasantly.

I had to concentrate to tap the letters. It took a few minutes and I could hear Kiki sigh across from me. I knew how I looked, too girly, too jacked up over crumbs Boyd threw my way. Kiki was not glad about it. She didn't even know Boyd. But I did—I could see him very distinctly in my mind just then, his grumbling sweetness, his spells of cold scorn, his bragging, his ridiculous illusions about what he could do, and the waves of tenderness I had for him, the sudden pangs of adoration. I was perfectly aware (or just then I was, anyway) that some part of my life with Boyd was not entirely real, that if I pushed it too hard a whole other feeling would show itself. I wasn't about to push. I wanted us to go on as we were. A person can know several things at once. I could know all of them while still being moved to delight by him—his kisses on my neck, his way of humming to the most blaring tune, his goofing around with Oliver. And I saw that I was probably going to help him with the cigarette smuggling too. I was going to be in it with him before I even meant to be.

I was going to ride in the car and count the cash; I was going to let him store his illegal cigarettes in my house. All because of what stirred me, all because of what Boyd was to me. All because of beauty.

I had my own life to live. And what did Kiki have? She had her job making deals between the very rich and the very poor. She had her books that she settled inside of in dusty private satisfaction. She had her old and fabled past. I loved my aunt, but she must have known I'd never listen to her.

When I stopped texting Boyd, I looked up, and Kiki was dabbing at her plate of food. "The hummus was good," I said.

"They say Saladin ate hummus," she said. "In the eleven hundreds. You know about him, right? He was a Kurd who fought against the Crusaders."

She knew a lot. She was waiting for me to make some fucking effort to know a fraction as much. Saladin who? In the meantime—anyone looking at our table could've seen this—we were having a long and unavoidable moment, my aunt and I, of each feeling sorry for the other. In our separate ways. How could we not?

Thomas Pierce

Ba Baboon

FOR A LONG TIME they do nothing but hide and wait. Very
little light creeps in under the pantry's double doors. Brooks
examines the cans on the shelf level with his head: beans, corn,
soup. This pantry does not belong to him—or to his sister, Mary.
They are in someone else's home. Mary has her eye pressed to the
door crack.

"Do you have to breathe so loud?" she asks. "I'm trying to
listen."

The pantry is small but not coffin-small, not so small that
Brooks can't stretch his arms wide like a—well, like a what,
exactly? Like a scarecrow on a pole. Okay, a scarecrow, sure, but
where did that image come from? From the muck of the way back
when, no doubt. "Your long-term memory seems to be hunky-
dory," Dr. Groom has told Brooks more than once, jubilantly.

Sure enough, a student theater production from almost thirty
years ago bubbles up fresh, unbattered: the out-of-tune piano at
the end of the stage, the hard crusts of chewing gum under the
seats in the auditorium, the flattened cereal boxes cut into rect-
angles and painted to look like a road of yellow bricks. Fourteen
years old, Brooks nearly landed the coveted Scarecrow role in

The Wizard of Oz, coveted because of the beautiful blond-haired fifteen-year-old playing Dorothy Gale, a girl who later, according to three Munchkins, gave it up to the Tin Man in the janitor's closet. It might have been Brooks she gave it up to if he hadn't screwed up in auditions and been cast instead as a member of the dreaded Lollipop Guild.

"If I only had a brain," Brooks sings.

"That's not funny," Mary says, and looks over at him. "I really wish you wouldn't say things like that. It's upsetting."

Say things like what? Oh, the bit about the brain. Brooks gets it now, why he's thinking about the mindless scarecrow after all these years. Somewhere up in his head is the Old Brooks, that asshole, and he's poking fun at this moodier, slower version of himself. "If you only had a brain," Old Brooks is singing, a malicious smile on his chubbier face, his brown hair combed over neatly, not cropped short with scabby scars across the scalp.

"You might feel irrationally angry sometimes," Dr. Groom has said. If he's feeling agitated, Brooks is supposed to ask himself why, to interrogate his agitation, but, God, does he want to punch something right now, anything, the angel-hair-pasta boxes or the cracked-pepper crackers, the clementines or the canned chickpeas, so many chickpeas, a lifetime's supply of chickpeas. He could punch the peas into a mash and lick his knuckles clean. Brooks has lost all sense of how long they've been hiding in this pantry. He plops down onto a lumpy dog-food bag beside his sister.

"I don't hear them anymore," Mary says. "They might be upstairs. Maybe they're asleep."

Brooks nods, then lets his eyebrows scrunch. He can feel his sister studying him.

"Have you forgotten why we're in here?" Mary asks. "Have you forgotten about the dogs?"

The events of the afternoon have been disassembled and constellated in his memory: a turkey sandwich, his sister's Taurus, a small brass key from under a mat, a tiled kitchen floor, two snarling dogs. It's like standing inches away from a stippled drawing and being asked to name the subject. And the artist.

Mary gives him one of her pity smiles, where her upper lip mushrooms around her bottom lip, consumes it. She is a compact, muscular woman, still a girl really, with a body for the tennis court, not the sort of person you could knock over easily.

The dog-food pebbles crunch under his sharp butt bones when he shifts. He's lost weight, probably twenty pounds since the accident. Brooks doesn't remember anything from that night, but according to the police (via his mother) he was alone at the time, unloading groceries from the back of his car on the street in front of his town house. Someone smashed the left side of his head with a brick. A brick! The police found it in some bushes down the street, along with bits of Brooks's skull. The assailant took the car (which still hasn't been recovered and probably never will be) and his wallet. "A random act of violence," his mother called it. "A totally senseless thing." Unnecessary qualifiers, he sometimes wants to tell her, as the universe is inherently a random and senseless place.

"I need to go," he says.

"We can't."

"Go, as in pee."

"Right," Mary says. "Of course. I'm sorry. Let's just give it a few more minutes. Just to be safe. The last thing we need is to go out there and get bitten."

He squirms.

"Here," she says, and offers him a third-full bottle of organic olive oil. "You can pee in this."

You can pee in this. Mary feels like one of the nurses. Brooks is staying with her for a month, while their mother is away, and that means she is responsible for his meals, for his entertainment, for getting him to all his appointments.

Yesterday they had to wait forty-five minutes for the doctor to return to the examining room. Brooks was a broken record while they waited: "Pencil box screen door pencil box screen door." Dr. Groom was to blame for this. One of his memory games. The doctor often began his checkups by listing a random series of words for Brooks to repeat later, on command, a test of his short-term memory. Before leaving, their mother had warned that Brooks might attempt to scribble the words on his hand when the doctor wasn't looking. Brooks, their mother had explained, wanted his independence back almost as much as they wanted to give it to him. But that wasn't possible yet. He still had what she called "little blips." He could be coherent and normal one minute and the next . . . well.

"Pencil box screen door pencil box . . ."

"You don't have to remember it anymore," she said. "The doctor already asked you, and you got it right. You already won that game."

That didn't stop him. He hammered each syllable hard, except for the last one, *door*, to which he added at least three extra breathy *O*s. He ooooohed it the way a ghost or a shaman might. Maybe he is a shaman. Who can say. What the doctors call hallucinations and delusions—maybe they are something else entirely. Mary read an article somewhere online explaining that people with brain injuries sometimes report unusual and even psychic side effects. There was a stroke victim who said he could read a book and be there—actually be *in the book*, tasting the food, smelling the air. A teenager in a car accident lost his sense of taste but said he could feel other people's emotions. It had something to do with unlocking previously unused parts of the brain.

Watching her brother clumsily tap his fingers on the shiny metal table, Mary wondered if it was possible he was in communication with something larger than both of them: a cosmic force, the angels, Frank Sinatra, anything. She doubted it. Her poor brother could barely button his shirt. And as for those words, the skipping record, maybe he'd fallen into some sort of terrible neural-feedback loop. He seemed to be saying it involuntarily now.

She was ashamed by how much she wanted to slap her brother. Her whole life, Brooks had been the one looking after her—and so what right did she have to be irritated now? When things got rough with her boyfriend after college, it was Brooks who drove all the way down to Atlanta and helped her pack her things. It was Brooks who defended her to their mother when she quit her job with the real-estate company. It was Brooks who wrote her a check to buy the Pop-Yop, her soft-serve franchise.

She worried that it would never be that way between them again, that the balance had forever shifted, and then she felt selfish for worrying about such a thing. Brooks needed her. It was her turn.

"Your pants, Brooks," she said, and handed him his khakis.

He stood there beside the exam table in white underwear and a wrinkled blue shirt, holding the khakis out in front of him like an unwanted gift. Mary was supposed to have ironed his shirt for him before they left the house that morning, and that she hadn't fulfilled this duty was obviously a source of some anxiety for her big brother. He could no longer tolerate creases—in clothes, in paper, in anything. Watching him step into his pant legs, she thought he might bring up that morning's ironing debacle again, but he tucked in the shirt and zipped his pants without comment.

His crease intolerance was one of many changes that had come with the accident. A longtime smoker, he now said that smoke made him feel sick. He had a closet full of dark clothes that these days he deemed depressing. In fact, his new favorite article of clothing was a tight, bright-pink-and-purple sweater that Mary wouldn't let him wear outside the house, because it wasn't his but their mother's.

When, finally, Dr. Groom came back, Mary stayed seated in her little plastic chair, eyeing all the instruments, the cotton swabs and the tongue depressors in the glass jars, the inflatable cuff of the blood-pressure device. The bigger, more impressive machinery was somewhere else, in another building. The nurses had trouble keeping Brooks still in those machines. Apparently, he got antsy.

"Pencil box screen door," Brooks blurted, all trace of shaman gone from his voice.

"Very good, Mr. Yard," the doctor said, and then leaned back against the table to explain the scans, how they were looking good, better than expected, given the nature of the accident and Brooks's age, which was forty-four. Of course, he said, it wasn't all about the scans. The scans wouldn't show any shearing or stretching, for instance. But Brooks was doing well, that was the bottom line. He wasn't slurring his words. His headaches were less frequent. Even his short-term memory was showing signs of improvement. A fuller recovery, the doctor said, might very well be possible.

Brooks is not sure how possible it will be to pee, cleanly, into a third-full bottle of organic extra-virgin olive oil, especially given the tiny circumference of its plastic top. The tip of his penis will not fit into that hole. The bottle is a little slippery. He pops off the black top that controls the outward flow of the oil and hands that to Mary. He turns away from her and unzips.

"I've got this can of Pirouette cookies ready if you run out of bottle," Mary says.

"I just need you to be quiet." He concentrates—or doesn't. What's required is the absence of concentration. That should be easy, shouldn't it? He's a pro at that now. He sees a yellow brick road. The urine comes in splashy spurts at first and then streams steadily. The bottle warms. The urine pools in a layer above the olive oil, all of it yellow. Thankfully, he doesn't need the cookie tin for overflow. Mary hands him the top when he asks for it and tells him job well done.

Bottle plugged, they decide to store it under the lowest shelf, out of sight for now. He plops back down onto the dog-food bags. If he had to, he could sleep like this.

He checks his wristwatch with the shiny alligator-leather strap, a gift from a long-ago girlfriend. Which girlfriend, he couldn't say.

"We've been in here for an hour," Mary says. She stands and peers again through the crack in the double doors. "Maybe we should just go for it. I don't see the dogs."

Her left eye still at the crack, she crouches down for a new angle on the outside world, her small hands on either side of the white door for balance.

"Let me," Brooks says, rising. He grabs the brass knob near her left temple, and Mary slides away to let him pass. He emerges from the pantry. To his right, through another doorway, he can see a kitchen with a high white ceiling and recessed lights. To his left, a long unfamiliar hallway unfolds, hardwood floors with wide dark-red planks, at the end of which an imposing grandfather clock ticks.

"Not that way," Mary says when he starts down the hall.

He hears a distant clacking of nails, a jangling of collars. Never has such a tinkly sound seemed so ominous. Mary is behind him now, tugging at his shirt, his arms, pulling him back into the sepulchre of the pantry. The dogs are approaching, their stampede echoing down the hallway. When his back collides with the food shelves, two fat cans drop and roll at his feet. Mary pulls the doors shut again. Seconds later, the dogs galunk into them. Their bulky, invisible weight shakes the flimsy wood so hard Brooks wonders if the hinges might pop. Mary holds the brass knobs tight, as if worried that the dogs are capable of turning knobs. The dogs growl. It's hard to think straight over that noise.

"I'm sorry," she says. "I shouldn't have let you go out there. That was dumb of me."

"What are they, exactly? What breed?"

"Rottweilers? Dobermans? I don't know what they are, but they're freaking huge. Biggest dogs I've ever seen. Genetically modified, maybe. Wynn would do that. Order a bunch of genetically modified military dogs. That would be so him. There are two of them, Baba and Bebe. Wait, let me try something. I think I just remembered it." The dogs are still clawing at the pantry doors. She sticks her lips to the crack and says, "Baba Beluga." The dogs don't stop their attack. "Bebe, Baba, Baba O'Riley. It's something like that."

"What is?"

"The safe command. Oh, Goosie, I'm sorry I got you into this."

Goosie. When was the last time she called him that? Back at his town house, in the drawer to the right of the stove (his mind still has that power at least, the power to conjure up images, to see things that aren't directly in front of him), he must have a hundred thank-you cards addressed to Goosie. Thank-yous for the loan, the money that helped her buy the soft-serve place that she had, until then, only managed. The golden egg, she called his loan. Him, the goosie.

"The safe command will make them docile," she says.

"Remind me again who Wynn is to you?" he asks.

"A friend," she says quickly. "He's out of town for a few days, and I agreed to feed his dogs and bring in the mail. He gave me the safe command before he left. I should have written it down."

"Could have just told me. I would have remembered."

She smiles.

"Let's just call someone for help," Brooks says.

"I would if I could. My cell is out in the car."

Brooks fishes around in his pockets.

"Yours is in the car, too," she says.

"Well, that's bad luck. What should we do now?"

"When they settle down again, we'll go together. There's a door in the kitchen. That's, what, like, thirty feet from here?"

Brooks isn't sure but nods. The dogs are no longer scrabbling at the doors but whining. They walk in circles, with clicking nails, outside. Mary reaches over Brooks's shoulder for a bag of pistachios. She rips open the plastic at the top and offers him some. "We missed breakfast," she says.

He doesn't want any nuts. He sits down on the dog food again, his head back against a shelf. His medication can make him groggy. He needs to rest his eyes.

He is halfway in a dream when Mary announces that it's time for another attempt to escape. The dream is about fishhooks. Well, not about fishhooks, but it involves them. He is looking for one in the bottom of a tackle box. Brooks hasn't gone fishing in more than a year, probably not since his last trip to Nicaragua. His company, which he started with a friend a decade ago, manufactures medical devices and has a factory outside Managua. The last time he was down there, Brooks took a few extra days and chartered a deep-sea-fishing boat out of San Juan del Sur. He caught a striped marlin, though it was the captain who did the hard work, setting up the rod, finding the right spot. All Brooks did was wait and take orders, reel when the captain yelled to reel. Going deep-sea fishing is, actually, kind of like how he lives now. Sure, he can fry a few eggs, but only if there is someone there to help him, to keep him on task, to clean up the mess when his hands fail him, to calm him down when he loses his temper, to reel him in.

"You have gunk on your face," Mary says, and wipes it away with a wet thumb. "I think it's old soy sauce."

"Are you sure we should go for it again?" he asks. "How long will the owners be away? We could survive in here for days."

"No," she says. "I got us into this mess. I'll get us out."

Brooks knows this is the truth, that his sister is to blame, but he can't let go of the feeling that he should be masterminding the escape. After all, he's the big brother. He's always taken care of her. That's just how it is. His former self, the Old Brooks, up there somewhere, would know exactly what to do in this situation. Old Brooks sees a solution, surely, but he's keeping quiet about it. He's enjoying all this confusion. "Try not to think about who you were before the accident," Dr. Groom has said, "and concentrate instead on who you want to be now. Accept the new you." Sometimes Brooks wants to toss Dr. Groom out the window.

. . .

Mary opens the pantry doors. She doesn't see the dogs. If only she had poison. She imagines Wynn coming home and finding both dogs dead. She imagines him cradling their bodies and weeping. No, Wynn wouldn't weep. He'd probably just buy two more dogs, recycle the names, and move on with his life. Mary has never killed an animal as big as a dog. She veered her car in order to hit a squirrel once and regretted it for two days.

She makes it a few steps into the kitchen before realizing that Brooks has fallen behind. He has stopped at the fridge. Photos and appointment cards are stuck to the front of it with magnets. He's looking at a Polaroid, one she can see—of two children, a tiny girl and an older boy, on a seesaw. Across the bottom someone has written "What goes up . . ."

She waves at him to get his attention. At least forty feet of tiled floor separate them from the back door. She considers sprinting for it, but they haven't discussed that as the plan, and she doesn't want to surprise Brooks. She takes two steps, then two more. It's when she reaches the entrance to the living room that she sees them in there, twenty feet away, the dogs, heads low, tails stiff, coarse black fur Mohawked up along their backs. Is it possible that the dogs have set an elaborate trap for them?

"What's wrong?" he asks, far too loud.

The dogs growl. Their heads drop even lower.

"Baa baa black sheep," Mary whispers. "Bibi Netanyahu." Maybe Wynn has changed the password. She hates him now more than ever. Her friends warned her about him. They'd heard strange things about him. Perverted things. According to a guy who used to work with him, he cheated on his wife constantly. He'd been with a hundred women. Probably his dick was contaminated, they said. At least make him wear a condom, they said.

Brooks can't see the dogs, but he hears them now. His sister inches backward. He could probably make it to the pantry in time. But not Mary. He looks around the room for something that might help them. He sees the cordless phone on the wall behind him. Mary could call her friend for the safe command, and all this would be over.

"Top of the fridge," he whispers.

"What?" She sneaks a look over her right shoulder.

Brooks leans back for the phone as Mary lunges for the fridge. When he turns, she's trying to use the ice dispenser as a foothold. The freezer door swings open. She slams it shut and scrambles up onto the soapstone counter. From there she pulls herself up onto the fridge. Brooks is not far behind her. Phone in hand, he flings himself onto the counter, belly first. He feels like a spider with all its legs ripped out. He's having trouble getting up onto his knees. He reaches for a cabinet knob. One of the dogs locks onto his ankle, and he screams. He writhes, swinging the phone back and forth. When the phone connects with the dog's head, he loses his grip on it and it goes clattering to the floor. But he's free now. He's able to clamber up beside his sister.

The top of the fridge is covered in dust. They have to crouch to avoid hitting their heads on the ceiling.

"You're bleeding," Mary says, bending down to his ankle.

"Don't bother with it now." He looks down at the dogs, at their giant stinking faces. One dog is on the floor whimpering, and the other is pogoing up and down the front of the fridge, knocking loose all the photos and appointment cards. Its back paws come down on the phone and launch it sideways.

"I dropped it," Brooks says. "The phone. Sorry. We could have called your friend."

Mary is prodding at his ankle unscientifically. "Don't worry about it. That wouldn't have worked anyway."

"Why, he's out of the country or something?"

"Well—"

"He doesn't know we're here," Brooks says.

His sister looks at him as if she were the one with the dog bite.

The night Wynn first brought out his video camera they were in Myrtle Beach, at his family's vacation home. Mary listened to the waves through the open window as Wynn fiddled with a tape. Wynn with his blue eyes, the perfect gray streak in his long, windswept hair, the difficult marriage to his crazy pediatrician wife, who was hardly ever around. Then he told her to start playing with herself. Already she could anticipate the regret. Maybe that was part of the fun.

Did she enjoy making the video? A little bit, sure. For the newness of it. But not for the sex itself. It didn't even feel much like sex to her. It was like something else. She was a planet, way out in space, out of its orbit, and he was an unmanned spaceship, taking measurements of the atmosphere. She was not suitable for habitation. The pillowcases smelled like potato chips and sweat. She wondered if he'd even washed the sheets, if maybe this was one of the kids' bedrooms. He smacked her bottom, and she almost laughed. It wasn't risqué, it was silly.

She broke off the affair a few weeks later, when he proposed a new video, this one in his bathroom at home. His wife was at work and the kids were at school. He already had the camera out.

"Do you ever watch these later?" she asked.

"Not really," he said. "It's not about that. Making them is what's fun. It is fun, isn't it?"

She was in a white towel, examining the shower. There was blond hair trapped in the drain. His wife's, no doubt. One of the drawers under the sink was halfway open, and she could see cotton swabs and a box of tampons. She opened the medicine cabinet and found three different kinds of antidepressants.

"Not mine," he said. "Let's start with you in the shower. You ready?"

She slipped back into her underwear and told him it was over.

"I don't understand," he said.

"I want the tape," she said. "From the beach."

"I erased it. I always tape over them."

She left him half naked in the bathroom. Later, she wondered if she might have got the tape from him then if she'd only been a little more persistent. She thought about it constantly. At work, ringing people up, she lost track of the numbers. She spilled a box of rainbow sprinkles, and what should have been a ten-minute cleanup took her almost thirty.

"You've got to get that tape," her friends said. "What if he puts it online?"

Online! She started visiting pornography sites, just in case. There were so many categories of sex. She couldn't believe all the categories: Mature, POV, MILF, Amateur, Ex-Girlfriend. How might Wynn have categorized her?

She called him and demanded the tape.

"I already told you," he said. "It doesn't exist anymore."

"I'll call the cops."

"Listen, if I had it I'd give it to you, but I don't. You can't just call me like this. I'm at work."

She imagined a locked desk drawer in his home study, a hundred tapes, each with a label, her name on one of them, the date, the location, the positions, the noises made, all of it charted out and diagrammed.

This was her situation to fix. Wynn kept a key hidden under a rock on the back porch. She remembered that. All she had to do was wait for the right day, the right moment.

"And so you think he has the tape here," Brooks says. "Somewhere in this house? And that's why we broke in?"

She nods.

"You could have just told me," he says.

"You would have judged me."

"Sure, but only a little."

"Would you have gone along with it? If you'd known we were breaking into someone's house?"

"No, of course not," he says. "I would have waited in the car."

She smiles at him, and he is relieved to see that it's a real smile, without a trace of pity. "So where is Wynn now?" he asks. "How much time do we have?"

"A few hours, maybe. They drove up to Chapel Hill for the day. His son's looking at colleges." She knows this because Wynn shares so much of his life online. When she was with him he was hardly ever without his phone.

"If I had a sex tape, I don't think I'd keep it in the house for my wife to find."

"You don't know Wynn."

The dogs have stopped barking. They sit patiently at the foot of the fridge. Brooks's ankle throbs. He doesn't know what to do next. If only he could curl up here and take a nap. But the dogs will never give up. They are trained to attack intruders, and that's exactly what he and Mary are. They're the intruders. He has broken into someone's home. He needs a brick. Where's his brick? Give him a brick.

Brooks jumps, not over the dogs and toward the door but to their left. He lands on both feet and sprints back down the hall. The dogs follow. He's the distraction, the bait. "Find it!" he yells back to Mary. He passes the pantry. Ahead of him is the grandfather clock. A blue Oriental rug shifts sideways as he turns left at the end of the hall. He runs up a wide staircase, hand on the rail, and at the top he sees that there are doors, three of them. They all look the same. It's like a terrible game show. He grabs the knob of the middle door, but his fingers won't grip right. "Some things will get better and others won't," Dr. Groom says, and Brooks will have to accept that.

But it's not his fingers, he realizes. The door is locked. He slings his shoulder into it with all his weight. Thankfully the lock is cheap and the door pops open.

Closing it behind him, he finds himself in a room with hot-pink walls decorated with gruesome movie posters. A stereo and a television barely fit on a small white desk beneath the window. In the dead, gray television screen, Brooks can see his warped reflection staring at him: his awful haircut, his skeletal face. Overhead, the ceiling fan spins. The bedspread moves.

Moves? A tiny wiggle at the corner of his vision. An almost

imperceptible change in the arrangement of wrinkles in the blanket. Like a scene from a horror movie.

In the months after the accident, Brooks experienced what he now knows were mild hallucinations. At the hospital he became temporarily convinced that a family of goats had taken up residence under his bed. They had gray coats and black eyes, and at night they came out to lap water from the toilet. If Brooks called for help, the goats would scatter in all directions. Dr. Groom had explained that Brooks could no longer implicitly trust everything he saw and heard. What Brooks needed, he said, was a healthy dose of skepticism. If goats were ransacking his room, he was supposed to remember that it would be very tricky for a goat to get past the hospital's front desk and take the elevator to the third floor. If the coatrack asked him for a grilled cheese, Brooks needed to remind himself that coatracks did not typically require human food, especially grilled cheese. If a bedspread sprang to life . . .

He steps toward the bed. There are pillows piled at the head and foot. In the middle, under the bedspread, is a person-size lump. He watches it closely.

"Who's under there?" he asks.

The lump is very still.

"I'm trying to leave," he says. "So don't be afraid. All of this was a big mistake. Us being here, I mean. We know your dad. We got trapped. By your dogs."

The lump doesn't move.

"I'm Brooks. I'm not sure if you're actually under there. Maybe I'm talking to nothing. I can get a little confused. I haven't always been this way." He steps toward the desk. "I'm moving your desk so I can go out the window. Your dogs want to eat me. So I'm going out the window. Sorry." An apology to a ghost.

He slides the desk toward the closet, everything on it rattling. A water glass topples over and the liquid rolls. He grabs a sock off the floor and sops it up before it reaches a closed laptop covered in pink monkey stickers. "I spilled some water," he says, "and I had to use one of your socks. Sorry. Your laptop is fine, I think." He gets the window open and pops out the screen, which lands below in some holly bushes. He sticks one leg out and straddles the sill. It's a long way down, but not so far that he will necessarily break a bone. Still, this is probably going to hurt.

"Ba baboon," the lump says.

"I'm sorry?"

"Say that to the dogs and they won't attack you."

"So you're really under there?"

The lump doesn't answer.

"Thank you. That's very kind. I'm Brooks."

"Yeah, you said that already."

"Aren't you supposed to be off with your family or something?"

"I got out of it. Please go now."

"I hope you're not just in my head," he says, and goes to the door. "Because that would mean *ba baboon* is total nonsense, and I'm going to get bitten again." The lump doesn't answer. He's about to turn the knob but stops. "By the way, just in case this ever happens again—"

"God. Why haven't you left yet?"

"I will. I'm about to. But next time this happens you should really consider calling the police—or at least your parents."

The lump is quiet.

"Just an idea," Brooks adds.

The lump sits up fast, the bedspread transformed into a mountain. "Look, my mom, like, stole my cell, all right?" the lump says. "And the only phone up here is all the way in my parents' room, and it's not like I had a ton of options, you know? I told you what to say, now go. Just get out of here."

Brooks isn't sure what to say. He considers apologizing again.

"Actually, I lied," the lump says. "I did call the police. They'll be here, like, any minute. You're going to jail."

"Okay," Brooks says, hand on the door. "I'm going."

When Mary climbs down from the fridge, part of her just wants to leave and forget the tape. But she can't do that. Brooks could be hurt upstairs. He could lose his way. He could trap himself in the linen closet and, in the dark, lose himself entirely.

Until her brother's accident, Mary never gave much thought to the idea that personalities may be not only malleable but also divisible from the self. There has to be more to us than memories and quirks that can get smashed away so easily. This raises questions of accountability. What part of her is accountable for her decisions if all that stands between Mary being Mary and not someone else is a simple bump on the head?

Wandering down the hall in search of the tape, she finds a room with a computer on a mahogany desk and a leather chair on a clear plastic mat over the carpet. Wynn's camera is on the chair, and in a metal tray beside the computer she finds a stack of small gray tapes. She can't sort through them here. She'll just have to take them all with her. She dumps out a bag of tangled cables, connectors, and startup disks and drops the tapes into the bag. Then she adds the camera, just in case.

The hallway is quiet. Brooks is upstairs somewhere—and the dogs? At the bottom of the stairwell, she hears their nails. "Get out, Brooks!" she yells, and runs back the way she came, down the hall, past the grandfather clock and the pantry, into the kitchen, all of it so familiar now. She goes out the back door and into the yard, the sunlight on her face, a stultifying whiteness. One day she will forget everything, and there will be nothing left of her except . . . This. Whatever This is. Total erasure, maybe.

She roams around the perimeter of the house, searching for any sign of Brooks up in the windows. She sees a popped-out screen in some bushes, but there's no sign of Brooks up above in the window. On the front porch, she leans into a narrow window beside the door with her hands cupped around her eyes. Through the thin white curtain she can barely make out a table in the foyer, a painting on the wall above that, and the base of the wide staircase. She rings the doorbell three times, hears it echo in the house. She is about to abandon the porch when through the window she sees feet, then knees, then a torso. Brooks is striding down the stairs as if he owns the place.

The dogs follow him, no longer vicious at all, their heavy dumb tongues lolling over sharp, crooked teeth. Her brother has tamed the beasts. The dead bolt clicks open, and there he is, framed in the doorway, her big brother.

The dog bite isn't deep enough to warrant a trip to the emergency room. "No more stitches," he says. "Please." Back at Mary's, he takes a hot shower and lets the water trickle over his wound. Blood swirls around the drain. He towels off and wraps his ankle with gauze and then falls into a long nap on top of the covers. When he wakes up, it's dark out. He does his exercises at the foot of the bed, then heads downstairs. In the den, the blinds are drawn and the television screen casts a blue light across the furniture. On the floor, stacks of gray tapes surround a video camera tethered to the television by a long cord.

Brooks sits down cross-legged and brings the camera into his lap. He can hear Mary in the kitchen, rattling pots, preparing dinner. The tapes all look the same. He picks one off the top and pops it into the camera. When he pushes play, he keeps his finger on the button, just in case he's presented with something no brother wants to see.

Two lines squiggle across the screen, and then a patio appears, a concrete space bright with sunlight. The camera is bouncy in someone's hand. Two kids are on the ground, dyeing Easter eggs in red Dixie cups. The boy, maybe twelve years old, gives an egg to his younger sister. Holding it between two fingers, she dips it in the cup.

"Hey, I didn't know you were awake," Mary says, striding into the den in an apron. When she sees what he's watching, she sighs and sits down beside him on the floor. They stare up at the television together.

It's been years, Brooks thinks, since he last saw this tape, but it's all coming back to him now: their dye-stained fingertips, Easter eggs buried in the pine straw, the smell of the azalea bushes, his mother lounging in the yard with her Bible and *People* magazines.

"Seems like yesterday that was us," Mary says.

The little girl on the screen knocks over the cup and colored water spills all over her dress, the blue dye splashed up across her chest. She faces the camera bewildered, looking for help or reassurance, maybe, and begins to cry.

"We shouldn't be watching this," Mary says, and grabs the camera from Brooks's lap. "It's wrong. Do you think I should try to return this stuff? I feel awful about it. I guess I could leave it all on the doorstep."

As she's saying this, a woman Brooks doesn't recognize rushes onto the screen with a handful of paper towels for the little girl's dress, and only then does he fully understand that this isn't their patio or their Easter or their mother. This isn't their childhood at all, and never was. "Stop clinging to the Old Brooks," Dr. Groom likes to say, "and guess what? You'll still be you."

He looks over at Mary, her finger poised on the stop button. But she doesn't press stop. She doesn't pull the cable from the camera or gather the tapes back into the crinkling bag, either. She is watching the boy, on-screen, as he holds up a perfect egg and then runs out of the frame. The little girl climbs onto her mother's lap and cries into her shoulder. The scene cuts: The kids are off searching for the eggs—in tree limbs, desk drawers, mulch beds, and, improbably, under a doormat. "Not there," Mary says aloud. "I mean, really." When the video ends, the room is dark, and they are quiet. Brooks waits a few seconds before sliding another tape across the floor to her. Mary's eyes dart up his arm to his face, her expression so serious that he wonders if she's really allowing herself to see him for the first time since the accident. He mushrooms out his upper lip, imitating her pity smile, and she rolls her eyes.

Then she loads the next tape.

Elizabeth Strout
Snow Blind

Bᴀᴄᴋ ᴛʜᴇɴ ᴛʜᴇ ʀᴏᴀᴅ they lived on was a dirt road and they lived at the end of it, about a mile from Route 4. This was in the north in the potato country, and back when the Appleby children were small the winters were icy and snow-filled and there were months when the road seemed impassably narrow. Weather was different then, like a family member you couldn't avoid. You took it without thinking much. Clayton Appleby attached a sturdy snowplow to his sturdiest tractor, and he was usually able to clear the way enough to get the kids to school. Clayton had grown up in farm country and he knew about weather and he knew about potatoes and he knew who in the county sold their bags with hidden rocks for weight. He was a closed book of a man, he inhabited himself with economy, but his family under-stood he loathed dishonesty in any form. He did have surprising and sudden moments of liveliness. For example he could imitate perfectly old Miss Lurvy, who ran the Historical Society's tiny museum—"The first flush toilet in Aroostook County," he would say, heaving back his narrow shoulders as though he had a large bosom, "belonged to a judge who was known to beat his wife quite regularly." Or he might pretend to be a tramp looking for food, holding out his hand, his blue eyes beseeching, and his children would laugh themselves sick, until his wife, Sylvia, got them calmed down. On winter mornings he let the car warm up in the driveway, scraping the ice from its windows, exhaust billowing about him until the kids tumbled down the salt-dappled snow of the steps. There were three other kids on the road—two boys in the Daigle family, and their sister, Charlene, who was close to the age of the youngest Appleby child, a strange little girl named Annie.

Annie was skinny and lively and so prone to talkativeness that her mother was not altogether sorry when she spent hours by herself in the woods playing with sticks or making angels in the snow. She was the only Appleby child to inherit the Acadian olive skin tone and dark hair from her mother and grandmother, and the sight of her red hat and dark head coming across the snow fields was as common as seeing a nuthatch at the bird feeder.

One morning when Annie was five and going to kindergarten she told the carful of children—her brother and sister and the Daigle boys and Charlene—that God spoke to her when she was outside in the woods. Her sister said, "You're so stupid, why don't you shut up." Annie bounced on the seat beside her father and she said, "He does, though! God talks to me." Her sister asked how did he do that, and Annie answered, "He puts thoughts in my head." She looked up at her father then, and saw something in his eyes as he turned to look at her that stayed with her always; something that did not seem like her father, not yet, something that seemed not good. "You all get out," he said, when he pulled up in front of the school. "I have to speak to Annie." When the car doors had slammed shut, he said to his daughter, "What is it you saw in the woods?"

She thought about this. "I saw the trees and chickadees."

Her father stayed silent a long time, gazing over the top of the steering wheel. Annie had never been scared of her father the way Charlene was scared of hers. And Annie wasn't scared of her mother, who was the cozier parent, but not the most important one. "Go on, now." Her father nodded at her, and she pushed herself across the seat, her snow pants squeaking, and he leaned and got the door, saying, "Watch your fingers," before he pulled it shut.

That was the year Jamie Appleby did not like his teacher. "He makes me sick," Jamie said, throwing his boots in the mudroom. Like his father, Jamie was not a talker, and Sylvia, watching this, had a quick flush come to her face.

"Is Mr. Potter mean to you?"

"No."

"Then what?"

"I don't know."

Jamie was in the fourth grade and Sylvia loved him more than her daughters; he caused an almost unbearable sweetness to spread through her. That he should suffer anything was intolerable. She loved Annie gently because the child was so strange and harmless. The middle child, Cindy, Sylvia loved with a mild generosity. Cindy was the dullest of the three and probably the most like her mother.

It was also the year Jamie saved up his money and gave his father a tape recorder for his birthday. This turned into a terrible moment because his father, after unwrapping the present with barely any rips to the wrapping paper, the way he always unwrapped things, said, "You're the one who wants a tape recorder, James. It's indecent to give someone a present you want yourself, though it happens all the time."

"Clayton," Sylvia murmured. It was true that Jamie had wanted a tape recorder, and his pale cheeks burned red. The tape recorder was put away on the top shelf of the coat closet.

Annie, talkative as she was, did not mention this to anyone, including her grandmother next door. Her grandmother's house was a small square house, and in the long white months of winter the house seemed stark and bare naked, the windows like eyes stuck open, looking toward the farm. The old woman was from the St. John Valley and was said to have been beautiful in her day. (Annie's mother had once been beautiful too, photos showed that.) Now the old woman was stick thin and tiny wrinkles covered her face. "I would like to die," she said languidly, from where she lay on her couch. Annie sat cross-legged in the big chair nearby. Her grandmother drew in the air with her finger. "I would like to close my eyes right now and pass away." She lifted her head of white hair and looked over at Annie. "I'm blue," she added. She put her head back down.

"I'd miss you," said Annie. It was a Saturday and it had snowed all day, the flakes big and wet and thick, sticking to the lower windowpanes in curves.

"You wouldn't. You only come over here to get a piece of candy. You have a brother and a sister to talk to. I don't know why the three of you don't play together."

"We're not in the appetite." Annie had once asked her brother to play cards and he had said he was not in the appetite. She picked at a hole in her sock. "Our teacher says if you look at the fields right after it snows and the sun is shining hard you can get blind." Annie craned her neck to see out the window.

"Then don't look," her grandmother said.

When Annie was in the fifth grade, she began staying at Charlene Daigle's house more. Annie was still lively and talked incessantly, but there had been an incident with the long-forgotten tape recorder—a secret that she shared with Jamie—and ever since the incident it was as though a skin was compressed round her own family; the farm, her quiet brother, her sulky sister, her smiling mother, who often said, "I feel sorry for the Daigles. He's always so grumpy and he yells at the kids. We're awfully lucky to have a happy family." All of it made Annie picture a sausage, and she had poked a small hole in the casing and was trying to squirm out. Mr. Daigle did not really yell at his kids; in fact, when she and Charlene took a bath he often came in to wash them with a washcloth. Her own father thought bodies were private and had recently become red-faced and yelled—yelled hard!—because Cindy had not wrapped her sanitary pad adequately with toilet paper before putting it in the garbage. He had made her come and get it and wrap it up more. It caused Annie to tremble inside; the skin of the sausage was shame. Her family was encased in shame. She felt this more than she thought it, the way children do. But she thought when she was old enough for that awful thing to happen to her own body she would bury the things outside in the woods.

So she went to Charlene's house after school and they made large snowpeople that Mr. Daigle sprayed with the hose so they would turn icy and glasslike in the morning. When it was too cold to be outside Annie and Charlene made up stories and acted them out. Her father, stopping by to get her, would stand with Mrs. Daigle and watch them. Mrs. Daigle wore red lipstick, there was something fierce about her; Clayton Appleby got a twinkle in his eye when he talked with her. It was not a look he got when he talked to his wife, and one Saturday afternoon Annie said quite suddenly, "This is a dumb play we made up. I want to go home." Walking back up the road to their house she still held her father's hand as she had always done. Around them the fields were endless and white, edged by the dark trunks of trees and their spruce boughs weighed down with the snow. "Daddy," she said, blurting it out, "what's the most important thing to you?"

"You of course." He did not break his stride. "My family." His answer was immediate and calm.

"And Mama?"

"The most important of all."

Joy spilled around Annie, and in her memory it stayed that way for years. The walk back up the road to her house, holding the hand of her father, the fields quieting in their brightness, the trees darkening to a navy green, the milky sun behind their house that was the color of the snow. Once inside she knocked softly on the door of her brother's room. He was in high school and small hairs were on his upper lip. She closed the door behind her and said, "Nana's just a mean old witch. Nobody likes her. Not one person."

Her brother kept looking at the comic book he held open. "I don't know what you're talking about," he said. But when Annie sighed and turned to go, he said, "Of course she's an old hag. And don't worry about her. You always exaggerate everything." He was quoting his mother, who said that Annie exaggerated things.

The farm had belonged to Sylvia's father. Clayton came from three towns away, and he had been raised in a trailer with a family that had no money, farm, or religion. He had worked on farms, though, and knew the business, and after he married Sylvia he took over the farm when his father-in-law died. At some point before Annie's memory, the house for her grandmother had been built. Until then she had lived in the main house with the rest of the family.

"Listen to this," Jamie had said, coming to Annie one day before supper, and they went to the barn and huddled in the loft. "I hid it under Nana's couch before Ma came over." The tape recorder clicked and whirred. Then there was the clear voice of their grandmother saying to her daughter, "Sylvia, it gags me. I lie here and I want to vomit. But you've made your bed. So you lie in the bed you made, my dear." And there was the sound of their mother crying. There was some murmur of a question. Should she speak to the priest? Their grandmother said, "I'd be too embarrassed, if I were you."

It seemed to be forever, the white snow around them, her grandmother next door lying on her couch wanting to die, Annie still the one who chattered constantly. She was now an inch short of six feet and thin as a wire, her dark hair long and wavy. Her father found her one day behind the barn and he said, "I want you to stop going off into the woods the way you do. I don't know what you're up to there." Her amazement had more to do with the disgust and anger of his expression. She said she was up to nothing.

"I'm not asking you, I'm telling you, Annie, you stop, or I'll see to it you never leave this house." She opened her mouth to say, Are you crazy, but the thought touched her mind that maybe he was, and this frightened her in a way she had not known a person could be frightened. "Okay," she said. But it turned out she could not stay away from the woods on days when the sun was bright. The physical world with its dappled light was her earliest friend and it waited with its open-armed beauty to accept her sense of excitement that nothing else could bring. She learned the rhythms of those around her, where they would be and when, and she slipped into the woods closer to town, or behind the school, and there she would sing with gentleness and exuberance a song she'd made up years earlier: "I'm so glad that I'm living, just so glaaad that I'm living—" She was waiting.

And then she wasn't waiting, because Mr. Potter saw her in a school play and arranged for her to be in a summer theater, and people in the summer theater took her to Boston, then she was gone. She was seventeen years old and the fact that her parents did not object, did not even ask her to finish high school, occurred to her only later. At the time there were various men, many of them fat and soft and with large rings on their fingers, who held her close in darkened theaters and murmured how lovely she was, like a fawn in the woods, and they sent her to different auditions, found her people to stay with in different rooms in different towns; people, she found, who were extraordinarily, unbelievably kind. The same compression of God's presence she knew in the woods expanded into strangers who loved her, and she went from stage to stage around the country and when she came back to visit the house at the end of the road she was really surprised by how small it was, how low the ceilings. The gifts she bore, sweaters and jewelry and wallets and watches—knockoffs bought from city sidewalk vendors—seemed to embarrass her family. Her very presence seemed to embarrass them. "You're so thespian," her father murmured in a voice coated with distaste.

"No I'm not," she said, because she thought he had said *lesbian*.

His face had gotten heavier, though he was still lean. He slid a watch across the table to her. "Find someone else who can use this. When have you ever seen me wear a watch?"

But her grandmother, who looked just the same, sat up and said, "You've become beautiful, Annie. How did that happen? Tell me everything." And so Annie sat in the big chair and told her about dressing rooms and small apartments in different towns and how everyone took care of each other and how she never forgot her lines. Her grandmother said, "Don't come back. Don't get married. Don't have children. All those things will bring you heartache."

For a long time Annie did not come back. She sometimes missed her mother, as though she felt across the miles a wave of sadness lapping up to her from Sylvia, but when she telephoned, her mother always said, "Oh, not much here is new," and did not seem at all interested in what Annie was doing. Her sister never wrote or called, and Jamie very seldom. At Christmastime she sent home boxes of gifts until her mother sighed over the telephone and said, "Your father wants to know what we're to do with all this rubbish." This hurt her feelings but not lastingly because those she lived with and knew from the theater were so warm and kind and outraged on her behalf. The older members of any cast treated Annie with tenderness and so without realizing it, she stayed in lots of ways a child. "Your innocence protects you," a director told her once, and in truth she did not know what he meant.

There is a saying that every woman should have three daughters because that way there will be one to take care of you in old age. Annie Appleby was everywhere—California, London, Amsterdam, Pittsburgh—and the only place Sylvia could find her was in a gossip magazine at the drugstore, where her name had been linked with a famous movie star. This embarrassed Sylvia; people in town learned not to mention it. Cindy was nearby in New

Hampshire; she'd had many children quickly and a husband who wanted her home. So it was Jamie who stayed at the farm, unmarried. Silently he worked alongside his father, who remained strong even with age. Silently he tended to the needs of his grandmother next door. Sylvia often said, "What would I do without you, Jamie?" and he would shake his head. His mother was lonely, he knew. He saw how his father increasingly did not speak with her. His father began to eat sloppily, which he had never done. The sound of his chewing was notable; bits of food fell down on his shirt. "Clayton, my goodness," Sylvia said, rising to get a napkin, and he shook her off. "For Christ's sake, woman!"

Privately Sylvia said, "What's wrong with your father?" But Jamie shrugged and they did not talk about it again until Jamie, going through the books, realized what was happening. Terribly, it all made sense: his father's querulousness, his sudden asking repeatedly where Annie was, "Where is that child? Is she in the woods again?" All this fell into Jamie's stomach with the silence of a stone falling into the darkness of a well. Within a year they could not care for the man; he ran away, he started a fire in the barn, he drove them insane with his questions: "Where's Annie? Is she in the woods?" And so they found him a home, and Clayton was furious to be there. Sylvia stopped visiting because he was so angry when she came, one time calling her a cow. The sisters were informed, and Cindy came home for a few days, but Annie could not. She said she could be there by spring.

When she turned off Route 4, Annie was surprised to find the dirt road had been paved, and it was no longer a narrow road. A few new and large houses had been added near the Daigle place. She would not have recognized where she was. Cindy was in the kitchen, which seemed even smaller than the last time Annie had come home, and when Annie bent to kiss her, Cindy just stood without moving. Their mother, said Jamie, was upstairs; she would be down after the kids had talked. Annie felt the physical, almost electric, aspects of alarm and sank slowly into a chair as she unbuttoned her coat. Jamie spoke carefully and directly. Their father was being asked to leave the home he was in; he was abusive to the orderlies, Jamie said, making sexual passes at all the men, grabbing at their crotches, and was altogether disruptive. A psychiatrist had seen him, and their father had given permission for their talks to be shared, though how a man with dementia could give permission Jamie did not understand, but as a result Sylvia had learned that for years Clayton had a relationship with Seth Potter, they were lovers, Sylvia said she had often suspected this, and Clayton was, demented as he might be, referring to himself as a raging homosexual, and he was very graphic in things he said; they would most likely have to put him in a far less pleasant place, there was no money unless they sold the farm and no one was buying potato farms these days.

"All right," Annie finally said. Her siblings had been silent for many minutes and their faces seemed so young and sad although they were middle-aged faces with middle-aged lines. "All right, we'll deal with this." She nodded at them reassuringly. Later she went next door to see her grandmother, who seemed surprisingly unchanged. She lay on the couch and watched her granddaughter go about turning on lights. "You came home to deal with your father? Your mother's had a hell of a time."

"Yes," Annie said, and sat in the big chair nearby.

"If you want my opinion your father went mad because of his behavior. Being a pervert. I always knew he was a homo, and that can drive you insane, and now he's insane, that's my opinion if you want it."

"I don't," Annie said gently.

"Then tell me something exciting. Where have you been that's exciting?"

Annie looked at her. The old woman's face was expectant as a child's, and Annie felt an unbidden and almost unbearable gash of compassion for this woman who had lived in this house for years. She said, "I went to the ambassador's home in London. They had the whole production there for dinner. That was exciting."

"Oh, tell me everything, Annie."

"Let me sit a minute." And so they were silent, her grandmother lying back down like a young person trying to be patient, and Annie, who up until this very day had always felt like a child—which is why she could not marry, she could not be a "wife"—now felt ancient. She thought how for years onstage she had used the image of walking up the dirt road holding her father's hand, the snow-covered fields spread around them, the woods in the distance, joy spilling through her—how she had used this scene to have tears immediately come to her eyes, for the happiness of it, and the loss of it. And now she wondered if it had even happened, if the road had ever been narrow and dirt, if her father had ever held her hand and said his family was the most important thing to him.

"That's right," she had said earlier to her sister, who cried out that were it true they would have known. What Annie did not say was that there were many ways of not knowing things; her own experience over the years now spread like a piece of knitting in her lap with shadows all through it. In her thirties now, Annie had loved men; her heart had often been broken. Currents of treachery and deceit seemed to run everywhere; the forms it took always surprised her. But she had many friends and they had their disappointments too, and nights and days were spent giving support and being supported; the theater world was a cult, Annie thought. It took care of its own even while it hurt you. She had recently, though, had fantasies of what they called "going normal." Having a house and a husband and children and a garden. The quietness of all that. But what would she do with all the feelings that streamed down her like small rivers? It was not the sound of applause Annie liked—in fact, she often barely heard it—it was the moment onstage when she knew she had left the world and joined fully another. Not unlike the feelings of ecstasy she'd had in the woods as a child.

Her father must have worried she would come across him in the woods. Annie shifted in the big chair.

"Did they tell you about Charlene?" her grandmother asked.

"Charlene Daigle?" Annie turned to look at the old woman. "What about her?"

"She's started a chapter for incest people. Incest Survivors I believe they're called."

"Are you serious?"

"Soon as that father died, she started it. Ran an article in the newspaper, said one out of five children are sexually abused. Honestly, Annie. What a world."

"But that's awful. Poor Charlene!"

"She looked pretty good in her picture. Heavier. She's gotten heavier."

"My God," Annie said softly. She stood to go, touching lightly the top of her grandmother's head, thinking how in the kitchen Cindy had said quietly, "We must have been the laughingstock of the county."

"No," Jamie had said to her. "Whatever he did, he hid."

Annie had seen how their distress showed in their guarded faces. "Oh," she had said, feeling maternal, protective toward them. "It doesn't really matter."

But it did! Oh, it did.

Back in the main house, Sylvia sat with her children for supper in the kitchen. "I heard about Charlene," Annie said. "It's unbelievably sad."

"If it's true," answered Sylvia.

Annie looked at her siblings, but they looked at the food they moved into their mouths. "Why would it not be true? Why would someone make that up?" Jamie shrugged and Annie saw—or felt she saw—that Charlene's burdens were nothing to them; their own universe and its wild recent unmooring was all that mattered now. Sylvia went upstairs to bed, and the three sat talking by the wood stove. Jamie especially could not stop talking. Their silent father in his state of dementia seemed unable to keep himself from spilling forth all he had held on to secretly for years, and Jamie, who had been silent himself, now had to tumble all he heard before them. "One time they saw you in the woods, Annie, and he was always afraid after that you'd find them." Annie nodded. Cindy looked at her with a pained face, as though Annie should have had more of a reaction than that. Annie put her hand over her sister's for a moment. "But one of the strangest things he said," Jamie reported, sitting back, "was that he drove us to school so he could, just for those moments, be near Seth Potter. He didn't even see him, dropping us off. But he liked knowing he was close to him each morning. That Seth was only a few feet away, inside the school."

"Oh God, it makes me sick," Cindy said.

Jamie squinted at the wood stove. "It puzzles me, is all."

The vulnerability of their faces Annie could almost not bear. She looked around the small kitchen, the wallpaper that had water stains streaking down it, the rocking chair their father had always sat in, the cushion now with a rip large enough to show the stuffing, the teakettle on the stove that had been the same one for years, the curtain across the top of the window with a fine spray of cobwebs between it and the pane. Annie looked back at her siblings. They may not have felt the daily dread that poor Charlene had lived with. But the truth was always there. They had grown up on shame; it was the nutrient of their soil. Yet, oddly, it was her father she felt she understood the best. And for a moment Annie wondered at this, that her brother and sister, good, responsible, decent, fair minded, had never known the passion that caused a person to risk everything they had, everything they held dear heedlessly put in danger—simply to be near the white dazzle of the sun that somehow for those moments seemed to leave the Earth behind.

Vauhini Vara

I, Buffalo

T HE EVENT IN QUESTION took place at the end of the summer. I don't recall which day. That summer the days failed to
distinguish themselves from one another, and given that failure,
I don't see why I should do the distinguishing for them. I can tell
you that this anonymous day began warmly. I know this because
I began the day on the bus and recall perching on the edge of the
seat so that my thighs wouldn't stick to the plastic. I had woken
early and, unable to sleep, decided to go to the park.

The only other people on the bus were a young black woman
and her son, who sat across from me. The mother wore a fur coat,
and the boy sat on her lap facing me with the hem of his mother's
coat tight in his fist. He might have been four years old.

"Hot day for a coat like that," I said to the mother.

"Pardon?" the mother said defensively, as if I had cast an accusation.

"Hot day," I said. "I'm going to Golden Gate Park."

The mother ignored me. The boy fidgeted and squirmed on
her lap and, finally, his mother said tiredly, "Baby, you want a
grenade?" The boy looked up at her with delight and nodded.

"What do you say?" she said.

"Momma. Give me a grenade."

"Nuh-uh. What do you say?"

"Please, Momma. Give me a grenade."

The mother seemed satisfied with this. She said, "All right," and reached into her purse.

As I watched her fumble, I realized I was sweating. The heat was part of it, but I was also starting to feel anxious. I had my hand on the bell cord, ready to pull at any time, as if it were some sort of alarm, but when the mother drew her hand from the purse and opened it to the boy, her thick-lined palm was empty.

"Here you go, baby," said the mother.

The boy took the imaginary grenade, pulled on an imaginary pin, and the next thing I knew, he had his eyes fixed on me and his arm pulled back. A gasp flew from my lips, and one of my own arms threw itself up in defense. I put it this way because they, the gasp and my arm, seemed to act of their own accord. I never would have done such a thing myself.

The boy froze, then turned to look at his mother, who shook her head at me.

"Child's just playing. Dang."

"I'm sorry. I've got a hangover."

I've always had a habit of sharing too much with strangers. In my youth, my mother coached me against this, and for a long time I held back. But over the past eight months, my opportunities for conversation had been limited. No more morning banter with the man and the dog. No more phone calls with clients. I couldn't help it.

"I don't drink," the mother said through pious pursed lips. "Haven't in five years." She indicated, with her chin, the boy.

"That's good," I said. "Nothing good comes of it." I added, "You hear stories like that—a woman has a child, and it saves her life." I wanted badly for the mother to think well of me. "I like your coat," I said, when she didn't respond.

But she didn't respond to that, either—only pushed a big

horse's breath of air through her nostrils, then turned her gaze toward the front of the bus and sat silently.

Nothing good does come of it. I wasn't lying about that, nor am I lying about anything else that happened that day. I haven't lied since I took an oath, long ago, to behave in a manner consistent with the truth. At the time I found the language strange—that I behave not necessarily in a truthful manner but only in a manner consistent with the truth—but after a while I got used to it.

That was a long time ago.

Still, I know some facts consistent with the truth.

I am a woman. I am thirty-six years old.

At the time of the event, my apartment had been recently vacated by the others who had formerly inhabited it with me—a forty-four-year-old man from Oregon and a sixteen-year-old dog of unknown breed. The man was a hopeful and bighearted man who demanded much goodness of others and was therefore often disappointed. I trusted him completely.

He had taken the dog, too.

They left behind them a great and holy emptiness. It resembled the alarming emptiness that cathedrals and mosques hold for those of us who believe in nothing beyond what is proven to exist. We feel ourselves surrounded only by unfilled space. That's where I lived at the time of the event.

I awoke that afternoon to the smell of spoiled fish and a fierce headache, and I could remember nothing of what had transpired between the bus and my awakening. Not a single detail. The morning on the bus seemed as far away as another continent.

This was not, I'll admit, an altogether alien feeling. I'll be direct. I've blacked out many times in my life. I was a teenager when it began. I'm ashamed of this. Any addict who says she's not ashamed is lying to you or to herself. I believe it makes matters worse if you don't fit a particular profile. You spend your days

322 / VAUHINI VARA

all buttoned up in your white shirt and pressed pants and iron-flattened hair like a perfect productive citizen. It's not a lie—it's not as if colleagues say, "Are you an addict?" and you say, "No way!" Still. *Fraudulent*—that's probably the term.

The smell of spoiled fish brought a couple of details back. At some point earlier in the day, I recalled, I had opened a takeout box of sushi and a bottle of wine. I had finished the wine. I had vomited.

That's all I had.

My apartment has two floors, which makes it sound larger than it is. I woke in my bed in the bedroom, which is upstairs, with the door open to the hallway. It seemed that the smell came from the hallway. I ventured out there and found that my hunch was correct: Out in the hallway, the smell was truly noxious, as if the entire, brackish marine world had washed up into my apartment. I felt a prick of recollection: Something had gone wrong. I hadn't reached the toilet in time; I hadn't reached a garbage can; I hadn't found my way to the kitchen sink.

But where had I done it, then?

Downstairs, the smell was fainter—enough that my sense of urgency diminished. In the kitchen, the sun shone warmly onto the countertop. The sky that day was fogless and clear and blue. I checked the living room, ducking to inspect the fireplace for good measure, but saw nothing. I felt clearheaded and alert as I went through these motions, but as soon as I became aware of this, my anxiety welled up again. I'd been through enough evenings like this. I knew the hangover was only dormant. It would surely come alive at some point later in the night. *Good God,* I thought. How had I slept so long?

That's when my sister called.

They were on their way up from Los Angeles for the weekend.

"Who?" I accused.

She and Sam and Mara, she said. Right now they were outside of Sacramento.

"You're staying here?"

"You're asking?"

"This is an ambush. Whose idea was this?"

"Where do you want us to stay? The Hyatt?"

"Did they put you up to it?"

"Oh my God. Are you seriously that paranoid? Hold on. She's being paranoid. Hold on. Mara's got an audition. She's all excited. Sam says we'll be there in a couple hours."

"Cool," I deadpanned.

"You act like you don't want us to come. Mara wants to know why you don't want us to come."

"Tell Mara it's because I know you have ulterior motives."

"She doesn't know what that means, ulterior motives. Hold on. Nothing, Mara. She says she does want us to come. Hold on. Mara wants to know what's for dinner."

"Dinner?" I said. "Pizza?"

"Takeout?"

"No. I don't know why you'd assume that."

"I'm not assuming anything. We get takeout all the time."

"It's not takeout," I said.

Because I know how to make pizza. In fact, I'd already had the idea earlier that week at the grocery store when I came across the cheap premade dough sitting next to the hummus like a bagged breast. I had tried to pick out good tomatoes for that purpose. To make good pizza sauce, you have to pick tomatoes that smell a certain way, according to an Italian friend of mine—yeasty, my friend said, almost like beer. So I had held a tomato to my face and sniffed. The tomato smelled only like itself—tomatoey. I had picked up another one and smelled, then another, then another. My mind had latched on to this one word, *yeasty*, and wouldn't allow me to move on. *Yeasty*, said my mind, *yeasty*, and finally I just picked the best-looking tomatoes, the reddest and closest to bursting, and continued to the meat department.

By the time I hung up with my sister, I'll admit, I'd forgotten all about the smell. I started making the pizza. I chopped the tomatoes. I rolled out the dough. I had a great satisfying sense of being a civilized person in a civilized world. Only when it was all ready to go did I pour myself a drink. A glass of wine. I can handle, you understand, a glass of wine.

At the sound of the doorbell, panic rose in my throat. I lit a vanilla-scented candle and set it on the kitchen table. The candle had already burned down nearly to the bottom. When I opened the door, and Mara came bounding inside and took a running leap into my arms, I can't explain the feeling I had. I want to call it euphoric. But I know how that makes me sound. As if this might have been the onset of some kind of episode.

"Auntie Sheila!" she said into my shoulder.

"Mars Bar!" I said. I'll tell you—I had nearly forgotten how much I love my niece. My Mars Bar. When was the last time we'd seen each other? I never saw her these days. Mara was wearing what looked like pajamas—a dinosaur-patterned jumper with built-in footies. Sam and Priya stood shoulder to shoulder in the doorway. They were the same height and had grown to look alike over the ten years of their marriage—the same mildly skeptical smile, the same slight stoop of their shoulders. "Let's play!" I said.

"It's almost bedtime," Priya said.

"She has to wake up early for the audition," Sam added.

Mara is a child actress. She auditions for all sorts of roles. I knew they sometimes traveled. But San Francisco? What kind of a film got made in San Francisco? Who had ever heard of that? Once Woody Allen made a movie in the Haight. A colleague of mine saw him at Zam Zam. So maybe this wasn't only a pretense for checking in on me. Maybe our parents hadn't put Priya up to this after all. I started to let my guard down. Then Sam sniffed at the air, and I felt a sharp synaptic twitch as I remembered the vomit. I shifted Mara's weight onto my hip.

"Come in, come in," I said to them all. "Give me your coat," I said to my sister. "I like your coat."

Et cetera.

I was trying to distract them from the smell.

"Give me your coat, give me your bags," I said. "Give me all of it—I'll put it up in the room. How was the drive?"

They didn't give me any of it. "Don't be so formal," Sam said. "We'll take it up, no problem."

But the smell, I told myself. *But you don't want to act weird,* I answered myself. "Whatever," I said.

While they went upstairs to put their bags down, Mara wandered around the living room, picking up various objects—a snow globe on the television, a framed photo of me and my ex that I couldn't bring myself to take down—and setting them down again. She wore enormously thick eyeglasses, and her hair was done up in a pair of uneven pigtails. Glasses aside, she looked strikingly similar to how Priya had looked as a child, despite Mara's bland-faced whitey of a father.

I suddenly remembered another part of what had happened between morning and evening.

"Hey, kiddo," I said, "you want to see a buffalo?"

"I've seen one," she said.

"Are you sure?" I said. "A real one?"

"They have them at the zoo," she said.

"This is different," I said. "These ones are in the park."

Because that's what I had been going to do that morning. I was on this kick. I had been treating myself to the sights of San Francisco that I had been too busy to visit during my working life. When I got off the bus, I stopped and bought a little bottle of bourbon. The smallest, cutest bottle. A child could hold it in one fist. The bourbon glowed from within like liquid sun. It took all my willpower to put the bourbon back in its paper bag and to hold that bag tight till I got to where I was going. Good God, it was hot. When I got to the paddock, I was drenched in sweat. There were supposed to be nine of them—three adults, six children, all female, because the park had moved the males when they figured out the obscene amount of humping all the males and females were doing—but I saw only one. She had the top-heavy build of a boxer—this barreled chest, these thick shoulders, this impenetrable wall of a forehead, all balanced on top of four matchstick legs. For her to stand on those legs and get from one place to another should have been impossible. It defied all good sense. Yet that's what she did. She walked with great grace, as if nothing mattered but to walk. Her shoulders pumped with strength. Her legs, truth be told, tottered a little. When she came to a patch of yellow grass where some wildflowers had sprouted, she stopped and lowered her head as if for benediction. She was massive and shaggy and humpbacked and ancient. Her grace made me feel like the smallest of creatures. She ate the flowers.

I pressed my face to the grid of the wire fence, cool against my skin, and I called out to her. "Hey, girl," I said. "Hey."

She ignored me. Truly, it was as if I wasn't there. And maybe I wasn't, I started to feel. There was not another human being in sight. Only me and the great animal. Who was I to allege that I existed? For what reason should I exist? Where was the proof?

And it's true that it was hot that day. And it's true that I was sipping from my bottle. But the strangest thing happened. Having eaten, the buffalo raised her head again, and I felt a great top spin of joy at this. She continued her walk in my direction. She was so close I could see her eyebrows, and this, too, seemed miraculous. An instant later, she tumbled to the ground on her side as if felled. Her body sent up a puff of brown dirt. In that moment, I had a really strange experience. I felt as if I had fallen to the ground myself. I could taste the dust in the air. Every muscle in my body relaxed. I was not a thinking being. I was free. This lasted for only an instant. Then the buffalo rolled onto her feet and stood, and I was myself again. I stood there gripping the fence waiting for the feeling to return, but it didn't.

Mara came across as very comfortable in her own skin, the way child actors often do.

"You want to know something interesting?" she said.

"What?"

"The Donners ate each other. You know them? The Donner Party?"

I was taken aback. I hadn't remembered her being this gruesome. By the time I thought of what to say—"Not personally," I wanted to say, to be a little funny—Mara had moved on. She was wandering around the room, every once in a while asking a question: "Who's this?" Or, pointing the remote control at the TV, "How does this work?" She moved really fast. I couldn't keep up.

"Sheila?" she said after some time.

"Yeah?"

"What's that smell?" she said.

"What smell?" I said. "Must be your upper lip."

Over dinner, they explained that Mara's audition was for a film about the Oregon Trail. Mara had been doing her research to get into character—getting Priya to take her to the local library and read to her from musty hardcovers. That was how she had discovered the story of the Donners, who had eaten each other.

"Gross," Priya said.

"I wouldn't eat you," I said to Mara, "unless I was really hungry."

"Come on!" Priya said.

I chewed on a pizza crust, took a swig of beer, and grabbed another slice. I had fled Mara's question about the smell by giving my flippant answer, then running to the kitchen to put the pizzas in the oven. Now all seemed nice again. *We'll go see the buffalo tomorrow*, I thought. *Maybe tomorrow the others will be out.* I would say to Mara, "Did you know that the American buffalo is the largest mammal in North America? Technically, they're bison. At one point there were sixty million of them in the United States alone. That was before the United States existed. Then people showed up and hunted them so bad that there were only a couple hundred of them left. They were about to go completely extinct. So some people decided to save the bison. They got together and put a bunch of them in Golden Gate Park, and maybe some other places, too, and all these bison had a bunch of babies, and now they're not even close to going extinct." All of this was true. I had been surprised by this information, which I'd found on a big, faded tablet in the park.

"Do you know what *extinct* means?" Priya asked Mara. "It's when every single animal of one kind of animal dies."

"Yeah, like the Donner Party," Mara said.

"Oh, God," Priya moaned. "Sam."

"She does this great cannibalism routine," Sam said. He took a giant bite of his pizza and chewed with his mouth open. Spit and cheese sprayed from between his teeth. "Nom-nom-nom," he said, and when he finished, he patted his stomach. I laughed. He had grown one of those soft, domestic paunches. My own, lost man had one of those. A place to cup your hand at night. A place consistent with the truth if ever there was such a place. My God, I had lost it. "Method acting," he said—this other man, Priya's man, said this.

"Don't make fun of me!" Mara clattered her fork against her plate. It seemed she would cry, but she started laughing shyly.

"Don't mess around, you guys," Priya cried. "Sheila, Sheila, this gruesome streak of hers, it's actually sort of freaking me out."

At first, I felt a surge of pride that my little sister would still confide in me, after all that had happened. Then I wondered if my sister was implying something else. The truth was this: I had been a dark and gruesome child. I would persuade my poor baby sister to watch as I stretched a live worm with my fingertips until the tiny creature snapped in two or allowed a mosquito to rest on my thigh and fill itself up with my blood before thwacking my palm onto the sucker and smearing the resultant brown gunk across Priya's face. But our parents had ignored this, in light of my excellence at school and in piano lessons, and had focused on berating Priya for her learning difficulties and clumsy-fingered musical efforts.

Now, I recognized what was happening: Priya must have been waiting to find me in a moment of weakness. Now, here was that moment, and here was Priya's chess move: "this gruesome streak"—the implication being that there was a direct line, one that our parents had willfully ignored, between my own childhood gruesomeness and my recent fall from grace.

Oh, that.

Fine.

I might as well tell you about it: the so-called fall from so-called grace. My scandal involved a high-profile, married client. He had been in San Francisco on business for a day and a night, and we had agreed to meet for a drink at the martini bar atop his hotel. We were supposed to discuss a case involving asbestos in a housing complex in the Western Addition, but after a few drinks, we discovered that we had both spent part of our twenties in Shanghai, and all of a sudden, we were trading obscenities in Mandarin. I turned to look out at the sunset. This was a historic hotel, the kind of place at which girls were said to have sat in their sailors' laps before sending them off into the cold Pacific mist, and, thinking of this, I slid my hand across the table until my fingertips rested atop his own.

I don't know what to say.

I was in a sort of fix with respect to my man.

We had been together for ten years. But recently he had proposed to me, and after this, I had found myself hating him. I hated him for wanting to commit himself to me forever. He was the only person who knew me to my core. Yet he would have himself committed to me forever. Was he some kind of idiot?

I had accepted, of course.

But now this.

Before long, my client and I were back in his hotel room, and I was sharing with him several lines of cocaine, and I flirted with him by admitting that for other clients—who I at least had the good sense not to name, though all that came out in the end—I charged a lot of money for my drugs.

Then we were jumping on the bed. We were touching the ceiling with our fingertips. We were having so much fun. I was sucking on his thigh. This was a foreplay trick that my man with the dog liked. My client was making these sounds. My client sounded different from my man. He also looked different. He had this massive orb-like stomach and a pink coloring to my man's slim brown self.

I was considering this when I realized that my client was sobbing. The sight embarrassed me, especially because I had mistaken his boyish little gasps for noises of anticipatory pleasure.

"Could you just hold me?" he whispered.

The fun seemed over much too quickly. But I shimmied up the bed's twisted sheets and allowed him to lay his bearded head on my chest and whisper about how little he loved his wife, whom he respected for her intellect but with whom he had no romantic chemistry. His tears and snot salted the valley between my breasts. But the kids were still young. They were all he had. He pulled his phone from his pocket. Would I like to see some pictures? On Facebook? Maddie at the beach. Rico on his birthday. It was for them that he made his living taking advantage of the vulnerability of undocumented immigrants, because, we might as well both face the facts, lawyer and client, this was what we were doing. "I plead guilty!" he said. "Ha-ha!"

At this, my horror was complete. I finally stood and brought a hand towel from the bathroom and dabbed forcefully at his tears and snot.

"This didn't happen," I said. "I swear to God."

My indiscretion was discovered within days: Due to a slip of the finger, the client accidentally sent a drably suggestive e-mail meant for me (he wanted me to know that he couldn't stop thinking about my mouth) to the office manager in my firm, who was also named Sheila. Soon after that, the client confessed all—I have no idea why he did such a thing, but he did. I was fired. Of course, I had to tell my man. You know the rest, about his departure with the dog, and the emptiness.

It was the cocaine that turned them all against me. I guess it was his first time. People could say about the other behavior:

Well, it happens to the best of us. But the best of us don't oper-
ate side businesses selling drugs to law clients. The best of us—
maybe you're among them—feel that if attorneys, who take an
oath to behave in a manner consistent with the truth, go around
selling drugs, then everything is permissible. Well, what if it is?
Can there be a fall, I ask you, if there is no grace?

I went to the sink to refill the pitcher of water. "That's how kids
are," I said. And I feinted: "In fact, just this morning on the bus,
a little kid tried to throw a fake grenade at me." After freezing
like a little statue, his arm pulled back, the boy had dropped his
hand to his thigh. While his mother had spoken, he'd filled his
cheeks with air and slowly expelled it, meanwhile drumming
his fingers on his leg.

"It's shocking," Priya said, "how many irresponsible adults
there are in this world."

None of us spoke. We bent our heads over our pizzas, we
munched our crusts from end to end, we pinched between our
fingers the bits of sausage and pepper that had fallen to our plates
and ate those, too.

Sam sighed and went to the fridge for a second beer.

Priya burped. "Oh, God," she said. "I'm tipsy."

"Are you kidding?" I said. "You're not drunk."

I hated those women who would have two drinks and claim
to be drunk. Ooh, my delicate constitution. I couldn't believe my
little sister had turned into one of them. And she used to be the
one our parents worried about. *Keep an eye on her,* they told me.
She's not studying. And now you looked her up online, and she had
this great social media presence. She wrote about being a stage
mom, or whatever you call it. She got invited to write these guest
posts on these blogs. Meanwhile, an online search for my name
turned up reams of lurid detail. I held out hope that other, more
prominent Sheila Reddys would soon overtake me. Most of them
seemed unlikely candidates: a self-published poet in Virginia, a
doctor in Detroit, and three engineers—two in San Jose, one in

the Seattle area. But some seemed promising. I had my eye on the freelance journalist who had recently published an essay in *Marie Claire* and the marketing vice president at Procter & Gamble who, according to LinkedIn, had been slowly moving up the managerial chain. I prayed for the rise of those Sheilas.

Now, Mara spoke again. "Sheila, seriously—what's that smell?"

Priya and Sam turned to look at me, and I stood to clear the table, making a noisy pile of the plates and then going to the sink to slide the scraps into the garbage disposal. I could feel pinpricks under my arms, and I wondered if I was visibly sweating. "What?" I said, but even as I spoke, I knew I sounded stupid. I had to confess. "The smell?" I said, still standing at the sink. I said, like it was nothing, "I threw up somewhere."

"Oh, Sheil," Priya said. I didn't know which was worse—my sister's passive aggression minutes ago, or her pity now.

"I don't know where it is," I said, feeling smaller than the smallest person ever to have existed. "It's weird," I said.

There was silence. Then Sam said, "That's okay!" He grinned. "That's okay, Sheil! It happens to everyone." Priya opened her mouth as if to protest—it does not happen to everyone—but Sam had already scraped back his chair and rolled up his sleeves. "We'll help you," he said.

I wandered around the kitchen. Priya was drawn to the laundry room. Mara went upstairs by herself.

"Found it!" she called out to us. We went scrambling up the stairs to where she stood peering down into the laundry chute. That dark limbo space of the house.

"Mara, move it!" Priya cried out. This was dirty business. Grown-ups only. Mara stepped back in alarm at the sharpness of her mother's tone, and the rest of us crowded around the laundry chute.

The vomit had dried middrip along one side of the chute into a purplish brown crust of yellowtail, tuna, and fish eggs, decorated with rice globules and seaweed bits.

"Whoa," Sam said. And suddenly—just like that—I remembered. I had found myself, after visiting the buffalo, in the BART station downtown. How had I gotten there? That I don't remember. It had been rush hour. This had felt strange, I remembered, to be there among you working people—you weary, bow-backed working people, your fingers working your phones as if they were rosary beads: You whom I once had been. You were not identical. I don't mean to suggest that you were. You were in fact quite the opposite—each of you so very different from one another, your private concerns yours alone. One woman perched in the hollow of a phone booth with an accounting textbook open in her palm. She pressed the other hand to her forehead and mouthed the words as she read. People passed by and didn't notice her, nor did she notice them. You were like trees to one another, or pylons in an obstacle course. You had once been trees and pylons to me, too.

But now, I was undergoing a change. I felt ghostlike that morning, as if I had left the world of the living and was now paying an invisible visit. I stood in one of the long and orderly lines and when the train screeched and shuddered into place, I closed my eyes against its wind and opened them only when the air stilled and I heard groans and sighs of frustration among my line mates. The door where we'd lined up was stuck shut—USE ANOTHER DOOR, said a sign—and now we all scrambled to the next car, and when I entered that car along with everyone, instead of staying put, I pushed open the door to the first one—the shut one—so that I could be in there alone.

There was a handful of others in the car, and we exchanged looks of complicity. And over the course of the ride I came to think of them all as my friends and was sorry when I left. I raised a hand in parting. Some of them raised hands back. And by the time I returned home, I'm pleased to admit: I was happy. Yes. Happy. I'd stopped to pick up some sushi and wine. Then I set the radio to play through all the speakers in my house, and I went to lie down on my bed. There was a French song on the radio. I don't speak French, but it was a nice song. The lyrics went something like "Eska poo poo yay yay yay! Vuh shashay la moonay pay!" And I stripped and dropped my clothes to the floor, and I went through the closet, putting on outfit after outfit. I stood before the mirrored closet door and shimmied and sang. "Eska poo poo yay yay yay! Vuh shashay la moonay pay!" I stood in my pile of clothes, and I trembled and sweated and felt joyful. I lifted my breasts and felt the cool air on their undersides. And then I felt nauseated.

"Of course Mara was the one to find it," Sam said. "Your sense of smell hits its peak when you turn eight and declines when you hit your twenties." How Sam loved to make perfect sense out of everything strange and mysterious in the world. He looked at Mara, who, in the wake of my sister's rebuke, stood quietly and lip-tremblingly to the side. He put a hand on her shoulder and said, "The first step is to clean what we can reach from up here." He held the laundry chute open and peered inside. "Sheila," he said, "do you have a sponge?"

I went down to the kitchen and got the dish sponge from next to the sink, then returned and handed it to Sam.

"Sam, let her do it herself," Priya said. "For fuck's sake. Mara, stay back."

"Oh, let me try," Sam said, and he gave Priya a look that was compassionate and trite. *Your sister is in trouble—we have to put aside our disgust and try to help.* Scrubbing with the dish sponge, he loosened and cleaned the crust around the top edges of the chute, and the fish smell tangled with the lavender scent of the detergent. But the vomit had dripped deep into the chute. Sam couldn't reach far enough to get all of it.

"I'll try," Priya said, avoiding my eyes. She took the sponge from Sam and stuck her arm into the chute, twisting at the waist to reach as far as she could. Her shirt lifted as she stretched, and I could see the light down of hair at the small of her back. Sam touched the small of Priya's back. *How bourgeois,* I thought, *for a husband to still be attracted to his wife.* "I can't get it," Priya said.

"My turn," I said. But I couldn't reach either.

The problem was that the space was too small for us; we were stymied at the shoulder. Priya had the idea to go downstairs to the laundry room and try to reach the vomit from below, and she took Sam with her to investigate while I stayed upstairs. Soon I heard my sister's voice bellowing up through the chute: All they could see were some drops of puke atop my towels in the laundry basket. "It's too far," Priya called. "It's all up there."

From the top of the chute I could see her poke a broomstick around. It made a hollow rattle. Mara crept closer, her eyes aglint. Was she thinking what I was thinking? I bent to her and waited for her to say it.

She did. "I could try," she whispered.

"You want to?" I whispered.

"I can?" she whispered. She touched her mouth.

"Shush," I whispered, "they'll hear. Let's get you in there." I handed the dish sponge to her. "Go at it, sweet pea."

What I did was, I hoisted her up by the waist and let her shimmy into the chute. Then I was holding her by the thighs, then by the ankles. Only then—when I had her by the ankles, all of her weight in my hands—did I realize how heavy she was. A full-grown child. I felt it in my forearms. I felt it in my back. "Gross," Mara said in a voice that seemed echoey and overlarge.

"Mara?" Priya sang out from the laundry room—two trembling notes, rising low to high. She could probably see Mara from down there. I don't know why she said it as if it was a question. Mara didn't respond. She only grunted like a mechanic.

"Sheil?" Priya shrilled. Her voice rose. "Mara, you in there? Sheil?"

Then came Priya surging up the stairs with Sam on her heels. You want hysterical? Here was hysterical. "For God's sake, pull her up, Sheila!" she cried. I hoisted Mara out by her ankles and deposited her on the carpet. Priya swooped in and picked Mara up in her arms.

"Mom, I'm fine," Mara said, and squirmed out of Priya's grip. "Gosh," she said. Standing, she smoothed her hair and scanned the faces of the adults.

The scent of lavender swelled in the hallway, and for a moment, it was all we could smell.

"Done," Mara said. She sniffed and smiled. "Actually, I love vomit," she said.

"Good girl," I told her.

Back downstairs, we washed our hands in turn. We didn't speak. We didn't make eye contact. We sat on the couch. I suddenly felt worn out and dirty. I felt vomit on my palms; I smelled it in the air. It turned my throat sweet.

The Donners ate each other, I thought.

"Priya, I want to make you a martini," I said.

"I'm wasted," Priya said.

"You're sleeping here!" I said. "Who cares?"

"I'll have one," Sam said.

"Sam," Priya said.

I felt impatient. I went to the kitchen. I made the martinis and brought them back on a tray. Sam took one. Priya hesitated. Then she took one and I took one. I felt great as soon as the gin touched my lip. It was like swimming in a long, deep pool and finally getting to the end of the lane. You come up for air and feel great before you've even taken a breath, because you're anticipating all the breathing you're about to do. That's how I felt.

"Sam, you have mine," Priya said softly. "I actually don't want it."

"Aw, babe, I don't think I can," he protested. "Don't drink it, then."

She glared at him. I knew what she was doing. What she was doing was straight out of some textbook. Some idiot's guide. But I felt great and would not be made to feel less great. "I'll have it," I

said, and I took the glass right out of her hand, and I had it. Right
there, on the spot, I had it, and then I finished my own, and I felt,
for the first time in months, a kind of triumph.

I sat back into the couch and watched Mara. She was building
a fort. She had pulled the cushion from the easy chair and taken
it to the wide space near the fireplace, where she dropped it. Now
she went to the dining room table and got a heavy, tall-backed
chair, which she carried, struggling, to the living room. Then she
went back and got another, then another. All these she arranged
into a tight enclosure. Finally she came and squeezed onto the
couch between me and my sister and regarded her creation.

"Nice fort, kiddo," I said, reaching down to take a swipe at
Mara's ear.

"Hey. It's a cave."

This struck me as a great thing for a child to say, smart and
original. "It's a cave." I wondered what other thoughts were whirl-
ing around in my niece's head. I thought about all that I was
led to believe in my childhood: Olives are bad for you; if you
don't brush your teeth at night, they will rot and fall out; blowing one's nose in a towel will leave a dark stain that can never be
removed; children have two stomachs, one of which is reserved
for dessert; and so on. But Mara could not be deceived! This
was not a fort! "It's a cave," Mara had said. "I love vomit," she'd
said. I was struck hard by the force of my love for this child.
Every other love of my life seemed small compared to this
love. I grabbed Mara by her arm and pulled her to me. "You're
perfect," I said.

"My arm," Mara said. "Stop."

"Sam," Priya said. She seemed tired and sad.

I let go. "Don't ever grow up," I said.

"Okay," Mara said, and she scampered across the room and
ducked into the cave.

"Remember how we used to do that?" I asked my sister. "We
used to make a fort and pretend to be wild animals living in
there?"

"I wanted to be the lioness," Priya told Sam. She was doing this thing where she wouldn't talk to me.

"No. You liked being the boar. I did your hair."

"This one time," Priya told Sam, "she did my hair in a braid and then she took the gum out of her mouth and wrapped it around the bottom of the braid instead of using a hair tie, and our mom had to cut it out."

"Oh, come on," I said. "It wasn't tragic," I told Sam.

Mara came crawling out from her cave. She surveyed the room, plucked a knitted blanket off the armchair, and put it over the front opening of the cave to make a door. Then she disappeared again.

"She has an artist's mind," I said. "I was thinking tomorrow we could take her to Golden Gate Park."

"Can't," Priya said to Sam. "The audition."

"After the audition?" I asked.

"Maybe?" Sam said to Priya.

Priya squirmed. "There's something under here." We all stood, and Priya lifted the couch cushion. There, among the lint and the hair, was a brown apple core. Frankly, I couldn't remember the last time I had eaten an apple. Yet there it was.

"Oh, God, Sheila," Priya cried out. Her face contracted, and I was afraid she would start sobbing.

"Don't be a baby," I said. "It's just an apple core."

Priya put her hand to her mouth. She was really crying. She really was. I hadn't seen her cry, I realized, since we were small. I looked to Sam, who put his hands on her shoulders. "Shh," he told her. "She's okay," he told her.

I actually thought for a moment they were talking about me. I felt touched. I felt, for a moment, that all was not lost.

"She could have fallen," she said. "Jesus Christ."

Sam glanced up at me, then down at his hands. "Let's get some fresh air," he said. "I'll have a cigarette."

Priya looked at the cave, at me, at him. Her gaze made a triangle. She tucked a loose strand of hair behind her ear and wrapped her arms around herself as if she was cold. "Okay," she said in a small voice.

I swear to you, the sound of her voice. It reached into me. It passed through some kind of barrier and got inside. I wanted to say something to her. But I didn't know what to say. What do you say? *I love you*? How insufficient. I couldn't. I couldn't even look at her. I don't even know what she looked like in that moment. But I felt so close to her. I don't know if she felt it. I guess she didn't. They stood. They put on their shoes. They went out the door. They shut it. All was quiet.

I stood. I sat. I stood again, stumbled, and fell to the floor. *Water,* I thought, and I went crawling to the kitchen. This was a good way to get from one place to another. I'd forgotten how good. I hadn't crawled in a long time. When I got to the sink I stood, steadied myself, and poured myself a glass of water. I drank. The water tasted healthful and mineral, as if I were sipping from the palm of God himself. The palm of truth. Your palm. I drank. I poured another glass. I drank and drank. I felt desperate. I remembered that I had shed my clothes earlier in the day and stood in the pile of shed clothes and sung. Now I mourned that moment and all the others that had died. I placed my glass on the counter and knelt on the floor, and once I was there, it seemed impossible that I could stand again. So I didn't. I got on my hands and knees. I padded across the kitchen and into the living room. My shoulders pumped. I felt nothing but the knowledge that I was to go to the cave. And when I arrived there and pulled back the blanket and peered inside, I found what I had known, on some level, I would find. There emanated from inside the cave—in the person of the child inside, may you bless her and keep her ever safe—the hot radiance of truth.

The cave was warm and dark and smelled of corn chips. The child lay curled on her side, her arms tucked at her chest, her cheek pressed to the floor. Her mouth hung open as she breathed, and a thin thread of drool dangled from the corner. Her bowed mouth was of the reddest red. I moved carefully into the cave, not touching the walls, and remained on my hands and knees before the sleeping child.

But I shouldn't say *I*.

I wasn't there.

The buffalo gazed upon the child and felt a deep sense of peace. The child's eyelids fluttered, and her mouth made little movements, and the buffalo held her breath and stayed still. Then the buffalo let herself fall down at the child's side and rolled so their bodies were close. She wanted to be closer still. She pressed her chest to the wings of the child's back, and she cupped in her paw the round of the child's belly, and she pushed her forehead to the child's soft neck, and she wept. For she had been alone for so long. And now this child with her warmth and goodness and her smell of childhood. Oh, God. Did she hold the child too close? Did she make some sounds that a child might find frightening? From outside the cave came the distant sound of a door opening and closing. The sound of a person calling the child's name.

What can I tell you?

An instant later, all would be lost—the walls of the cave torn asunder so that all the goodness and warmth dissipated; the child's mother flying in, pulling the child out from the buffalo's grasp. Then I lay alone. What more can I tell you? Good God, I would tell you if I were the buffalo, let it be. Enough with all these words. Enough with the endless questions and endless answers. It's cold out here in the kingdom of man. But it seemed, for a moment, that this one child's heat might warm a creature amid the dying of her species.

Elizabeth McCracken

Birdsong from the Radio

L ONG AGO," LEONORA TOLD her children, and the telling
was long ago, too, "I was just ordinary." Of course they didn't
believe her. She was taller than other mothers, with a mouthful
of nibbling, nuzzling teeth and an affectionate chin she used as
a lever. Her hair was roan, her eyes taurine. Later the children
would look at the few photographs of their mother from the time,
all blurred and ill-lit, as though even the camera were uncertain
who she was, and they would try to remember the gobbling slide
of her bite along their necks, her mouth loose and toothy. She was
voracious. They could not stop laughing. *No! No! Again!*

Children long to be eaten. Everyone knows that.

Those were the days before the buses came in. The children
could hear from their bedroom windows the screech of the trolleys up the hill. Their father ran his family's radio manufacturers,
and there were radios in every room of the house, pocket and
tabletop, historic cathedrals. His name was Alan. "Poor Alan,"
Leonora called him, and they both understood why: He was
in thrall to his wife. He was a very bus of a man, practical and
mobile, and he left the children to Leonora, who had a talent for
love, as he had a talent for business.

Winters she took the children tobogganing. Summers they

piloted paddleboats across the city pond. She never dressed for the weather. No gloves, no sunhats, no shorts, no scarves—she was always blowing on her fingers or fanning her shirt. Sunburn, windburn, soaking wet with rain. The children, too. Other mothers sent them home with hand-me-down mittens and umbrellas.

Not surprising, said those mothers later, she never took care of her little ones.

Rosa, Marco, Dolly: Leonora brought them to see the trolleys the last day they ran. She wore a green suede coat, the same color as the cars, in solidarity. It closed with black loops that Leonora assured her children were called frogs.

"It's raining," said Leonora. "The frogs will be happy."

"Those aren't frogs," said Marco. He was five, the age of taxonomy.

"They are," said Leonora. "I promise. And my shoes are alligator."

"Why are we watching the trolleys?" he asked.

"There's no beauty in buses," Leonora said. "A bus can go anywhere it likes. Trolleys are beautiful."

"Oh yes," said Rosa, who was seven, "I can see."

Leonora was as melancholy as if the streetcars had been hunted into extinction. They were lovely captives who could not get away, and they left only their tracks behind.

Her coat fastened with frogs, her shoes were alligator. Perhaps she was already turning into an animal.

The children grew bigger, and bony. Leonora grew worse about love: She demanded it. She kissed too hard. She grabbed the children by the arms to pull them close. "You *seized* me," said Dolly, age six. "Why did you seize me so?"

"I was looking for a place to nibble," said Leonora. But Dolly was a skinny girl.

Leonora bit. She really did now. Moments later, contrite, writhing, she would say, "The problem is I love you so. I do. Can I be near you? Do you mind?"

What had happened to Leonora? Perhaps it was the sad story that ran through her family—a great-grandfather had lived three decades in an asylum, an aunt had killed herself. Perhaps she had a fall in the bathroom and it broke all the vials that contained her essence; the chemicals of her body mixed inside her and foamed and smoked and ran over. Perhaps she missed her children, who were growing up.

The doctors prescribed pills that she refused to take.

She still tried to eat the children, but they were afraid of her. She had to sneak. The weight of her as she sat on the edge of their beds in the middle of the night was raptorial: ominous yet indistinct. At any moment she might spread her arms and pull the children from the sheets, through the ceiling, and into the sky, the better to harm them elsewhere. The children took to sleeping in the same bed. Rosa, Marco, Dolly. Too old to sleep together, but they had to. They chose a different bed every night, and lay still as they heard her go from pillow to pillow, the unfurling flump of the bedclothes like the beat of the wings they thought they could see on her back.

"Come back to sleep," said Poor Alan from the hallway in a terrified voice. "Come listen to the radio and fall asleep." The top of his head was bald. The light from the bathroom pooled in a little dent in his scalp, just below his summit.

The children had radios in their room, too, of course. He snapped one on, to the classical station, to calm them down. "You never need be lonely with a radio!" he always said, but they knew it wasn't so. A radio station was another way grown-ups could talk to children without ever having to listen.

It was Rosa who told Poor Alan they had to go. She was fifteen. "We're leaving," she said. "You can come if you want to, but Marco and Dolly and I are going." Then, seeing his face, "We'd like you to come."

"She needs help," he said.

"She won't get it."

He nodded. "How will we manage?"

"We're not managing now," said Rosa. "In a year I'll get my license. I'll drive the little kids to school." The little kids. She was only two years older than Marco, who was three years older than Dolly.

"What will happen to your mother?" said Poor Alan, wringing his hands.

"Whatever it is, it's already happening," said Rosa.

"She's a wonderful mother. You must remember that."

"I don't," said Rosa. "I can't. Not anymore."

He wasn't a bad man. He could be forgiven for thinking it was a war, an ancient one, and that she would fight against the rest of them as long as they were near. In the spring he took Rosa and Marco and Dolly to a new house, and Leonora was left behind. He arranged for her disability checks. He did not take her off the bank account.

"If you get help, we'll come back," he told her.

Poor Alan hired a nanny, Madeline, a jug-eared, freckled beauty. A good girl, as her father later described her to the news cameras. She picked up the children every day after school. Rosa worshipped her; Dolly and Marco merely loved her. This went on for eight months, until the day after her twenty-first birthday, when she woke at noon still drunk from the first legal cocktails of her life, in late December, and loaded the children into the car, and found the car was too hot; and as she tried to wrench her black peacoat off one shoulder, and as she felt the last of the Black Russians muscle through her veins, and as she hit a patch of black ice, she understood that there would be an accident. She could see the children hurt in the backseat, the windshield gone lacy. Herself, opening the door and running away, away, away. *When the car stops, I'm going to leg it*, and that was the last thought Madeline or any of them ever had.

No children, thought Leonora. She had intended to get herself upright and go looking for them. She should have eaten them when she could.

For a while she tried to distract herself with the radios. Each bore Poor Alan's family name like a badge on the pellicle of the speaker. She went from room to room and turned them on, but then she thought she could hear—behind the sonorous day-long monologue of the news station, or the awful brightness of Vivaldi—the voices of her children. She worked the volume and tuning knobs in mincing little oscillations, then there they were: the tootling rhythm of Dolly, the defiant hum of Rosa, Marco sighing. She wondered if they had their own stations, or even their own radios. No: They would be cuddled up together in one frequency, the way they liked.

But she could never tune them in clearly, and slowly the sound turned feral, howling, chirping, shrieking: a forest empty of children. Then she knew they were gone.

The radios wouldn't turn off tight enough; the voices of strangers leaked through. She unplugged the cords, knocked the batteries from the backs. She could still hear that burble, someone muttering or the sound of an engine a block away.

She lay in bed. At her ear thrummed the old clock radio, with the numbered decagons that showed their corners as they turned to indicate that a minute had ended, or an hour, the thrum a little louder then. She felt her torso, where her children would have been, had she managed to eat them.

Not everyone who stops being human turns animal, but Leonora did.

The top of her back grew humped with ursine fat, and she shambled like that, too, bearlike, through the aisles of the grocery store at the end of the street. She shouldered the upright fridges full of beer, she sniffed the air of the checkout lanes. Panda-eyed and eagle-toed and lion-tailed, with a long braid down her back that snapped as though with muscles and vertebrae. Her insides, too, creatures of the dark and deep. Her kidneys, dozing moles; her lungs, folded bats. The organs that had authored her children: jellyfish, jellyfish, eel, eel, manatee.

I am dead. I am operated by animals.

Her wandering took her to the bakery, where she'd taken her children every Saturday morning of their early childhood, to let Poor Alan sleep in. In the slanted case she saw the loaves of challah. There was something familiar about them.

"Can I help you?" said the teenager behind the counter. His T-shirt had a picture of the galaxy on it, captioned YOU ARE HERE.

She tapped the glass. "Please," she said, and he pulled out a loaf, and she said, "I don't need a bag."

He'd already started angling the loaf into the bag's brown mouth. Who didn't need a bag for bread?

"I don't need a bag," she repeated. She counted out the money and set it down. "Just the paper."

He handed the bread self-consciously across the counter. When it was in her hands she adjusted the wax paper around it, admired the sheen of the egg wash, its placid countenance. Then she carried it to a table in the window and spread out the paper and set the loaf upon it.

She saw a sleeping baby in the shape of the bread, knees and arms akimbo, head turned, as always, to the left. *Marco.* The girls had cast different shadows. She put her hand on the loaf to check for oven warmth. Not on the surface. Maybe at the heart. Later she wouldn't care what people thought of her, she'd cradle the loaf in her arms before eating, but now she patted the bread, and then, with careful fingers, pulled it apart. Yeast, warmth, sweetness, a very child. Her mouth was full with it, then her head and throat and stomach. She felt the feral parts of her grow sleepy and peaceable.

I am eating Marco. I am eating my boy.

Thereafter, every morning she went to the bakery and bought a challah and pretended it was one of her children. Rosa slept with her bottom in the air. Dolly, alone of them, liked to be swaddled. Marco, akimbo. She carried the day's loaf in her arms to the table. She patted it. Then she ate it. Not like an animal. Knob by knob, slowly: One loaf could last for hours, washed down with water from the crenellated plastic cups the bakery gave away for free.

That was her nourishment. She lived on bread and good manners and felt sick with her children.

The new mothers of the neighborhood wished the bakery would throw the bulky, unkempt woman out. As they wished, they felt guilty, because they were trying to teach their children tolerance. But then they looked at the slanted case. The center bay was filled with glittering sugared shortbread cookies, decorated according to the season. Hearts, shamrocks, eggs, flags, leaves, pumpkins, turkeys, candy canes, hearts again. Evidence: Bakeries were for children, and children were frightened of Leonora.

Sometimes a mother and child would walk by her table, and Leonora could see the tight, unhappy discomfort of judgment on the mother's face.

"Say hello, Pearl," the mother would tell her child, and Pearl, dutifully, would say hello, and Leonora would wave; she knew the mother was thinking, *Thank God she doesn't know what I'm thinking.*

These children neither pained nor interested her. They weren't her darlings. But every now and then a Pearl or a Sammy would smile at her, and even giggle, and she would want a nibble, a taste, in the old way. A raspberry blown on a neck, a kiss with a bite at its heart: *nibble, nibble, yum.* They weren't hers, but they were sweet. Yet if you were the mother of dead children that was over. You weren't allowed.

On those days she ordered a second loaf of bread, which she dragged home and tore apart.

Five years passed like nothing. She was recognized in the neighborhood as the monument she was, constructed to memorialize a tragedy but with the plaque long since dropped off. She was Leonora. Nobody imagined that she was a person who'd always been exactly as she was—poisoned, padded, eyes sunk into her

348 / ELIZABETH McCRACKEN

face. She existed only at the bakery, at the table in the window, eating in her finicky way. She spoke to the people behind the counter. That was all. Some were patient, and some weren't.

Then one day a man came in, caught her eye, and smiled.

Poor Alan, she thought reflexively, but then she recalled Poor Alan was dead, though he'd remembered her in his will and set up a trust to take care of her. This man wore a green wool hat like a bucket, which he pulled off to reveal a full head of white hair. The hat looked expensive, artisanal. No, he was never Poor Alan, who'd lost his hair long before it faded. But she did know him. He sat across from her. The tabletop was Formica, the green of trolleys.

"Mike Wooster," he said.

"Hello, Mike Wooster," said Leonora. She could smell her own terrible breath. She still slept in a bed and washed herself, but she did not always remember to brush her teeth. Why would she? She scarcely needed them.

He bounced the hat around on his fists, then set it in front of him. She had a sense that he wanted to drop it over the remains of her loaf: Dolly this time. He said, "I'm Madeline's father."

She heard the present tense of the sentence. "I know who you are," she said.

Everything about him was rich and comforted. "I heard you came here," he said. "That bread good?"

She tore off a brown curve. A cheek, a clenched hand. She sniffed at it before she pushed it in her mouth.

He cleared his throat. "We're having a memorial service. And my wife and I and our kids—well, we thought of you." He picked the hat back up, brushed some flakes of challah from the brim. "I've thought of you." He said that to the hat. "Every single day I've thought of you. You know, they turned my daughter into a monster, too."

The alcohol, the coat, the ice. Everybody said that if one of those things hadn't been true they never would have crashed.

"Too?" she said. The animals of her body were roaring back to life.

They—whoever *they* were—had not turned Leonora into a monster. They had erased her. Newspapers, television, the horrible gabbling radio, which spoke only of the children's father, the left-behind man, the single parent. That poor man, looking after his children. To lose all of them at once.

Poor Alan had a memorial service, too, had invited her. Though he'd asked her to come to the front, she'd sat alone, at the back of the church—a *church!* since *when!*—drunk and stunned. No one else spoke to her. She was a mother who'd let her children go, a creature so awful nobody believed in her. She'd had to turn herself into a monster, in order to be seen.

"Madeline never got a chance," said Mike Wooster. "To redeem herself. But you could. You could be redeemed."

She laughed at that, or part of her did, a living thing sheltered in a cave inside of her. "Redeemed," she said. "Like a coupon."

He shook his head. "Like a soul. Your *soul* can be redeemed."

"Too late," she said. "Soul's gone."

"Where?" he said.

"Where do you *think*?" she said.

He took her hand. "This only feels like hell," he said. "I know. I do know."

She shook her head to refuse his sympathy: She could smell the distant desiccation of it. *No.* Why had he come here? He had a dead child, too, of course. She could feel the loss twitching through his fingers, the sorrow, the guilt, like schools of tiny, flicking fish that swim through bone instead of ocean. He was not entirely human anymore, either. She heard the barking dog of his heart, wanting an answer. Her heart snarled back, but tentatively.

If she accepted his sympathy she would have to feel sorry for him. She would have to *transcend*. Some people could. They could forgive and rise above their agony.

Her organs turned in their burrows, and she felt an old emotion, one from before. Gratitude. She was thankful to remember that she was a monster. Many monsters. Not a chimera but a vivarium. Her heart snarled and snarled and snarled. She listened to it.

"The thing is," said Leonora to Mike Wooster, as she pulled her hand from his, "you can't unbraid a challah."

"No?" he said. "Well, I'd guess not."

"Would you like some?" she asked.

He looked at the rubble of the day's bread. "Oh, no. That's yours."

"Let me get you one. Please."

"I don't need—"

Leonora said, rising, "It will be a pleasure to watch you eat."

Reading *The O. Henry Prize Stories 2015*

The Jurors on Their Favorites

Our jurors read the twenty O. Henry Prize Stories in a blind manuscript. Each story appears in the same type and format with no attribution of the magazine that published it or the author's name. The jurors don't consult the series editor or one another. Although the jurors write their essays without knowledge of the authors' names, the names are inserted into the essay later for the sake of clarity. —LF

Tessa Hadley on "A Ride Out of Phrao" by Dina Nayeri

I like everything about this striking, original, unexpected story. Its subject is a middle-aged Iranian doctor who made a new home years ago in America with her daughter but has never quite felt at home there. She goes to Thailand to work with the Peace Corps in a village near the city of Chiang Mai, where there are few modern conveniences and no air-conditioning, where the toilet is a hole in the floor, where she dreads the lizards climbing her walls at night. This sounds as if it might turn out to be a hand-wringing story about the guilt of privilege or the tragedy of underdevelopment—but actually it's such a gentle, haunting, private, funny little exploration. Much of its effort is to catch the character and experience of this particular rather extraordinary woman: resilient, unreliable, generous, prone to untruth, anxious over certain social superstitions (she mustn't let her "seams show"), modest in her sense of her own entitlement.

And yet audacious too! How brave she is to make a new life in an utterly strange place, twice over. She has no idea that she's brave, however, and has rather a low estimate of herself—although she spends no time dwelling on that and doesn't indulge in self-pity. We don't feel her character at the level of her ideology, or through learning what she wants to get out of the world for herself, or because we're invited to engage with her angst. Sentence by delicate sentence, the writer pieces together the richly muddled comedy of this woman's history, and her thoughts and fears: We dwell with her rare open spirit—open to her new life, her own past, to the others she encounters and works with. She is so alive to every moment, and curious, alert in all her senses—"enthralled," for instance, by the wonderful Thai fruit she learns to peel, and to name. Dr. Rin, as the villagers call her, has planted herself—but so modestly, with no presumption that she could ever make sense of any of it—at the intersection of several different worlds, which might as well be different planets: America, Iran, Thailand. In its modest refusal to judge, or to lead us to any portentous conclusions or doomy moralizing, the story models such an appealing position, imaginatively, for our relations to our global world.

The subject of the story is important, but of course it only works because of how it's done. The narrative is so subtly and intelligently positioned, inside Dr. Rin yet also able to give us a perspective on her from outside, as if we were watching her. And it's built out of such good detail—all the telling detail that gives us Dr. Rin's Iranian past, her Thai present, and her American interim. The detail is complex and nuanced—a rich ragbag of finely observed fragments—and yet somehow the steady, intelligent sentences find a way through it all so that we're never muddled or confused. The story finds its clear, pure line through its material; the writing is beautiful because it doesn't try too hard. "The rain blurs the lines of their faces and bodies, and their movements become dreamlike." Every observation is wonderfully exact. A seamstress has "a browning half tooth."

Dr. Rin teaches English in a Thai school, and makes friends with an awkward boy, odd and physically unappealing, who may be slightly autistic, and whose father hits him. The boy tries to touch her breast, and she doesn't know whether this is moving or distasteful. Her thoroughly Americanized daughter, Leila—who can't forgive her mother for her lies, her bankruptcy, her quixotic hopes, her "running away"—comes from America to visit, but Leila can't bear the dreary poverty of the place, or do without a flush toilet. Yet the story doesn't set itself crudely up against Leila, it doesn't score points against her; she's lovely and young and strong and full of appetite, and we can imagine just how she finds her mother exasperating. This writing doesn't pretend to understand the world, or sum it up; there's no clinching resolution to any of the questions it raises. We never quite know what the boy wants from Dr. Rin, and there's never ever any confrontation with the boy's father—in fact he's the one who finally drives Leila back to Chiang Mai, to bathrooms and civilization. The story's language is plain, and never overwrought, yet it closes with an exquisite metaphor that feels like a leap of vision when it comes. Dr. Rin remembers the fruit—the Iranian persimmon, or the Thai mangosteen—in which sweet flesh is separated from foul by such a fine membrane.

Tessa Hadley was born and raised in Bristol. She's written five novels, including *The Master Bedroom*, *The London Train*, and *Clever Girl*, and two collections of short stories, as well as a book of criticism, *Henry James and the Imagination of Pleasure*. She is a professor of creative writing at Bath Spa University and reviews regularly for *The Guardian* and for the *London Review of Books*.

Kristen Iskandarian on "Birdsong from the Radio" by Elizabeth McCracken

This story glows with an eerie incandescence and has the aura of a fairy tale. "'Long ago,'" it starts—but the telling is through a character, Leonora, whose reliability we are made to doubt almost immediately, "and the telling was long ago, too." And so, we have a story that begins with a story, told to children who are no longer alive, through their mother who wanted to eat them, because, of course, "[c]hildren long to be eaten. Everyone knows that."

There are many things to love about "Birdsong from the Radio": the images, indelible brushstrokes of language—"the unfurling flump of the bedclothes like the beat of the wings they thought they could see on her back"—the musicality of the sentences, their rhythm mirroring the stalking, lurking pulse of Leonora herself as she becomes something subhuman but also superhuman. The subject matter, which seems to encompass the whole of our human condition but also something deeply and dearly specific: a mother's love and need for her children—primal and unrelenting—set in stark relief to a father's love for radios, and his fear of his wife's rabid love.

But the most captivating trait of the story, for me, is the voice—it comes from the belly of a timeless and placeless place, from the nowhere/everywhere where fables get forged. Its author-less authority means that its demands, which are great, must be met within the sphere of its own rubric and logic. That's a lot to ask of a short story, which is to say, this story asks a lot of itself, but it succeeds prodigiously. The starting point here is a mother's love writ as spectacle, as atrocity: love and madness as bedfellows in a tiny bed.

We say that a mother's love is all-consuming, but here, we see it enacted almost in reverse—the love is the children, embodied in the figures of Rosa, Marco, and Dolly, and the love is a hunger, a sickness, something threatening, so that Leonora's only mode of survival is to try to eat them. First, in playful nibbles, and gradually, in fervent, frightening bites. When they, along with her husband, leave her, the radios that used to bring her comfort start taunting her—through the static she hears the whinny of their voices, "cuddled up together in one frequency," as though they have formed a team against her.

After the children's quick, tragic death—dying as they lived, as a unit—Leonora's hunger becomes a feral grief. She turns more and more animal, "humped with ursine fat," "bearlike," "panda-eyed," and pronounces herself dead. But her hunger outlives her, gnaws like a second animal within her. To quell it, she turns to bread, that first, fundamental food: "Yeast, warmth, sweetness, a very child." The pared-down language manages to stay rich and evocative without cushioning or embellishing Leonora's anguish. The challah is as vivid as if it were painted and comes as much as a palliative to us, the readers, as it does to Leonora—"the sheen of the egg wash, its placid countenance." Her ritual, buying and eating a daily loaf, soothes her, saves her—which is what all of our rituals are meant to do.

Perhaps the most satisfying element of this story occurs toward the end, when Leonora sits face-to-face with the father of the girl who killed her children, along with herself, in the car accident. Unkempt, unhinged, unwanted, Leonora sees in this broken, polite, civilized man a shard of her own reflection. Her way of reaching out toward it is to reach for more bread, giving it to him in an effort, it seems, to both massage and aggravate her own agony. It is an invitation to partake in the feast of her misery, or to create from the crumbs of their collective sadness a trough where they may feed side by side. Leonora recognizes that if she "accepted his sympathy she would have to feel sorry for him. She would have to *transcend*"—but she is unwilling to do this, unwilling to rise over and above the pain that has forged her, the children who have nourished her. And so the question becomes—and it's such a good one, for a short story, since short stories have long been saddled with the burden of redemption—

what if someone doesn't want to be saved? Leonora's transformation is not static but rather infinite, holographic—from human into monster, monster back to human. For some of us, and certainly for her, sorrow is the beginning, the denouement, and the end.

Kristen Iskandrian was born and raised in Philadelphia. She received her BA from the College of the Holy Cross and her MA and PhD from the University of Georgia. Her work has been published in *Gulf Coast, Denver Quarterly, American Letters & Commentary, Memorious, La Petite Zine, Fifty-Two Stories, PANK, Tin House*, and many other places, both in print and online. She lives in Birmingham, Alabama.

Michael Parker on "Cabins" by Christopher Merkner

Since I read and comment upon stories to put bread on my table, I am forever making lists of Things I Need for Stories to Do in Order to Win Me Over. Although the items on my list often change, there are staples, mostly obvious ones: I need to be surprised; I need to be invested in all that is at stake for the characters; I need to be able to follow the access road so that it will lead me, surely and subtly, to the astral plane; I need for the rhythms of the story, in both sentence and form, to convey the desire that drives it. I need to, as Flannery O'Connor said, "feel the extra dimension that comes about when the writer puts us in the middle of some human action as it is illuminated and outlined by mystery."

"Cabins" satisfied all my requirements. It had me by the third line. The slip into present tense from the established past, the sudden truncated rhythm of the sentences, the repetition of certain words: Something's up here. Sit up, slow down, pay attention. On the first read my footing was unsure. The numbers preceding each section might imply linearity, but the story roots around in the manner of memories involuntarily assembled. The structure perfectly mimics the narrator's anxiety. He has a lot to be anxious about. He and his wife of six years are expecting a baby. He's recently had a heart attack and bypass surgery. He is involved in a lockdown while visiting a prison, during which he witnesses an inmate kicked repeatedly in the head. Everyone he encounters—most of them acquaintances rather than close friends—is getting a divorce.

"Cabins" is not short on dramatic action, but the deepest and most satisfying tensions occur when the reader, along with the narrator, attempts to construct some logical narrative from these disparate scenes. Of course the narrator is a step ahead—he has, after all, selected and distributed the interactions and details of the plot. But he's also confused, aimlessly in search of assurance, if not certainty, that his marriage is safe. When he visits the prison with a former neighbor who has started a therapy group for "inmates who were, had been, or feared they would soon be divorced by their partners or spouses," he listens to his neighbor thank the prisoners for "their willingness to 'see the world beyond love.'" The narrator, so aware and fearful of the fragility of marriage, attempts to see the world beyond love, but his fantasies of a remote cabin where he might live apart from his wife are, however distracting, ultimately empty.

All of the above makes the story sound terribly serious. In fact, it's a scream, though our laughter is of the uneasy variety. The narrator has ridiculous conversations with his friends in hookah bars and on basketball courts. The details of the narrator's imagined cabin are hilariously absurd. The narrator and his friends are melodramatic if not bathetic, but their inflated emotions arise out of their vulnerability.

What moved me most about "Cabins" was the way its shape offered resolve from a situation forever unresolvable. There are no glib attempts at answers here, only the mysterious transformation of doubt into brittle but vigilant faith.

. . .

Michael Parker was born and raised in North Carolina. Twice an O. Henry Prize winner, he is the author of two story collections and six novels, including, most recently, *All I Have in This World*. He is the Vacc Distinguished Professor in the MFA Writing Program at the University of North Carolina, Greensboro. He lives in North Carolina and Texas.

Writing *The O. Henry Prize Stories 2015*

The Writers on Their Work

Molly Antopol, "My Grandmother Tells Me This Story"
My relatives love to tell stories, but the one place I never heard about was Antopol, the Belarusian village, virtually destroyed in World War II, where my family originated. A little more than a decade ago I was living in Israel and wound up at a holiday party in Haifa where I met an elderly woman from Antopol who had known my family. It was an extraordinary moment in my life. She led me to an oral history book about the village, written in Hebrew, Yiddish, and English. The moment I finished reading it, I began working on this story.

But it ended up taking me almost two years to get the story where I wanted it to be. I read every memoir and biography of partisan life near Antopol that I could get my hands on, spent months in different archives, and traveled to Eastern Europe to visit partisan bases and conduct interviews. But it was only when I realized, after more than a year of wrestling with the story, that the tension in the piece was as much about why the granddaughter was so obsessed with these dark periods of history (a question I've been struggling to answer about myself for years) as it was about the war that the story really cracked open for me.

Molly Antopol was born in Connecticut and raised in California. She was selected as one of the National Book Foundation's

5 Under 35 honorees, and her debut story collection, *The UnAmericans*, was longlisted for the National Book Award. She teaches creative writing at Stanford University, where she was a Wallace Stegner Fellow, and is at work on a novel. She lives in San Francisco.

Russell Banks, "A Permanent Member of the Family"

Sometimes a work of fiction can be too closely based on reality. I wanted to write this story decades ago, when my children were young and their parents' divorce was still a fresh and painful memory for everyone involved. But the accidental death of the family dog, the central event in the story, as I understood it back then, was too punishing, for me as much as for my children and ex-wife. So, yes, it actually happened pretty much as the story has it. But I had to wait until all the principals had forgiven one another before I could subject the material to the pressures, needs, and requirements of fiction. Perhaps I also had to wait until I could forgive myself, so that I could imagine the father as a sympathetic character without sentimentalizing or judging him.

Russell Banks was born in Massachusetts. He is the author of eighteen works of fiction, including the novels *Continental Drift*, *Rule of the Bone*, and *Lost Memory of Skin*, as well as six short-story collections. Banks is a member of the American Academy of Arts and Letters and was New York State Author (2004–08). He lives in Miami, Florida, and in upstate New York.

Lydia Davis, "The Seals"

I had written a very different version of this story five years earlier, much shorter and angrier in its tone. The general situation was the same: the narrator, presumably an office worker of some kind, traveling by train on Christmas Day and musing on her older sister and Christmases past. But I allowed her to be—as she seemed to want to be—narrow and resentful, unwilling to admit that she was angry with her sister for dying.

Although the story was effective in that form, I was not satisfied with it—I felt it could be larger in every sense, more generous in spirit and embracing more of the positive as well as the negative in her memories of her sister. It could also extend further back in time, to include the years when she was much younger. And so I decided to write a longer story based on, or starting from, the shorter version. I let it grow quite freely. What surprised me then was that, as though unbidden, the narrator's father, who had died soon after the older sister, entered the story too, as though of his own accord, so that as the story evolved it embraced the two of them, and even their relationship, as the narrator imagines it, after death. It is most moving to me, as a writer, when that happens—when a piece of writing goes in its own direction, of its own volition.

Lydia Davis was born in Massachusetts and grew up there, as well as in New York City and Vermont. She is the author of seven collections of stories and one novel, *The End of the Story*. She is also the translator of many works from the French, including Proust's *Swann's Way* and Flaubert's *Madame Bovary*, and, more recently, from the Dutch, the stories of A. L. Snijders. She is a 2003 MacArthur Fellow and a chevalier of the Order of Arts and Letters, and she was the recipient of an American Academy of Arts and Letters Award of Merit medal and the Man Booker International Prize, in 2013, among other honors. She lives in upstate New York.

Percival Everett, "Finding Billy White Feather"

This story grew out of my short time living in Wyoming and on the Wind River Indian Reservation of the Arapaho and Shoshone peoples. While there I listened to the way mundane stories can become spiraling tales. I am always interested in how language and stories shape identity. I never say what I have meant to do in a story because that doesn't matter. Meaning gets made over and over again, differently each time depending on the reader and the circumstances of the reading. This is an obvious and pedestrian idea, but no less exciting for that fact. I will say that for me the birth of the twin horses in the story is the most intriguing part. Make of that what you will. I like horses.

Percival Everett is author to more than twenty books, among them *Erasure*, *I Am Not Sidney Poitier*, and *Percival Everett by Virgil Russell*. His latest story collection is *Half an Inch of Water*. Everett lives in Los Angeles.

Lynn Freed, "The Way Things Are Going"

Almost everything I've written seems to center around place and displacement, home and exile. I don't know how to account for this story other than to say that South Africa is a country that has always been fraught with irony. And that of all the people I know in post-apartheid South Africa, of any race, there is not one who has not personally known someone who has been murdered. Their stories haunt me. And so does what becomes of them when they decide to leave.

Lynn Freed was born in Durban, South Africa, and came to the United States as a graduate student. Her books include six novels, a collection of stories, and a collection of essays. Her work has appeared in *Harper's*, *The New Yorker*, *The Atlantic*, *The New York Times*, *The Washington Post*, *The Wall Street Journal*, *National Geographic*, *Narrative*, *Southwest Review*, and *The Georgia Review*, among others. She is the recipient of the inaugural Katherine Anne Porter Award in fiction from the American Academy of Arts and Letters, two O. Henry Prizes, and fellowships, grants, and support from the National Endowment for the Arts and the Guggenheim Foundation, among others. She lives in Northern California.

Becky Hagenston, "The Upside-Down World"

My husband and I were in the South of France in 2010, visiting friends who live in Aix-en-Provence. We took a bus to Nice and wandered around that bright, gorgeous city—we swam in the Mediterranean, walked in the heat to the amazing Chagall museum, had an insanely overpriced drink at the Le Negresco hotel bar. We were walking down the Promenade des Anglais—the beach boulevard—and witnessed the aftermath of what looked like a horrifying accident. All we could see was a smashed car windshield and a woman's shoe. I kept thinking: *Who was that person? Could she possibly be okay?* Later that day, we found out that a couple staying at our B & B had been pickpocketed in broad daylight and had to go to the embassy in Marseille to get new passports. Everything suddenly seemed so precarious, so dangerous, even in that beautiful city.

I took a lot of notes, but all of this information and strangeness was completely unfocused for a long time. I tried to write about a couple in the South of France—first a young married couple, then an old married couple—but nothing happened until I realized they were middle-aged siblings. Why would middle-aged siblings be in Nice? That's when the story took off. When Gertrude's bag disappeared from the beach, I needed to know who took it, and that's how Elodie came about.

Becky Hagenston grew up in Bel Air, Maryland. She received her BA from Elizabethtown College and graduate degrees from the University of Arizona and New Mexico State University. Her first collection of stories, *A Gram of Mars*, won the Mary McCarthy Prize; her second collection, *Strange Weather*, won the Spokane Prize for Short Fiction. Her stories have appeared in *Crazyhorse*, *The Southern Review*, *Indiana Review*, and many other journals, as well as *The O. Henry Prize Stories 1996*. Her awards include the Reynolds Price Short Fiction Award, the Great Lakes Colleges Association New Writers Award, and the Julia Peterkin Award.

She is an associate professor of English at Mississippi State University and lives in Starkville, Mississippi.

Naira Kuzmich, "The Kingsley Drive Chorus"

When I was growing up in East Hollywood, a lot of young men from my Armenian community were finding themselves in trouble. These were cousins, neighbors, classmates. This story was born out of the love I had for the mothers of these boys, women I had long admired and feared in equal measure. Because I was so young, there was much I was unwilling to ask these women and much they were unwilling to tell me. I was forced, then, to wonder. Now I still wonder, but also imagine. Now I write and try to empathize. Only now have I begun to understand.

Naira Kuzmich was born in Yerevan, Armenia, and raised in the Los Angeles enclave of Little Armenia. Her stories and essays have appeared in *The Threepenny Review*, *West Branch*, *Blackbird*, and elsewhere. She lives in Missouri.

Elizabeth McCracken, "Birdsong from the Radio"

On the most basic level, this was an assignment: The wonderful Kate Bernheimer, editor of *Fairy Tale Review*, asked me to contribute to a collection of stories based on myths. For a long time I cast around wondering what myth I might choose. Many of the myths that really meant something to me seemed too obvious—Icarus, for example—and then one day my children suggested that my New Year's resolution might be biting them less. They said this in a cheery way, in the same cheery way, in fact, that I bit them, a progression from the usual way a lot of parents threaten to eat their babies up. Before I had children, I'd always found this proposed cannibalism unfathomable, but now: Well, I never sunk my teeth in when I bit, but I would bury my face in their necks and know that at some point they'd grow out of it and I never would and they were the ones who got to decide. I got to thinking about Lamia—I'd loved the rather glamorous Keats poem about her—and when I read more and learned that in some versions she was a woman who'd gone mad from grief after the death of her children, and therefore turned into an animal, well, it all made sense to me. Also: I'd always wanted to write about the end of the trolleys in my childhood neighborhood.

Elizabeth McCracken is the author of two story collections (*Here's Your Hat What's Your Hurry* and *Thunderstruck & Other Stories*), two novels (*The Giant's House* and *Niagara Falls All Over Again*), and a memoir (*An Exact Replica of a Figment of My Imagination*). She teaches at the University of Texas at Austin and lives in Austin, Texas.

Christopher Merkner, "Cabins"

"Cabins" emerged from the experience of having a good friend—or someone I'd thought was a really close friend—very casually tell me over a pastry and coffee one afternoon that he and his wife were divorcing. I remember getting the chills, thinking, *My God, I can't believe this is happening to them*, and I told him I was so sorry, and he dismissed my concerns and just continued on with the elaborate details of the divorce—his affair, his wife's affair, etc.—all of which was a shocking explosion of new information for me to process—and though he reported this information with sincerity and detachment and objectivity, he was also making it clear to me that he'd already told this information to something like fifteen or so other people before me. And so once my mystification thinned out, I started thinking about that, about how the real divorce in our conversation was my divorce from this close friend's personal reality. And also my divorce from the lives of these other fifteen people he'd already told, all of whom were mutual friends of ours, and none of whom mentioned a word of this to me. The problem of course, and the thing that most bothered me at the time, was that I'd foolishly assumed I had some sort of intimate arrangement with the details of these people's personal lives. Obviously that wasn't the case, and I remember thinking, as I was working through this story, just how many lives I find myself assuming I know but ultimately know nothing about at all, or just very tiny bits and pieces.

Christopher Merkner was born and raised in northern Illinois. His fiction has appeared in *The Best American Mystery Stories*, *Black Warrior Review*, the *Chicago Tribune*'s *Printers Row Journal*, *The Cincinnati Review*, *CutBank*, *DIAGRAM*, *Fairy Tale Review*, *The Gettysburg Review*, *Gulf Coast*, *Hotel Amerika*, *New World Writing*, *The Collagist*, and elsewhere. He is the author of the story collection *The Rise and Fall of the Scandamerican Domestic*. He lives in Denver, Colorado.

Manuel Muñoz, "The Happiest Girl in the Whole USA"
My father didn't become a US citizen until the late 1980s. He was deported many times. As a child, I didn't know to be alarmed at my father's sudden disappearances, since he always returned. I had a very naive idea of what it meant to be deported and it wasn't until I was a young adult that I understood the different circumstances that led to his deportations and how involved my mother was in getting him back home.

My parents are very good but reluctant storytellers. It takes work to get them to talk about a past our younger memories can't confirm. They prefer retelling stories everyone around the kitchen table can vaguely remember; they recognize that already knowing a story is a magic quite different from surprise.

The stories of the deportation years have come more easily now, because they watch the news and see what is happening on the border, the ways in which families are torn apart. "Things are so much harder now," my father says in Spanish. In the 1980s, my parents had no money, no credit cards, and sometimes no transportation. Yet my mother always brought my father back home. I think of the waiting game at the two parks—a detail of their story that once tested my notions of plausibility—and have humbly accepted that I have a lot of work to do on what it means to have faith, to endure without ever losing hope.

Manuel Muñoz was born in Dinuba, California. He is the author of a novel, *What You See in the Dark*, as well as two short-story collections, *Zigzagger* and *The Faith Healer of Olive Avenue*, which was shortlisted for the Frank O'Connor International Short Story Award. The recipient of a Whiting Award, he lives and works in Tucson, Arizona.

Dina Nayeri, "A Ride Out of Phrao"

In the summer of 2012, in the midst of a divorce, I went on a trip to Thailand. It was the first time I had traveled alone in a long time, and the place I was headed was my mother's home in Phrao, a tiny village outside Chiang Mai. The village was just as I've described in the story, but the circumstances were very different. Unlike the mother and daughter in my story, who are disconnected from each other and have deep unspoken issues, my mother and I spent most of our time laughing and exploring her new Thai life (she had a machete!). I had a difficult first night, which inspired the final scene of the story, but after some adjustment and a few pep talks, my mother gave me a backpack and some comfortable Thai dresses and we set off on a journey to see the temples of Chiang Mai, to eat street food in Bangkok, and to swim in Phuket. We are big talkers, and so we told each other everything about our lives, and she helped prepare me for my upcoming singlehood. During one of our talks, my mother told me about a boy in her class who grabbed her breast. She said, "What do you think that was?" and we laughed it off as instinct. Over those weeks, she told me other tales of her double culture shock (as an Iranian and a naturalized American) and I began to imagine the story that eventually became "A Ride Out of Phrao."

When I returned home, I wrote two pieces. The first was an essay that eventually appeared in *The Wall Street Journal* about coming to terms with my own weaknesses after watching my mother adapt easily to Thailand. The second was this story. To create the main character, Shirin, I used another woman in our family as a model—a timid and insecure woman, the kind of person who spends fifteen minutes ironing a blouse for her widow's group—imagining how she would behave in my mother's situation. She would be less graceful, for sure, but also in a kind of lonely turmoil, a shell she can't break because of her need to keep certain images of herself intact. Years later, when both stories were out in the world, my mother read them. She said, "Are you allowed to imagine the same trip for two completely different stories?" I said, "Of course!" And she said, "That makes no sense, but okay." She sent me her diaries from Thailand so I could write a book about the many changes we both experienced during those two years.

Dina Nayeri was born in the middle of a revolution in Iran and moved to Oklahoma at the age of ten. Her work (including her novel, *A Teaspoon of Earth and Sea*) is published in more than twenty countries and was selected for *Granta*'s "New Voices," Barnes & Noble's Discover Great New Writers, and other honors. Her stories and essays have appeared in *The Wall Street Journal*, *The Atlantic*, *Vice*, *Guernica*, *The Southern Review*, *Marie Claire*, and elsewhere. She holds a BA from Princeton, an MBA from Harvard, and an MFA from the Iowa Writers' Workshop, where she was a Truman Capote Fellow and Teaching-Writing Fellow. She lives in New York City.

Brenda Peynado, "The History of Happiness"

I wrote this story the first semester of my MFA program. I was trying to figure out how to write about my travels as an IT auditor, living three hundred days out of the year in hotels. I had met two incredibly kind Indian men while at a bar after working through an account's disaster recovery plan (if a tsunami, for example, wipes out the mainframes, how are they set up to stay online?) and spent the night talking with them on a Singapore beach.

When I started my MFA, the world had impressed upon me how lucky I was to have gone where I had, met the people I had, been taught by such amazing dynamos of spirit. Even the narrow escapes had still been miraculous escapes. Caught in a riptide, I was able to cling to an abandoned bridge. A taxi driver tried to rob me, but when I opened the door mid-traffic and jumped out, he sped off. Men followed us home but veered off when we reached our destination. Traveling was one of the most sustained periods of happiness in my life. How magical the world is! Through the process of writing this story I had to unlearn all that. What if the people I met hadn't been good? What if I had less good intentions? What if I didn't even know what happiness felt like?

That was my entrance into the story about those two nice men in Singapore. However, for so many drafts, the worst happened that night she spends with Anil and Satik, but then I realized that her yearning wasn't figuring out how to be happy despite being a victim; it was the opposite. It had to do with struggling with her own complicity in her unhappiness, in wanting so much from the world that she was willing to take it. She wanted to be a victim, and this character had the most to learn by not getting that victimhood. And there I had my story and a lesson that would spur me through the rest of my writing: What do my characters want desperately, and with what quiet disasters does the world defeat them, defeat us?

Brenda Peynado was born and raised in Florida and spent her childhood summers in the Dominican Republic. She received her BA in computer science from Wellesley College and her MFA in fiction from Florida State University. Her fiction has appeared in *The Threepenny Review, Mid-American Review, Black Warrior Review, Colorado Review, Pleiades,* and others. In 2013, she was on a Fulbright grant to the Dominican Republic, working on a novel. She lives in Cincinnati, Ohio.

Thomas Pierce, "Ba Baboon"

Many years ago my grandfather was in an accident on his farm and suffered a traumatic brain injury. He was a different person afterward—with different likes, dislikes, wants, habits. I found these personality changes both frightening and fascinating. I think most of us like to assume we are who we are and will be that way until we die. It can be an unsettling thought, the extent to which our identities are so malleable, the degree to which we are barely ourselves, even from one moment to the next. I suspect there is something nonmaterial involved in all of this—a fragment that can't be bashed, bruised, or aged away—but somehow I doubt that the soul has anything to do with something so crude as a personality.

I'd long wanted to write a story that grappled with these questions, but for years I struggled to find the right structure and characters. I had an engine but no car. I only got moving once I had an image of Brooks and Mary, brother and sister, trapped in someone else's pantry, a pair of vicious dogs outside the door.

Thomas Pierce was born in South Carolina in 1982. He is the author of the short-story collection *Hall of Small Mammals*. His stories have appeared in *Oxford American*, the *Virginia Quarterly Review*, *The Atlantic*, *The Best American Nonrequired Reading*, and elsewhere. He was a Poe/Faulkner Fellow at the University of Virginia, where he received his MFA. He lives in Charlottesville, Virginia.

Emily Ruskovich, "Owl"

"Owl" began with a single image: a woman lying in the grass at night, shot down by a group of boys who had mistaken her for an owl. I didn't know anything else for a very long time. I wrote several partial drafts of this story in different voices over a period of three years. A few of these drafts took place in the modern day, and a few of them contained a third member of the family, the couple's young son. But these versions didn't satisfy me. It felt like I was forcing plots upon a premise whose hold on me I had yet to fully understand. It was only when other vivid images began to gather in my mind around the central image that the story opened up, and opened up fast. The coffee grounds spread on the dirt floor, and the giant-headed inbred cats. These details came from my family history, the coffee grounds from my mother's side, the cats from my father's. I knew these two real images were related somehow to the one I had invented, but I didn't know how—so that's what I set out to discover. Solving my own mystery, I invented someone else's. The various histories merged into a strange genealogy. The cats, the coffee, the woman-not-owl. I put them together for a while, and the result was a fifteen-year-old girl tied up in a buggy on her wedding day, pregnant with a pig thief's child.

Emily Ruskovich grew up in the Idaho Panhandle. She is a graduate of the Iowa Writers' Workshop and was a fiction fellow at the University of Wisconsin. Her fiction has appeared in *Zoetrope: All-Story*, the *Virginia Quarterly Review*, and *Inkwell*. Her first novel, *Idaho*, and first collection of short stories are both forthcoming. She teaches at the University of Colorado in Denver and lives in the mountains west of the city.

Lynne Sharon Schwartz, "The Golden Rule"

That this story exists at all is really a fluke. I wrote it a couple of years ago and wasn't quite happy with it. I knew it needed something but didn't know how to complete it. I set it aside and pretty much forgot it. Then a magazine editor asked me to contribute a story; I hunted around in my files and found "The Golden Rule." Strange how feeling wanted by an editor—having an assignment, so to speak—gave me the impetus to return to the story. What had seemed unclear and undoable became clear at once, and the finishing touches weren't nearly as difficult as I had imagined.

As far as the subject, I've been living in New York City apartment buildings for more than forty years and have closely observed all the interactions in those buildings. I even based a novel, *In the Family Way*, on the antics and fictional goings-on in one such building. So the subject is dear to me; urban apartment buildings are a microcosm of society at large. I've also been thinking a lot about aging, and how the "getting old" observe the truly old, in anxious anticipation of their own futures.

Lynne Sharon Schwartz, a native New Yorker, is the author of twenty-three books, including the novel *Two-Part Inventions*; short stories; nonfiction; poetry; a memoir, *Not Now, Voyager*; and translations from Italian. Her latest is a collection of essays, *This Is Where We Came In*. Her novel *Leaving Brooklyn* was nominated for a PEN/Faulkner Award, and *Rough Strife* was nominated for a National Book Award and the PEN/Hemingway Award for Debut Fiction. Her work has been reprinted in *The Best American Short Stories*, *The O. Henry Prize Stories*, *The Best American Essays*, and other anthologies. She has received grants from the Guggenheim Foundation, the National Endowment for the Arts, and the New York State Foundation for the Arts, and she teaches at the Bennington College Writing Seminars and Columbia University's School of the Arts. She lives in New York City.

Lionel Shriver, "Kilifi Creek"

Like Liana in the story—like most adults, I imagine—I keep a growing list in the back of my head of the times I almost died. What interests me about the nature of these disparate brushes against nonexistence isn't the practical "lessons" I derive from them (look both ways before you cross the street, etc.). Many of these moments are dumb. For example, I had the most ludicrous bike accident in Manhattan last summer. Had the spill occurred in front of an overtaking truck, I would hate to read the subsequent obituary: "Ms. Shriver was suddenly forced to slow down so drastically that the bicycle would no longer stay upright and it fell over." No matter the circumstances, all these encounters teach the same lesson. It's the sheer brutality of the message that stays with you. Only in the immediate aftermath of having been a hairsbreadth from permanent oblivion have I ever truly believed that I could die. I've wanted to write a story about these moments for a long time.

When I read in *The New York Times* about the fate of an attractive young woman in Manhattan, something clicked. She was out on the balcony of her apartment, socializing with a date. The balcony railing gave way, and she plummeted to her death. Something about this story had the hallmarks of This Could Be You. It linked in my mind with all the times that, had matters gone just a little differently, I wouldn't be here.

Lionel Shriver was born and raised in North Carolina. She is the author of eleven novels and is known for *The New York Times* bestsellers *So Much for That* (a finalist for the 2010 National Book Award and the Wellcome Book Prize) and *The Post-Birthday World* (*Entertainment Weekly*'s Book of the Year), as well as the international bestseller *We Need to Talk About Kevin* and her more recent novel, *Big Brother*. Winner of the 2005 Orange Prize, *We Need to Talk About Kevin* was adapted for an award-winning feature film. Both *Kevin* and *So Much for That* were dramatized for BBC Radio 4. Shriver's work has been translated into twenty-eight languages. She writes for *The Guardian*, *The New York Times*, London's *Sunday Times*, the *Financial Times*, *The Washington Post*, and *The Wall Street Journal*, among other publications. "Kilifi Creek" won the BBC National Short Story Award in 2014. She lives in London, England, and Brooklyn, New York.

Joan Silber, "About My Aunt"

When Hurricane Sandy hit New York in 2012, the radio had a story about older people in housing projects who were unfazed

374 / *Writing* The O. Henry Prize Stories 2015

at being without electricity and water, much to the surprise of volunteers. (My neighborhood, the Lower East Side, was in the dark zone—but I could get out to lean on friends in the lit parts of town.) I began to think about self-reliance as a key trait, which led to the character of Kiki. I leaped at the chance to invent her background in Turkey, which I've visited a few times, a culture different enough to illustrate her pliancy. And I wanted Kiki viewed by a younger female character, with her own ideas about risk and obligation and her own love complications. I liked the sense of these two, aunt and niece, understanding each other just fine but viewing each other across the great divide of age, where neither envies the other.

I assumed this story was done when I finished it, but it has become the first chapter of a novel.

Joan Silber was born in New Jersey. She is the author of seven works of fiction, including *Fools* (longlisted for the National Book Award and finalist for the PEN/Faulkner Award), *The Size of the World* (finalist for the Los Angeles Times Book Prize in Fiction), *Ideas of Heaven* (finalist for the National Book Award and the Story Prize), and *Household Words* (winner of the PEN/Hemingway Award). Her stories have been in four *O. Henry* collections. She is also the author of *The Art of Time in Fiction*, a critical study. She teaches at Sarah Lawrence College and lives in New York City.

Elizabeth Strout, "Snow Blind"

In truth, it is always difficult for me to know where a story comes from. With "Snow Blind," I know that I had an abiding image of snow, lots of it, like there used to be in my childhood in New Hampshire. But I set the story in the potato lands of Maine, because I had been there recently and the scenery was fresh in my mind. I was interested mainly in this child and her relationship to the natural world, how she could not keep herself away from those moments of ecstasy she felt by herself. The rest of it unfolded from that.

Elizabeth Strout was born in Portland, Maine, and is the author of four books of fiction. *Amy and Isabelle* won the Chicago Tribune Heartland Prize and also the Los Angeles Times Art Seidenbaum Award for First Fiction. It was also shortlisted for the Orange Prize in England and the PEN/Faulkner Award. She is also the author of *Abide with Me* and *Olive Kitteridge*, which won the Pulitzer Prize in 2009, and most recently *The Burgess Boys*, nominated for the Harper Lee Prize for Legal Fiction. She lives in New York City.

Emma Törzs, "Word of Mouth"

Here is the order in which some of the elements of this story came together, over about a year of writing it on and off.

1. I had a job, finally, at a new restaurant called—well, it wasn't called the Whole Hog, but aside from that, the first paragraph of the story is completely true. I waitressed three months at a barbecue restaurant doomed for failure, and many strange things happened to me there, none of which made it into this story. I took the setting only, how beautiful it was and how absurd.

2. I was (am) fascinated by the idea of the "missing girl." But what had happened to mine? Answering this question was one of the main thematic challenges in the story and I went back and forth a lot. In one draft she was eaten by a mountain lion.

3. My friend told me about a landlady he'd had, whose situation I stole for Miranda nearly in its entirety. The real Miranda was a pianist and woke my friend playing concertos on the piano in the living room, and in fact it was this detail that most impressed me, and that I most wanted to use in a story, but the piano ended up a clumsy metaphor for God-knows-what and was cut.

4. The grandmother appeared only in the final draft. I knew the narrator had "run" from something, and through much of the writing I was hoping I could get away with being mysteriously vague about what exactly she'd run from. But more often than not, vagueness is just an amateur attempt at creating tension, and in order to finish the story I knew I had to decide what exactly had happened to my narrator. Enter Grandma.

Emma Törzs was born in Massachusetts in 1987 and received her MFA from the University of Montana, Missoula. Her stories have appeared in journals such as *Ploughshares*, *The Cincinnati Review*, *Narrative*, and *Salt Hill*. She teaches and waits (tables) in Minneapolis, Minnesota.

Vauhini Vara, "I, Buffalo"

When I first moved to San Francisco after college, more than ten years ago, I was captivated by the city's beauty. I liked to take long walks and, on one of these walks, came across the bison paddock in Golden Gate Park. Bison! In the middle of a city! What? I tried, back then, to write a story about a girl who takes walks around San Francisco; I sent her to the bison paddock, among other favorite places of mine. The problem was that nothing much happened in the story. Years later, in graduate school, I was working on a new story about a woman, Sheila, whose life is falling apart. Sheila happened to live in San Francisco, and when I thought about how she might fill her days, after having lost her job, I remembered the earlier protagonist's trip to the bison paddock and thought it was exactly the sort of thing Sheila would do. I didn't realize until later that the experience would end up at the emotional center of "I, Buffalo."

Vauhini Vara was born in Regina, Saskatchewan, in Canada, and was raised mostly in Prince Albert, Saskatchewan, and in suburbs of Oklahoma City and Seattle. She is a graduate of the

Iowa Writers' Workshop and has been at the MacDowell Colony and Yaddo. Her short stories have been published in *ZYZZYVA*, *Glimmer Train*, and elsewhere. She writes for the website of *The New Yorker* and was a reporter at *The Wall Street Journal* for nearly a decade. Her journalism has been anthologized in *Dogfight at the Pentagon*, a collection of page 1 features from the *Journal*. She lives in Colorado.

Publications Submitted

Stories published in American and Canadian magazines are eligible for consideration for inclusion in *The O. Henry Prize Stories*. Stories must be written originally in the English language. No translations are considered. Sections of novels are not considered. Editors are asked not to nominate individual stories. Stories may not be submitted by agents or writers.

Editors are invited to submit online fiction for consideration, but such submissions must be sent to the address on the next page in the form of a legible hard copy. The publication's contact information and the date of the story's publication must accompany the submissions.

Because of production deadlines for the 2016 collection, it is essential that stories reach the series editor by July 1, 2015. If a finished magazine is unavailable before the deadline, magazine editors are welcome to submit scheduled stories in proof or manuscript. Publications received after July 1, 2015, will automatically be considered for *The O. Henry Prize Stories 2017*.

Please see our website, www.ohenryprizestories.com, for more information about submission to *The O. Henry Prize Stories*.

The address for submission is:

Laura Furman, Series Editor, The O. Henry Prize Stories
The University of Texas at Austin
English Department, B5000
1 University Station
Austin, TX 78712

The information listed on the following pages was up-to-date when *The O. Henry Prize Stories 2015* went to press. Inclusion in this listing does not constitute endorsement or recommendation by *The O. Henry Prize Stories* or Anchor Books.

Alimentum
PO Box 210028
Nashville, TN 37221
Paulette Licitra, editor
editor@alimentumjournal.com
alimentumjournal.com
as of 2014, online with continuous
    publication of new material

Amoskeag
School of Arts and Sciences
Southern New Hampshire
    University
2500 North River Road
Manchester, NH 03106
Benjamin Nugent, editor
b.nugent@snhu.edu
amoskeagjournal.com
annual

Bellevue Literary Review
NYU Langone
Department of Medicine
550 First Avenue, OBV-A612
New York, NY 10016
Danielle Ofri, editor
info@BLReview.org
BLReview.org
semiannual

Border Crossing
Lake Superior State University
650 West Easterday Avenue
Sault Ste. Marie, MI 49783
Julie Brooks Barbour, Mary
    McMyne, Jillena Rose, editors
bordercrossing@lssu.edu
lssu.edu/bc
annual

China Grove
Lucius Lampton, editor
chinagrovepress@gmail.com
chinagrovepress.com
semiannual

CutBank
University of Montana
English Department, LA 133
Missoula, MT 59812
Allison Linville, editor
editor.cutbank@gmail.com
cutbankonline.org
semiannual

Dappled Things
Meredith McCann, editor
dappledthings.editor@gmail.com
dappledthings.org
quarterly

Eleven Eleven
California College of the Arts
1111 Eighth Street
San Francisco, CA 94107
Hugh Behm-Steinberg, editor
elevenelevenjournal.com
semiannual

Fairy Tale Review
Department of English
Modern Languages Building
University of Arizona
Tucson, AZ 85721
Kate Bernheimer, editor
fairytalereview.com
annual

Fiction River
WMG Publishing
PO Box 269
Lincoln City, OR 97367
Kristine Kathryn Rusch, Dean
    Wesley Smith, editors
fictionriver.com
semimonthly

Fourteen Hills
Department of Creative Writing
San Francisco State University
1600 Holloway Avenue
San Francisco, CA 94132
Heather June Gibbons, editor
14hills.net
semiannual

Free State Review
3637 Black Rock Road
Upperco, MD 21155
Hal Burdett, J. Wesley Clark,
    Barrett Warner, Raphaela
    Cassandra, editors
editors@freestatereview.com
freestatereview.com
semiannual

Grain Magazine
PO Box 67
Saskatoon, SK S7K 3K1
Canada
grainmag@skwriter.com
grainmagazine.ca/about
quarterly

Harper's Magazine
666 Broadway, 11th Floor
New York, NY 10012
Ellen Rosenbush, editor
harpers@harpers.org
harpers.org
monthly

Image
3307 Third Avenue West
Seattle, WA 98119
Gregory Wolfe, editor
image@imagejournal.org
imagejournal.org
quarterly

Little Patuxent Review
PO Box 6084
Columbia, MD 21045
Steven Leyva, editor
editor@littlepatuxentreview.org
littlepatuxentreview.org
semiannual

Lumina (print)/Lux (multimedia edition)
Sarah Lawrence College
1 Mead Way
Bronxville, NY 10704
Jessica Denzer, editor
lumina@gm.slc.edu
luminajournal.com
annual

MĀNOA
Department of English
University of Hawai'i
1733 Donaghho Road
Honolulu, HI 96822
Frank Stewart, editor
mjournal-l@lists.hawaii.edu
manoajournal.hawaii.edu
semiannual

Mid-American Review
Department of English, BGSU
Bowling Green OH 43403
Abigail Cloud, editor
casit.bgsu.edu/midamericanreview
semiannual

Midwestern Gothic
Midwestern Gothic/MG Press
PO Box 3447
Ann Arbor, MI 48106
Jeff Pfaller, Robert James Russell,
    editors
info@midwestgothic.com
midwestgothic.com
quarterly

Mississippi Review
118 College Drive #5144
Hattiesburg, MS 39406-0001
Andrew Malan Milward, editor
msreview@usm.edu
usm.edu/mississippi-review/index
    .html
semiannual

New Ohio Review
English Department
360 Ellis Hall
Ohio University
Athens, OH 45701
Jill Allyn Rosser, editor
noreditors@ohio.edu
ohio.edu/nor
semiannual

Oxford American
PO Box 3235
Little Rock, AR 72203-3235
Roger D. Hodge, editor
editors@oxfordamerican.org
oxfordamerican.org
quarterly

Poets and Artists
GOSS183
604 Vale Street
Bloomington, IL 61701
Didi Menendez, editor
didimenendez@gmail.com
poetsandartists.com
published 6–8 times a year

Prairie Schooner
123 Andrews Hall
University of Nebraska–Lincoln
Lincoln, NE 68588-0334
Kwame Dawes, editor
prairieschooner@unl.edu
prairieschooner.unl.edu
quarterly

Printers Row
Chicago Tribune
435 North Michigan Avenue
Chicago, IL 60611
Jennifer Day, editor
jeday@tribune.com
chicagotribune.com/printersrow
weekly

PRISM international
Creative Writing Program
University of British Columbia
Buchanan E462
1866 Main Mall
Vancouver, BC V6T 1Z1
Canada
Nicole Boyce, editor
prismprose@gmail.com
prismmagazine.ca
quarterly

Raritan
31 Mine Street
New Brunswick, NJ 08901
Jackson Lears, editor
rqr@rci.rutgers.edu
raritanquarterly.rutgers.edu
quarterly

Redivider
Department of Writing, Literature
    and Publishing
Emerson College
120 Boylston Street
Boston, MA 02116
Pamela Painter, editor
fiction@redividerjournal.org
redividerjournal.org
semiannual

Red Rock Review
English Department, J2A
College of Southern Nevada
3200 East Cheyenne Avenue
North Las Vegas, NV 89030
Todd Moffett, editor
redrockreview@csn.edu
sites.csn.edu/english
    /redrockreview/index.htm
semiannual

Relief
Brad Fruhauff, editor
editor@reliefjournal.com
reliefjournal.com

Salamander
Suffolk University
English Department
8 Ashburton Place
Boston, MA 02108
Jennifer Barber, editor
salamandermag.org
semiannual

Salmagundi Magazine
Skidmore College
Attn: Salmagundi Journal
815 North Broadway
Saratoga Springs, NY 12866
Robert Boyers, editor
salmagun@skidmore.edu
skidmore.edu/salmagundi
quarterly

Scribendi
c/o UNM Honors College
MSC06 3890
1 University of New Mexico
Albuquerque, NM 87131
Jordan Burk, editor
scribendi@unm.edu
scribendi.unm.edu
annual

Sheepshead Review
UW–Green Bay
Attn: Sheepshead Review
2420 Nicolet Drive
Green Bay, WI 54311-7001
Roberto Rodriguez, editor
sheepsheadreview@uwgb.edu
blog.uwgb.edu/sheepsheadreview

Slice
Beth Blachman, editor
editors@slicemagazine.org
slicemagazine.org
semiannual

Southern Humanities Review
Department of English
Auburn University
9088 Haley Center
Auburn, AL 36849-5202
Chantel Acevedo, editor
shr@auburn.edu
southernhumanitiesreview.com
quarterly

Southern Indiana Review
Orr Center, #2009
University of Southern Indiana
8600 University Boulevard
Evansville, IN 47712
Ron Mitchell, editor
usi.edu/sir
semiannual

Sou'wester
Department of English
Box 1438
Southern Illinois University
    Edwardsville
Edwardsville, IL 62026-1438
souwester.org
semiannual

Southwest Review
Southern Methodist University
PO Box 750374
6404 Robert Hyer Lane,
    Room 307
Dallas, TX 75275-0374
Willard Spiegelman, editor
swr@smu.edu
smu.edu/southwestreview
quarterly

Subtropics
Department of English
University of Florida
PO Box 112075
4008 Turlington Hall
Gainesville, FL 32611-2075
David Leavitt, editor
subtropics@english.ufl.edu
english.ufl.edu/subtropics
triannual

The American Literary Review
PO Box 311307
University of North Texas
Denton, TX 76203-1307
Bonnie Friedman, editor
americanliteraryreview@gmail
    .com
americanliteraryreview.com
semiannual

The American Reader
Uzoamaka Maduka, editor
editors@theamericanreader.com
theamericanreader.com
semimonthly

The Antioch Review
PO Box 148
Yellow Springs, OH 45387
Robert S. Fogarty, editor
mkeyes@antiochreview.org
review.antiochcollege.org/antioch
    _review
quarterly

The Asian American Literary
    Review
Lawrence-Minh Bùi Davis and
    Gerald Maa, editors
editors@aalr.binghamton.edu
aalrmag.org
semiannual

The Briar Cliff Review
3303 Rebecca Street
Sioux City, IA 51104-2100
Tricia Currans-Sheehan, editor
tricia.currans-sheehan@briarcliff
    .edu
bcreview.org
annual

The Carolina Quarterly
510 Greenlaw Hall
CB# 3520
The University of North Carolina
    at Chapel Hill
Chapel Hill, NC 27599-3520
Lindsay Starck, editor
carolina.quarterly@gmail.com
thecarolinaquarterly.com
triannual

The Chattahoochee Review
Anna Schachner, editor
thechattahoocheereview.gpc.edu
semiannual

The Cincinnati Review
PO Box 210069
Cincinnati, OH 45221-0069
editors@cincinnatireview.com
cincinnatireview.com
semiannual

The Farallon Review
1017 L Street
Number 348
Sacramento, CA 95814
Tim Foley, editor
editor@farallonreview.com
farallonreview.com
annual

The Fiddlehead
Campus House
11 Garland Court
PO Box 4400
University of New Brunswick
Fredericton, NB E3B 5A3
Canada
Ross Leckie, editor
fiddlehd@unb.ca
thefiddlehead.ca/index.html
quarterly

The Georgia Review
706A Main Library
320 South Jackson Street
The University of Georgia
Athens, GA 30602-9009
Stephen Corey, editor
garev@uga.edu
garev.uga.edu
quarterly

The Gettysburg Review
Gettysburg College
Gettysburg, PA 17325-1491
Peter Stitt, editor
pstitt@gettysburg.edu
www.gettysburgreview.com
quarterly

The Greensboro Review
MFA Writing Program
3302 MHRA Building
UNC–Greensboro
Greensboro, NC 27402-6170
Jim Clark, editor
tgronline.net
semiannual

The Hudson Review
33 West 67th Street
New York, NY 10023
Paula Deitz, editor
info@hudsonreview.com
hudsonreview.com
quarterly

The Iowa Review
The University of Iowa
308 English-Philosophy Building
Iowa City, IA 52242
Harilaos Stecopoulos, editor
iowa-review@uiowa.edu
iowareview.org
triannual

The Kenyon Review
Finn House
102 West Wiggin Street
Kenyon College
Gambier, OH 43022-9623
David H. Lynn, editor
kenyonreview@kenyon.edu
kenyonreview.org
published six times a year

The Literarian
The Center for Fiction
17 East 47th Street
New York, NY 10017
Dawn Raffel, editor
submissions@centerforfiction.org
centerforfiction.org/magazine

The Literary Review
Fairleigh Dickinson University
285 Madison Avenue
Madison, NJ 07940
Minna Proctor, editor
info@theliteraryreview.org
theliteraryreview.org
quarterly

The Long Story
18 Eaton Street
Lawrence, MA 01843
R. P. Burnham, editor
rpburnham@mac.com
longstorylitmag.com
annual

The Louisville Review
Spalding University
851 South Fourth Street
Louisville, KY 40203
Sena Jeter Naslund, editor
louisvillereview@spalding.edu
louisvillereview.org
semiannual

The Malahat Review
University of Victoria
PO Box 1700
Stn CSC
Victoria, BC V8W 2Y2
Canada
John Barton, editor
malahat@uvic.ca
web.uvic.ca/malahat
quarterly

The Missouri Review
357 McReynolds Hall
University of Missouri
Columbia, MO 65211
Speer Morgan, editor
question@moreview.com
missourireview.com
quarterly

The New Yorker
1 World Trade Center
New York, NY 10007
Deborah Treisman, editor
fiction@newyorker.com
newyorker.com
weekly

The Paris Review
544 West 27th Street
New York, NY 10001
Lorin Stein, editor
queries@theparisreview.org
theparisreview.org
quarterly

The Pinch Literary Journal
English Department
University of Memphis
3720 Alumni Avenue
Memphis, TN 38152
Tim Johnston, editor
editor@pinchjournal.com
thepinchjournal.com
semiannual

The Saturday Evening Post
1100 Waterway Boulevard
Indianapolis, IN 46202
editors@saturdayeveningpost.com
saturdayeveningpost.com
published six times a year

The Sewanee Review
The University of the South
735 University Avenue
Sewanee, TN 37383-1000
George Core, editor
sreview@sewanee.edu
review.sewanee.edu
quarterly

The Southeast Review
Department of English
Florida State University
Tallahassee, FL 32306
Erin Hoover, editor
southeastreview@gmail.com
southeastreview.org
semiannual

The Southern Review
338 Johnston Hall
Louisiana State University
Baton Rouge, LA 70803
Jessica Faust and Emily Nemens,
    editors
southernreview@lsu.edu
thesouthernreview.org
quarterly

The Threepenny Review
PO Box 9131
Berkeley, CA 94709
Wendy Lesser, editor
wlesser@threepennyreview.com
threepennyreview.com
quarterly

The Worcester Review
1 Ekman Street
Worcester, MA 01607
Diane Vanaskie Mulligan, editor
twr.diane@gmail.com
theworcesterreview.org
annual

Third Coast
Western Michigan University
English Department
1903 West Michigan Avenue
Kalamazoo, MI 49008-5331
Laurie Ann Cedilnik, editor
editors@thirdcoastmagazine.com
thirdcoastmagazine.com
semiannual

Tin House
PO Box 10500
Portland, OR 97210
Rob Spillman, editor
info@tinhouse.com
tinhouse.com
quarterly

Tweed's
Randy Rosenthal and Laura Mae
    Isaacman, editors
tweedsmag.org
semiannual

Virginia Quarterly Review
5 Boar's Head Lane
PO Box 400223
Charlottesville, VA 22904
editors@vqronline.org
vqronline.org
quarterly

Water-Stone Review
MS-A1730
1536 Hewitt Avenue
Saint Paul, MN 55104-1284
Mary François Rockcastle, editor
water-stone@hamline.edu
waterstonereview.com
annual

Western Humanities Review
University of Utah
English Department
255 South Central Campus Drive
LNCO 3500
Salt Lake City, UT 84112-0494
Barry Weller, editor
whr@mail.hum.utah.edu
ourworld.info/whrweb
triannual

Willow Springs
668 North Riverpoint Boulevard
    2 RPT
Suite 259
Spokane, WA 99202-1677
Samuel Ligon, editor
willowspringsewu@gmail.com
willowsprings.ewu.edu
semiannual

Witness
Black Mountain Institute
University of Nevada, Las Vegas
Box 455085
Las Vegas, NV 89154-5085
Maile Chapman, editor
witness@unlv.edu
witness.blackmountaininstitute.org
annual print, semiannual online

Workers Write!
PO Box 250382
Plano, TX 75025-0382
David LaBounty, editor
info@workerswritejournal.com
workerswritejournal.com
annual

Zoetrope: All-Story
916 Kearny Street
San Francisco, CA 94133
Michael Ray, editor
info@all-story.com
www.all-story.com
quarterly

Zone 3
Austin Peay State University
Box 4565
Clarksville, TN 37044
Barry Kitterman, editor
zone3@apsu.edu
apsu.edu/zone3
semiannual

ZYZZYVA
57 Post Street
Suite 604
San Francisco, CA 94104
Laura Cogan, editor
editor@zyzzyva.org
zyzzyva.org
quarterly

Permissions